Murdering
Ministers

Books by Alan Beechey

The Oliver Swithin Mysteries
An Embarrassment of Corpses
Murdering Ministers
This Private Plot

(with Gina Teague)
Culture Smart! USA

Murdering Ministers

An Oliver Swithin Mystery

Alan Beechey

Poisoned Pen Press

Copyright © 1999, 2014 by Alan Beechey

First US Trade Paperback Edition 2014

10 9 8 7 6 5 4 3 2 1

Library of Congress Catalog Card Number: 2014930263

ISBN: 9781464202452   Trade Paperback

Poisoned Pen Press
6962 E. First Ave., Ste. 103
Scottsdale, AZ 85251
www.poisonedpenpress.com
info@poisonedpenpress.com

Printed in the United States of America

for Mary

Come to my woman's breasts
And take my milk for gall, you murdering ministers,
Wherever in your sightless substances,
You wait on nature's mischief.
—William Shakespeare, *Macbeth*

Prologue

Billy Coppersmith realized he was possessed when he caught himself thinking about breasts during the Lord's Prayer.

If it had been the sermon, he wouldn't have been worried. Everybody's mind wandered then, especially when Parson Piltdown got onto one of his tedious theological kicks. But it had begun during the second hymn, when sixteen-year-old Michaela Braithewaite, standing one pew in front of him and slightly to the right, took in a deep breath for the last verse. And now, nothing could get the profile of her tight sweater out of Billy's mind.

It *had* to be an evil spirit. What else would make a fourteen-year-old boy think about sex all the time? Nigel warned that they were all around, waiting to snatch at the souls of the innocent and lead them into sin. Billy resolved to ask Nigel to drive out the demon when the group met for lunch after the morning service. He knew Nigel could do it. Surely he'd agree, now that they'd shared secrets? No demon was any match for Nigel's profound and infallible faith.

Billy had witnessed that faith in action a few weeks earlier— Nigel grappling with the spirit of blasphemy that possessed Troy, his thin fingers gripping Troy's forehead like twin spiders, the two men shaking convulsively in unison. And then that great cry of "Satan, come out!" when Nigel flung his arms wide and crumpled senseless to the floor. "Pray!" Heather had screamed, and they all felt the spirit scuttling about the living room, searching frantically for a new host, the temperature suddenly dropping in the presence of evil, while they desperately babbled prayers for the protection of their young souls.

Or at least, Heather said that's what she felt—she swore she could almost see it—so that's what the teenagers all agreed had happened, even using the same words. It was certainly the story he told his mocking school friends the next morning, as he tried in vain to get them to come to Nigel's prayer group. (Every new member was a victory for Christ, Nigel and Heather told them.)

Troy was the latest recruit. He was eighteen and he must have had lots of girls, but Michaela had made him join Nigel's group before she'd agree to go out with him. And Nigel spotted Troy's evil spirit the moment he swaggered into the room. Now Troy was born again, his evil dispersed to the air. Did that mean he and Michaela would have to be chaste? Or did they pray first and then make out, aware of God's eyes on them? Maybe, despite her reputation at school, Michaela was still a virgin? If so, Billy was one better than her—or worse, depending on Who was judging you. Nigel hadn't judged him.

But Billy had seen the works of good spirits, too, at Nigel's house. And like the others, he'd been struck with the Holy Spirit itself, those evenings when the excitement within the young group was palpable, almost hysterical, and Nigel had touched their foreheads, one by one, holding their gaze and muttering prayers, until he tossed them backwards and they fell to the carpet like toppled statues. And one time, Michaela had started to writhe on the floor and make strange noises that were almost like words, but not words Billy had ever heard before, and then Heather piped up that she has been visited by a spirit of interpretation, a gift from the Lord, and she began to translate the strange prophecies—something to do with sterility and error in God's house, and about a sign that would be coming soon. (Well, it was certainly getting close to Christmas, Billy noted, and wondered if he'd have to get Chrissie a present, even though they had broken up since that one time.)

Michaela had been speaking in tongues, Nigel explained later. It was a special gift from God. Billy started to wonder why God couldn't have delivered the message in English in the first place, but he quickly concluded that questioning God was sacrilege and wished instead that he could speak in tongues, too. Though perhaps with nobody else present at first, in case he said something embarrassing.

There was Nigel now, on the platform at the front of the barn-like church, sitting behind the Communion table with that prating idiot Parson Piltdown and the other deacons, including Billy's mother. They were all such hypocrites, not even true believers, not by Nigel's lofty standards. Parson Piltdown came from the Church of England, so it was doubtful he was even a Christian.

This was Nigel's first Communion service as a deacon. He'd already sung for them, playing that twelve-string guitar so hard to keep in tune in the cold church. (Would Nigel invite him to play his electric guitar next time he performed?) The stale pellets of bread had been distributed and consumed. Now it was time for the wine.

Parson Piltdown—it was Nigel's name for him; Billy had to remember to call him Mr. Piltdown if they spoke—lifted the chalice.

"After the same manner also He took the cup," he intoned, in that stupid posh voice he used for readings, "when He had supped, saying, 'This cup is the new testament in my blood: this do ye as oft as ye drink it, in remembrance of me.'"

And Nigel himself brought the wine to the congregation! Billy snatched the tiny shot glass from the tray as Nigel passed it. Their eyes met, and Nigel gave him a small smile, an acknowledgment of the promises they had made to each other. Communion wine was awful, Billy had already discovered, with a foul, lingering aftertaste and no alcohol to speak of. But he'd enjoy this glass.

After the wine was distributed, Piltdown served the deacons on the dais. Then he took a glass for himself. He turned to the quiet, expectant church, raising his glass as if proposing a toast.

"Let us drink together, in remembrance of Him."

He drained the glass and sat down again, on the largest chair in the middle of the platform. The small, scattered congregation drank their wine, dropped their empty glasses into metal rings attached to the pews, and bent their heads in noiseless prayer. An odd, reverent silence fell over the church.

Billy didn't lower his head—he didn't know why not. But that meant he was able to watch as Nigel, setting his glass clumsily on the table, rose slowly to his feet. Was he going to speak?

Nigel coughed twice, the second cough folding into a gurgle, as if unseen hands were pressing on his throat. The deacons, disturbed in their meditations, lifted their heads one at a time to watch him. Even Michaela and Troy looked up from the depths of their prayers.

Nigel stood, breathing heavily. Then he pressed his hands to his face, his eyes staring in astonishment at something only he could see, floating above the pews. Billy saw Piltdown exchanged a worried look with his mother, sitting beside him. Only old man Potiphar, the oldest deacon, seemed undisturbed and rapt in prayer.

Now Piltdown crept over and tried to whisper in Nigel's ear. But Nigel paid no attention. He continued to stare ahead, as if his neck had turned to stone, like Lot's wife gazing at the cities of the plain. His breath had become labored and audible. Piltdown looked awkward and lost.

Suddenly, Nigel gave a great cry, and his arms began to tremble. The noise continued, animal-like and increasingly desperate. He moved forward on unsteady legs, twitching, like a badly manipulated puppet. Then, with an intense convulsion, his legs flailed and he tipped forward, pivoting over the rail that ran along the platform.

Troy leaped to his feet. "He has been struck by the Holy Spirit!" he shouted, his voice drowning Nigel's thick groans. "Praise the Lord!"

And now Michaela jumped up and left the pew, standing in the aisle and lifting her arms in supplication. This time, Billy didn't notice her chest.

"Praise the Lord!" she cried. "God is with us."

The familiar murmur passed among the other teenagers in Nigel's group, and Billy too found himself rising and shouting his praises as the young people danced into the aisle and gathered around Nigel at the front of the church. The man was now lying on his back on the dusty floor, his arms and legs convulsing, making strange, breathy noises as he shook.

"He's speaking in tongues," squealed another girl. "Who has been given the gift of interpretation?"

"I have," shouted Michaela quickly. "This is the sign! This is the sign of a new day, when the children shall lead and the old shall be driven from the temple. Praise the Lord! Hallelujah!"

The others took up the cry, and one began to sing a mindless, repetitive chorus. Soon they all joined in.

In that moment, Billy understood all that Nigel had been teaching. And although he was singing and dancing with the others, part of him watched the scene with fascination: his young friends jumping around the body, their arms clutching at heaven like windswept palm leaves; the deacons on the platform struck dumb and motionless in their spiritual impotence; the other communicants standing in their places, trying to see what was happening but not daring to step forward.

And Nigel himself, Nigel now revealed at last as the great prophet of the Second Coming, as he'd surely hinted, almost levitating from the ground in his desire to float up to his God, his whole body one uncanny arc, with only his head and heels in contact with the floor. Hallelujah! Praise the Lord, indeed!

But who was that woman, Billy wondered—the one now sprinting down the aisle from the back of the church, her amazingly curly hair floating wildly around her head? She wasn't a church member. Was she some sort of messenger from God? An Angel?

Then he remembered: She was that good-looking police detective who'd been asking all those questions yesterday. What was she doing here, at church, on this Sunday morning of all mornings? And what was she shouting, trying to make herself heard above the elated, singing, dancing teenagers?

"Let me through!" she was yelling. "Let me through, and stand back, everybody! Please!"

"Nigel is bringing us God's word," Michaela protested, weeping with joy.

"He's not bringing you anything," the detective snarled, as she tried to pull the dancing children out of her way. "Can't you see? He's dying!"

Chapter One

Tis the Season to Be Jolly

Sunday, December 14 (Third Sunday of Advent)

Sitting down had clear advantages over kneeling, Oliver Swithin had decided. If anyone ever asked him to create a new religion— "Swithinism" had a lilt to it, but it might be a bit hard on lispers—he would make sure that everybody sat down for the prayers. For one thing, the position was more natural—rather like perching on the toilet, with much the same spirit of supplication and hope for a blessing.

And it was quicker. At his parents' parish church, the vicar's call to prayer would have been followed by several noisy seconds of cracking knees and the odd territorial grabs for hassocks. (Or were those cushions called "cassocks"? Not being much of a churchgoer, he could never remember the difference. Both words sounded vaguely like Scottish mountain ranges. Or indelicate parts of the body.)

"Amen," said the minister, at the end of a brief prayer that seemed largely improvised, like the many others that had preceded it. The tiny congregation mumbled a brief echo of the word, and Oliver realized that his mind had been wandering again. He shifted position on the uncomfortable pew and scribbled "Cassocks?" on his reporter's notepad.

"My text for today's sermon," the young man in the pulpit continued, "can be found in the gospel according to Saint Matthew, chapter fifteen, verses ten and eleven."

"And the best I can get, even with four-hundred-speed film, is a thirtieth of a second at f-two-point-eight," Ben Motley whispered loudly into Oliver's ear as he loaded a new roll of film into his Canon.

"Our days are numbered," murmured Oliver.

"I'm reading from the Revised English Bible," the minister continued. A thick-necked, elderly man sitting in the pew in front of Oliver and Ben stopped flipping the pages of his well-thumbed King James's Bible and snapped it shut.

"'He'—that is, Jesus, of course—'called the crowd and said to them, "Listen and understand! No one is defiled by what goes into his mouth; only by what comes out of it."'"

The minister repeated the last sentence with quizzical pauses, a look of concentration on his ruddy, good-natured face, as if he'd momentarily forgotten why he'd chosen the text. The elderly man and his wife seemed to take it as scriptural dispensation to unwrap sweets.

Ben lurched away and tiptoed closer to the front of the church, training his camera on a small group of sullen teenagers sitting close to the left wall. Apart from this cluster, there were about a dozen worshippers, but the large, plain, nineteenth-century building with its parallel rows of high-backed pews could clearly hold a congregation thirty times as large. A group of older ladies had huddled like shamefaced latecomers in the rear pew, under the shelter of a dark balcony, although Oliver knew they'd been there at least twenty minutes before the service began.

The minister had already explained to the congregation that the evening's service would be photographed by Ben Motley, a man famous for his "spirited pictures of sporting women." Since Ben's notoriety actually came from his portraits of female celebrities and society dames at the point of orgasm, Oliver had to credit the clergyman's subtlety. And once past the embarrassment of being stared at by churchgoers, he was equally relieved to hear himself introduced as a "leading writer of instructive works for children," who was there to write an article about the United Diaconalist Church. If the congregation had found out the whole truth, they might have regarded Oliver's presence as one of the first signs of the Apocalypse.

Strictly speaking, it wasn't going to be Oliver's article, but the work of Finsbury the Ferret, the character he had created for his series of children's books called *The Railway Mice*. After several slender volumes of innocent tales (and months of negligible royalties), published under Oliver's pseudonym O.C. Blithely, the introduction of Finsbury into the series had made each subsequent book an automatic best seller, and gave British popular culture a new hero in the shifty, foulmouthed, evil-tempered beast. Oliver's friend and housemate, Geoffrey Angelwine, was a member of the public relations team devoted to squeezing as much mileage out of Finsbury as possible, and he had pushed Oliver into writing a piece for *Celestial City*, a new online guide to London Sundays, as a dry run for Finsbury's potential career as an opinionated commentator on the foibles of bipeds.

The editor of *Celestial City*, fearful of missing the bandwagon for the zeitgeist du jour (although Oliver had speculated that you had to be really slow to miss a bandwagon), had jumped on the publication of an ex-Spice Girl's recovered memories of her former life as Saint Theresa of Avila as a harbinger of the nation's millennial spiritual awakening. He had decided that an atheist ferret's satirical take on a small suburban church would make pleasant online reading for Christmas, especially if the pages included pictures by an absurdly handsome photographer whose career was entirely based on sexual ecstasy.

Oliver always liked working with Ben, partly because his friend and landlord owned a black Lamborghini, and partly because the attention Ben inevitably attracted gave Oliver an excuse for barely being noticed himself. Now in his mid-twenties, he had more or less accepted that, Ben or no Ben, his unkempt fair hair, cheap glasses, and that certain absence of firmness about his jaw were hardly the assets that would capture the interest of a sultry stranger across a less-than-crowded place of worship. Besides, he reflected proudly, he had a steady girlfriend now.

But what had intrigued Oliver about the assignment was the name of the minister of the selected church: the Reverend Paul Piltdown. Oliver had gone to school with a Paul Piltdown. And a call to the manse in the north London suburb of Plumley confirmed that this was indeed the same Pauly Piltdown who'd shared his first copy of *Playboy* and with whom he'd played baccarat during long winter lunchtimes, using rules learned from a James Bond novel. Which explains why Oliver was sitting in church that Sunday evening, thinking of rude things for Finsbury to say about the service and, despite his agnosticism, feeling thoroughly guilty about it.

Oliver had long suspected that his school friend would find a vocation in the church, ever since Pauly's whispered confession as a twelve-year-old that he thought he might look good in a cassock.*(Ah, that's the difference!)* But this church? In the sixth form, Piltdown had been addicted to High-Church Anglicanism, and when Oliver had last seen him, seven years earlier, he'd been heading off to Cambridge with ambitions for a bishopric, an almost gymnastic addiction to genuflecting, and a best blazer that always smelled faintly of incense. Yet instead of the surplices and stoles he had coveted as a teenager, Piltdown's only religious attire this evening was a white clerical collar, worn with a rumpled navy-blue suit that sat awkwardly on his hefty, rugby-player's body.

His surroundings were similarly unadorned. Above the dark oak wainscoting, the only ornamentation on the sallow walls was a row of dimly glowing electric heaters, which were doing little to lift the temperature on that damp December evening. Since there was no altar, Piltdown had conducted most of the simple service from behind a sturdy wooden table, set firmly on the lowest level of a carpeted platform. This platform, which stretched almost the full width of the building, rose a couple of levels behind the minister, presumably for a choir, but instead of an elaborate reredos or dazzling stained glass window, Piltdown's backdrop was the pipe array of a sizeable organ, painted an ugly battleship gray. (The hymns, however, had been accompanied by a young woman who played an upright piano, on the floor to the left of the platform.) The space struck Oliver as more like a theater than a church.

Piltdown had only left his station to deliver the sermon, when he had climbed the steps to a high pulpit, rising out of the right-hand side of the stage like a submarine's conning tower. The one touch of color in the church was a garish, appliqué banner pinned to this pulpit, proclaiming JESUS IS LORD in childish lettering.

"As we draw close to Christmas," the minister was saying, unconsciously patting his thatch of thick, wild hair, "our thoughts naturally turn to that well-known story of our Savior's birth. Perhaps we first learned it from Nativity pageants performed by children, just like the one our own Sunday School will be performing during our Christmas Eve carol service. I myself can remember playing a king one year, wearing a splendid cardboard crown covered with silver foil and my new dressing gown with the gold piping as a robe…"

Piltdown glanced across to the younger people, seeking a smile or nod that would accompany a similar reminiscence, but they remained unmoved. Most were staring dully at their hands while he spoke, avoiding his eyes. They had shown little enthusiasm during the earlier parts of the service, rising wearily to mouth the three or four hymns and bending over so deeply in the pews during the long prayers that they practically disappeared. Perhaps they were playing baccarat?

"And what do we find when we actually study the Christmas story in the scriptures?" Piltdown went on. "Do we find a harsh innkeeper turning Mary and Joseph from the door of the crowded inn, with his tender-hearted wife running after the couple to offer accommodation in their stable? No. Do we find an ox and an ass? No. Nor do we find a stable, for that matter. Or three kings, whom tradition has named for us."

"If I could get up to that balcony," Ben whispered, perching beside Oliver as he reloaded his camera again, "I could do a great overhead shot pointing down on the pews. But the door's locked."

Oliver swiveled to look up at the shallow balcony behind and above them, but from the low angle he could only make out more high-backed pews in the darkness. Lowering his gaze, he met the stern eyes of a middle-aged woman in the rear pew. She winked at him. He smiled weakly and turned around again, wondering what he was missing on television at that moment.

Paul Piltdown had been speaking now for fifteen minutes on the need for Christians to promulgate the biblical facts of the Nativity story without the accretions of tradition and myth. He paused suddenly, and although he did not utter a blessing, it was clear the sermon was over. Piltdown beamed around the church, coughed, and glanced down at his notes.

"Now before our final hymn," he continued, "I'm going to ask our good friend Nigel Tapster to share his musical witness."

Piltdown sat down in the pulpit, sinking from sight, and a man sitting among the teenagers rose to his feet and sidled out of his pew. He was tall and rangy, with a balding head and a sparse, straggling beard that had been fussily shaped to his chin. His gray suit seemed a size too small. He stooped to pick up a large twelve-string guitar, which had been lying in a case beside the piano, and passed its leather strap over his head and one arm. The teenagers all seemed suddenly far more animated, and smiled and whispered to each other as Tapster reached the platform.

He paused, his head down, as if listening intently to words whispered urgently into his ears. Ben's camera clicked several times. Then Tapster lifted his gaze, looking around the church with dark, intense eyes.

"Friends, dear friends," he said, his voice reedy and nasal. "The Reverend Piltdown has just told us what the world believes when it shouldn't. I'd prefer to sing about what the world doesn't believe when it should." He strummed the guitar strings, wincing momentarily.

"It's no good, I'll have to send it back to the shop to be tuned," he said apologetically, stepping off the platform and rummaging in the guitar case. One of the boys in the group let out a short, loud laugh. It echoed sharply off the bare walls of the church, as if the building was swatting away the unfamiliar sound. Tapster blew softly into a pitch pipe, fiddled with the tuning heads, and returned to the platform. "You know, not many people play the twelve-string guitar," he muttered, "because it takes a lot of pluck."

The joke was old and weak, but perhaps it was new to the young people, because they all laughed heartily for as long as it took Tapster to finish tuning the instrument. He played an E major chord, nodded with satisfaction, and began to strum in a different key. It was hardly an infectious rhythm, but within two bars, the young people were already swaying in time with the music. Tapster began to sing, very badly.

The song seemed to consist of little more than three chords and the word "Alleluia," but the youngsters were clearly enjoying it more than anything else in the service. Two or three of them began to clap, and the woman who had been playing the piano earlier now started to shake a tambourine in an arrogant fashion.

The performance ended, and Tapster stepped down from the platform, reverently replacing the guitar in its case. Oliver noticed that the young people mostly had their eyes closed now, with half-smiles on their faces, and one was raising a hand to the ceiling, as if asking God for a bathroom break. The old man in front of Oliver grunted.

Piltdown rose in the pulpit and announced the final hymn. The tambourine player stepped over to the piano and played the introduction to "As With Gladness, Men of Old." Oliver wondered if Tapster would return the earlier compliment and accompany her on the maracas.

After a final blessing and a moment of silent prayer, Piltdown came down from the pulpit and stalked along the aisle on the right-hand side of the church. His flock meanwhile began to gather personal belongings and fidget in their pews. The young people were the first to escape, shuffling up the left aisle and through a heavy velvet curtain that hung below the balcony and separated the sanctuary from the narthex beyond. Tapster stayed behind, collecting his guitar. The pianist waited for him. Oliver passed his hymn book to a young girl of around thirteen, who was already steadying a teetering pile with her chin. She grinned and hurried away.

In the pew in front, the older couple stood as if on cue and turned simultaneously. Though they were both clearly in their seventies, Time had so far treated them with uncharacteristic decency. The woman was tall and straight-backed, with milky skin and a braid of thick white hair. Her husband was stocky-framed, and his hair, while fine and thinning, still covered his scalp and was largely dark. The way he fixed Oliver with a critical gaze from his small, brown eyes indicated he had no need of spectacles.

"Cedric Potiphar," he announced solemnly, with a noticeable Cornish accent and a volume level that showed Time could still be a bastard. Oliver shook the large, dry hand and managed to introduce himself without mispronouncing his name. Potiphar took in this new information. "My wife, Elsie," he added eventually, as if unsure of the propriety of exposing her to a writer. Mrs. Potiphar rewarded Oliver with a nervous smile, but didn't speak. The couple then repeated the entire exercise with Ben.

"May I welcome you both to the Lord's tabernacle on this Sabbath day?" Potiphar intoned loudly.

"Thank you very much," said Oliver.

"We outstretch the hand of fellowship to all," Potiphar conceded. "No matter how unworthy," he added more quietly, with a sidelong glance at Tapster and the pianist, who were ambling past the pew. He fell silent. The girl with the pile of hymn books paused and watched Tapster until he disappeared through the curtain at the back of the church.

"I suppose the guitar-playing is a way to involve the younger folks," said Ben quickly, correctly guessing that the fishlike expression on Oliver's face masked a fruitless and increasingly desperate attempt to think of any conversational comment to make to the Potiphars. Although Oliver was the most polite individual he knew, Ben was also aware that his friend was utterly inept when it came to sustaining small talk.

Potiphar glared at the photographer as if he'd offered to take a set of boudoir shots of his wife. He tapped on the leather cover of his well-worn Bible. "There's nothing in God's word about preaching through entertainment," he grumbled.

"Nothing about hearing aids either, cocky, more's the pity," muttered his wife under her breath. Potiphar appeared not to notice.

They had edged their way to the aisle and joined a queue of people slowly passing through the curtain. The Potiphars seemed content to let Oliver and Ben precede them, and as the two men slipped through into the church's entrance hall, they saw the reason for the hold-up. A one-man receiving line, Paul Piltdown was now greeting each congregant in turn as he or she headed for the front door and the chilly night air of north London.

Ahead of them, Tapster and the woman had collected their out-door wear—a worn anorak for him, a buttonless crimson overcoat for her—and were now speaking to Piltdown simultaneously in low, urgent voices. The genial expression had left the minister's face.

"Good evening, Cedric," said a middle-aged man, who had just collected an overcoat from a peg on the narthex wall. Not waiting for Potiphar to attempt an introduction, the man turned briskly to Oliver and Ben.

"Sam Quarterboy, deacon and church secretary," he announced crisply, as Oliver found his hand being drawn into a hearty and skillful handshake through some hypnotic force he couldn't explain. Quarterboy was clearly practiced in the presentation of a public self, from his shiny brogues to his tight, glossy bald pate. He was of medium height and build, but his stiff bearing and florid face implied that he had ordered his skin one size too small and a much fleshier man was pressing out the wrinkles from the inside.

"I trust you're going to give us a good write-up, Mr. Swithin," he stated. It was not intended as a question, and Oliver was relieved that he wasn't expected to answer. "It's about time people realized that the United Diaconalist Church is very much part of the English landscape. There are a couple of hundred thousand of us around the country. Nothing odd here, as you can see. Just hymns, prayers, sermons. None of this New Age mumbo-jumbo or hysterical charismatic nonsense. Very solid foundation, this church. Very solid."

Quarterboy tapped his foot on the tiled floor and grinned humorlessly, showing more straight white teeth than Oliver imagined could fit in just one set of jaws. Oliver recalled that his dictionary of religion had described the Diaconalists as "nonconformist separatist protestant dissenters"—four words that said what they were against, but not what they were for. But he was saved from thinking of something to say to Quarterboy by the conversation between Piltdown, Tapster, and the woman, which was no longer being conducted in whispers.

"It's the youngsters I'm thinking of," Tapster was saying urgently as he pulled on his anorak. "There are already so many conflicting messages in the world. I'm surprised to hear freethinking from the pulpit."

"*From* the pulpit," the woman echoed, as if Tapster hadn't just used the words.

"Nigel, nobody cares for the children more than I," Piltdown protested. "I truly think you're overreacting."

"We'll see." Tapster picked up his hard guitar case and stared into Piltdown's face. "You know I'm saying these things out of Christian love, Paul. God has plans for Plumley. He has told me."

Piltdown smiled uncomfortably. Tapster opened the narthex door for the woman and followed her through it in a noisy rustle of nylon and Velcro. The pair joined the gaggle of waiting teenagers and drifted away into the darkness.

"Bless me, Father, for I have sneezed!" Oliver called to Piltdown's back. There was a slight pause, then Piltdown turned with a broad smirk and grasped Oliver's hand as if it were a lifeline. Oliver introduced Ben, and they stood to one side while Piltdown ceremonially bade farewell to the remaining congregants.

"Go in and make yourself at home," Piltdown was saying as Cedric and Elsie Potiphar cautiously made their way down the frosty church steps. "I hold an open house at the Manse after the service," he explained to Oliver. "Sandwiches and tea and a little fellowship. If you're not rushing away, perhaps you'd care to join us?"

"A cup of tea, Vicar?" said Oliver, silently checking for Ben's assent. "That would be lovely."

"Jolly good, but for the sake of your article, remember that I'm a minister, not a vicar," Piltdown said genially. "It makes a difference. I'm a servant of this congregation, not the representative of a higher authority."

He stepped through the narthex doors, crossed a shallow vestibule, and tugged the church's main door closed, making sure the catch had clicked into place.

"Does that mean your members are free to challenge your sermons?" asked Oliver as Piltdown came back into the narthex. "Sorry, we couldn't help overhearing the tail end of your conversation with the—for want of a better word—musicians."

Piltdown led them through the darkened church, turning off the heaters as he passed. "That was Nigel Tapster and his wife, Heather. She's filling in as the pianist for our services. Well, yes, authority in the United Diaconalist Church is not central, as in the Church of England. We don't have bishops or cardinals or anything like that. Each congregation is independent, supervised by its elders—deacons, hence the name 'Diaconalist.' As their minister, I'm only a sort of full-time professional super-deacon, with more responsibilities, including leading the worship, but no greater authority. And anyone in the congregation can be a 'prayer minister,' if the Spirit moves them."

"And this Nigel Tapster's one of your deacons?" Ben asked.

"Actually, no. Nigel's fairly new to the church, but he has a marvelous way with the young people—he's attracted quite a few new members in the months he's been with us. They're good people, he and his wife." Piltdown made the comment as if it was a reminder to himself. "We're having our annual church meeting this Friday, when we elect deacons for the coming year. I believe Nigel will be standing for election. If you want to find out more about the church, Ollie, you're welcome to come and observe."

"I'd like to but I have to see my uncle's Bottom," Oliver claimed with a snigger. Ben sighed. They had passed through a doorway beside the pulpit and were now standing at one end of a dim, musty-smelling corridor that ran the full width of the building.

"Ah yes, your uncle, the Scotland Yard detective," said Pilt-down, without a pause. "I remember that he was fond of amateur dramatics. At school, we used to envy you enormously for having an uncle who was Chief Inspector Mallard *and* a Shakespearian actor, to boot. I presume from your comment that he's perform-ing in *A Midsummer Night's Dream?*"

He broke off as Ben burst in sudden peals of laughter and thumped Oliver soundly on the back.

"Did I say something funny?" Piltdown asked apprehensively, noticing Oliver's crestfallen expression.

"Not intentionally, Paul," Ben spluttered, attempting to recover his breath. "It's just that Oliver's been going round for weeks bleating 'I'm going to see my uncle's Bottom' and hoping that somebody would fall for it."

"Oh, sorry, Ollie," said Piltdown contritely. "Would it help if I roared and split my sides now?"

"That won't be necessary," Oliver muttered.

"How is your uncle, by the way? Still a detective?"

"Yes. He's a superintendent now."

"Promoted to glory. Well, not in the biblical sense," Piltdown added hastily. "Not that the expression has a biblical origin, of course, it's just…" He let the remark trail off and tilted his head on one side. In the silence, they could hear sounds from the far end of the corridor—coins and glassware clinking, not neces-sarily in the same room. Nobody was in sight, but light shone through a couple of transoms.

"I don't want to lock anybody in," Piltdown mused, toying with a bunch of keys.

"Who would still be here?" Oliver asked, privately amazed that the dank, cheerless building could keep anybody from a warm home now that the service was over.

"I imagine one of the deacons is counting the offering, and there could be someone in the kitchen wrapping up the church flowers." Piltdown gestured to a door beside them "Look, why don't you two go next door to the Manse and make yourselves at home? I'll be along shortly."

Oliver and Ben let themselves out into the chilly night air and cautiously traced an overgrown path that skirted the building. Light from the streetlamps ahead of them glinted off cigarette butts, broken beer bottles, and a couple of discarded condoms among the nettles, indicating that God's name may have been called upon outside as well as inside the church. The path led them to a small, gravel car park in front of the building, separated from the main road by a low wall.

"Has organized religion had any impact on your life, Ben?" Oliver asked cautiously, as they turned into the street. There was little traffic on the road that Sunday evening.

"Yeah, when I was growing up, there was that hour every Sunday evening."

"When you went to church?"

"No, when we turned off the television because all the channels were showing religious programs. I've always hated Sundays, Ollie. London Sundays are a black-and-white day in a technicolor week. They're like that squishy package you got among your Christmas presents—the one from your father's childless aunt that always turned out to be socks."

"I never minded socks," Oliver reflected. "Should I get Effie socks for Christmas? Not very romantic, I suppose."

They turned into the gateway of the manse and studied the facade of the large, square, nineteenth-century house. It had been denied any of the ugly ornamental features that later generations would pretend to adore, in a desperate attempt to believe that most Victorians were whimsical madcaps. Instead, the manse stood behind a shallow but well-tended front garden and scowled glumly at the road with the half-naked bulkiness of a sumo wrestler.

The front door was ajar, although there was nobody in the hallway. They heard voices and a few notes from a piano in the large reception room on the left. Ben took Oliver firmly by the elbow and guided him into the room, aware that the prospect of stepping into a room full of people he didn't know would be enough to keep his friend studying the hallway long-case clock all evening.

The girl who had been picking out "Wonderwall" on the poorly tuned piano seemed too young to have seen a lot of westerns, but she still stopped playing abruptly. Everyone in the room stared at the new arrivals. Oliver realized with relief that he had already met more than half the room's occupants—the Potiphars sitting stolidly on a hard couch in front of the bay window, Sam Quarterboy perched on a dining chair beside the upright piano, and the young teenage girl on the piano-stool, whose face he'd last seen above a pile of hymn books. There were only two strangers: a woman in a deep armchair beside Quarterboy and a slim young man in his twenties, sitting at the far end of the room on another hard dining chair.

Quarterboy leaped up and drew the visitors smoothly into the room, introducing the woman as his wife, Joan, the girl as his daughter, Tina, and the young man as Barry Foison, before splitting them as neatly as a pack of cards. Oliver found himself irresistibly guided to a raffia-topped stool between the Potiphars's sofa and Joan Quarterboy's armchair, while Ben took a seat between Tina and Foison.

Joan Quarterboy was in her late thirties and clearly believed in going to church dressed in her Sunday best. She wore a blue two-piece suit, artificial pearls, and an odd hat shaped uncomfortably like an overturned dog dish on her frizzy hair, which was already styled in anticipation of her retirement years. Her small features seemed to huddle for protection in the middle of her face. Lipstick was her only makeup, exactly the same shade of orange as the spine of a Penguin novel. Oliver took one look and guessed that Joan had never owned a pair of jeans in her life.

Both she and Potiphars were smiling encouragingly at him, as if willing him to speak. Ben was already deep in conversation with Foison and the girl, and Oliver once again envied his handsome friend's confidence and social ease. Being alluring like Ben must be like having your self-consciousness surgically removed at birth, and Oliver remembered his fear that even the harshly professional Effie Strongitharm would not be immune to the good-looking photographer's potent pheromones, back in the days when Oliver was nobly but inexpertly concealing his passion for his uncle's Sergeant. But Effie had chosen him, and the last four months had been the happiest in Oliver's life. He wished she were here now. No, definitely something more romantic than socks. He swallowed and tried to think of a question for his neighbors.

"Er, have you been members of the church long?" he asked nobody in particular. Joan Quarterboy looked abruptly terrified and turned toward her husband.

"My wife and I moved to Plumley when we got married," Sam Quarterboy cut in, to Joan's evident relief. "The Quarterboys have been Diaconalists for generations. But the record at this church is held by young Cedric here. He's been serving the Lord as a deacon now for more than forty years, without a break. Isn't that right, Cedric?"

Cedric Potiphar was staring ahead of him as if he hadn't been listening, but he spoke in his deep Cornish tones.

"'For he that is called in the Lord, being a servant, is the Lord's freeman.' One Corinthians, chapter seven, verse twenty-two."

"Very true, brother, very true," Quarterboy agreed, and Oliver found himself nodding sagely with the others. But only he seemed to hear Elsie Potiphar's whisper:

"Needs a servant himself, to pick his dirty knickers off the bedroom floor."

Oliver looked at her quickly, but she seemed lost in thought. He realized it was time to pose another question.

"So, Mr. Potiphar, I imagine you must be an honorary deacon for life by now?"

Potiphar frowned, and looked as if he was going to dredge up another biblical reference, but again Sam Quarterboy spoke first.

"Every deacon has to be elected, Mr. Swithin, every year at the annual church meeting. In fact, it's taking place on Friday evening. There are four places on the diaconate—Cedric and I are humbly putting our names forward for consideration, as we do every year. And Patience Coppersmith and Dougie Dock are also standing again—I imagine you'll be meeting them shortly."

Oliver noticed that Quarterboy hadn't mentioned Nigel Tapster. Didn't Paul say he was running, no doubt on the bearded twit ticket?

"Why don't you join us on Friday at the church meeting?" Quarterboy continued. "I'm sure it would give you some valuable information for this article of yours."

"Your minister already invited me," Oliver replied swiftly. "But on Friday, I'm scheduled to see my uncle's Bottom."

There was an uncomfortable silence, apart from a small suppressed squeak from Elsie Potiphar. The smile drained from Joan Quarterboy's face.

"I'm not sure I understand you," said Sam Quarterboy tentatively.

"Oh. Well, my uncle's playing Bottom in Shakespeare's *A Midsummer Night's Dream*, you see, and I'm going to a performance."

Oliver waited in vain for the comprehending laughter. Quarterboy adopted a look that suggested he was about to explain Diaconalism to a slow eight-year-old (something he might have attempted). "Then perhaps, you could have put it that way in the first place," he said starchily. "I'm sure you didn't mean it, but your comment implied you were going to look at a close relative in an unclothed state."

"It's just as well our Tina didn't hear," whispered Joan. They all looked across to where their young daughter was talking animatedly to Ben Motley and Barry Foison. Ben glanced up at that moment and noticed Oliver's shamefaced expression.

"Oliver," he called quickly, interrupting the girl's flow of words, "you should really hear this. Tina's been telling us how much she likes writing."

Tina Quarterboy swivelled on the piano stool and fixed her intense brown eyes on Oliver. Her face had a permanently eager expression, as if someone had grasped her nose and pulled it forward slightly, dragging the rest of her features after it. Oliver just had time to notice her long dark pigtail and the casual clothes on her thin body, which were mercifully contemporary, when she began speaking to him, very rapidly.

"Oh yes, I love writing," she said, beaming. "I write all the time. I was just telling Mr. Motley here that I want to be a writer when I grow up. Every evening, you know, instead of watching television, I take out my journal and put down everything that happened and everything I've thought of during the day. I don't mind at all. I'd spend my whole day writing if I could—stories, poems, my thoughts, my ideas, anything and everything. I just want to be a writer."

Ben interrupted quickly. "Yes, I was just saying, Ollie, that since you're a writer yourself, Tina might want to pick your brains, gather a few tips."

"That's so interesting," Tina cut in again. "It must be wonderful to be a professional writer. What sort of things do you write?"

"Well, I write stories for children," Oliver began cautiously.

"How marvelous!" cried Tina. "I'd like to write stories for children. I've done some adventure stories, imagining myself in all kinds of peril, but they're really for grownups. How do you think of your stories, Mr. Swithin?"

"Now that's an interesting question. I suppose—"

"I really don't know how I think of *my* stories," Tina interrupted. "They just come to me. I was writing this really fascinating one the other day..."

The front door to the manse slammed. Tina trailed off as Paul Piltdown appeared in the doorway, to Oliver's great relief, since the beaming Quarterboys showed no inclination to wrestle their daughter to the ground and gag her. Piltdown greeted his guests and immediately took orders for tea and coffee.

"Patience and Dougie will be joining us shortly," he added. "They're just running the church flowers round to poor Mrs. Aymis, who's been in bed with her leg."

Oliver sniggered, but nobody else seemed to see the humor, so he turned it into a throat-clearing.

"Let me give you a hand," said Joan Quarterboy, making no attempt whatsoever to rise from her comfortable chair.

"No, let me, I know where things are," shouted Tina, to Oliver's relief, and she bounded off the piano stool and followed Piltdown toward the kitchen.

"The minister thinks a lot of our Tina," Joan said softly. She signaled this family victory with a peculiar smile, which actually turned the corners of her narrow mouth downward. "She's very fond of him."

"He's a good man," Sam Quarterboy cut in, as if the remark were a work in progress rather than a final judgment. "Of course, there were those of us who didn't take to his High Church ways at first. And there's a little too much theology in his sermons, for my taste. But we've come to respect him."

"Well, I for one prefer a little meat on the bone of my sermons," cried Barry Foison unexpectedly, in a high-pitched voice. "I found this evening's sermon refreshing and thought-provoking, and frankly, I'm disgusted that horrible man Tapster had the gall to criticize Paul in front of the whole church."

"The question I ask myself," said Potiphar, stirring to life, "is who granted this Nigel Tapster the dispensation to preach unto us this evening? The elders of the church were not consulted. Is this to become a regular part of our worship? There's nothing in my Bible about guitars." He fondled the book, which lay in his lap.

"The young people seemed to enjoy Mr. Tapster's music," Oliver commented as he wrote some thoughts in his notebook. When nobody answered, he looked up. Eventually, Joan Quarterboy broke the clumsy silence.

"We're a little concerned about Nigel's influence over our young people, Mr. Swithin," she explained, leaning forward as if sharing a secret, although the entire room was following the conversation. "We're rather afraid he wants to alienate the children from the church. They've taken to meeting privately in the Tapsters' home after the evening service, and sometimes during the week, too. Nigel and Heather Tapster have some odd ideas, it seems."

"Odd ideas?" Oliver echoed. Joan seemed to warm to her new role as storyteller.

"Well, Patience Coppersmith's son, Billy, is about the same age as our Tina, and he got her to go with him to a couple of Nigel's prayer meetings. But she came back with some very peculiar stories, about spirits making her do things, hearing people speak in tongues, and the like. She's at that impressionable age, you see, Mr. Swithin. So Sam put his foot down and insisted that she come home with us after church from now on. Billy is still part of Nigel's little group, though, and I know Patience is sick with worry about him. Apparently, Nigel tried to do the same thing at his last church, Thripstone Central. But there was some sort of scandal, and he was asked to leave."

"What sort of scandal?" Oliver pressed, sensing fodder for his story. Joan looked uncomfortable.

"I believe it had something to do with a girl," she said, mouthing the last word as if she was referring to a gynecological problem. "Barry can tell you. He used to go to Thripstone."

Foison crossed his slim legs and wrapped his right shin behind his left calf. "This was a couple of years ago, before Heather and Nigel got married," he claimed. "They'd only just met. She was a missionary in Brazil for most of the time Nigel was at Thripstone."

"Now, now, Barry," Quarterboy interrupted, "I'm sure we don't want to give Mr. Swithin the impression that we sit around after church gossiping like a lot of old women."

The criticism found its mark. Foison seemed to shrink inside his large, baggy sweater, aware of the eyes watching him. Behind

Oliver, Elsie Potiphar mumbled something that sounded like "lot of old women, yourself, tosh," but when he turned, she was staring into space. Ben diplomatically started a conversation with Foison.

"If Tina's friends continue to go to the Tapsters' meetings, aren't you worried she might still be drawn to their circle?" Oliver asked Joan quietly.

"She'd never defy her father," Sam cut in, with a small self-satisfied smile. "We only had to have that conversation once. I see it as my parental duty to protect her from wrong-thinking people who'd fill her little mind with things we don't agree with. That includes smutty talk, which is why I may have seemed a little old-fashioned about your unintended remark earlier, Mr. Swithin."

"As it is, Tina will lose her innocence soon enough," Joan quavered sadly. "In fact, Sam and I have been discussing when we should do this."

Oliver started. He was unaware that virgin sacrifice was one of the rituals of the United Diaconalist Church. Now this would make the article a little more interesting. But it quickly occurred to him that the Quarterboys equated the word "innocence" with a basic ignorance of avian and apian matters. "Surely she's already had some sexual education in school?" he suggested. Sam winced at the word.

"Oh, we've insisted that she be removed from those classes," he replied.

"We told Tina that babies are a gift from God to a mother and father," said Joan. "Which is true, of course. And then we made it clear that we wouldn't answer any more questions, so we know she doesn't have any."

Sam sighed. "I wouldn't trust schoolteachers to tell my child the facts of life. They're bound to make copulation sound pleasurable. If we left our children in ignorance a little while longer, we'd have far fewer teenage pregnancies and nobody would be murdering unborn children—"

He stopped himself abruptly as Tina paced slowly into the room, holding the handles of a large wooden tray. She placed it on a coffee table and began to hand out small plates and paper napkins to the group. Then she passed around a platter of bread rolls, cut in half and slathered with butter and fish paste.

"Aren't you having some, too?" Oliver asked her, taking a roll and balancing his plate on his thigh.

"No, that stuff makes me blow chunks," Tina answered blandly. Joan tutted, but Sam, now drawn into the conversation with Ben and Barry Foison, didn't notice. "A lot of things make me puke these days," the girl continued. "Besides, I'm on a diet."

"Where do they get these ideas?" asked Joan in wonderment, as if her daughter had just declaimed Newton's first law of motion in High German.

"It's true, Mum, I've been putting on weight lately."

"But that's normal, lovey, you're a growing girl. You know, Mr. Swithin," Joan added, after Tina had slipped out of the room again, "I wonder if we need to have that conversation sooner rather than later. Oh dear."

They heard the front door open and close, and a slim woman in her late forties came into the room. In contrast to the other women, she was smartly dressed, in a way that suggested style had won out over fashion, and her graying hair was expensively cut into overlapping spikes that folded around her skull like flower petals. She had just been introduced as Patience Coppersmith when Piltdown finally made an entrance, carrying another large tray laden with cups, saucers, and an enormous teapot under a bright quilted cozy. Tina trotted in behind him, reverently clutching a coffee pot.

"Is Dougie with you?" Piltdown asked Patience.

"He's just parking the car."

Joan Quarterboy tapped Oliver on the arm. "Have you met Dougie Dock yet?" she asked softly.

"I'm afraid not."

"Oh, he's a character, you'll like him." She leaned in close and whispered, as if giving Oliver a secret password. "He's a bit of lad, on the quiet." Oliver, not knowing what this expression meant or why it seemed to be a confidence, took a bite out of his roll and wondered why Ben was suddenly frowning at him.

"I'm sorry it's all a little basic," Piltdown said apologetically as he poured tea and handed the cups around the room.

"You do very well, considering you're on your own," declared Patience. Her voice was clear and musical, as if she were used to addressing children. There were polite murmurs of agreement around the room. "But it's about time you started looking for a wife, Paul," Patience continued. She grinned. "I can say that because I'm nearly old enough to be your mother."

"But not quite," laughed Barry Foison. "And you are available, Patience."

Piltdown smiled without meeting anybody's gaze. "I'm not sure being a Diaconalist minister's wife is an attractive prospect for today's young women. But someday I'll get around to it."

"He's waiting for me to get older," Tina asserted, which provoked more laughter.

"We never see *you* with a girlfriend, either, for that matter," Joan Quarterboy said to Barry Foison. The smile faded from Foison's face again, and he pretended to be fascinated with the pattern on his plate. The front door slammed, and a middle-aged man in a blazer and sheepskin-lined car coat came into view.

"Ah, Dougie, good," Piltdown announced. "Now we can say grace."

Dougie Dock hovered in the doorway and the church members bowed their heads as Piltdown delivered a brief prayer. Oliver did his best to hide the large bite he had already taken from his roll.

"I know I'm popular, but there's no need to give thanks every time I arrive," Dock caroled. He was of medium height and had a thin face, decorated with heavy-framed spectacles and very blue jowls and chin. The lank black hair that still remained on the sides of his head was brushed backwards and hung over his collar. His remark received a mixed reaction from the audience, from deprecating tuts to polite chuckles, but nobody laughed longer than Dock himself. Piltdown introduced Oliver and Ben.

"Ooh, hell-oo," Dock crooned, with a peculiar singsong tone to the second syllable. He executed a theatrical half-bow where he stood, then picked his way across the room to shake hands with Ben and then Oliver.

"And while I'm over here," he continued, in a nasal voice the swept good-humoredly into the falsetto range, "I must grab a kiss from the youngest dolly-bird in the room." He leaned over Elsie Potiphar and planted his lips on her cheek. Joan Quarterboy laughed indulgently and nudged Oliver.

"Now don't you go getting jealous, Cedric," Dock said with a wink, stepping away, but managing to nudge Oliver from the other side as he passed. Potiphar grunted amiably, and some of the others laughed again. Only Oliver heard Elsie Potiphar mutter the word "Prick!" vehemently under her breath. Dock tugged playfully at Tina's pigtail as he passed. She cried "Ow!" with unnecessary vigor and scowled at him, but he just grinned and took an unoccupied chair beside the door.

"Did I understand you're writing an article about us, Oliver?" Dock asked. "You ought to come to the church's annual business meeting on Friday and see what goes on behind the scenes."

"Yes, thank you, Mr. Dock—"

Dock held up an admonitory hand. "Please, I'm Dougie to everyone. Jesus used his first name, and if it was good enough for him, it's good enough for me, eh?" He chortled for some time at the remark. "Besides, if you call me 'Dock,' people might think I really am one."

"What?" asked Ben.

"A doctor. Or one of the seven dwarfs, eh, Tina?" Dock laughed again and pulled at the girl's pigtail. She moved out of range sullenly. "So you'll come on Friday then. Oliver?"

"Actually no," Oliver replied carefully. "I have a prior engagement. My uncle's drama group is performing *A Midsummer Night's Dream*."

"Ooh, I say, are you going to see your uncle's Bottom?" Dock interrupted emphatically and subsided into guffaws of laughter, without taking his gaze from Oliver's face. Tina spluttered, some of the others laughed aloud, and to his irritation, Oliver noticed that even Sam and Joan Quarterboy were smiling faintly, although shaking their heads.

"I don't know how I think of them," cried Dock as he wiped his eyes, complimenting himself quickly in case nobody else did. Oliver, feeling the amused eyes of Ben and Paul Piltdown on him, bent forward and took another mouthful of fish paste roll.

It was close to ten o'clock when Ben's Lamborghini hurtled away from the curb in front of the church and the sudden G forces caused Oliver to rediscover prayer. They had spent the bulk of the evening in the clutches of Dougie Dock, who had produced a large wallet of color prints from a summertime trip to Canada and proceeded to give them an illustrated lecture without once asking Ben's professional opinion as to why half the pictures seemed to be studies of his camera's flash, reflected in the window of a moving tour bus. Dock broke off only once to show a card trick to Tina, provoking loud mutters from Cedric Potiphar about "the Devil's picture-book" and quieter grunts of "Get a life" from Elsie, although Oliver could not be sure whom she was referring to. The magic trick failed because Tina apparently took the wrong card. Unlike most children, she did not ask the conjuror to do it again.

At last, Oliver's social torture ended, and the visitors collected their coats and vanished into the night, but not before Dock had produced a fifty-pence piece from behind his ear twice.

"What did you make of them?" Oliver asked as they sped along the Westway toward their home in Holland Park. Ben hesitated, pretending to concentrate on an unnecessary gear change.

"Pleasant," he said eventually. "Hospitable. Devout. Sincere. Virtuous, I'm sure."

"Dull?"

"Er...possibly."

"Yes," Oliver agreed. "They certainly seem to have chosen a dull way to spend a London Sunday: badly sung hymns in a chilly church, hard pews, and a fifteen-minute sermon, followed by fish paste sandwiches. It was a bit like stepping though a time warp and finding yourself back in the seventies."

"The fifties," Ben murmured caustically.

"I wish Geoffrey hadn't got us into this. They're decent, ordinary people. There's nothing there for Finsbury the Ferret to make fun of."

Ben thought for a moment. "What about this Nigel Tapster?" he asked. "They all seem to think he's trouble, with the possible exception of your friend Paul. Speaking in tongues, exorcizing evil spirits—no wonder young Tina Quarterboy wanted to be part of Tapster's private club. Casting out demons is a bit more entertaining than Dougie Dock's tired conjuring tricks. Finsbury could go to town on that stuff."

The Tapsters left as foul a taste in Oliver's mouth as three cups of Piltdown's cut-price tea. But Ben had a point. Could "Finsbury the Ferret Meets the Exorcist of Plumley" suit *Celestial City's* needs?

Oliver looked out over West London and sighed. He might have shown more interest if he'd known that Nigel Tapster would be dead within a week and he'd already encountered the murderer.

Chapter Two

Save Us All from Satan's Power

Thursday, December 18

Detective Superintendent Timothy Mallard was worried, for the wrong reason.

There were plenty of right reasons. For one thing, he was sitting on the receiving end of an oversized desk in the office of his boss's boss, Assistant Commissioner Weed. Out of onomastic necessity, Weed had spent at least fifty percent of his professional life cultivating a personal style so instantly forbidding that, as a protective reflex, the brains of his inferiors had learned to repress any conscious association between the AC's unfortunate surname and its common botanical meaning. As a result, many a chief inspector in Weed's area had found his or her sleep disturbed by dreams of menacing six-foot dandelions.

But when Mallard had discovered, shortly after joining the police force some thirty-five years earlier, that he did not possess the innate ability to intimidate, he had resolved that he was not going to let himself be intimidated by anyone not actually in possession of a weapon that goes bang. Young Weed held no terrors for him, despite the AC's best efforts over the years. Mallard did not even have the native fear of authority, which left his nephew-by-marriage Oliver tongue-tied in the presence of a peaked cap.

Nor was Mallard worried about the following evening's opening night of *A Midsummer Night's Dream*. He was immune to stage fright (although the audience for the Theydon Bois Thespians' Christmas productions rarely outnumbered the cast), he was confident of his lines, and he had even bought into the director's interpretation of the play.

Humfry Fingerhood's late-summer production of *Macbeth* had been a surprising triumph with local playgoers, largely because the director's emphasis on bare flesh and copious blood had unwittingly turned a tragedy into a comedy. Humfry now seemed determined to reverse the process with the *Dream*. He had ditched the horror movie setting he'd used for the previous play, to the disappointment of the more satirical Thespians, who thought *A Midsummer Night's Scream* would make a good sequel to *Dracbeth*. To their initial disappointment, the three large women who had stripped to the buff as Macbeth's witches had all been asked to keep their clothes on to play Titania's fairies, and Humfry had limited his trademark nudity to the quartet of young lovers, who would enter the forest in the stiff unyielding costume of the late Victorians and then gradually shed their celluloid collars, waistcoats, petticoats, corsets, and other clothing, as appropriate to their gender. Finally, the lovers would symbolize their early morning awareness of Truth at the beginning of Act Five by skinny-dipping in the orchestra pit.

(The pit's regular occupant, a pasty-faced voyeur who played the piano for the Thespians, had been looking forward to this coup de théâtre until he discovered that in "a statement about ageism and homophobia in modern society," Humfry had cast four overweight middle-aged men as the lovers. The pianist had not been seen since last night's dress rehearsal. Nobody missed him.)

Mercifully, Humfry's only instruction to Mallard was to "play it straight." This had puzzled Mallard at first, who had always innocently assumed that the "Pyramus and Thisbe" play-within-a-play was a farcical send-up of amateur dramatics. But he deferred to Humfry and had found what he believed to be the key to this unorthodox approach. His only niggling concern was fitting himself into his costume, which had come from a job lot of surplus costumes donated by the Royal Shakespeare Company, from a time when the RSC clearly stressed S&M. He was conscious that the lace-up trousers he had chosen were meant for a much slimmer man and had quietly added a tin of talcum powder to his makeup box.

Not that Mallard was carrying any surplus weight on his tall, thin frame. Growing older was yet another thing he refused to worry about. His health was much better than it should have been, given the stressful hours he put in each day as a Scotland Yard detective, followed inevitably by a long, wearying commute home because of his insistence on spending every night with his wife, Phoebe. Despite his thick, white hair, he managed to look younger than his age, perhaps because his lined face was partly obscured by nondescript spectacles and a slightly disreputable moustache.

He was mentally prepared for the passage of time, too. Mallard had spent a very high proportion of his adult life doing the two things he enjoyed most, which were solving crime and loving his spouse, and he felt this track record would spare him from regrets on this side of the grave and from judgment on the other.

So it was odd that a man with no fear of intimidation, public display, or mortality should be apprehensive of a buff folder, lying closed on Weed's enormous desk. Mallard knew what it was and he feared it.

Weed·cleared his throat and glared at Mallard, his small eyes as dark and round as bullet-holes under dense, black eyebrows like a pair of crows' wings. His mouth opened, a sudden gash appearing in his face, and the tip of his tongue probed around the edges of this entrance, as if feeling for lips that weren't there. Mallard, who knew Weed well by now, returned the smile.

"Well, Tim," Weed began, in his faint Yorkshire accent, "look what I have here."

"What is it?" Mallard replied cautiously. Weed picked up the folder.

"It's your personnel file, Superintendent. And from the look of it, I'd say it's been out of circulation for some time."

"Really?"

"Yes, really. The most recent date in it is 1976."

"How strange," said Mallard, not casually enough. He crossed his legs, still not casually enough, and failed to ask the question Weed was expecting.

"It turned up out of the blue during a routine audit the other day," Weed persevered. "We found it inside the criminal record of one Vic Pilchard, currently serving five years for video piracy in Holloway."

"Holloway is a women's prison."

"I didn't say your file was the only mix-up in this case," Weed admitted, looking slightly uncomfortable. "Frankly, we were wondering why Pilchard hadn't applied for parole. But do you have any idea where your file was *before* Pilchard's conviction? Or how a senior Scotland Yard detective's personal information found its way into the National Identification Bureau in the first place?"

"I couldn't begin to guess."

"No, I don't suppose you could." Weed glowered, sensing that the formality of Mallard's answers, as well as his fidgeting, masked some deeper concern. Mallard attempted to deflect the conversation.

"But this doesn't seem to have affected my career," he stammered. "I mean, I have had a promotion or two since 1976. I was a detective sergeant then, I recall, working for Chief Detective Inspector Cadwallader. Cadwallader the Cad, we called him, although he was actually quite a gentle man, and devoted to his family. His wife was once a Wopsie; they met on a case—"

"Yes, most interesting," Weed interrupted, as aware as Mallard that his own career with the Yard did not go back half as far. "Naturally, you haven't been the Invisible Policeman since 1976, and your computer records are all up-to-date. But that's the odd thing."

Weed opened the folder and shuffled some of the loose pages. Mallard tensed.

"I did a quick check against these old application forms and data sheets, just out of curiosity, and it seems there are certain… discrepancies."

Now for it. Mallard swallowed noisily. Weed's face darkened in a clear attempt to be conciliatory.

"Tim, the computer thinks you're five years younger than you really are. You're overdue for retirement."

Mallard allowed no expression to cross his features.

"Well, that's nice to know," he began amicably, "but I'm not sure I'm ready to hang up the handcuffs just yet. Maybe in a year or two. I'd like to see young DS Strongitharm make it to inspector first."

Weed leaned forward and assumed an expression that had once made a burly detective inspector lose control of his bladder in the same chair. "I'm not sure you understand me, Tim. We knew you were well past the *recommended* retirement age for police officers. At your level, and with your experience, we have the discretion to ignore that. But what this means is you're older the *mandatory* retirement age of fifty-five, and no amount of discretion can keep you here once you pass that point."

"Rules are made to be broken," Mallard suggested hypocritically, since he had always held that the remark belonged with the collection of ready-made expressions that only stupid people used to account for anything that happened, such as "There are more things in heaven and earth" and "God moves in a mysterious way" and "A bad dress rehearsal means a good opening night." Five actors had said that one, like a mantra, the night before.

"Not this rule." Weed sat back and adopted what he thought was a sympathetic look, although on the receiving end, it looked as if the AC was signaling lack of responsibility for a fart. "But surely, Tim, retirement's something you'd be looking forward to? I can't think how someone like you, who came of age working for the great detectives—men like Cherrill and Beveridge and Cadwallader—could stomach the way the Yard works these days. It's been a bloody long time since a Scotland Yard super-intendent's name was a household word, front page news, and all that. Today, investigators depend so much on the scientists."

"We always have," Mallard growled.

"What I mean is, it's all computerized, decentralized. Every area, every region has its own murder experts right there on the ground."

"Maybe, but while there's still a need for a Murder Squad, no matter how diminished, I'd like to be part of it, even if I'm the last one in the frame."

Weed shuddered. "Now there you go, Tim. 'Murder Squad.' How many times do I have to tell you, it's supposed to be Serious Crimes. You're the last of a dying breed, Superintendent."

"All the more reason for some conservation," Mallard replied darkly. Weed wagged a finger at him.

"Now, now, Tim, I know why you're putting up a fight, I know what you're thinking."

Mallard found that hard to believe, since it involved an intimate knowledge of fourteenth-century Huguenot torture methods. "You do?"

"Oh yes. You think that since it's an official mistake, we should cut you some slack. And you'd be right. We can still be flexible. So there's no need to worry."

"No?"

"No, we'll up your pension to take account of the payments you've already missed."

Mallard did not answer. He stared out of Weed's window at the gray London roofscape. Yes, he expected to retire someday, sometime in the next few years; he and Phoebe had already planned the round-the-world cruise they would take before selling their Theydon Bois house and buying that rundown farmhouse in Dorset, which he would painstakingly renovate while first writing his memoirs and then rewriting them in a series of soft-boiled police procedurals. But was that supposed to happen so soon?

"So here's what I want you to do," Weed was saying. "There's only a couple of weeks before the end of the year, and I know you and DS Strongitharm don't have a case at the moment. I'm giving you some additional paid leave, starting tomorrow. You could probably use it with Christmas coming. Why don't you take the time to think about the situation, and then we can start you on your pension in January."

"What about Strongitharm?" Mallard asked nervously.

"Effie will be fine," Weed assured him. "You've trained her well. Besides, I've got something for her to do until we reshuffle the teams in the new year."

Mallard studied the nameplate on Weed's desk. "Who knows about this?"

"Just you and me, for now. I presume you'd like it to look as if it's your own decision to retire. In fact, I'd like it to be your decision, which is why I'm giving you time to get used to it. Come back the Monday after Christmas and bring in your official notification in writing. For the records."

He stood up. The interview was clearly at an end. Mallard pushed his chair back and reached casually for his file.

"Can I take this?" he asked. "For old times' sake"

Weed placed a stubby finger on the folder, pinning it to the desk-top. His eyes narrowed, almost disappearing under the shaggy eyebrows, and his face seemed to split and gape again, revealing lower teeth like a line of tipsy snowmen. Mallard had never seen him so happy.

"I think I'll keep it. For now," he said. He slipped the folder into a drawer in his desk.

Mallard shuffled from the room, unaccountably thinking of stinging nettles. And where he'd like to stuff some.

◇◇◇

It was five-thirty, and almost dark when Oliver stepped out of the Plumley Central Underground Station, tried first to guess the way to the Tapster's home, and then reluctantly accepted the symbolic castration that went along with asking for directions at a nearby newsagent.

After several days of procrastination, he had finally decided to pursue Ben's suggestion and see if an interview with Nigel Tapster would provide some feisty, festive, Finsbury prose. He called the Tapsters and found that the lay preacher would be delighted to meet him on Thursday evening. Oliver was almost looking forward to the meeting. It made a pleasant change after several frustrating hours on the telephone with the manufacturer of his laptop computer, which had stubbornly failed to boot up that morning. He had just exhausted his third service representative, when he noticed that someone had turned down the brightness control on his display, and the computer had been working perfectly all the time.

The Tapsters lived in a surprisingly large semidetached house on a quiet residential street, which was clearly within walking distance of the church. Certainly Paul Piltdown showed no sign of looking for a parked car as he hurried out of the Tapsters' front garden, slamming the wrought-iron gate behind him and striding rapidly along the street toward Oliver.

"Nice day for a walk, Vicar," Oliver said cheerfully when Piltdown drew level with him. Piltdown continued to barrel along the pavement for a second, as if Oliver's comment needed more than one attempt to clear the bar of his attention. Then he stopped abruptly and spun around, frowning.

"Ollie, it *is* you," he exclaimed. "Sorry, I thought I must be dreaming. You're the last person I expected to see." He looked away, and Oliver realized the comment was not motivated by joy. Piltdown began to adjust his clerical collar fussily.

"I'm paying a visit to Nigel Tapster," Oliver declared. "I presume you had the earlier appointment."

"What?"

"You've just been to see the Tapsters?"

"Oh yes. Yes, I saw him." Piltdown thrust his hands into the pockets of his overcoat.

"I'm surprised he didn't tell you I was coming. I'm planning to interview him for the article—to get the full breadth of Diaconalist belief."

Piltdown didn't react, but studied his feet thoughtfully. Oliver wondered if he was feeling cold.

"Look, I don't want to keep you," he continued brightly, "but since I'm here in Plumley, I was hoping I could drop round to the manse later, after I'm finished with the Tapsters."

"Finished with the Tapsters," Piltdown echoed. He looked up suddenly. "Sorry, Ollie, what? You want to come round later?"

"If that's all right. We didn't really get much of a chance to talk the other evening."

"Yes, that's okay," Piltdown said distractedly. "Whenever you like. I'll be in."

Oliver's desire to catch up with his old friend was genuine, but he also felt he owed the minister an explanation and an apology. He suspected that when the editor of *Celestial City* had selected Piltdown's church for the forthcoming article, he had not explained that the piece was going to be satirical. Despite the possibility of disappointing Ben and the certainty of annoying Geoffrey Angelwine, Oliver had more or less decided to abandon the assignment, unless Nigel Tapster proved to be the Antichrist and so a worthy target for the ferret's scorn. But was Piltdown in the forgiving vein? Oliver wondered, as the minister stood awkwardly in the street, his face and collar yellow under the streetlamp.

"Paul, I don't mean to pry, but are you all right?"

Piltdown frowned again and blinked several times. "I'm sorry, Ollie. No, there's nothing wrong. Nigel and I just had some words, if you must know—a few doctrinal differences. It's probably my fault, I may have let those comments last Sunday rankle a little. I think I need to cool off." He smiled weakly. "Come around later. I'll be fine by then."

He turned abruptly and headed off down the street without looking back. Oliver approached the Tapsters' front door, realizing that he had forgotten to ask Piltdown for directions to the manse. He could hear loud music, which did not break off after he rang the doorbell. He tried the bell again, but the music finally stopped when he resorted to a loud rattle of the knocker.

A moment later, Heather Tapster opened the door and ushered him into the hall.

"We didn't get to meet the other evening, Mr. Swithin," she said pleasantly, taking his coat. "I'm so glad that my husband's words made you want to learn more about our witness and our ministry with the young people. Perhaps you may become a regular visitor yourself? You're always welcome to our prayer meetings, or to join us for private prayer and spiritual fellowship."

Heather paused in her expert evangelism and Oliver had his first opportunity to see her close up. She was a little older than him, clearly attractive, but either oblivious or contemptuous of the fact. Not only did she wear no makeup, but she didn't seem to use the remedial cosmetics that would have reduced her skin's oiliness and eliminated the small outcrop of pimples on her forehead. Her long brown hair was unstyled and hung limply on either side of her head, as if she had delegated its care to gravity.

"I'm afraid Nigel is currently occupied," she continued, having given Oliver a similar mute appraisal, which for some reason broadened her smile. "The Reverend Piltdown paid us a surprise visit. But you're welcome to join us in the living room until Nigel's free."

Oliver became aware of a thin teenager standing in the doorway to the front room. He was about fourteen, with reddish hair and a face that reminded him of somebody he'd seen recently. A battered Fender Stratocaster hung on a strap around his torso, and a coiled red wire trailed into the room.

"I just passed Paul on the street," Oliver informed her.

Heather looked surprised. "Really? I didn't hear him leave. But then Billy and I were practicing for the Nativity play and we do tend to get a little enthusiastic. I wonder why Paul didn't pop in to say good-bye? That's very rude, especially for a minister of the church. And where's Nigel in that case?"

As if in answer, a toilet flushed upstairs, followed by the sound of running water. Oliver remembered that Patience Coppersmith's son was named Billy and understood the resemblance he had noted, although the youth's hair was longer than his mother's. A door opened above them.

"Is that our guest?" The lanky figure of Nigel Tapster came into a view, treading carefully down the stairs, and not taking his eyes off Oliver.

When Oliver had first seen Tapster the preceding Sunday, he had placed the preacher in the category of people who were better suited to casual dress than more formal wear, at least judging from the way Tapster's long limbs had easily outdistanced the arms and legs of his cheap, wrinkled suit. But he looked almost as uncomfortable now, in an old pair of gray flannels, a shapeless red sweater, and the same black socks and black wing-tips that he must have worn for work.

It took Oliver about a second to assess Tapster's clothes. And that was all the time he had before he became distracted by the intensity of Tapster's dark-eyed gaze, which hadn't left Oliver's face. It was as if, for those few moments, every other human being in the world had ceased to exist for Tapster. Dimly, Oliver noticed that his host was reaching down a hand, and he let his own hand be clasped in a firm, damp handshake.

"Good evening, Mr. Swithin," Tapster said in that nasal voice that should have begun to undo the spell he had cast on Oliver, but didn't. "Forgive me, I didn't dry my hands very thoroughly after washing them. But you can be sure they're clean." He had stopped on the first stair and beamed around at his audience. "We're great believers in hygiene in this household, aren't we Heather? Aren't we Billy? Cleanliness being next to godliness, as they say."

Heather murmured her joyful assent to this banality, and Billy laughed triumphantly as if Tapster had just delivered a successful commentary on the Dead Sea Scrolls.

"I trust your journey here was a satisfying one, Mr. Swithin?" said Tapster, catching Oliver again in his hypnotic gaze.

"It was fine. A little slow. Rush hour; you know."

"Rush hour." Tapster savored the phrase, as if the words were new to him and he was relishing their fresh-minted strangeness. "Yes, how trying."

"I always carry a book to read," Oliver added.

"A book? How wise. How very wise. Your mind must be in a state of constant nourishment. I admire that. Truly, I do. And I pray that you feel our meeting will continue to feed you, perhaps spiritually as well as mentally. Well, why don't you follow me upstairs to my study, so we don't disturb these accomplished musicians."

"Would you like some tea?" Heather asked, as Tapster began to climb the narrow staircase. He stopped, his head bowed, as if the question had untold theological significance for him. Oliver predicted that he was going to repeat "some tea" thoughtfully and then comment on his wife's generosity. And indeed he did.

Tapster had turned one of the bedrooms into his office, which was decorated with several bright South American paintings— naive scenes of country life or possibly Bible stories that hung incongruously over the faded wallpaper. A low, overflowing bookcase was also a stand for a collection of carvings in black wood, which seemed both religious and pagan at the same time. Similar carvings stood on the windowsill and on Tapster's battered desk.

"A remarkable collection," Oliver commented politely, sitting in an easy chair placed at the end of the desk.

"In many ways. They are Heather's, from her time as a missionary in South America. She was there for eight years altogether. Unfortunately, these trinkets are not all tokens of the Lord's coming triumph, but symbols of the warped religious practices she was battling."

"Is that how you met?"

Tapster pinned Oliver with his dark stare again. "Alas, Mr. Swithin, I have not had the opportunity to serve my heavenly father overseas. A bout of rheumatic fever in my childhood means I have to avoid the kinds of stress that Heather faced with such courage in Brazil. No, Heather and I met two years ago, when we were both worshipping at the same church a few miles from here, in Thripstone. She had just returned from South America."

"That must have been quite a contrast—from the darkest Amazon jungles to the London Borough of Thripstone."

"Yes, it must," said Tapster approvingly, as if the thought had never occurred to him. "Although her time with the savages was limited. She spent most of her time in the city of São Paulo, working in the favelas with the poor, trying to convert them to Christianity."

"I applaud her humanitarian work, of course, but I thought Brazil was already Christian?"

"Oh no, the Roman Church is very strong there, I'm afraid, but Heather won many souls for Christ. For a while, she was considering a new mission to Spain, to bring lifelong Catholics to true Christianity. But she chose to join me in my ministry here, and I thank the Lord for her help every day. Her price is above rubies."

"Above Ruby's?" muttered Oliver distractedly, choking back his astonishment at this casual intolerance, even hatred of another denomination. Surely they had the same goals? What about Christian unity, ecumenism? Tapster smiled indulgently and stood up to answer a thump at the door.

"'Who can find a virtuous woman? for her price is far above rubies,'" he quoted. "'The heart of her husband doth safely trust in her, so that he shall have no need of spoil.'" He opened the door for Heather, who carried a tray into the room and placed it on the desk. Tapster kissed her on the cheek.

"'She will do him good and not evil all the days of her life.'" he concluded, resuming his seat. "Proverbs thirty-one. Thank you, my dear."

"I didn't hear the parson leave," Heather commented coldly. "He didn't stay long."

"You and Billy were making sweet music all the way through his visit," said Tapster fulsomely. "My wife is the musician in the family, the partnership, I should say. The Lord has blessed her greatly. Do you know, she has perfect pitch? I, alas, cannot equal her in talent. It's as much as I can do to hit the right notes."

Don't flatter yourself, thought Oliver, remembering Tapster's thin singing voice and his labored attempts to tune his twelve-string guitar. Heather left the room, and Tapster poured two mugs of tea. A few moments later, the piano music resumed downstairs, punctuated by sustained wails from an electric guitar.

"Forgive me this impertinence, Mr. Swithin," said Tapster, "but I must ask you something very important at this stage."

Here it comes. Are you saved? Do you believe? Have you given your life to the Lord? How would Tapster phrase it?

"Would you like milk or sugar?" Tapster continued, smiling slyly in a way that suggested he had followed Oliver's thoughts. "Or honey, perhaps? Personally, I take my tea flowing with milk and honey, if you'll pardon my playing with the words of the Good Book. Exodus, I believe."

"I beg your pardon?"

"The promised land—a land flowing with milk and honey. First mentioned in the book of Exodus."

"Oh." Why did Oliver feel he was being patronized? Time to get back into the game. "Of course, you could 'pile honey upon sugar, and sugar upon honey.'"

Tapster knitted his eyebrows. "A biblical reference?"

"No, it's from Lamb's essay, 'A Chapter on Ears.' He claimed not to have one. An ear. Musical, that is." (*Like you,* Oliver added silently.)

Tapster looked surprised and gratified at the literary turn. "Lamb," he said appreciatively.

By now, Oliver had been studying Tapster's style for ten minutes, and found himself developing a perverse admiration for the preacher's technique. Nobody could feel insignificant in Tapster's presence—and despite the thinning hair and sparse, untidy beard, you could not deny that the man had presence. When you were the focus of those intense brown eyes, he made you feel that it was a permanent appointment, and that whoever may have held his attention a moment earlier had slipped out of the galaxy in the meantime. At a social gathering, Tapster would never look over your shoulder for other, more interesting encounters, or check his watch or fiddle unconsciously with his car-keys. Small talk would rapidly grow up. Your every utterance would be treated as a profundity, and no remark, no matter how mundane or facetious, could escape without being carefully weighed and hailed as a new discovery. No wonder adolescents flocked to him, especially those with old-fashioned parents like the Quarterboys, who were uncomprehending of their children's slavery to peer approval and of the hormones sloshing though their sprouting bodies. What teenager could fail to believe that Tapster truly understood and respected him or her?

"You hold meetings with the young people in your home," Oliver was saying. "Why do you feel the need for a separate community from the main church?"

Tapster put his mug down and licked a stray trickle of honey from his fingers. "We are not separate, Mr. Swithin. All are welcome to join us here. Every house can be a house of worship, and every man a minister of the Lord's word. The very earliest Christian communities met in the homes of believers, and witnessed many miracles of the spirit, despite being persecuted and despised."

"But they had no alternative. Over time, those early communities grew into the churches we have today. Why start all over again? Doesn't this contribute to the further fragmentation of the Christian Church?"

Tapster idly picked up one of the wooden carvings on his desk, an ebony paca that looked alarmingly like the pictures of Finsbury in Oliver's books. "Are you familiar with homeopathy, Mr. Swithin? Heather became adept with homeopathic medicine in Brazil, it spared her from the tragedy of worms—a diet of worms, so to speak. As you may know, when you practice homeopathy, you dilute and dilute and dilute the toxin until, mathematically, there should be no molecule left of the original. And yet it works, because the *essence* of the substance is still there. I think we can apply this metaphor to the Christian Church. No matter how much we divide the church, the essence of God, which we call the Holy Spirit, will still surface among the fragments. Some of them, anyway," he added slightly caustically. "I prefer to take my instruction directly from that essence rather than through self-appointed, self-interested intermediaries, such as priests and theologians."

"Doesn't that make you an intermediary too? Why should the children of Plumley listen to your interpretation of God's will instead of the minister's?"

Oliver was despairing of finding any angle for his story. Could Tapster be trapped into denouncing Paul Piltdown, a man who, nominally at least, was supposed to be singing from the same Diaconalist hymnal?

"I have no quarrel with the church here in Plumley," Tapster said cautiously. "By the grace of God, I'm standing as a deacon at tomorrow night's meeting. Heather plays the piano for the church services. Why would we do that if we wanted to create a barrier between the church and my fellowship? My desire is to do what I can to help the whole community find strength and comfort in the presence of the living God."

"Does that include speaking in tongues, casting out demons, and the other activities that are rumored to take place here?" Oliver pressed. "These somewhat medieval practices don't seem to tie in with mainstream Diaconalist thought." Although Oliver had wondered if demonic possession accounted for Dougie Dock. Tapster looked pained, as if disagreeing with Oliver caused bodily distress. He dropped the carving on his blotter.

"Pardon me, Mr. Swithin, but I don't possess the arrogance to dismiss these phenomena as medieval. As our Lord says, in the Gospel according to Mark, 'These signs shall follow them that believe: In my name shall they cast out devils; they shall speak with new tongues; they shall take up serpents; and if they drink any deadly thing, it shall not hurt them.'"

Oliver started to interrupt, but Tapster held up a hand. "I know what you're going to say," he declared, closing his eyes. "These evidences of spiritual activity can easily be confused with well-documented psychological phenomena. But to call something 'glossolalia' rather than 'speaking in tongues' doesn't alter the fact that it brings us the word of the Lord. Whether I drive out a demon or heal a dissociative disorder, it's still a miraculous cure, thanks be to God."

Blast him, thought Oliver, *he did know what I was going to say*. I bet he wouldn't be so sympathetic to modern psychology in front of his more impressionable acolytes.

"But these are children at your meetings, Nigel," he riposted heatedly. "Susceptible children, easily convinced that they're in the presence of something transcendent when they may only be having an emotional reaction. Can you be sure you're not taking advantage of their innocence, inadvertently I'm sure? Why—"

"Why do you people always reject emotion?" Tapster interrupted suddenly, as if he had been waiting for the topic to arise. He had thrown himself forward in his seat and was now staring intently at Oliver. "Intelligence and common sense, though God-given, aren't always going to lead you back to Him. You may just have to stop thinking and let your emotions lead you instead, Oliver!"

Oliver was almost mesmerized by the intensity of Tapster's expression. Was this the moment when an enthralled teenager, trapped in that precise, seductive gaze, would be commanded to prophesy and would instantly find the nonsense syllables rising through her throat and babbling from her mouth, seemingly beyond her control?

And then what? More spiritual conjuring tricks, more vacuous arguments, more analysis of prophetic writings until the disciples were convinced—if they even needed to be—that across the vast landscape of Mankind's history, the truth about God had been revealed to only one human being, and by the strangest quirk of fate, they were fortunate enough to be in his charismatic presence? You are the chosen. Follow me, step into this world of unconditional love, and you'll never have the burden of exercising your free will again. Now win more disciples for me, leave your family, sleep with me, give me the money for another Rolls-Royce, but don't dare try to escape from us, from our community, from our fenced-off compound.

For I am the way, I am the only way, and my obscure, simplistic banalities about the Light and the Force and Love are all you need to understand the Universe. And by the way, the Great Spaceship is just behind the next comet, ready to take us to our home world on the Planet Ultra. Now, cut off your balls and drink this drink. Don't worry that it tastes funny.

Oliver ran his tongue over suddenly dry lips. "I'm English," he replied at last. "I try to keep my emotions out of everything."

Tapster relaxed and laughed. "I can see I'm not going to win you to my point of view," he said cheerily. "Not yet. But why don't you stay and worship with us? There's a group coming over tonight for fellowship and praise."

But Oliver knew he needed to escape Tapster's presence. The brief interview had polarized his opinions: Tapster was either very genuine or very fraudulent indeed. If the former, Oliver had no quarrel—and, decidedly, no article. Every time he came close to losing all patience with organized religion—usually after reading about the private lives of American televangelists—he remembered the many, many people who had led exemplary lives of sacrifice, or even given up those lives, in the name of their God. Whatever he chose to believe or not believe for his own life, Oliver felt it was impolite to challenge another person's faith, and he refused to toss his tiny satirical pebbles at the vast bulk of Christianity for fear of hitting Dietrich Bonhoeffer or Mother Teresa.

But if Tapster was a humbug, and he could prove it, then a right good Ferreting would seem to be in order. Perhaps Paul Piltdown could be coaxed out of his diplomacy this evening?

As Oliver came down the stairs, he was surprised to see Paul waiting with Heather Tapster in the entrance hall. Heather glanced up at him and then hurried toward the kitchen. The occasional atonal rumble from the front room suggested that Billy Coppersmith had been left alone, and was testing his abilities on the piano.

"Ah, Oliver, good," said Piltdown quickly. "I came back because I realized you wouldn't know how to get to the manse. I've been waiting to take you away."

"You needn't have troubled yourself," Tapster said with some surprise at seeing the minister. He had ducked into the bathroom after the meeting to wash off the traces of honey. "I'd have been happy to give Mr. Swithin directions."

"No trouble, I assure you, Nigel," Piltdown continued with a weak smile, his hand on the front door latch.

Oliver collected his coat, thanked Tapster politely for his hospitality—Heather did not return—and followed Piltdown through the front door. They set off at a brisk pace along the dimly lit Plumley streets.

"You seem pretty settled here," Oliver commented as they passed a group of carol-singers gathered on a corner around a portable harmonium.

"Oh yes, I have a perfect record. Every couple I've married in the last three years is still married. And everybody I've buried is still dead."

"Tell me about the United Diaconalist Church."

"Well, as a separate religious group, the Diaconalists go all the way back to the English Reformation. We started as part of the Baptist movement, but the Diaconalists formed their own church in the early eighteenth century."

"Why?"

"It was a protest against factionalism. Fifty years later, after an argument over the need for church unity, we divided into the General Diaconalists and the Reformed Diaconalists. But then a few years later, half of the Reformed Diaconalists—the New Reformed Diaconalists, that would be—united with the General Diaconalists to become—"

"The United Diaconalists. I see."

"No, the Particular Diaconalists. We didn't become the United Diaconalists until earlier this century. That was when the Particulars—or, by then, the Reformed Particulars—joined up with the New Independent Diaconalists. They were an offshoot of the Strict Reformed Diaconalists, who were left over from the Reformed Diaconalists when the New Reformed Diaconalists split."

"So the United Diaconalists are now everybody?"

"Well, there are still some members of the Strict Reformed Diaconalists who were not part of the Independent Diaconalist movement. All that's left of them is a family of evangelical nudists in Hartlepool. So I think you can say we're united."

"Was it a hard transition from the Church of England?"

Piltdown chuckled. "I took quite a ribbing when I first came, because I was trailing clouds of Anglicanism. Apparently, my predecessor—who held the post for nearly twenty years—didn't wear any clerical garb and never once set foot in the pulpit, preferring to face the congregation at eye level."

"So you use the pulpit to assert a higher authority?" Oliver asked.

"Actually, I use it so those ladies who habitually take the back pew can see me better."

"Until you sit down."

"True. But I'll let you into a secret. I can still see them, even when I'm out of their sight."

"A periscope in the pulpit, Padre?"

"No, there are all these little fretwork holes cut into the pulpit's surround. If I position myself, I can survey the entire church and see which of my flock is yawning."

They turned a corner, and Oliver could now see the pale bulk of the mid-Victorian church, squatting behind its low crumbling wall. Only the vaguely classical frontage was stone. The side walls were old, brown brick, which clearly needed repointing. The slate roof was also in poor repair.

"But don't get me wrong, Ollie," Piltdown said, pausing in front of the church and looking critically at a wooden notice board, which stood in the shallow forecourt like a wayside shrine. "They're all good people. They make time to do good things. And I've got to admit, it's getting better for me here, too."

Oliver observed that his friend used the phrase "good people" with more sincerity than when he had applied it to Nigel and Heather Tapster a few days earlier. As they walked on, Oliver spotted a figure waiting by the manse's garden gate—a girl or a young woman, well wrapped against the cold, with long red hair that flowed from under a dark beret. She was too far away to make out her features, and as she caught sight of the two men hurrying toward her, she turned and walked quickly in the opposite direction. If Piltdown noticed her, he didn't comment, and he unlocked the front door without speaking.

"This is a big place for one man, living alone," Oliver commented, as he joined Piltdown in the manse's unenticing kitchen. He had been wandering through the ground floor rooms while his friend prepared some tea. "Do you have any help?"

"The church can barely afford an unmarried minister, let alone a housekeeper as well," he said absently. "I manage all right on my own. Clergymen are supposed to have plenty of time on their hands for cooking and cleaning—we only work on Sundays, after all."

Oliver saw that the dirty cups and plates from the previous Sunday were still waiting in the sink, supplemented now by several plates and breakfast bowls. Ignoring Piltdown's faint protests, Oliver filled a plastic washing-up bowl with water and added a generous amount of Fairy Liquid.

"No sign of someone to share your life?" he said, tossing a tea towel to Piltdown.

"Not unless you're still available," said the minister, with a lopsided grin. "No, things are a little uneventful on the romance front. Just as well, given my vocation."

"So the love that dare not speak its name…?"

"Had better hold its tongue as far as the Diaconalist Church is concerned. One whiff of my extracurricular interests and I'm out on the street. No, I'm applying my own 'Don't ask, don't tell' policy."

"Does it worry you to be alone?"

"I've accepted it for now. The old dog collar's a bit of a turn-off at the local disco, and there aren't many who'd look forward to being carried over this particular threshold."

"So why did you step over it?" Oliver asked, handing Piltdown a slippery dish. "The last time I saw you, you were so keen on the Church of England that I thought of using my pocket money to buy you a pair of gaiters for Christmas. What's a nice vicar like you doing in a church like this? Especially given your preferences."

Piltdown leaned against the kitchen table and adopted the same expression he had used when stalking through the church after his sermon.

"A man's spiritual journey lasts his lifetime," he said. "I wanted a deeper knowledge of God than I could find in the tired rituals and dusty theology books. So I explored other denominations, found the stripped-down worship and plain man's faith of the United Diaconalist Church to my taste, and when I graduated from Cambridge three years ago, I immediately applied for the position here as minister."

Oliver wiped his hands on a tea towel and tipped the soapy water from the bowl into the huge, square sink, where it seemed to want to stay for the night.

"What about Nigel Tapster, then?"

"What about him?"

"On the surface, he seems to be the very model of the simple, fervent spirituality you're seeking for yourself. But none of your deacons seem to trust him, there are rumors of a murky past, and he's clearly not your favorite person."

Piltdown thrust his hands into his trouser pockets and glared at his shoes. Oliver wished his old friend were a poker player.

"I said before," Piltdown answered eventually, "Nigel and Heather are good people. The youngsters love them. And whatever passed between Nigel and me this evening is a private matter."

There was still a trace of bitterness in his voice.

"From what I heard this evening, he might well be a saint," Oliver conceded. "But he could also be the Pied Piper of Plumley, enchanting the children away from the church. Aren't you afraid that you might have the beginnings of some weird kind of cult on your hands?"

"Nigel Tapster is hardly a Jim Jones or a David Koresh or any brand of Bhagwan."

"Not yet, but they all had to start somewhere. And if Nigel is just starting out on that path, isn't this the best time to fight him?"

Again, Piltdown seemed to think for several seconds before attempting an answer. "Nigel can't take the children away from the church if he's part of the church. That's why I encouraged him to run in tomorrow night's election."

"Bring him into the fold. He may be the devil, but at least he's our devil."

"Something like that," said Piltdown with a humorless laugh. "Not all the church members think he's bad news, you know."

"But there are only four diaconal positions. If Nigel gets in, one of the current deacons will have to stand down."

"Afraid so," said Piltdown, as he turned off the kitchen light and ushered Oliver through the door.

Which would it be? Oliver wondered. The first face to loom from his memory was Dougie Dock, and he immediately resented the dedication of so many neurons to the process. He had pegged Dock as one of the "clowns of private life" that W.S. Gilbert so wisely condemned to a beheading on Koko's list. Just the kind of man who would strike up a conversation with a stranger in an elevator, and then continue to make announcements as if he were in a department store—"Third floor, leather goods and ladies' underwear"—long after it had stopped being funny, if it ever started, punctuated with little puffs of self-congratulatory laughter. Then there was Sam Quarterboy, the last Victorian father. And scripture-spouting Cedric Potiphar, whose peculiar wife seemed to put the "mental" into his fundamentalism. But who was the fourth deacon? Was it the epicene young man

Ben had been talking to? What was his name? Barry...Poison? Foison, that was it. No, he wasn't a deacon. The fourth man was a woman, Patience Coppersmith. She had seemed blessedly normal, but Oliver could easily believe she might be concealing considerable uneasiness about her son's attachment to Tapster.

"Does your encouragement of Tapster run to voting for him?" he asked Piltdown.

"It's a private ballot," said the minister uneasily, standing in the dark for a moment. "That's the beauty of democracy."

The telephone in the hallway was ringing as Oliver let himself into the Edwardes Square townhouse.

"Yes?"

"Oliver Swithin, this is the police."

"What are you wearing?" he asked huskily. Effie Strongitharm giggled, which signaled that for once she had some privacy at her Scotland Yard desk.

"Just the usual plus fours and gas mask. Listen, where was that church you went to on Sunday?"

Should he make a joke about sudden elopements? Better not; their relationship wasn't that well established. And that reminded him, he still hadn't bought her a Christmas present.

"Plumley," he told her. "I just got back from a follow-up visit, as it happens."

"I thought you said Plumley. It's my new manor, starting tomorrow. Did Tim tell you he was taking leave until the end of the year? So rather than leave me kicking around the Yard with no guvnor to bother, I've been temporarily assigned to the CID in Area North West. They're a bit short-staffed, apparently, for the pre-Christmas crime wave. It's a bit of a slog to get there from Richmond, but it'll make a change from murder, and it's only for a couple of weeks. Do you remember Detective Sergeant Welkin?"

"Face like a week of wet Fridays?"

"No, that's DS Moldwarp. He's still here at the Yard. Welkin's a heavyset character, face like a boxer. Very strong Cockney accent. Breeds Burmese cats."

"Yes, of course. He always reminds me of my great-uncle Henry."

"Really? He reminds me of my dry cleaner. Anyway, Welkin was promoted to detective inspector a couple of months ago and transferred to Area North West, so I'll be working for him. He requested me, apparently."

"Uncle Tim hasn't said anything about a vacation," said Oliver thoughtfully.

"Perhaps he wants to concentrate on his stage career. Which reminds me, can you get out to Theydon Bois under your own steam tomorrow night? Since I'll be in Plumley anyway, it'll be easier for me to drive straight there. I'll bring you home afterwards."

Their conversation continued with further brief expressions of affection and mild lust, and then Effie was interrupted by the arrival of DS Moldwarp, who was covering her duties until she returned to the Yard. Oliver hung up the telephone regretfully, and was about to go to his bedroom when he caught sight of his reflection in the hallway mirror. His left ear was black.

Chapter Three

To Human View Displayed

Friday, December 19

Not her dry cleaner, Effie speculated, looking curiously at the policeman's harsh features. Perhaps it was the man who ran the pet shop on the street where she grew up? No, it had to be that actor who'd been in the movie she'd watched last week on Channel Four.

Detective Inspector Lenny "Spiv" Welkin finished his phone conversation, and Effie momentarily gave up wondering who he reminded her of. They were sitting in his office, a tiny, glass-walled room that completely failed to separate him, visually or acoustically, from the criminal investigation area in the small Plumley subdivisional police station. It was her first morning on her temporary assignment, and her unannounced appearance at the station had clearly provoked some curiosity among her new colleagues. From her seat, she could see several of the younger detectives appraising her frankly while pretending to take phone calls or check for data on computer screens. (Her hair, particularly, seemed to feature in their sign language.) Let them look, she thought. If they cross the line, she had her defenses.

"Congratulations again on your promotion, Spiv," she said. Although Welkin had worked only briefly for Mallard, she had known him for several years and respected him. Despite the tough visage and the unrelenting Cockney accent, she knew him to be a fair man, devoted to a house full of pedigree Burmese cats.

"Ta, Eff. I think I'm going to like it here, although it's been nothing but paperwork since I arrived a couple of weeks ago. Still, that suits a man in my condition."

He gestured at a walking stick propped behind the door. Their one assignment together had resulted in a rather energetic arrest for Effie, but a shattered tibia for Welkin, and while his leg was out of its cast, it was clearly not fully functional. "That's partly why I asked for you to come 'ere. It's only a small station—most of the big stuff goes on over at the main Thripstone cop shop. But we're a bit short-staffed, even for us. Two detective constables are out on the panel and my usual sergeant's gone off on honeymoon."

"You asked for me personally?" Effie said with surprise.

"Oh, yeah. I was talking to Assistant Commissioner Weed, and 'e let slip that Tim Mallard might be taking some time off, leaving you at a loose end until the New Year. So I made a grab for you. Figuratively speaking, of course," he added hastily, although he wasn't sure the qualification was an improvement. Welkin tensed, knowing only too well what Effie could do to him if she sensed anything untoward.

"In that case, I'm flattered," she answered, to his visible relief. "But are you expecting any bloodbaths in Plumley High Street between now and Boxing Day?"

Welkin laughed. "If the worst thing that happens is a double-parked sleigh and an unlicensed reindeer, that would suit me down to the ground. No, Sergeant, while your talents as a homicide detective are only to be envied, I was hoping you could help me with something else." He nodded in the direction of the large room outside. "You may have noticed that you've already attracted some admirers."

Effie did not alter her gaze. "You mean the prematurely balding stick insect playing pocket billiards, the pint-sized Casanova with the scrubby moustache and acne who keeps moving his chair so he can see up my skirt, or the chicken wearing glasses who keeps making odd hand gestures, as if he's shaking up an invisible bottle of medicine? A rather small bottle, I might add."

"I see you need no introduction to your colleagues on the shift," said Welkin wryly. "Don't worry, I'm working on their reeducation, and a splendid time is guaranteed for all. This morning, you're merely serving as a distraction from their normal victim, Detective Constable Tish Belfry. That's her in the corner."

Effie turned, and two of the male detectives outside suddenly became very interested in items on their desktops, although they did look up swiftly and grin at each other for no apparent reason. The third, the shorter man with the moustache, had now maneuvered his chair too far from his desk, so he pretended instead to be lost in thought in the middle of the room, tapping a pencil against his untidy teeth. Behind them, a dark-haired young woman in a severe navy suit was looking worriedly at a file. Her apparent obliviousness to the men's muttered conversation was so complete that Effie knew she hadn't missed a word.

"I don't have to spell it out, do I, Effie?" said Welkin. "Tish is a promising copper. I think she'd really benefit from a few days in your company. Come on, I'll introduce you."

He eased himself to his feet and limped to the door, allowing Effie to hold it open for him as a matter of pragmatism, not affirmative action. Picking up the walking stick, he led her across the main room, ignoring his male subordinates who began practicing sly Long John Silver impressions behind his back, and tapped Belfry lightly on the shoulder.

The speed with which DC Tish Belfry spun around and the intense scowl she assumed were promising, Effie thought, but she had to lose the flicker of apprehension, a true tell for the experienced bully. Tish appeared relieved when she saw Welkin and even managed a smile when he introduced her to Effie. She had strong Indian or Pakistani coloring, with straight, glossy hair cut to the level of her chin. But there was also the suggestion of European genes that added a sallowness to her clear complexion and lightened her eyes from espresso to a strong cappuccino.

Probably on her father's side, to judge from the family name, but the strong nose and angular chin that detracted only slightly from her general attractiveness could have come from either heritage. Tish's accent as she greeted Effie seemed local, and Effie found herself constructing a life story for the young woman (child of mixed race, probable disapproval of the parents' marriage from both sides of the family, only child or at least no brothers or she'd be better prepared for the indignities of life as the token female in a CID unit, most likely a single-sex school) before she reminded herself she wasn't dealing with a murder suspect. Mallard had trained her too well—Tish would probably answer personal questions without demanding legal representation.

"Effie's not too familiar with the manor," Welkin was saying, "so I thought you might start with a quick tour, show her the sights."

"Of course, Inspector."

"I could show her a few sights without leaving the station," muttered one of the men behind them. Welkin turned quickly, just as the stick insect began to limp across the room in another parody of the burly inspector's gait. He swiftly adjusted it to a scuttle.

"What are you doing?" Welkin asked, in long-suffering tones.

"Oh, just showing the lads my impression of the Hunchback of Notre Dame, Boss," the stick insect replied, crossing the room with bent knees, one shoulder higher than the other.

"That's your Richard the Third," sniggered the chicken.

"Nah, this is my Richard the Third," the stick insect responded, dropping his shoulder and lifting the other one. The other men snorted with messy laughter. A telephone began to ring in Welkin's office, and he hobbled back to answer it.

"Aren't you going to introduce us to the new girl, Tish?" asked the undersized Casanova. He was still draped like a starfish over the office chair. "I'd offer to get up, love, but I'm up already, if you get my drift."

His colleagues groaned and laughed again. Casanova assumed a poorly arranged expression of sincerity and looked up at Effie.

This was his mistake.

He had just moved on from admiring her copious, curly hair to gazing at her light blue eyes, when an odd sensation began. It wasn't that she changed her demeanor or even moved a muscle in her face, but suddenly he saw behind those appealing features the long-suffering, quizzical, slightly pained, but vaguely pitying countenance of every woman who had ever judged him in his life. He had the impression that a vast pair of scales was being created in his mind, and into one pan went all the instances of human decency and nobility that had moved him to tears since his childhood, from Henry V's St. Crispin's Day speech to Neil Armstrong's voice declaring "The Eagle has landed," while into the other pan went every example of his own unworthiness, freshly and vividly recalled (such as the time he had gone three stations past his stop on the Underground because the City secretary crammed in beside him had left one button of her blouse undone), every spiteful joke he had passed on, and every fierce suggestive remark he had ever whispered or shouted at a vulnerable woman whom he knew could not fight back. A great voice seemed to toll in his head "You have been weighed in the balance and found wanting!" This unfamiliar emotion that now coursed through every bodily canal—is this what shame, abject shame feels like? It made him want to shrink down below the floor and pull the linoleum over his head, so that he'd never have to face anyone or anything again. Especially Effie's ice-blue eyes. Instead, he slid off his chair.

The stick insect and the chicken guffawed as it rolled away on its castors, leaving him flat on his back.

"That put you in your place," shouted the chicken. "I don't think you're her type, mate."

"That'll do," murmured Welkin, stepping out of his office.

"Hey, maybe she doesn't like men at all," said the stick insect with exaggerated surprise, as if he had just discovered a pulsar in his bathroom.

Casanova had clambered to his feet. "Knock it off, lads," he muttered nervously backing away from Effie without daring to look at her. The chicken and the stick insect paused and stared at their colleague.

"What's the matter with you?" the chicken asked suspiciously.

"Nothing, nothing," said Casanova, risking a glance back at Effie, who had not moved since he had approached her that lifetime ago. "I'm just concerned that we're not creating a good first impression."

"Do what?"

"We're not being very polite to our guest, that's all."

"A guest who outranks you all, incidentally," Welkin announced smugly. "You can call off the guided tour for now," he continued quietly, after the three chastened men had absorbed the news and slunk away to their desks without speaking. "I have a real job for you both."

"I'd love to know what happened back there," Tish said, as she and Effie disappeared through the door. Welkin smiled again, knowing that what Tish was to learn privately was worth three months of classroom-based training. He had only once been on the receiving end of Effie's "Look," for a mild infraction, but she had elicited one of the half-dozen memories that always provoked a physical shudder. He shouldered his walking stick as if it were a rifle, and limped slowly back to his office, pausing only to crook the handle around the stick insect's unsuspecting neck and pull him backwards.

"And if I see any more Hunchbacks of Notre Dame, Constable," he hissed into the detective's ear, "I'll personally kick you in the bells."

◇◇◇

Oliver Swithin despised Finsbury the Ferret. He found it a constant effort to dream up despicable schemes for the evil beast to inflict on the hapless Railway Mice family, and he daily thanked Providence that the stories were published under his pen-name, O.C. Blithely, which—like Charles Lutwidge Dodgson before him—let him avoid responsibility for his character when it suited him.

Oliver couldn't even relieve his irritation by laughing all the way to the bank. The success of the Railway Mice books should have given him a decent income, but all of his earnings were currently sitting in an escrow account, managed by his publisher, Tadpole Tomes for Tiny Tots (although Oliver had wondered why this account was held in Switzerland). This was because the original illustrator of Finsbury—a callow art student on her first freelance assignment—was now suing the publisher for a sizeable share of the ferret's profits, past, present, and future. An interim judgment had recently allowed Tadpole Tomes to pay Oliver a stipend to cover his daily expenses, which freed him from the need to find a day job. Unfortunately, it also gave him more time to work on the Finsbury saga.

Not that he had any choice. Just before Finsbury's arrival in the Railway Mice books—an appearance that started out as a quick, private caprice, but accidentally found its way to the printed page—Oliver had signed a long-term contract with Tadpole Tomes, and the publisher was not going to back out of its only moneymaker, even if that money was currently a set of glowing numbers on a computer screen in Geneva. And the public appetite for the stories showed no sign of abating. Imitators had attempted to duplicate Finsbury, of course, but Willesden the Weasel and Slaithwaite the Slug, among many others, had failed to find an audience. For true depravity, there was still nothing like an original Finsbury the Ferret escapade, to Oliver's continued annoyance.

Tadpole Tomes had even hired a public relations firm, Hoo Watt & Eidenau, to think of new outlets for Finsbury, and Geoffrey Angelwine, who worked for this company, had exploited his long friendship with Oliver Swithin to finagle himself onto "the Blithely Account." Since Geoffrey now saw Oliver's continued productivity as the key to his own professional advancement, he was constantly urging new Finsbury-related projects onto the author, including the assignment on religion for *Celestial City*. And because Geoffrey lived in the same house as Oliver, he would often materialize at odd times and berate Oliver for not writing enough. So with wealth and fame out of the picture—the former unrealized, the latter unwanted—the primary motivating force in Oliver's working day had become avoiding Geoffrey.

This was easy if the weather was fine. Oliver would grab his laptop computer, walk to Kensington Gardens, settle himself under a tree with a flask of tea and a croissant, and reluctantly devise vile plots for Finsbury, pausing only to smile at a passing nanny, or tourist, or dog, or if his surroundings failed to distract him, playing solitaire until his battery ran out.

But on colder, wetter days, Oliver would creep moodily from room to room of the Edwardes Square townhouse he shared with Geoffrey, Ben Motley, and Susie Beamish, looking for distractions. Ben, the owner of the house, had converted the top floor into his photographic studio, and had taken to pretending he had a client whenever he heard Oliver's footsteps on the landing. Since his subjects all wanted to be photographed at the height of sexual ecstasy, Ben had learned to be creative with his vocalizations, and Oliver had often gone back down the stairs wondering why so many of Ben's clients sounded like Darth Vader sucking helium when they got aroused. Sex mystified him, as he had once said to Effie, who didn't seem surprised by the comment. Although she had never complained either.

That Friday afternoon, Oliver was camped in the shared kitchen at Edwardes Square when the oven timer rang to tell him it was time to leave for Theydon Bois. He shut down his laptop with his new Railway Mice story (*The Railway Mice and the Vertically Challenged Vole*) barely started and his solitaire winnings at minus £3,000, grabbed the slice of frozen pizza that he had slid into the oven ten minutes earlier, and headed downstairs to his bedroom.

He was only dimly aware that something was wrong when he noticed that his door was standing wide open. It was normally his habit to close it while he was out. The room beyond looked odd too, misty and slightly out of focus, as if seen reflected in a dusty mirror. Oliver made a mental note to get his eyesight tested again, stepped through the doorway, and collided with nothingness.

Well, obviously not nothingness. It must have been something that brought him almost to a halt, squashing the pizza into his face and causing cheese and tomato sauce to cascade down his clean shirt. But he couldn't see it. It was almost as if the room had been filled with water and then deprived of gravity, so that he had walked into a vertical wall of something clear and slightly yielding.

Oliver dropped the pizza slice and snatched at the film that was now wrapping itself around his face and chest. Plastic wrap! Somebody had taken lengths of plastic kitchen wrap and stretched it tautly across the doorway, leaving Oliver to bounce off the transparent barrier like a sponge hitting a drum.

"Gotcha," said a voice behind him, with a giggle.

"Geoffrey!" cried Oliver, trying to disentangle himself from the skeins of wrap, which were now bandaging his limbs so that he looked like an exhibitionist mummy. Geoffrey Angelwine's birdlike face emerged from the shadows, his beady eyes bright with amusement.

"You blithering moron!" Oliver exclaimed. "Look at my shirt! What do you think you're doing?"

"It was a practical joke."

"What? This is no time for practical jokes!"

"When is?" Geoffrey asked innocently, pulling the wrap off his friend. "Did you know some people will pay good money to have this done to them?"

"Have you totally lost your mind?" muttered Oliver. "This is just—"

"—like something Finsbury would do," Geoffrey interrupted. Oliver was not going to say that, but he knew that Geoffrey's habit of finishing other people's sentences was often a way of taking over a conversation, and he hoped it would lead to an explanation. Not that he had time for one.

"Exactly," Geoffrey went on. "Finsbury would do that. Do you remember when we were at University, it was a good party joke to stretch kitchen wrap over the toilets and wait for someone to take a pee?"

"Yes, bloody hilarious." Oliver screwed up the last of the wrap into a large, noisy ball and flung it at his friend. It stuck to his hand.

"So I simply applied the method to the whole body. You'll thank me for it."

Oliver exhaled noisily. "Geoff, I'm startled, I'm stained, I nearly dropped my computer, and I'm going to be late now to see—"

"Your Uncle Tim's Bottom?" Geoffrey butted in, grinning. "I never get tired of that one."

"To see Effie," Oliver stated emphatically. "So I sincerely doubt I'm going to thank you for anything right now, unless you spontaneously combust. Now, I'm going to get cleaned up as quickly as possible. And if I find that you've cut the buttons off all my shirts and put that kind of soap in the bathroom that blackens your face, you are a deader man than you are already."

"Just listen to my idea," Geoffrey pleaded, trotting after Oliver. "We need to find spin-off ideas for Finsbury the Ferret, right? Hence my concept: *Finsbury the Ferret's Guide to Being Absolutely Beastly*. One hundred and one original and innovative ways to annoy your friends. I've just given you one, and I have lots of other suggestions."

Oliver, who also had lots of suggestions at that moment, paused on the stairs up to the bathroom he shared with Geoffrey and Susie.

"Just a minute," he said, turning angrily on his friend. "Now I see it all. It was you who turned off my computer screen yesterday. And you were the one who smeared shoe polish on the hallway telephone."

Geoffrey smirked. "Good one, huh?"

"Good one?" Oliver exploded. "I've a good mind to—" He checked his watch and himself. "Geoffrey," he continued firmly, "forget it. The answer is no. No, no, no! I'm sick of that bloody ferret. I only write the Railway Mice books because I'm contractually obligated. And I'm certainly not interested in thinking of ways to be absolutely beastly. Although if I were, trust me, you'd be the first to know about it."

He disappeared into the bathroom, slamming the door in Geoffrey's face.

"I'll take that as a 'maybe,' then," said Geoffrey, as he slunk down the stairs again to short-sheet Oliver's bed.

One of the advantages of having Effie Strongitharm as his girlfriend, Oliver reflected, is that she is instantly recognizable, even from the back and in a dim light. He had finally reached the Theydon Bois Underground station just one minute before curtain time for the opening night of *A Midsummer Night's Dream*, but finding no minicabs in the station car park, he had to make a five-minute sprint across the frosty Green to the Theydon Bois Thespians' theater. The theater was one-quarter full for the opening night, which was a groundbreaking turn-out by the company's standards, but Oliver's Aunt Phoebe had elected to go to a later performance—assuming there would be one—since her aikido class was on Friday evening. This meant Effie would be sitting alone, and Oliver had no trouble making out her distinctive, bushy mass of curly hair, silhouetted against the stage lights in the front row. He had always been an enthusiastic ten minutes early for every meeting so far, and so he didn't know how she responded to being kept waiting. Knowing her reputation for imperiousness among her colleagues at Scotland Yard, he feared the worst. Perhaps, since the play had already started, she would have to hold her tongue until the interval. If he was unlucky, she'd hold his.

He waited until the stage cleared of goose-stepping fairies in storm-trooper uniforms, performing an unscripted entr'acte to a recording of Wagner, before he scurried down the aisle.

"I'm so sorry," he whispered, sliding into the seat beside Effie.

"Are you all right?" she replied, her blue eyes showing concern. "I was just starting to get anxious."

"Not cross?"

"Of course not." She leaned over and kissed him beneath his ear. "Ollie, I know you wouldn't be late if you could help it. I was worried that something might have happened to you."

Oliver sighed with relief. "That's what I love about you, Effie. You don't see this relationship as an opportunity to score points."

"*That's* what you love about me?"

"Well, there's the hair, too."

"I should think so."

She patted down the springy coils while Oliver started to explain why he had been held up, but he broke off when the stage lights came up again and the Athenian mechanicals made their way onto the stage. They were all dressed in contemporary clothes, including Mallard as Bottom in a corduroy jacket with patched elbows, jeans, Reeboks, and, incongruously, a paisley ascot tucked into a gray silk shirt. He had removed his glasses, and makeup made him look younger. The actors pulled chairs into a semicircle at the front of the stage.

"Is all our company here?" began the actor playing Peter Quince. Mallard/Bottom lay back casually in his chair and flicked a disdainful finger at Quince.

"You were best to call them generally, man by man," he said languidly, stifling a yawn, "according to the scrip." Then he began to examine his fingernails.

Oliver was puzzled, and his puzzlement grew as the scene progressed. He was all prepared for a traditional bombastic Bottom, the coarse amateur actor who tried to grab every role for himself with little subtlety, pompously overacting his heart out. But Mallard was avoiding the humor, treating the lines as if they were perfectly serious, in contrast to the other performers, whose antics seemed merely to exasperate him. Bottom did not interrupt Quince because he wanted to play every part in "Pyramus and Thisbe." His comments were the machinations of a world-weary, somewhat pretentious actor who really wanted to direct.

And yet, it was funny. At first the audience seemed as baffled as Oliver. But gradually they accepted the interpretation, starting with Bottom's demonstration of tyrannical acting, which was not emoted with the full force of Mallard's lungs but mumbled like a latter-day Marlon Brando. Titters were heard, followed by more sustained laughter. At the end of the scene, with Bottom's exhortation to "hold, or cut bowstrings," followed by hugs all around, the audience was roaring. They clapped loudly as the scene ended, and by the interval, they were applauding Mallard's every entrance.

"So how's the Plumley Plod Squad?" Oliver asked Effie, while they drank stale, overpriced coffee from an urn at the back of the theater. "Did they welcome you with open arms and an honor guard of raised truncheons?"

Effie sniggered. "Something like that," she said. "Detective Inspector Welkin now reminds me of Ozzy Osbourne."

"Talking of resemblances, don't you think Uncle Tim's Bottom seems vaguely familiar?"

"It's a good job I know what you're talking about," she remarked wryly. "However, while we have a moment, I'd actually like to pick your brains on a case."

Oliver glowed inwardly. Six months earlier, she would have been eaten with resentment if Mallard had approached him for help. It's amazing how love can alter your perspective.

"Pick anything you like," he caroled, instantly regretting the phrase. "What is it, a nice juicy murder?"

"No, it's a missing persons case. A thirteen-year-old schoolgirl."

"Not guilty."

"Nobody's guilty. Everything points to her being a runaway, not an abductee. But I think you may know her. When you were in Plumley last weekend, did you encounter a couple called the Quarterboys? They said they went to your friend's church, so I put two and two together."

"Sam and Joan. Yes, I met them. Why?"

"It's their daughter, Christina, who's done a bunk. Did you meet her, too?"

"Yes…look, are you sure Tina's run away?"

"Well, her parents were convinced at first that she'd been kidnapped by Mormons, but it's clear she went off of her own free will. A bag is missing, some of her clothes, some food items from the kitchen. And she left a note to her mother, saying not to worry, although Joan was positive that it was written at gunpoint. But why were you doubtful?"

Oliver brushed his hair out of his eyes and tried to revisit his time with the Quarterboys the previous Sunday.

"Sam and Joan seemed to be remarkably strict in controlling what Tina could and couldn't do, Sam especially," he told her. "I think young Tina has been brought up to believe that her number-one priority in life is to please her parents, never mind what she wants for herself."

"Sounds like the perfect recipe for creating a runaway daughter."

"I agree, but I didn't think Tina was quite mature enough for a teenage rebellion. Of course, all this is based on seeing her only for an hour or so. What have you been doing to find her?"

"I've been steeped in gore so long, thanks to Tim, that I'm a bit rusty on the standard procedure. Fortunately, my new partner, Tish Belfry, is fresh out of Police College and knows the drill. We've circulated the girl's description around the manor, checked the hospitals and shelters and bus stations, that sort of thing. I spent the day at her school, talking to teachers and school friends. Just in time—they broke up today for the Christmas holiday. The evening shift's taken over now, but I have to be back early tomorrow, so I'm afraid I'll have to drop you off at your flat tonight and then go home to Richmond. I may need to work the whole weekend. Sorry."

Oliver nodded glumly. At least the Christmas break was nearly here. He would have to go to his parents' home in the country for the day itself, but surely he'd be able to snatch some time with Effie?

"Tell me a bit more about the church," Effie said quickly.

Oliver briefed her on his two evenings with the Plumley Dia-conalists, including the tension over Nigel Tapster's arrival. "And tonight is their big night," he concluded. "The church meeting. Will the Exorcist of Plumley get a seat on the diaconate?"

"Do you think Tina might have run away to join Tapster's fledgling cult?"

"I doubt it. I recall her mother saying she'd been to a couple of the meetings, but Daddy Quarterboy put an end to those excursions when he heard about the weirder stuff. Tina seemed to have accepted her father's authority."

"What about your friend, the eligible Reverend Paul Pilt-down? Could he be eloping with the Lolitas of the parish?"

"Hardly. Officially, he's celibate, although it's not a job requirement. Between you and me, he's gay. He had to learn *something* at Cambridge. But I think Tina's very fond of him. Perhaps he may have some insight into what she's going through, if it's not betraying the confidence of the confessional or whatever they have in the Diaconalist Church. But didn't you meet him?"

"No. Why?"

Oliver scratched his head. "I'd have thought Sam and Joan would have called in spiritual reinforcements in this time of trial."

"Once they accepted that Tina had run away, they were adamant that they wanted to keep it in the family. Sam insisted that we didn't do a local house-to-house because of what the neighbors might think. I told them that once we started making our inquiries at Tina's school, it wouldn't be a secret much longer." She shrugged. "So there's nothing else I should know about the United Diaconalist Church? No human sacrifices or ritual cannibalism?"

Oliver smiled. "That might have made last Sunday evening a bit more interesting."

"You'd probably find any church service dull."

"Not at all," he protested. "I used to love going to evensong in my parents' village, all Stanford and stained glass. Especially on a snowy winter evening, with a brisk trot home through the moonlight afterwards, and the promise of mulled wine and warm flannel sheets. And I can vividly recall a summer evening on the promenade in Folkestone, listening to a Salvation Army brass band play 'For Those in Peril on the Sea' in the gathering twilight, with the waves breaking endlessly on the shore behind them. A magical moment."

"Oh, Oliver," Effie sighed, brushing his fringe aside with her fingertips, "you're really quite spiritual. If you only worked out, you'd be perfect."

He ignored the sly joke about his thin body, since he knew she equated muscularity with male narcissism. But religion had never come up before. It would be depressing, at this stage, to find out she was a Moonie. "So do I take it you're not much of a believer yourself?" he asked her casually.

Effie frowned. "That's rather a deep question for this stage of our relationship," she answered coldly. "Are you already planning our children's religious education?"

"Good heavens, no," he stammered, aware that his face must be reddening. "Nothing could be further from my thoughts. Well, not further, just not yet. I mean it's all too soon isn't it? Or don't you think it's too soon? Not that there's anything wrong in thinking about those things, and as far as that goes, I'd love to have your children, Effie. Sorry, I mean I'd love to get you pregnant. No I don't. Well, I do, but not without your knowing. Of course, you'd know eventually, but I was hoping we could practice a few more times first."

He broke off, convinced that he could say nothing further to extricate himself, and wilted under Effie's icy stare. Suddenly, she let out in a peal of laughter.

"Oh, Ollie, you're so easy sometimes," she chuckled. "This *is* going to be fun."

The lights in the hall flashed, and the playgoers started to wander back to their seats. There seemed to be more of them, as if word of Mallard's popularity had spread around the village during the interval.

"There is one thing I've remembered," Oliver whispered as the play began. "Tina's a thin thing, but she was complaining about gaining weight and feeling nauseous."

"So?"

"Well, I was wondering if she had the beginnings of some kind of adolescent eating disorder. Bulimia or anorexia nervosa. Maybe that's how her frustrations with her parents are emerging?"

The reappearance of the actors ended the conversation. They settled back to watch the second half of the play.

Once again, Mallard's performance was the triumph of the production. His Nick Bottom, portrayed as a pretentious director wannabe, more than compensated for the disturbing concept of the fairy world as a bunch of pre-war Nazi sympathizers and the antics of the cross-dressing Victorian male lovers. The problem with four naked middle-aged men leaping gracefully into an orchestra pit was that they had to clamber back onto the stage afterwards, which they accomplished with considerably less elegance. "I've just remembered, we have to buy some Christmas tree ornaments," Effie murmured idly. Oliver preferred not to watch.

The audience brightened as the "Pyramus and Thisbe" play-within-a-play approached, and erupted into spontaneous applause when the Athenians strutted out for the dumb show, dressed in RSC hand-me-downs. They assumed Mallard's discomfort in the skin-tight leather breeches was part of the act, and this comical counterpoint meant that his perfectly straight, almost moving delivery of Pyramus' ludicrous lines, as well as his exasperated asides to the heckling noblemen, continued to evoke gales of laughter. Finally, the moment came for Mallard as Bottom as Pyramus to stab himself with his sword. The deed done, Mallard stood facing the audience and an expectant hush fell throughout the theater. He let the weapon slip noisily from his hand.

"Now am I dead," he stated hoarsely. "Now am I fled. My soul is in the sky."

He tried to lift a hand to gesture toward heaven, but the weight of encroaching death was too much, and his arm dropped abruptly. The playgoers watched, enthralled.

"Tongue, lose thy light. Moon take thy flight."

This was the cue for the actor portraying Moonshine to reverse off the platform with a much-rehearsed silly walk, but nobody noticed. All eyes were on Mallard.

"Now die," he whispered, his head drooping almost imperceptibly. "Die," he breathed again. His knees began to buckle, and he let the momentum turn his body until he was facing upstage. He cried "die" twice more, once quizzically and then as if all the answers to the human condition had flooded into his wasting mind in the intervening microseconds. He collapsed onto his knees, still with his back to the audience, who by now were holding their breaths.

With a final "die" that was no more than the last intake of air leaving a tortured body, Mallard fell forward onto his outstretched arms, about to subside into a lifeless heap.

And then, releasing a small puff of talcum powder, the seat of his trousers split open.

"Well, Ollie," Effie shouted, barely audible over the cheers and rapturous ovation of a delighted audience, "now you really *can* say you've seen it."

Chapter Four

With the Poor and Mean and Lowly

Saturday, December 20

Tish Belfry was already at her desk when Effie arrived at the Plumley OCU on Saturday morning.

"Did Tina turn up?" Effie asked immediately.

Tish shook her head. "I called in on the Quarterboys on the way here," she reported glumly. "They haven't heard a thing. I hate this part of the job. I only had to appear on the doorstop to create a disturbance. Mr. Q thought I had the girl in the car, so he was pissed off at me, Mrs. Q was convinced I was there to tell them she'd been fished out of the river, so she was relieved."

"A fifty percent success rate, anyway," said Effie, hanging up her heavy wool coat and ripping down the mistletoe that somebody had taped above the CID room's coat-stand. "Do you really hate your job?"

Tish sighed. "No, I love police work. But it seems we women always get stuck with the soft stuff. Missing children, battered wives."

"Those are pretty important cases."

"Oh, I know, I know, Sarge. That's the point. The men *don't* think they're important, which is why they fob them off on us.

They only want to work on incidents that give them a chance to show how tough they are."

"Call me Effie. Okay, let's remind ourselves of what we know."

Tish checked a page of notes, neatly written out in her small handwriting. "Tina went to school as usual on Thursday. She left at about four o'clock, but didn't get home till nearly six. Her mother doesn't know where she was during these two hours, but she wasn't unduly worried because Tina takes part in after-school activities one or two nights a week, and Mrs. Q assumed this was one of those nights."

"Were there any activities at the school?"

"Only the regular meeting of the computer club. Tina's not a member and she wasn't there."

"How about irregular activities? Any pre-Christmas sporting events? Carol singing?"

"Nothing."

"And we know Tina didn't hang out with her friends during that time. All the girls I spoke to said she left as soon as school ended and they hadn't seen her since. I couldn't find anyone who could think of a reason why she should run away."

"Me neither. Although one of the girls I interviewed said she seemed withdrawn, thoughtful. Apparently she's usually something of a chatterbox. A bit full of herself."

"She's not quite fourteen," Effie mused. "Give her a year and she'll find herself taking a back pew to the boys in her class. Any boys in her life, by the way?"

"When I asked if she could have been meeting a boy after school, her friends seemed to think it was rather ludicrous. Tina spent a lot of time at this funny church her parents go to, and she came in for ribbing from her less religious peers."

"Was there anything happening at the church that evening?"

"I doubt it. The Quarterboys would have known, wouldn't they? Isn't he some kind of bigwig?"

"Church secretary, if I remember rightly," Effie said thoughtfully. Oliver had been out at Plumley during Tina's missing hours, or somewhat later. Had he said anything about meetings or events?

"Okay, so Tina arrives home at six," she picked up, remembering her own interview with the Quarterboys the previous day. "She claims to be feeling unwell, doesn't want any tea, and takes herself off to her bedroom. Mr. Q gets home at seven, looks in on her and has a few brief words. He notices that she's writing and assumes she's now doing her homework, so he leaves her alone. At nine-thirty, she calls downstairs to say she's going to bed. Mother looks in on her at ten-thirty and she seems to be asleep. Next morning, the bird has flown, leaving only a note. When she doesn't appear at school, Mum and Dad call the cops demanding bloodhounds and search parties. Let's see that note again."

Tish passed over a sheet of paper torn from a school exercise book, which Tina had left on the kitchen table. On it, she had written:

Dear Mum
   Don't worry about me. I'll be alright.
   I just don't want to disapoint Dad.
   Please don't worry.
Love
Tina

"I wonder what would disappoint Dad?" Tish asked. "Sam and Joan said they had no idea what she meant."

"From what I hear, Mr. Q. has high standards and expects her to run her life by them. A sneaky ciggie or a glimpse of *Playgirl* may be enough to plague her conscience for a fortnight."

"Still, to run away…"

Tish broke off, looking apprehensively at the door to the large room. Casanova, better known as Detective Constable Trevor Stoodby had sidled through and was trying to shed his oversized parka without letting go of a large paper bag.

"Oh, good morning, Ma'am," he said humbly to Effie.

Her first reaction was to correct the honorific, since it belonged to an officer with a higher rank—preferably female.

Her second reaction was to let it stand. Stoodby hung up his parka, and then approached the women, pulling various paper cups, packets, and stirrers from the bag.

"I thought you might like some nice hot coffee, Ma'am," he whispered, "seeing that it's a bit nippy out. I brought you some too, Tish. Black, one sugar, right?"

He smiled at Tish hopefully, who snatched away Tina's note before he could put her coffee cup on it.

"White, no sugar," she said scornfully. "But there's no reason why you'd know that." Stoodby looked downcast.

"Well, I didn't put the sugar in," he said contritely, "and there's milk in those little cartons. But I'll try to remember in future." He turned away and drifted toward his desk, muttering "White, no sugar" several times under his breath.

"Trevor," Effie called. He spun around, delight and apprehension fighting for the right to contort his features.

"Thank you," she said.

"Yeah, thanks Trev," Tish added reluctantly. In the battle for Stoodby's face, relief elbowed delight and apprehension aside and won by a nose.

"Where do you think Tina was during those missing hours?" Effie asked Tish.

"Maybe she was wandering around, afraid to go home? We could walk the route from school to home, ask people on the street if they saw her. It's largely residential in those areas, a couple of parks, although they wouldn't be too crowded in this cold weather."

"Shops? Chip shop? Some place to play video games?"

"Not where she lives, it's the posher part of town. She'd have to go well out of her way to reach the shops where the kids like to hang out."

"She had two hours. Maybe she was up the High Street, buying some Christmas prezzies for Mum and Dad? Let's try some street interviews this afternoon."

"It's a shame today's Saturday, though—there won't be the same traffic patterns as there would be on a weekday."

Saturday, thought Effie. She had planned to spend the day with Oliver. "Try it anyway," she said. "And look out for dog-walkers."

"Dog-walkers?"

"They often keep to a regular pattern. A dog's digestive system doesn't know it's the weekend. Don't focus just on Thursday evening—she may have been seen in the area since then. Tina doesn't seem a particularly worldly child, and I have a hunch that she won't have gone too far. My guess is she could be staying with someone. A friend, a relative, perhaps a sympathetic adult, who's letting her calm down before sending her home again."

Effie thought for a second. "How was her health?"

"Okay as far as we know. It sounds as if she was only pretending to be sick when she came home as an excuse to stay in her room, out of the way of her parents."

"I'd still like to know if she's been ill recently. Particularly if she's been showing any signs of an eating disorder. After all, she completely avoided her tea that evening."

"Another hunch?"

"A little piece of inside information. I have my sources."

"How mysterious!" exclaimed Tish. "But all right, I'll track down her doctor. Let's hope he or she is cooperative and not all fluffed up about patient privacy."

"The girl's underage and missing. Make that clear if you get any resistance. Okay, you call the Quarterboys, get the name of the doctor, and follow up there. Warn them that I'm coming over this morning. Then get more copies of Tina's photograph and line up some plods for street interviews this afternoon. I wonder if uniform have come up with anything, based on the circulation of her description?"

"They haven't," said Stoodby sorrowfully. He glanced up, seemingly surprised that the women were looking at him. "I checked on the way in. I didn't mention it sooner, because I didn't want to interrupt you."

"Well, thank you, Trevor."

"Don't mention it," he said, almost flushing. "Say, Tish, put me down for the street interviews this afternoon."

"Don't you have other cases to be working on?" Tish asked acidly.

"Oh yes, but this seems rather more important," Stoodby said, brimming with earnestness. "I hate to think of that poor little girl being away from her mum and dad, what with the cold weather and Christmas coming. I'll ask Mr. Welkin if I can lend a hand."

Tish stared at him. Effie was more circumspect.

"You've got enough to keep you busy?" she asked Tish.

"Yes. What are you going to do?"

"Me? I'm going to make a phone call. Then I'm going to drop in on the Quarterboys. And then I'm going to church."

◇◇◇

Geoffrey Angelwine woke with the cloying taste of chloroform still in his nose and mouth. His immediate reaction was amazement, first at finding himself alive and then at finding himself upright after so many hours of unconsciousness. But he quickly realized that his position was secured by manacles and chains that pinned him to the wall behind him.

Geoffrey opened his eyes, to little purpose. There was no light. Was it a room? It was cold, and he sensed the air moving on his face, as if some unseen ice giant were breathing on him in the darkness. As he tentatively moved his hands across the surface of the wall, it seemed uneven and strangely sticky.

He had been in bed, that he remembered, thinking with a quiet satisfaction of the several practical jokes he had played on Oliver during the day—the depilatory in the shampoo had been particularly effective—when the noises began. Scratching, rustling, and a high-pitched breathiness, like suppressed squeaking, coming from under his bed. He was leaning over, lifting the edge of the counterpane, when something—no, several things, furry, with short arms and sour breath—had shot out, pressed the wet handkerchief over his face, and held it there.

He tried to move his arms, but the manacles were tight and strong. If only he could see. But wait—there was a light! In the distance, a flicker of flame, coming toward him along a long, rocky passageway. And two strange pink dots, glowing above it. They were like eyes, but he knew nothing or nobody that had pink eyes, apart from a rabbit maybe or a...

A cold sensation gripped his heart and caused him to sweat from every available pore. He started to quake, rattling the chains around his body. Geoffrey knew this wasn't fear. He had experienced fear before, and this new feeling was far, far worse. There was only one word that Geoffrey could squeeze through his trembling lips, and that was..."Finsbury!"

The ferret stopped and smiled. "The same," he drawled, lifting the candle high and forcing the shadows to shrink like rapidly drying stains around the cave walls. "Welcome to my guest room."

"Oh my God," cried Geoffrey, struggling with the iron chains, "somebody help me! Help!"

Finsbury stroked his whiskers fastidiously with the back of a paw, and placed the candlestick on an old packing case, the cave's only furniture.

"Shout all you like," he crooned. "That shmuck little Billy and all his ghastly family can't hear you down here."

He produced a turd-sized cigar from his velvet dressing gown and lit it in the candle's flame, taking a few leisurely puffs.

"What do you want with me?" Geoffrey stammered.

"Want?" the ferret echoed, with mock astonishment. "Isn't it obvious? I want you to suffer, as all practical jokers should suffer." He blew a mouthful of foul-smelling smoke into Geoffrey's face. "I hate practical jokers, Angelwine. I believe that every idiot who spends the morning on April the First telling his trusting friends that their flies are open and collapsing into helpless laughter, simply because they look, should be drowned in a dribble glass and buried in a coffin filled with whoopee cushions."

"But I was only doing it for the book," Geoffrey whined.

Finsbury smirked and stepped back. He perched himself on the packing case, crossing his legs and letting a Turkish slipper dangle from his elevated paw. He sucked contentedly on the stogie.

"What are you going to do me?" Geoffrey quavered, after several seconds of unbearable silence. He was unable to break his gaze from those porcine-pink eyes. "What fiendish yet strangely apt tortures do you have planned, you weasel from Hell? Is it the joy-buzzer that's hooked up to 40 million volts? The fake buttonhole that squirts sulphuric acid? The gun that's really a cigarette lighter that turns out to be a gun after all? What? For God's sake, tell me!"

"How unsubtle," sighed Finsbury with a languorous yawn. "No, I have something special planned for you, Mr. Angelwine. I'm going to sit here…and abuse the English language!"

Geoffrey frowned. "What? Nothing more insidiously painful? Excruciatingly agonizing? Diabolically though somehow deliciously evil?" He looked puzzled. "Frankly, Finsbury, I expected something more beastly than that."

Finsbury shrugged. "None of us are perfect," he said casually.

"Is," Geoffrey muttered.

"I beg your pardon?"

"Is perfect. None of us *is* perfect. You said 'None of us are perfect.' But 'none' is singular."

"I shall have to be more careful," said the ferret apologetically. "I'll try to make less mistakes in future."

"Fewer."

"I'm sorry?"

"*Fewer* mistakes, not less. 'Mistakes' is a number, not a quantity, so it takes 'fewer.'"

"I see. Thank you. But irregardless of these niceties—"

"Oh for heaven's sake, there's no such word as 'irregardless,'" Geoffrey interrupted crossly. "Good Lord, Finsbury, you of all people—sorry, polecats—should know better than to indulge in such solecisms. They set my teeth on edge. Honestly, if there's one thing on earth that drives me to utter distraction, it's—"

He stopped abruptly, watching the slow grin spread across the vile creature's jaws.

"Now you get the idea," Finsbury purred, making himself more comfortable on the crate. "Oh yes, Mr. Angelwine, it's going to be long, long afternoon for you and for I."

"You, you archfiend," shouted a struggling Geoffrey, through pain-gritted teeth...

The ringing telephone caused Oliver to break off his free-flowing fantasy and peevishly save the document. He had longed to use the word "archfiend" in a Railway Mice story, and it sounded just right bleated in his imagination by Geoffrey's voice. And for once, he wasn't procrastinating, even though it was Saturday morning and he didn't have to work. Geoffrey's name would eventually be replaced with some poor woodland creature, but Oliver was pleased to have come up with a new perversion for Finsbury that had real educational possibilities for his young readers and didn't involve the use of questionable household implements. (The hapless victim would be saved by the explosion of Finsbury's cigar, which turned out to be a trick one sneaked into his pocket by the irritatingly resourceful Billy Field Mouse.)

"Yes," he snapped, impatient to return to work.

"Oliver? This is your Uncle Tim."

Oliver brightened. "Uncle Tim! Hey, you certainly answered that question."

"What question?"

"The one in *A Midsummer Night's Dream*. 'Doth the moon shine that night we play our play?'"

"Very funny," Mallard grunted at his chuckling nephew. "I had quite enough of your jokes last night."

When Oliver and Effie had gone backstage the previous evening, they had found a embarrassed Mallard sitting disconsolately in the tiny dressing room he shared with Puck and Oberon, while the play's producer, Humfry Fingerhood, was marching in circles in the small space, clearly agitated. Mallard had hastily completed his "Pyramus and Thisbe" scene wrapped in a Nazi flag, which he had grabbed from the back wall of the set, and by the time he returned for a shamefaced curtain call, he had changed back into his regular Bottom costume—patched corduroy jacket, jeans, Reeboks, paisley ascot, and gray silk shirt.

"I just don't understand it," Fingerhood was moaning. "They *laughed*. The audience actually *laughed* at your performance."

"I know, I know," Mallard muttered, dropping his head into his hands.

"It wasn't supposed to *be* funny," Fingerhood complained, nervously examining his fingernails. "It was my conception of what Bottom would be like if he were an ordinary amateur drama enthusiast, not some kind of clown."

"I'm sorry, Humfry," said Mallard. Fingerhood stopped and looked down with concern at his star actor.

"Oh, good heavens, Tim, darling," he said quickly. "If I implied that your performance was more than the width of gnat's eyebrow from perfection, you can beat me black and blue with a begonia. No, you played it exactly the way I wanted you to. Exactly the way I would have done it myself, in fact. It must be my conception of the part that's at fault. Ah well, I'll leave you to your guests. But I simply can't fathom what made it all so risible…"

Fingerhood hugged Mallard and flounced pompously from the room, a short figure in a patched corduroy jacket, jeans, Reeboks, paisley ascot, and gray silk shirt. As Mallard lifted his head to watch his producer leave, Oliver was sure he saw a slight twinkle in his uncle's eye. But it was rapidly replaced by a look of abject shame.

"Effie," Mallard began, "I'm so sorry you had to witness that, er…"

"Base display?" Oliver asked brightly.

"Unfortunate accident," Mallard concluded, with a momentary scowl at his nephew.

"I've seen worse," she replied with a smile. "You should take a look at what's left in the photocopier room after the squad's

Christmas party. But just out of curiosity, why weren't you wearing any underpants?"

"It made it easier to get those tight leather trousers on," mumbled Mallard, his voice sinking lower. "Sorry."

"Never mind Effie, how about apologizing to me?" Oliver piped up. "You're my uncle, so that makes it almost a Freudian experience."

Mallard stared at him. "I'm your uncle by marriage," he stated, "and if *you* want an apology, you can whistle for it. You didn't see anything of mine this evening that I haven't seen of yours dozens of times."

"True," said Oliver, "but if I recall—and actually I don't—those occasions all happened before I was a year old, when I could often be observed posing naked for the adoring masses on a bearskin rug."

"He'll still do it if you slip him fifty pee," said Effie cheerfully.

"You have just told me more than I wanted to know," groaned Mallard, standing up and gathering his possessions. "Phoebe will be waiting for us. And for God's sake, don't say anything about what happened tonight. I'll break it to her later that—"

"Her husband couldn't keep his assets hidden?" Oliver suggested, as they drifted toward the door. Mallard grabbed his arm. Effie had already passed into the corridor.

"The only reason I haven't throttled you is because I need to talk to you," he whispered urgently. "Privately. I'll call you tomorrow."

The concern was still evident in Mallard's voice the next morning. "I'm in trouble," he was saying on the telephone.

"I'm sure Aunt Phoebe will forgive you," Oliver replied. "It can't be the first time in your marriage that you've made a bit of an ass of yourself."

"Your aunt was very understanding and sympathetic about last night's fiasco."

"When she stopped laughing, I bet. I suppose the tricky part will be to get the trousers to split at exactly the same time tonight."

"Will you shut up about those bloody trousers!"

"So what's the trouble?" Oliver asked soothingly.

"It's professional."

"Ah. Is this something to do with this sudden Christmas vacation you seem to be taking out of the blue, thus obliging my girlfriend to work on weekends?"

"Exactly. It was forced on me by Assistant Commissioner Weed."

"Getting a little behind with your work?"

There was a noise on the line that suggested Mallard was either choking or practicing Japanese. After a pause, he spoke.

"Weed has turned up my personnel file. So they know about that mistake over my birthdate. He wants me to retire, starting more or less now."

"Bummer."

"If you make one more buttock joke, you little prat, I'm sending your Christmas present back!"

Christmas present! Oliver scribbled a reminder to think of something for Effie.

"I'm not ready to retire," Mallard was saying. "This is too soon, too sudden."

"But—"

"I warned you!"

"No, this is a real but," said Oliver sympathetically. "What can we do?"

"I was hoping you might have some bright ideas. Can you think about it over the next couple of days, anyway?"

"Certainly. It will take my mind off what I want to do to Geoffrey."

"What's young Angelwine been up to this time?" Mallard asked, and Oliver told him about the book proposal and the sequence of practical jokes, which had culminated that morning in the removal of every nut and bolt from his ancient bicycle.

"I was left just holding the handlebars," he complained. "I had to walk to Harrods to stalk and capture the *pains au chocolats.*"

"It's odd to think of Geoff as a practical joker, though, when he's practically a joke himself," Mallard said pensively. "Where is he now?"

"At work. Weekends have no meaning for the ambitious flack."

"Tell you what, give me his work number, I'll have a word with him."

"You'll threaten him with the long arm of the law if he doesn't desist forthwith?"

"Er, yeah, something like that. Although I can't threaten him with anything official if I'm on holiday. Now, what about this missing persons case Effie was telling us about last night? Think she needs a hand? Unofficially, of course."

"Busting in unannounced on her first assignment without you, Uncle Tim? Isn't that showing rather a lot of cheek? Even for you…"

Oliver listened placidly to the beginning of Mallard's stream of invective and then quietly hung up the phone. "Christmas present," he read off a sheet of notepaper. What did that mean?

The telephone rang again, putting the thought out of his mind.

Commentators who lament the triumph of conformity over individuality in English society should consider the semi-detached house. These paired dwellings, joined at the seams, were designed by their architects to be perpetual mirror-images, facing leafy residential streets in a perfect symmetry of form and decor. But like Siamese twins who rebel against being dressed identically, English homeowners have other ideas about their metaphorical castles. As Effie pulled into the Quarterboys' cul-de-sac, about a mile from the church, she was struck by the mismatches: Fake Tudor half-timbers, strapping half a frontage like a bondage outfit, jostled relentlessly modern picture windows; faux Jacobean cladding and diamond-pane windows stood cheek by jowl beside pebbledash and frosted-glass porches; and the Quarterboys' blue paintwork and off-white stucco competed blatantly with the brown and beige color scheme chosen by their neighbors.

The street was eerily silent for a Saturday morning, the cold weather keeping its children indoors. Joan Quarterboy answered the door and fussed Effie into the front room, which was clearly kept for the entertainment of visitors. It was warm, but there was a faint dampness in the air that implied the radiators had been turned on only recently. Effie knew that the rear sitting room contained the working fireplace and the family's modest Christmas tree.

Joan, too, seemed dressed to entertain strangers. Her skirt, blouse, cardigan, and outdoor shoes seemed unnecessarily formal for a Saturday morning. "My husband isn't here, I'm afraid," she announced nervously. "He couldn't sit still. So he's taken the car and he's driving the streets, just to see if he can spot our Tina."

Effie nodded and took in the room. It was sparsely furnished, with the bare minimum of good quality items to make entertaining tolerable—gold three-piece suite with fussy fringes, coffee table, unmatched end tables, small bookcase, and an odd étagère made of chrome and yellow glass, crowded with ornaments. The bookcase contained mainly religious books, including several different translations of the Bible. Nothing to indicate the presence of a thirteen-year-old in the household, except for a partially wrapped Christmas gift that Joan swept from the sofa to make room for Effie.

She had noticed this yesterday. Apart from some brightly colored outerwear in the hall, Tina's possessions were restricted to her bedroom, and even in this sanctum, there were clear indications of her parents' taste. She doubted that the girl would have chosen the old-fashioned dressing table complete with pink-draped pouffe or the faded eiderdown with its pattern of climbing roses. The walls were glaringly devoid of pictures of kittens, horses, or—if Tina was on schedule—pop singers and teenage television stars. There was only an Advent calendar, now two days behind schedule. The room's neatness meant Joan had easily spotted the space on top of the wardrobe from which Tina had removed her small suitcase.

"You must excuse me, Sergeant," Joan continued. "This business has left me very flustered. You're not the policewoman who telephoned earlier? I know I should be paying attention."

"That's all right, Mrs. Quarterboy," Effie said gently. "No, that's my assistant, Detective Constable Belfry." *My assistant.* She couldn't recall having used the phrase before. It had a nice ring when it wasn't applied to her.

"She wanted the name of Tina's doctor," Joan said. "I can't think why. Tina hasn't been to the doctor for months."

"Perhaps she went without your knowing?"

"She wouldn't do that sort of thing behind our backs. She knows better."

"Perhaps she just didn't want to worry you," Effie offered. "Although I should say that we have no reason to think she'd been to the doctor. It's just the sort of routine inquiry we have to make, in the circumstances."

"You do this a lot, do you?" asked Joan hopefully. "Find missing children, I mean."

Never having sought a missing child, Effie had no idea how to answer the question. She had helped to find the murderers of several missing children, but she didn't think Joan would appreciate hearing that. Fortunately for her, the woman had a limited capacity for listening to anything that lifted her out of her own narrow world. She prowled the surface of words, pouncing on opportunities to interrupt with her own beliefs and experiences.

"I suppose it's something a policewoman would be good at," she continued, filling the silence. "They leave the rough stuff to the men. I've noticed that on television."

"Most of the children reported missing turn up within twenty-four hours," Effie blurted defensively, having rejected the temptation to boast of her black belt at karate.

"But it's been more than twenty-four hours already," Joan wailed. She snatched a handkerchief from the sleeve of her cardigan and sat heavily on the arm of an armchair.

"Only just," said Effie, privately bemoaning her blunder. She perched beside Joan and put an arm around her shoulders.

Joan sobbed into the handkerchief for a few moments and then blew her nose.

"I'm sorry," she said. "I should be strong. Sam says we have to be strong. He says the Lord is testing us, and if we put our faith in God, everything will turn out fine."

Whatever works, thought Effie, although she wondered how Sam Quarterboy would twist that theology if Tina was in worse danger that she suspected.

"Would you like me to call the minister of your church?" she asked. "Wouldn't his help and guidance be a comfort while you're waiting for Tina to come home?"

"The only comfort I could have is for Tina to march through that door right now and say 'Hello, Mum,'" Joan replied, her eyes tearing again. "No, I don't want to call anyone at the church. Sam doesn't want them to know we're facing this shame. He's a proud man, he'd be humiliated if it looked like Tina was turning out to be a troublemaker or a juvenile delinquent. It was bad enough that we had to miss last night's church meeting for the first time in more than fifteen years."

"Just because Tina's run away, it doesn't mean she's a trouble-maker, or that she's at fault."

"What else could it be? What did *we* do that was wrong?"

Effie stood up. "Mrs. Quarterboy, we know for a fact that Tina chose to leave, which is good news, because we can rule out foul play. That puts the whole investigation onto a very different footing from the start. She's not an adult, but at thirteen, she's clearly old enough to have some idea where's she's going and how to look out for herself. As I said, I'd be very surprised if she doesn't come home by herself, today or tomorrow at the latest."

She knew Joan was no longer paying attention to the meaning of her words, but was sifting them for an opening for her own opinions. Effie noticed through the window that a maroon Ford Escort had pulled into the driveway, with Sam Quarterboy at the driver's wheel. She spoke quickly.

"When she does come home, Joan, the very last thing you or your husband should do is accuse her of being a troublemaker or get angry with her because of the fear and worry she's caused. There'll be time to get to the bottom of her disappearance. But first, make her feel welcome and forgiven. And above all, loved."

Joan Quarterboy looked up, with horror on her small features. "What kind of a parent do you think I am, Sergeant?" she demanded angrily. "Of course I love my daughter. And so does Sam. You don't have children, so you don't understand."

Effie waited until her instinctive irritation with the woman had subsided. She weighed her responses. *What makes you think...How do you know...* Too challenging. "How can you tell that I don't have children?" she asked, hoping the concession to Joan would disguise her impatience. Her gloved hand hid the absence of a wedding ring.

"You wouldn't be working if you had little ones, would you? Not as a policewoman."

The front door opened. Joan rushed into the hallway but stayed in the 1950s. "Did you find her?" she gasped.

Sam shook his glossy head without breaking his step and closed the door firmly behind him.

"I've just been—" He stopped, spotting Effie behind his wife. "Why are you here? Is there any news?"

"I'm afraid not."

"Then I can't think why you're wasting time here when you could be out looking for Christina."

Effie swallowed again. "We're doing all we can. I needed to ask you some questions."

"Questions, questions, it's all questions," Sam muttered, taking off his suede car coat and placing it on a hook beside Tina's anorak. Although he was wearing a thick, V-necked sweater, he still wore a silk tie with his nylon shirt, and his trousers looked as if they were half of a suit. He turned back to Effie irritably. "We're not holding anything back, you know. If we knew anything that would get our girl home sooner, we'd have told you by now."

"I'm sure of that, sir."

Effie held her ground, refusing to give him the signs of intimidation that he clearly expected. But she found herself excusing his frustration more easily than Joan's proud foolishness. Sam suddenly seemed too drained to compete.

"I hope at least you used an unmarked police car," he snapped. "We don't want the neighbors to think there's any trouble in this house."

"We're trying to be as discreet as we can in our inquiries," Effie replied, "but we do need to ask the general public if they may have seen Tina. If she doesn't come home today, you might consider an appeal on television. If Tina can see how much you're concerned about her, it may make her come home all the sooner."

"She's not stupid, she must know how concerned we are," he said stubbornly, fiddling with his car keys.

"Please, Mr. Quarterboy."

For all his faults, Sam Quarterboy was intelligent and decent, and in the face of Effie's firmness, he became aware that this untypical belligerence was not helping. He beckoned her into the front room and sat down wearily in an armchair. Joan followed.

"So what are these new questions?" he asked. Effie did not sit down.

"I want to know who Tina's friends are at the church. There's a chance she may have tried to contact one of them."

"Why would she do that instead of calling her parents?" asked Joan. "And anyway, Sam doesn't want people at the church knowing about this."

"It's all right, love," he said. "I've just come from seeing the minister. I told him everything."

"Him!" Joan blurted scornfully. "He didn't even have the decency to call round last night, after the meeting. You're the church secretary after all."

"I told Paul Piltdown we weren't going to the meeting because we were all down with a tummy bug. He didn't want to disturb us last night. In fact, he was coming over this morning when I turned up."

"By rights, they should have canceled the meeting altogether," Joan grumbled, not wishing to waste the mood of dissatisfaction that had enveloped her. "I trust at least that you were reelected, even if you weren't there."

"Yes, I was reelected to the diaconate," said Sam. "But there's bad news, too. Nigel Tapster was made a deacon. Poor Cedric Potiphar had to stand down. Perhaps if we'd been there, our votes would have made the difference."

"That man!" Joan began, but Sam interrupted her.

"This isn't helping Constable Strongitharm find our Tina," he declared. Effie chose not to correct him. "Now, who were Tina's friends at church?"

Joan subsided onto the sofa, nervously stretching the small handkerchief that she held in her lap. "Well, there aren't too many children of her own age, these days. They grow up and drift away. If their parents aren't in the church, we don't seem to be able to keep them."

"Is there a youth club or some other association?" Effie asked.

"There used to be, but it sort of died. We were hoping that Paul Piltdown, being a younger man, might make the difference, but so far, he hasn't attracted many new young people. Dougie Dock runs the local group of the Victory Vanguard, but it's for boys only. No, the only thing happening at the moment is the Sunday School Nativity play, which is going to be part of the Christmas Eve carol service. Tina was going to be in that—she'd been chosen to play Mary. But the other children in it are all younger. She was really looking forward to it. She was supposed to be at a rehearsal this afternoon."

Joan began to weep softly. Her husband reached across and touched her arm gently.

"I understand Mr. Tapster's become something of a youth leader," Effie said quickly.

"Unappointed and unwanted," Joan snorted, despite the tears.

"Nigel's prayer meetings aren't officially sanctioned by the church," Sam explained diplomatically, unaware that Effie had been well briefed about the Tapsters' practices.

"Did Tina go to these meetings?" Effie asked, trying to confirm what Oliver had told her. "Is there any chance that Mr. Tapster or his wife may be able to help us find her?"

"Once Tina told us the goings-on at Nigel Tapster's house, I kept her away," said Sam forcefully. "That was weeks ago, and I know for a fact that she hasn't been anywhere near them since. No, if anything, she was much closer to Paul Piltdown, our minister."

"I was hoping to drop in on Mr. Piltdown later," said Effie. "Now that he knows about the situation, he—"

The telephone rang in the kitchen. Joan looked up at her husband with a terrified expression on her face, but Effie suspected it was her regular habit. She hurried from the room. Sam and Effie followed her.

Joan was frozen, her back to the others, listening closely to the telephone. Then she turned. Her face was joyous. She mouthed the words: "It's her!"

"Keep her talking," Effie whispered to Sam and snatched her mobile telephone from her handbag, switching it on and cursing inwardly that she hadn't programmed in any telephone numbers for the Plumley OCU. She scrabbled in her bag for her diary.

"Why don't you come home, lovey?" Joan asked, tears running down her cheeks. "We've been so worried."

Effie punched in the number for the CID. "I'm going to try and have the call traced," she explained softly. "But it's going to take some time."

"All right, dear. All right," Joan was saying, in a tone that suggested she was nearing the end of the conversation. Sam suddenly snatched the receiver from her hand.

"Christina, this is your father," he announced. "Tell me where you are and I'll come and pick you up. What do you mean, you—"

He stood motionless for a second. Then he slowly replaced the telephone on the hook. "She hung up," he said incredulously.

Effie recognized the stick insect's voice on her mobile phone, but she disconnected the line without speaking. Maybe the telephone company would still have a record of the call?

"She hung up on her father," Sam repeated. Joan covered her face with her hands.

"Gawd, Effie, you don't do things by halves," Detective Inspector Welkin was complaining. He was less wary of antagonizing her when she was on the other end of a telephone.

Effie was parked on a double yellow line near the entrance to Plumley Central station, and she was using the time to catch up on the investigation. She had already called Tish Belfry to report that Tina was alive and clearly staying away from home of her own volition. Joan thought the call had come from a public telephone, but although the girl was coherent and intelligible, she hadn't given any clues to her whereabouts. Effie told Tish to contact the telephone company and then continue with the afternoon's sweep of the area between Tina's school and her home. Then she called Welkin to ask for permission.

"I've just had bloody Trevor Stoodby in my office trying to get all of his mates involved your case," Welkin continued. "Listen, Eff, I appreciate the crash course in sensitivity training, but we can't have the entire CID out looking for a runaway on the last Saturday before Christmas."

"Agreed," said Effie, silently thanking Stoodby for securing her a strong negotiating position. "That's why I just want Tish and a few uniforms—the ones who'd be on that beat anyway. You can keep the rest."

"I suppose I can let you have Trev, since he seems so keen. Keeps bleating 'poor little Tina' and mumbling about *his* first Christmas without his mum and dad. I think he was twenty-four at the time. The others don't seem interested. I'm going to send them up the High Street for some undercover work among the shoppers. So what do you think, is the kid going to be home in time for the Queen's speech?"

"I hope so, but I don't think it'll be today. She's scared of Dad for some reason, although he says they didn't have any sort of argument, and he's not aware of anything she's done that would get him angry."

"Maybe that's the problem. Only *she* knows and she's scared to tell him."

"I think you're right," Effie agreed, noticing the man who had appeared at the tube station exit and was now standing uncertainly on the pavement. "I'll check in again later, I've just seen someone I want to interview."

She folded the phone and tossed it into her bag. Then she climbed out of the car, ran over to the man, and kissed him very hard on the mouth.

◇◇◇

"Well, this is a very unexpected pleasure," said Paul Piltdown, ushering his visitors into the manse. "Oh, perhaps not entirely unexpected in the case of Sergeant Strongitharm, since I heard the news about Tina Quarterboy this morning. Very distressing."

Oliver and Effie followed him into the large living room where Oliver had met the deacons six days earlier. This time, he took the sofa in front of the window. Effie sat beside him.

"You two look like a young couple who want me to marry them," said Piltdown jovially. Seeing their immediate discomfort, his face fell. "Oops, sorry. Clearly a bit premature for that sort of pleasantry. Effie, I'm sure Oliver will tell you that I'm a past master at putting my foot in it."

"I'm sure it all goes back due to his influence in your youth," she replied graciously. Oliver, startled, embarrassed, and now slighted, chose to look grumpy. Piltdown smiled.

"Ah good, you seem to have the measure of this old reprobate. Now, forgive me for my ignorance of police matters, Effie, but I understood you investigated murders with Oliver's Uncle Tim? I trust this doesn't indicate pessimism about poor Tina?"

Effie quickly explained why she was assigned to Plumley.

"I see," Piltdown said thoughtfully. "And you wanted to ask me if I knew where Tina was. I should warn you that even though the United Diaconalists do not practice formal confession, I would have to regard any conversations between myself and Tina as off-limits. Fortunately, that's not a problem in this instance, since I didn't know she'd run away until Sam came to see me this morning, and I have absolutely no idea where she is now. Or should that be 'unfortunately,' because if I did know, I would beg her to go home to her parents. Tea?"

He slipped from the room to put the kettle on. Piltdown had struck Effie as personable, with an open and appealing face that fell slightly short of being attractive. He was clearly at ease with women, although she could see that no woman under sixty had had any influence on the decoration of the manse, which clearly pre-dated Piltdown's arrival.

"I like him," she murmured. "He's a bit like a pious, over-grown teddy bear."

"Being virtuous goes with the job," Oliver replied. "I told you, he'll be very cooperative. You don't need me here as an excuse for interviewing him."

"But would you have come all this way if I'd said I just wanted to see you for a couple of hours?" she asked, squeezing his hand tenderly.

"Of course."

"Good boy. Now I won't have to break your fingers after all."

They snatched their hands apart guiltily as Piltdown returned with a tea tray, trying to hide his amusement at their reaction. He put the tray on a small table and sat down on a stiff-backed chair.

"I wanted to offer you some biscuits, but I seem to have run out. Liquids only, I'm afraid. I could have sworn that there was an entire packet of Jaffa Cakes in the pantry the other day. Alas, Oliver knows my housekeeping is not all it should be."

"He leaves his vests in the pantry and his pants in the vestry," Oliver murmured. The others ignored him, and Piltdown busied himself with the tray.

"It's sad to think that Tina herself was playing mother in this very room last Sunday evening," he commented ruefully. He paused, and tea slopped from the teapot into a saucer.

"Something occur to you?" asked Effie.

"Something ironic, I suppose," Piltdown answered. "Tina was 'playing mother,' as the expression goes, by pouring the tea for everyone. And she should be playing the mother of God right now in the children's Nativity play. They're rehearsing next door, even as we speak."

"Were they rehearsing last Thursday evening?"

"Oh no. All the rehearsals to date have been during Sunday School. But since the performance is going to take place in the church as part of the carol service on Christmas Eve—goodness, that's this Wednesday, how time flies!—they're meeting now while the building's empty. Barry Foison is the director, writer, and composer. He says it's going to be a Nativity for our time. Frankly, I'm dreading it."

"There was no other church event that Tina may have gone to after school on Thursday?"

Piltdown shook his head. "That was the evening I met you, wasn't it, Ollie?" he asked casually, passing Oliver a cup of tea on a mismatched saucer.

"That's right," Oliver answered. "You'd been to see Nigel Tapster. Hey, how did the church meeting go last night? Did you cast the Tapster out into the desert?"

Effie knew the answer, but she let the minister respond. It might be informative. Piltdown rubbed his hands together nervously.

"Nigel was elected as a deacon," he answered. Oliver whistled his surprise.

"How did that happen?" he asked.

"He won enough votes, of course," Piltdown answered blandly. "I told you, Ollie, we're a democracy. Nigel must have been sneakily doing the rounds of church members, persuading them to put a fresh face on the diaconate. And with Sam and Joan AWOL, he managed to squeak by, by one vote."

"So Sam's lost his daughter and his seat, all in twenty-four hours?"

"No, Sam's all right. Our deacons are of the old school. They've been brought up to believe it's not cricket to vote for yourself. They arrange to vote for each other. Patience votes for Dougie, Dougie for Sam, and so on."

"Who's the unlucky devil who should have received Sam's vote?"

"Cedric Potiphar. Hardly a devil. It's the first time in nearly a hundred years that a Potiphar hasn't been a deacon in Plumley, and the first time in forty that the Potiphar hasn't been Cedric. He was devastated to point of catatonia. I'm not sure he's really taken it all in."

"Why didn't you just postpone the meeting when you heard about Sam and Joan?"

"Some members made that suggestion, but others stated that church rules should prevail. We had a quorum, so the election had to take place. There's no requirement that all the current deacons be present, or the church secretary. Or the minister, for that matter."

"And was Nigel Tapster himself one of the people insisting on the letter of the law?" Oliver asked slyly, hoping to see a crack in Piltdown's stony facade. He had always sensed a much deeper resentment of Tapster than his friend had revealed.

"What do you think?" was Piltdown's reply. "Of course, if I'd known the true reason for the Quarterboys' absence, I would have made a stronger case for postponement. But they had merely called in sick. Sam has his pride, apparently, and Cedric has paid the price for it."

"Just out of curiosity, who did you vote for?"

"We're getting a long way from Tina and the reason for Effie's visit," Piltdown said pointedly, shifting noisily on his chair. He turned to Effie. "Can I help you with anything else?"

Effie had been glancing through her notebook. "Who were Tina's friends at the church?" she asked. "Who would she have confided in if she had any problems at home?"

"I'd like to think she might have confided in me. She used to be friendly with Patience's son, Billy, but I rather feel they've spent less time together since he became one of Nigel Tapster's circle. The other girls in Tapster's group are a little older—old enough to regard young Tina as a different species. You might talk to some of the other kids in the Sunday School, but since Tina was older than most of them, her role was more one of mother hen than boon companion."

"That was Billy Coppersmith at Tapster's house last Thursday?" Oliver asked.

"That's right. He and Heather were having a rather noisy rehearsal for the Nativity play."

"We're trying to track Tina between the time she left school at about four o'clock and the time she got home two hours later," Effie informed him. "Where were you at that time?"

"Gosh, am I being grilled?"

"It may jog your memory."

Piltdown ran a hand over his untidy hair. "Let's see, I was here until about a quarter past five, which is when I set out to walk to the Tapsters'. It takes ten minutes or so. I stayed for about quarter of an hour with them. Well, with Nigel—Heather and Billy kept up that infernal piano and guitar music all through our meeting. So it must have been about a quarter to six when I left and ran into Oliver. And you say Tina is accounted for at that point?"

"Until sometime during the night, when she ran off," Effie told him. "There's no chance that she might have gone to the Tapsters'?"

"I didn't see her there that evening."

"I meant during the night."

"The Pied Piper of Plumley, I think you called him, Ollie?" Piltdown said, collecting the cups and saucers. "No, I'm fairly certain that Tina wouldn't have sought sanctuary with the Tapsters."

"She wouldn't have run off to join Nigel Tapster's cult, despite her parents' attempts to keep her away from his influence?" Effie asked.

"Or because of them?" Oliver added.

Piltdown looked from one to the other. "There is no 'cult,'" he said quietly. "We admittedly have some theological differences among church members, even among deacons, but that's a family affair, nothing that we need the police to sort out for us. Just as I'm sure that when Tina turns up, we'll be able to address her problems within the Diaconalist family."

Oliver sensed that the interview had turned inexplicably icy, and while he knew that he had hardly uttered a word since their arrival, he felt responsible. He cleared his throat.

"Paul," he began tentatively, "as my girlfriend, Effie's naturally heard my opinion of Nigel Tapster's mission and the tension he's been causing within the church. As a police officer, she's only concerned with bringing Tina home safely to her parents. You can trust her to keep the roles separate."

"Of course," Piltdown replied. He grinned self-consciously. "Sorry, Effie, that little speech came out much more harshly than I intended."

"That's all right, Paul," she said, closing her notebook and slipping it into her handbag.

"And as I said," Piltdown continued, "I have no idea where poor Tina is right now. More tea?"

"Thank you, but we have to go," Effie claimed, jumping to her feet. Oliver, who wanted more tea, followed loyally.

"Oh Paul," she asked at the front door, "would it be possible to look in on the Nativity play rehearsal? You never know, one of the children may have heard something about Tina."

"Of course. You'll need to go down to the side door of the church. Partly my fault, I seem to have mislaid my set of the church keys, and Barry Foison only has a key to the side door. Oliver, you met Barry on Sunday, so he'll know you aren't the drama critic for *The Guardian* or some other interloper."

He closed the front door instantly. Oliver and Effie walked through the manse garden and into the street. A small break in the clouds allowed watery afternoon sunlight to wash the classical facade, giving the stonework a silvery finish. The rotting notice board in the shallow forecourt included a bright, homemade poster announcing the Christmas Eve carol service, with a child's painting of an angel blowing a long trumpet.

"You know," said Oliver, looking back along the street, "you jogged *my* memory about Thursday evening. Paul and I were walking back to the manse, and we were just about here when

I caught sight of a girl hovering by the manse gate. She turned away when she saw us."

"Could it have been Tina?"

"Not sure. It was dark, and there are no streetlights by the gate. If forced to guess, I'd say no. This girl seemed a little bigger than Tina and I had an impression of long red hair, whereas Tina's is dark."

"What time was this?"

"Just about seven o'clock."

"If Joan is right about the time Tina got home—and I think she is, because she's a mother—then it couldn't have been her. Did Paul see this girl?"

"If he did, he didn't react. I suppose that's odd, in retrospect. The girl was fairly conspicuous and seemed to be waiting for him. Even if he didn't recognize her, he'd surely have made a comment about a possible visitor."

They turned into the church's small car park and Oliver lead the way past Effie's Renault toward the overgrown path that ran beside the building, parallel with the manse's garden.

"So you're changing your mind about my old friend?" he asked.

"Not at all. I still think he's very nice."

"Even after it turned awkward over that Tapster business?"

"Paul wasn't awkward because he was being unpleasant. He was awkward because he was lying to us and he felt bad about it."

"He was lying?" said Oliver, aghast. "A man of the cloth?"

"You think every word a priest says is true? In and out of the pulpit?"

"What did he tell us that wasn't true?"

"Nothing. But I'm sure he didn't tell us the whole truth, even though I sense he really wanted to."

"So he knows where Tina is?"

"No, he would have told us or the Quarterboys if he knew that. It's more that I think he knows why she ran away. But as he said, that's really a family matter. Your intervention at that point was very welcome, incidentally. I was just starting to feel like smacking him, dog collar or no dog collar."

"Ah. And my wise comment helped you recover your professionalism."

"Sort of. Your 'wise comment' was just patronizing enough to make me want to smack you instead," she said sweetly.

The side door to the church was old and warped, and Oliver had to push hard before it opened with a shudder. Effie stepped ahead of him into the darkness, and immediately found herself in front of a spiky-haired, leather-clad biker with a harsh seven o'clock shadow and sunglasses. She stopped, noticing that his dirty jeans were unzipped and hanging around his hips. He stared at her, his tongue protruding a little between wet red lips.

"Do you want some help with those?" she said gently, indicating the biker's jeans.

"Yes please, miss," the biker whispered, pulling up his leather jacket and T-shirt to reveal a white belly above underpants with a Wallace and Gromit pattern. Effie dropped to her knees and pulled the boy's jeans up firmly to his waist.

"I had to go to the toilet, but the zip's too stiff for me to do up," complained the six-year-old. Effie finished tidying his clothes and leaned back, looking at him critically.

"You look very scary," she confirmed. "What's your name?"

"Kurt, Miss."

"Pleased to meet you, Kurt. My name's Effie. You need a shave."

The boy grinned. "That's make-up," he said shyly. "And I'm not supposed to be scary."

"Oh, I thought you were a Hell's Angel?"

"No, I'm a Heaven's Angel. I'm the angel Gabriel." He struck an odd pose that was clearly intended to make him look dangerous, but actually made Effie want to hug him. Then he deflated slightly. "It's only for the Nativity play," he whispered. "I can't really ride a motor-bike."

"That's just as well," said Effie, "because then I'd have to arrest you."

Kurt's eyes opened wide. "Are you a policeman?" he asked, with innocent sexism.

"Oh yes. Just like on 'The Bill.'"

Kurt glanced at Oliver, who was still standing in the doorway. "Is he a policeman too?" he asked.

"No," said Effie. She smiled slyly. "Kurt, have you ever heard of Finsbury the Ferret?"

"Here we go," muttered Oliver.

"I'll say!" exclaimed Kurt, his face brightening. "I've got all the books."

"Well, this gentleman is one of Finsbury's henchman. It's all right, though. He's under arrest."

Kurt looked critically at Oliver. "He doesn't look evil enough to be one of Finsbury's henchman."

"That's because he's a master of disguise. He's really very bad indeed."

"Shouldn't he be wearing handcuffs, if he's under arrest? Why doesn't he run away?"

Effie stood up. "Because he's given me his word that he won't. Life is so much easier when you trust people. Isn't it, Hrothgar?"

She addressed the last remark to Oliver, who smiled sarcastically but said nothing. Kurt stared at him for several seconds and then clearly lost interest in the conversation. They followed him through a door that led into the sanctuary of the church.

In daylight, the church seemed austere and uninviting, and its need for fresh paint and plaster was more apparent. Even the colors on the bright banner pinned to the pulpit seemed to recede. Oliver's earlier impression, that it seemed more like a theater than a place of worship, was reinforced by what was taking place. Barry Foison was sitting in the third pew, wearing the same loose sweater that he'd worn the previous Sunday, studying a script. To the left of the platform, Heather Tapster was sitting at the upright piano, which had been wheeled away from the wall and slightly dismantled. Billy Coppersmith was standing beside her, still wearing his Stratocaster, which was plugged in to a small practice amplifier at his feet.

"All right," Foison called wearily, "we've done the bit with the kindhearted hotel manager, and Joseph and Mary have stashed their moped in the garage. Cut to the shepherds. Kylie, you'll be a shepherd on Christmas Eve, so you can stop being Mary for a while."

A small girl was sitting on a folding stool in the center of the highest tier of the platform, immediately in front of the gray pipes of the unused organ. An older boy sat beside her, wearing a shiny lounge suit, and a lifelike baby doll lay in a metal toolbox between their feet. At Foison's command, the girl picked up the doll and started to clump down stage.

"Kylie, where are you going with baby Jesus?" Foison asked, his high-pitched voice reaching even higher to express his surprise.

Kylie stopped and thought for a second. "I'm taking him to work," she explained. "My mummy takes me to work with her."

"Yes, but you're not baby Jesus's mummy. Put him back."

"Yes I am. Mr. Dock explained all that in Sunday School last week. God inseminated me…" She knitted her brow in concentration. "In-tra-ut-er-ine-ly," she continued slowly. "It's Joseph who's not his biological father. We're an extended family."

Foison sighed deeply. He had clearly passed the point of seeing the humor in anything uttered by a seven-year-old. "I mean, you're not Mary now, darling. Tina Quarterboy is going to be Mary, but she couldn't be here today, so you're just standing in for her."

"Can't I take baby Jesus with me anyway?" Kylie pleaded, cuddling the doll. It burped realistically.

"You're going to be one of our shepherds," said Foison firmly. "Shepherds don't have babies. Well, they do, but they don't take them out at night."

"Can I have a lamb, then?"

"It's not that sort of shepherd," Foison began, but was cut off by Kylie's scream, which echoed around the empty building. The boy playing Joseph had finished inspecting the contents of his left nostril and had sneaked up behind Kylie, snatched the doll from her arms, and was now attempting to see if its head was detachable. Kylie turned and pushed him. He pushed back. The doll burped again. Foison covered his face with his thin hands, while Heather Tapster bolted from the piano stool and tried to separate the two children.

"Good afternoon, Barry," said Oliver. "I don't really want to stop the show, but is this a good time to ask you a couple of questions?" He had sidled over to the young man, who looked up, startled to hear the voice.

"Oh, it's Mr. Swithin, isn't it?" he said with a nervous smile. He glanced over to the stage. Joseph was back on the stool, idly kicking the doll, which he was dangling between his legs. Heather had led Kylie through a door to the left of the church, which presumably connected with the rooms behind the sanctuary wall.

"I think we have a minute or two," Foison said. "Kylie has to change costume. Is this about your article?"

"Not really. It's about Tina Quarterboy."

Oliver beckoned to Effie, who came over and introduced herself. If Foison was surprised to meet a police officer in this odd way, he showed no sign. Effie and Foison talked about Tina for several minutes, but the young man could offer no reason why the girl had run away and had no clue where she might be. He seemed open and genuinely concerned for Tina's safety. From a distance, Oliver studied him carefully. Foison was about his age, and yet the young man had called him "Mr. Swithin," without any hint of sarcasm. This meant he had either forgotten Oliver's name or that it was an habitual affectation, which was odd. Ben had spent more time talking to Foison on the previous Sunday evening—Oliver would have to compare notes with his friend.

"It's so strange that she should just disappear," Foison concluded. "Quite unlike her. She was so looking forward to being the Virgin Mary in our little play."

"She was going to wrap the babe in swaddling bands and lay him in a toolbox?" Oliver queried, after Effie had privately signaled that her interview was over. Foison laughed, covering his mouth with his fingertips. His teeth were very white.

"I thought the children might enjoy it more if we updated it somewhat," he said.

"Well, Joseph was a carpenter, so I suppose a toolbox is appropriate."

"Actually, in this version, Joseph is an IKEA salesman. But we'd better press on."

Heather Tapster had resumed her seat at the piano, and following a cue from Foison, struck two very loud chords. Billy joined in, with an odd wailing tune that slithered across several keys, thanks to Billy's liberal use of the guitar's tremolo arm and his habit of bending every note across the fretboard until the string seemed about to snap. It took a minute for Oliver to recognize the melody as "While Shepherds Watched Their Flocks By Night."

Three children filed glumly out of the door by the piano and paced across the lowest tier of the platform. Kylie was now dressed in a nurse's uniform, another girl was wearing a smart dress and carrying a briefcase, and a boy was clearly supposed to be a policeman, although it wasn't immediately obvious why he was carrying a crook. Nor could Oliver fathom why he also had a long, white cotton-wool beard.

"Garth!" Foison yelled, jumping to his feet. "What are you doing?"

Garth thought about the question for several seconds before delivering his considered response. "What?" he said.

"Lose the beard, Garth. And the crook."

"But I'm supposed to be a shepherd," he protested.

"Only metaphorically. You're a policeman—a modern-day shepherd, the sort of person who'd be on watch at night in today's world."

"Why can't we just be real shepherds, like in the Bible?" asked Kylie petulantly. "Then I could have a lamb. And I want a beard like Garth's."

"You're a nurse, sweetie," said Foison, drawing on his dwindling reserves of patience. "And Garth's not supposed to have a beard."

"Can't I still have a beard if I'm a policeman?" Garth asked.

"No, and that's not a regulation beard anyway. Take it off, please."

Garth reluctantly put the crook down and removed the beard. Foison covered his face with his hands again and took several long deep breaths. When he looked up again, the other girl was wearing the beard.

"I bet there are social workers with long white beards!" she protested, as Foison marched over to the platform and silently took the beard away. Oliver and Effie tiptoed across the church and took a seat close to the piano, waiting for an opportunity to talk to Heather and Billy.

"All right, let's start again," said Foison. "Go off and come on again when you hear the music." The three children groaned.

"Do we have to hear Billy play the guitar again?" said the social worker. Billy scowled at her.

"It's rock music, Danni. It's modern. Don't you like it?"

"Can't we just sing a nice carol?" the girl continued.

"About a lamb?" Kylie added.

"All right, all right, we'll assume you've heard the music and you're all on stage. Garth, you start."

Garth took three steps toward the front of the platform, clasped his hands behind his back, and flexed slightly at the knees.

"Evening all," he intoned. "Blimey, it's a bit parky round the houses tonight. What I wouldn't give to be curled up back at the nick with a nice cuppa and me copy of the *Socialist Worker*, thus proving that the Filth aren't all a bunch of pig-ignorant fascists..."

Foison turned and smiled weakly at Effie, who beamed graciously back. While the three children practiced their scene, Oliver sidled across to the piano and peered over it at Heather Tapster.

"I understand congratulations are in order," he whispered. Heather frowned, as if she didn't understand. She seemed distracted.

"Nigel's elevation to the peerage," Oliver continued softly.

"Oh, yes," she said softly. "Thank you, Mr. Swithin. We're truly grateful that the Lord has blessed our efforts."

"I have a police detective with me," he said, still keeping his voice low, "and she's looking into Tina Quarterboy's disappearance. Is this a good time to ask you and Billy some questions? It won't take long."

Heather glanced away quickly at the stage. Foison was reminding the children of their lines. "Well, all right. But I'm not sure that I can help. I don't know Tina very well, and I haven't seen her since last Sunday's service. It's quite a shock to hear she's run off."

"Do you have any idea where she may have gone?" asked Effie, who had slid in beside Oliver. She waved her warrant card. "Were there any friends who may have taken her in for a couple of nights?"

"Taken her in," Heather repeated slowly. She tossed her head, as if trying free herself from a cobweb. "Billy knows her better than I do. Perhaps he can tell you."

She called quietly to Billy, who took off the guitar and joined the group at the piano. Effie explained who she was, which seemed enough to terrify the teenager, and he answered her questions more or less monosyllabically, with frequent glances at Heather for moral support.

"And you didn't see her on Thursday evening, after school?" she concluded.

"We don't go to the same school," Billy said.

"But did you see her?"

"I went round to see Nigel and Heather," he answered cautiously. "We were rehearsing for Barry's Nativity play. He saw us." He gestured to Oliver. "So are you a copper, too?" he asked.

Oliver shook his head. "You and Tina used to be friends, I understand," he commented.

Billy studied his sneakers. "We broke up. Her Mum and Dad didn't want her to come with the rest of us to Nigel's house after church."

Effie turned back to Heather. "Is there any chance your husband may have seen the girl, or that she may have confided some of her troubles in him?"

Heather shrugged. "You'd better let him answer that. He'll be at home this evening, if you'd care to drop round. We're having the young people in for some seasonal prayers. Maybe you'd like to join us?"

"Unfortunately, I have to be somewhere this evening," Effie said quickly, which was news to Oliver. "How about tomorrow? Assuming Tina hasn't turned up in the meantime."

"We'll be at church in the morning," Heather replied. "It's Nigel's first Communion service as a new deacon."

Foison clapped his hands. "Music cue," he trilled. "Appearance of the angel Gabriel to the shepherds."

Billy picked up his guitar, seemingly grateful to break away from the detective, and waited for Heather to strike a bright chord. He improvised a loud pentatonic fanfare, jamming his foot hard on a sustain pedal on the floor. The music died away, not quickly enough for Oliver's taste. He was amazed at how long a guitar solo could be sustained without the application of either a plectrum or any appreciable talent.

"Gabriel!" Foison shouted. "The angel Gabriel! Kurt, that's your cue!"

The heavy curtains at the back of the church twitched, and a very short biker stepped through.

"Yo!" he shouted. He took a comb from his pocket and swept it theatrically through an imaginary pompadour. Then he adjusted his black leather jacket with a twitch and swaggered down the aisle.

"Don't have a cow, dudes and dudettes," Kurt crooned. "For word to your mother! The Notorious G.O.D. sends a wassup to you and your posse, knowwha'I'msayin'? There be some heavy shit coming down in the city of my man David…"

"Don't say sh—Don't say that word!" said Foison with a wince. "Start again and do it right."

"Let me be Gabriel instead of the Sentimental Socialist Worker," said Danni, as Kurt retreated dejectedly to his starting point. "My mummy says I'm her little angel."

"I'm sure she does, dear," Foison murmured, "but Gabriel was a boy angel."

"Angels have long golden hair and they wear nighties," Danni protested. "That makes them girls."

"Not in my experience," said Foison under his breath.

"All the angels I've seen were girls," Danni continued.

"You've never seen an angel!" Kylie cut in.

"I have. I've seen lots of angels. In fact I saw one just a minute ago. Flying up there in that sunbeam!" Danni pointed into a bright ray of sunlight streaming through a circular window above the church's disused balcony. "And it was a girl," she added defiantly.

"Bloody little liar," snapped Garth. Danni stared at him, then burst into tears. The boy playing Joseph, who had wandered off to stuff chewing gum into the organ pipes, noticed the commotion and threw baby Jesus at Garth, with the aim of knocking off his helmet. The doll hit Kylie, who also burst into tears.

"Gabriel's musical cue, quickly please," shouted Foison, attempting to break up the brawl between his shepherds. But before Heather could strike the keyboard, a different musical fanfare sounded raucously from the back of the church, and a troupe of six or seven small boys in uniform blazers and scarlet forage-caps came through the curtain. They were each blowing a bugle. Dougie Dock swaggered in behind them, wearing an adult-size version of the same uniform.

"I brought your heavenly host, Barry," called Dock, as the boys ran down the aisle, exchanging high-fives with Kurt. "We've been up the High Street, giving the shoppers a tune or two."

He marched pompously up the aisle to the front of the church, while Foison shuttled the new arrivals through the door by the piano, calling out instructions. Dock greeted Heather and, without asking, sat beside her on the piano stool and laboriously picked out the broken-chord accompaniment to "Heart and Soul." Heather moved away.

"I thought you were going to join in on your electric twanger, young Billy," Dock said, after playing the chord sequence many more times than called for by his skills. He glanced up and noticed Oliver and Effie, immediately leaping to his feet and hurrying over to them with an affected balletic lope.

"Well, hell-oo," he sang, with the same cadence that had made Oliver wish to avoid him on the previous Sunday. Reluctantly, Oliver took the proffered hand.

"And how's my old friend, Oliver?" he asked, grinning broadly behind his thick-framed glasses. Even though it was earlier in the day than their last encounter, his cheeks and chin were as blue as Kurt's, but without the aid of makeup, suggesting that Nature was wasting testosterone on entirely the wrong people. "I say, did you ever see your uncle's Bottom?"

Dock laughed heartily at his joke, and then turned and explained it at some length to Heather and Billy. Effie prodded Oliver.

"Tell me you didn't," she groaned. "Not to him."

"And who is this lovely lady?" Dock was now asking in fulsome tones, politely lifting his forage-cap. A couple of long, stray hairs went with it.

"Effie Strongitharm," she said, before Oliver could remember her name.

"And are you, my dear?" Dock retorted, taking her hand.

"Am I what?"

"Strong in the arm?" He squeezed her hand slightly and felt for her biceps with his free hand, as if assessing her strength, but something made him abandon the joke abruptly and step back. Oliver was not sure if Effie had given him a flash of the famous and feared Strongitharm Look or if Dock had actually found her biceps, which was remarkably firm and taut due to years of karate.

"You've been in the High Street, Mr. Dock?" Oliver asked quickly.

"Now, Oliver, I asked you to call me Dougie, didn't I?" Dock replied with a nudge. "Jesus used his first name, and if it was good enough for him, it's good enough for me, eh? Besides, if you call me 'Dock,' young Effie might think I really am one."

Effie, who was searching in her handbag for her warrant card, did not ask the obvious question, and Dock hurried on.

"Yes, I took some of my Victory Vanguard boys out for a march to work off some energy, bring the color back to their little cheeks. Here, since I'm in uniform, I'll give you the official VV salute."

He held up both hands, first and second fingers extended in a double Churchillian victory sign. It was vaguely reminiscent of Richard Nixon's final gesture on the steps of the helicopter that took him away from the White House for the last time. Behind Dock's back—and to it—a couple of the boys delivered their own colorful variation on the salute.

"It was quite funny, actually," Dock continued. "We gave the Christmas shoppers a rousing rendition of 'Ding Dong, Merrily on High' on our bugles—of course, we can't play all the notes—and after we'd blasted out the 'Gloria' chorus, one of my lads turned to me and asked 'Is that what the angel meant by "Glory to God in the High Street"?' It's so sweet, isn't it? He's only eight, such a dear little soul."

Dock seemed almost misty-eyed at the reminiscence, but Effie's announcement that she was actually Detective Sergeant Strongitharm brought him sharply back to reality. He expressed surprise to hear that Tina had run away, but could offer nothing that would help Effie find the girl. Effie concluded the interview and indicated to Oliver that she was ready to leave the church. Dock confirmed that he had unlocked the building's front door on the way in and trotted away, already preparing a retelling of the incident for his boys that would no doubt cast himself as some sort of special constable.

In the narthex, Oliver slipped an arm around Effie's shoulders, gently pivoted her toward him, and kissed her.

"I'm on duty, you know," she cautioned him quietly as they broke apart and then launched herself at his lips again. They held each other for a few seconds in the dark space. Outside, the daylight was fading.

"Alone at last," Oliver mused, absentmindedly caressing the curves of her bottom, but a gently cleared throat from the doorway told him he was wrong again.

"Helping the police with their inquiries, sir?" said a young woman with dark hair. She stepped toward them. "Well, Effie, I suppose this is your mysterious inside source."

"Hello, Tish," said Effie coolly. She stepped away from Oliver, who was far less adept at handling unexpected shame, and introduced him to her assistant. They shook hands.

"Inspector Welkin said you were here," Tish told Effie. " I thought I'd check in with you, before we start the street interviews. I tried your mobile first, but there was no reply."

"I must have left it in the car," Effie confessed.

"No joy with the Quarterboys' family doctor, by the way. He hasn't seen Tina in months. Did you get anything useful?" Tish asked, glancing slyly at Oliver.

"Nothing that will help us find the girl," said Effie. She turned to Oliver. "Ah well, Ollie, you have delighted me long enough. I'll take you back to the train station."

"What time do you get off?" he asked.

Effie sighed. "Since we haven't found Tina, we don't. At least not till late. After we finish the interviews, Tish and I are going to check out some of the shelters and other haunts where the runaways end up in the West End. The evening is the best time to do that. It might be a long night, and I have to be back here in the morning to see Nigel Tapster and some of the other church people. So once again, I'll go home to sleep when I finish. Sorry, Ollie."

"You onto something here, then?" Tish asked hopefully. Through the curtains, they heard the piano and guitar playing the rhythmic patterns that accompany rap music.

"I don't know," said Effie, leading them through the narthex doors and across the church's vestibule. Tish's car was parked beside hers. "But I'm more convinced than ever that Tina is a lot closer to home than the West End. If only we knew where to look."

Chapter Five

How Still We See Thee Lie

Sunday, December 21 (Fourth Sunday of Advent)

When Effie returned to the church the next morning, the car park was full, and she reluctantly left her Renault on the street opposite. She had tried to time her arrival with the end of the morning service, to waylay some of the departing congregants, but she was clearly early. She got out and leaned on the car, knowing that she would probably doze off if she stayed inside. The sound of church bells from a few streets away signaled the superior punctuality of Anglicans.

Yesterday had been a very long day. At four o'clock exactly, half an hour after she had watched Oliver disappear glumly into Plumley Central Underground Station, she had begun the slow walk from Tina's school to her home, while Tish Belfry, DC Stoodby, and a couple of uniformed officers followed other possible routes that Tina might have taken through the middle-class mean streets of suburban Plumley. But none of the pedestrians they stopped could positively remember noticing Tina on Thursday afternoon or seeing her since, and the few leads that emerged were vague and certain to be sterile, the imagined sightings of a public eager to help a child, rather than true memories. The telephone company had so far been unable to trace Tina's phone call the previous morning.

And so, after an early dinner in a High Street café crowded with short-tempered Christmas shoppers, the three detectives had taken the train to Leicester Square to begin the tour of the shelters and youth centers where many of the capital's runaways gathered for free food and medical attention and, occasionally, salvation. Tina's description had been circulated as soon as she had gone missing, and the police and social workers associated with the shelters were conscientious, but Effie knew they were also overwhelmed with similar descriptions from police stations all around the country, especially as the holiday season increased the tensions within families. She and Tish could focus on Tina alone, and try to edit from their minds the dozens of other children they would see hanging up sparse tinsel and homemade paper chains on the bare walls of the shelters, or hovering in nervy flocks around Piccadilly Circus, or, as the cold evening wore fruitlessly on, gathered beside fires in the Dantesque cardboard cities that had grown up under the city's bridges and overpasses. For all her self-confidence and skills at self-defense, Effie was secretly pleased that Trevor Stoodby had tagged along with them.

She wanted to find Tina now for more than one reason. Obviously, she wanted to bring the child home safely to her parents. But Effie was growing aware of a personal need to see Tina with her own eyes, face to face. She had stared at the photograph Tish had obtained from the Quarterboys so often—that thin, impish face, the audacious nose that she may yet grow into, the long, dark pigtail—that it occasionally startled her to remember she had never met the girl. She needed to be sure that Tina would still look the same in person, and not turn up with the haunted, defiant, vulnerable eyes of the teenage girls and boys she had seen on the streets and in the shelters, or with a gaunt, bruised body that might already be tainted with heroin or desecrated by sexual predators.

Their energy had run out at three in the morning, long before they had exhausted every possible site. Effie took a taxi to her flat in Richmond, slept for four hours in her clothes, and, freshly showered and changed, made her way back to Plumley by train on Sunday morning, fighting to stay awake in case she missed her stop. She was pleased to see that her Renault had survived the night in the police station car park, having little faith that the location was any deterrent to enterprising car thieves.

Poor Ollie. It was the first time since they had become a couple that her job had completely edged out an entire weekend, apart from the couple of hours she had engineered the day before. She knew how he must be feeling, if he knew what was good for him. After years of not caring whether or not she had a man in her life, she could not, for now, imagine being without Oliver. She mourned the lost opportunity, but Tina had been gone for longer than the magic, meaningless twenty-four hours, and she could not walk away, knowing that DI Welkin had nobody else to put on the case. Fortunately, Tish understood this too, and was once again at the station on Sunday morning before she arrived. So was Trevor Stoodby, looking different. He had shaved off his ludicrous moustache that morning, and the ribbing he received from his male colleagues, who were prepared to mock any change for no logical reason, lasted until Welkin ordered all three of them back to their undercover duties in the shopping center.

Effie decided she would find a way to make it up to Oliver. She really ought to think of a memorable Christmas present for him before it was too late. Surely Tina would be home before Christmas Day?

It was midday when she spotted Barry Foison jogging toward her along the alleyway beside the church. He ran over to an old Fiat parked in the car park, rummaged for something in the glove compartment, and then scuttled back the way he had come, without seeing her. She crossed the street and cautiously climbed the three steps in front of the church entrance, noticing that there was no wheelchair ramp. It had been a long time since she had attended a church service, and she didn't know what to expect.

The main doors of the church were open, but they led only to a shallow vestibule, and a pair of closed inner doors kept in the warmth. Effie passed through these doors into the church's narthex. Nobody was in sight, but she heard the congregation singing on the other side of the heavy velvet curtains that separated this space from the sanctuary. It was "O Little Town of Bethlehem," sung to the old English folk song that had been turned into a hymn by Vaughan Williams. She loved this carol.

They were singing the final verse as she found a gap in the curtain on the left side of the church.

"O holy child of Bethlehem,
Descend to us, we pray…"

Effie sent her wish to whatever higher power might be listening that a certain missing child would descend to her. She slid into a rear pew, recalling the words of the carol from her own childhood and joining in as Heather Tapster struck the piano keys for the last quatrain.

"We hear the Christmas angels
The great glad tidings tell:
O come to us, abide with us,
Our Lord Emmanuel."

Effie sat down. Then she noticed that the rest of the congregation was still standing and got to her feet again. Paul Piltdown was in the pulpit, diagonally across the church from her. He spoke into the microphone, startling Effie, who hadn't noticed the loudspeaker mounted on the wall above her head.

"Once again, friends, we invite you to remain with us as the table is prepared for the Lord's Supper. And now the grace of our Lord Jesus Christ, the love of God, and the fellowship of the Holy Spirit be among and remain with you, now and forever. Amen."

Effie had some vague idea that she was supposed to cross herself at these words, but nobody else did. There was the low-frequency rumble of a sotto voce "Amen," and then Piltdown sat down in the pulpit. The worshippers also, sat, leaning forward in prayer. Heather turned away from the keyboard and seemed to be feeling for something on the floor, but the piano cut off Effie's view of her. She reappeared with some sheet music and launched into a gentle arrangement of the Wexford Carol. Piltdown climbed down from the pulpit and walked the length of the aisle opposite where Effie was sitting, apparently deep in thought. The worshippers stirred from their prayers, and some gathered Bibles and handbags. Several young children scurried into the church through the door near the pulpit that she and Oliver had used the day before—she recognized Kylie and Kurt among them. Dougie Dock followed, beaming broadly. The children slotted themselves into various family groups, which then headed for the exit along with some individual worshippers, no doubt to be greeted heartily by the minister. Outside, Effie could hear more children's voices and footsteps running along the alleyway beside the church. But about a dozen people stayed in their pews, some continuing to pray, others idly flicking through their hymn books or chatting quietly with their companions.

Of course, this was a mass. Not a mass, that was Catholic. Not a Eucharist, either. A Communion service, that was it, held after the main service had finished. Hadn't Heather mentioned it the previous day? Her husband's first as a deacon. Effie would have to wait until it was over before she could speak to him. Well, if she remembered the drill from her parish church, you didn't have to join in the parade to go up to the altar rail if you didn't want to participate. Where *was* the altar rail? The balustrade that ran along the lowest tier of the platform was too high. Behind it was a large table, covered with a white linen cloth, with several heavy wooden chairs, like armless thrones, lined up behind it.

Heather stopped playing, and after a brief exchange with a group of young people sitting near the piano, she walked toward the back of the church. She did not acknowledge Effie as she passed. Wouldn't she stay to see her husband's first performance, if that was the right word? Or was she like Phoebe, superstitious about attending one of Tim's opening nights, despite the risk that it might also be the closing night? And where was the famous Nigel Tapster anyway?

Barry Foison came into the church through the door to the left of the platform, wearing a double-breasted suit that seemed too large for him, and carrying two platters, which he placed on the Communion table. Then he padded away again. Meanwhile, Piltdown made his way back through the church, presumably having said his farewells to the congregants who couldn't wait to get the roast in the oven. Some people rose from their seats and joined Piltdown on the platform. Effie recognized Dock and Sam Quarterboy—she knew from an earlier phone call that Sam felt his place was in God's house, while Joan felt hers was at home beside the telephone. There were three others. A tall, balding man had come in through the same door Foison had been using. That had to be Nigel Tapster, from Oliver's description. A smart woman with stylishly cut gray hair had to be Patience Coppersmith, Billy's mother, the only woman on the diaconate. Yes, there was a certain resemblance between her and the sullen sandy-haired teenager, whom Effie could see among the youngsters. And that should have been it, according to Oliver's briefing: four deacons, with the minister in the middle. But who was the other, an old man, moving stolidly toward the platform, climbing the step, and settling himself onto one of the oak thrones? She saw Quarterboy tap Piltdown on the shoulder and point toward the man. Piltdown looked surprised, but made a gesture of helplessness. Tapster also stopped and glared at the old man, who seemed oblivious to the fuss but simply stared ahead, clutching a Bible.

Foison made a second appearance, this time carrying two odd trays that looked like cake stands with tall handles. He placed them carefully on the table, and then took a seat in the third pew. Piltdown sat down in the center chair, immediately to the left of the old man. Sam Quarterboy sat on Piltdown's left, with Patience taking the outer chair on that side. That left one chair on the old man's right, with both Dock and Tapster hovering beside it. Finally, Tapster mimed that Dock should have the special chair. He stepped off the platform, grabbed the piano stool that Heather had vacated, and carried it back with him. The old man still seemed unaware that anything was going on.

Piltdown rose to his feet. The church fell silent. Heather had not returned.

"Friends, whenever we meet around the Lord's Table, it is a special and solemn occasion. Today, it is…er…especially special, since we mark the first participation of our brother deacon, Nigel Tapster, as an officiant in the sacrament, and we also mark the long and historic diaconal career of our dear brother, Cedric Potiphar."

That explains that, thought Effie. The old boy's cuckoo. Didn't Piltdown say he'd had trouble convincing Potiphar that he had lost his deposit?

"To celebrate this event, we are not going to sing the usual Communion hymn this morning. Instead, Nigel is going to lead us in our musical worship with a seasonal song."

Tapster smiled broadly and once again walked off the platform. He collected a guitar from an open case beside the piano and returned, tentatively testing the strings with a plectrum. Then he tried a chord, grimaced, and turned to the congregation.

"This is going to be a little Chinese number," he announced, leaving an expectant pause. "Called 'Tu Ning,'" he added eventually.

The deacons remain stony-faced, but the teenagers groaned in unison and continued to laugh noisily at the joke while Tapster went back and rummaged in his guitar case.

There was a laugh at the rear of the church, too. A child's laugh. Effie turned, but she was the only occupant of the back row of pews; three elderly women who were sitting across the aisle from her had filed out before the Communion service. Nobody was there. It must have been an echo from the front, bouncing off the plain walls, or perhaps a stray laugh picked up by the pulpit microphone.

Tapster was back on the platform. He played another chord, and the guitar seemed to be in tune now, although he was still looking pained. Perhaps the constant back and forth was too much exercise for one session, Effie reflected wryly. Tapster sucked thoughtfully at a forefinger for a second, as if waiting for inspiration. Then he strummed the guitar and began to sing. Effie's amusement rapidly vanished.

It was a shame that Tapster failed to carry the melody, if there was one, because it left his audience with nothing but the words to focus on. These seemed largely to be branding the entire planet, believers and nonbelievers alike, as hypocrites, with the notable exception of the enlightened lyricist and, by extension, the singer. But this aspersion must have been lost on the cluster of teenagers at the front of the church, who cheerfully joined in the unmemorable chorus as if they'd been rehearsed. The chorus contained the song's only sop to the season, which begged God to send his "true spirit of Christmas Present" to dwell among us, clearly on the assumption that it hadn't been here before the songwriter demanded it. Effie could almost hear the whirring from Dickens's grave.

Tapster finished the song, took one more trip on and off the platform to place his guitar in its case, and settled back for the Communion service itself, which began with a long prayer conducted by Piltdown. Effie dared not close her eyes. She had placed herself directly underneath a glowing electric heater, and despite the cold weather outside, she was feeling snug and sleepy. Her drowsiness was intensified by the reverent hush that had fallen over the church. She slipped out of her wool coat and placed it beside her on the pew.

Piltdown ended his largely improvised prayer and segued neatly in the Lord's Prayer. The congregation murmured the well-known words with him. Effie joined in, mainly out of respect for their beliefs, but she found the prayer comforting and timely, following the nightmare visions of the previous evening. *Thy will be done. In earth as it is in heaven.* (Why "in" earth?)

After the amen, and another period of silence, Piltdown began to deliver some set lines over the bread—not a Communion wafer, she noticed, but a slice of a white loaf.

"On the night that he was betrayed," the minister intoned, "our Lord took Bread, and when he had given thanks, he brake it, and gave it to his disciples, saying, 'Take eat, this is my body which is given for you: this do ye in remembrance of me.'"

He tore the slice down the middle, and placed each half on a plate on either side of the table. He handed the plates to Sam Quarterboy on his left and to Dougie Dock on his right. The two deacons left the platform and began to make their way up each aisle, offering the plate to the communicants, like a flight attendant distributing boiled sweets.

The nearest communicant to Effie was a tall, old woman whose thick white hair was braided into a bun, sitting in the middle of the church. Dock would have to walk the last thirty feet of the aisle with the sole aim of offering bread to the detective. She tried to signal that she did not wish to participate, but as he neared, he recognized her and assumed this was some sort of greeting. He mouthed his trademark "Hell-oo" but then set his features rigidly, as if to teach her that a Communion service was not an occasion for social chat. Effie found herself mutely taking a piece of bread, like a small crouton.

When the servers had returned to their seats on the platform, Piltdown took one of the plates and passed along the row of deacons. Each took a piece of bread. Finally, he took one himself and turned to the congregation.

"Let us eat together, in remembrance of him."

He placed the bread carefully in his mouth. The other communicants followed his lead, and the aweful silence of private prayer returned. Effie contemplated dropping her bread into her handbag, but had some odd notion that this might be a sacrilege beyond her comprehension. She reluctantly ate it, chewing it so long that she tasted sugar in her mouth.

Piltdown stood up and picked up a silver chalice.

"After the same manner also he took the cup," he said, "when he had supped, saying, 'This cup is the new testament in my blood: this do ye as oft as ye drink it, in remembrance of me.'"

He put down the chalice and picked up one of the odd con-
traptions that resembled a cake stand, handing it cautiously to
Patience Coppersmith. Then he passed the other to Nigel Tapster. Each deacon left the platform and followed the same path
up the aisles as their colleagues who had distributed the bread.

Tapster served the cluster of teenagers first, with a brief smile.
As he reached the old woman, she seemed to whisper something
while taking a glass of Communion wine from the stand. Tapster
raised his eyebrows and moved on.

It was Effie's first good view of the man she had come to interview, and he held her gaze as he approached, his intense, dark
brown eyes scrutinizing her face. Certainly, despite the shabby
ordinariness of his body and the clothes he wore, Tapster's eyes
could command attention, could make you believe this man had
secrets, maybe could offer impressionable children mad glimpses
of different worlds.

Then Tapster's eyes narrowed and a small crease appeared
beside his mouth, and Effie knew with disgust how he was
appraising her. She looked away. Only when he reached the end
of her aisle did he realize she was refusing the wine. He inclined
his head and turned away.

A sudden chilly draft from the main entrance made her
regret removing her coat. She gazed around the church, noticing
the cracks and damp patches in the cream-colored plaster. You
could almost make out faces in the patterns, just as the devout
can sometimes spy the face of Jesus in an oil spill or a spaghetti
advertisement. She knew it was only an accident of the mind,
programmed from birth to turn two blobs of the right size and
distance into a pair of eyes. An optical illusion for an overtired
brain. Like the way she was imagining Tina's disembodied head,
floating in the air at the back of the church.

Effie sat upright.

It *was* Tina.

She would know that face anywhere. And she wasn't floating.
The girl had poked her head through a gap in the velvet curtains
at the end of the other aisle and was watching the service intently.

Why was she here? To see her mother or her father presumably. And finding her mother wasn't here, would she run away again?

Effie knew that if she could slip out through the curtains on her side, she could pass through the church's narthex and come up behind the child. As long as Tina didn't notice her. The girl seemed fascinated by the events on the platform—Effie risked a glance, Piltdown was serving wine to the deacons. She started to edge her way along the pew, sliding across the worn oak, keeping her eyes on Tina's profile. So far, the girl hadn't noticed the movement.

Effie reached the end of the pew. She had to rise to get over the pew's arm and into the aisle. She braced her feet and began to rise.

Tina turned and saw her. The head ducked away.

Effie flung her coat onto the floor and ran toward the gap in the curtains on her side of the church. There was a loud cry from the platform behind her, but she did not turn. Perhaps someone had been startled to see a communicant bolt for the exit? She shut it out of her mind, groping for the way through the velvet.

The narthex was dark and seemed empty. But could the girl be hiding among the winter coats hanging from pegs along one wall? Effie stopped and listened for the faint sounds of a thin body scurrying away, but there were more shouts coming from the church behind her—loud cries of children singing praises to God. She must have left the service at the very second it turned—rather unexpectedly—from veneration to celebration.

The narthex door was propped open! That's why she had felt the sudden draft. Effie bolted through the door, across the bare vestibule, and down the steps in front of the church.

There was no sign of the girl.

She ran straight across the car park, vaulted the low wall and stopped on the street, trying to assess all the escape routes. Nobody running in the road. Only houses and small commercial buildings across the street, nothing to offer cover in such a short space of time. Plenty of parked cars she could duck behind.

Effie looked behind her, swiftly weighing her options. Was the girl under a car in the church's car park? Had she ducked along that path beside the church, or scaled the fence and dropped into the manse's garden?

She paused again to listen. Still that noise of shouting, coming through the open door to the church, but no other telltale sound of escape. If the girl had fled the building, there was no way Effie could find her alone. Why hadn't she brought Tish with her? Damn. Damn damn bugger damn.

She strode back into the church, pausing in the vestibule. There were doors on either side of the space, presumably leading to broom cupboards or electricity meters, but both were clearly locked.

Could Tina still be in the narthex after all? Effie passed through the inner doors and closed them behind her. The shouting had turned to singing, although someone was still keeping up an odd, breathy grunt, out of time with the music. Like a dog or a pig in intense pain. Good God, Oliver hadn't warned her about this part of the service. It sounded even worse than Nigel Tapster's carol.

She parted the curtains and stared.

The older congregants were standing in their pews, rigid, almost as if they had no idea what to do at this point in the ritual. The deacons were also frozen on the platform, one or two of them whispering to each other. Tapster was gone. But the half-dozen young people had left their pews and were swarming in front of the platform, singing and chanting and performing an odd dance around something on the ground that Effie couldn't quite see. That's where the noise was coming from.

Nobody would notice her. She stood on a pew to get a better view of whatever was on the floor. A man's stomach rose into sight.

Effie began to sprint down the aisle. "Let me through!" she shouted. "Let me through, and stand back, everybody! Please!"

"Nigel is bringing us God's word," protested a teenage girl. She was weeping, hysterical.

"He's not bringing you anything," Effie said sharply. She pulled the children aside, trying to get to the convulsing figure on the floor. They were so far lost in rapture, what would it take to convince them there's a real problem here? "Can't you see?" she yelled. "He's dying!"

Her words made no impression on the children, who continued to sing tunelessly, but they seemed to bring the hesitating deacons to life. Piltdown raced down from the stage, followed by Dock, and tried to clear some space around the body. Effie could now see for certain that it was Tapster, lying breathless and delirious, the eyes that had checked her out five minutes earlier now rolling helplessly in their sockets.

"We need a doctor," she shouted to Dock. "Is there a doctor or a nurse in the church?"

Dock shook his head. Effie looked around frantically and noticed that one sandy-haired teenager had stopped dancing and was watching Tapster, trembling with fear.

"Billy," she said, gesturing toward the back of the church. "Go to the back pew and get my handbag. Now!"

The tremble turned into a sudden start, and Billy hurtled away.

Tapster was whimpering, clearly in intense pain, but unable to speak. Effie felt for his pulse, but it seemed that her touch increased his agony.

"We'd better all stand back," she commanded as Billy returned with her bag. She opened it and grabbed her mobile phone. "Does anyone know if he's an epileptic?" she asked.

A hand closed suddenly on her wrist.

"He's not sick," cried the girl who had spoken before, expressing a perfectly balanced mixture of pity and contempt for any mortal who did not possess the wisdom of her sixteen years on the planet. "God is speaking through him. I should know, I've been given the gift of prophecy! Hallelujah!" She let go of Effie and spread her arms wide, turning her head to the ceiling, but more of the teenagers had stopped dancing now and were hovering on the edge of the group, uncertain and frightened.

"Hallelujah!" the girl defiantly shouted again. Tapster squirmed, as if just the sound of the voice was giving him additional pain. "Oh, you just don't understand, you silly people! Come on, everybody, let's sing to the Lord."

Patience Coppersmith strode into the group, pulled the girl aside roughly, and slapped her across the face. "For God's sake, Michaela, get out of the way," she snapped.

Astonished, Michaela stayed where she was, a hand on her red cheek, until a tall youth gently drew her into a side pew. Meanwhile Effie called for immediate medical assistance, describing Tapster's symptoms. They reminded her of something she had read about once.

"Everybody stay very quiet," she ordered, as softly as possible. "Noise seems to bother him. And don't touch him."

But nobody seemed inclined to approach the man squirming on the ground. The teenagers withdrew fearfully to the pews they had been sitting in, except for Billy, who had moved to his mother's side. The other deacons who had left the platform stood helplessly. Most of the communicants had come forward from their pews, forming clusters of observers in each aisle.

"I think it's going to be all right," Effie whispered to Dock, who was closest to her. "An ambulance is on its way."

There was a sudden scream from Tapster, and his whole body quaked. The guttural noises that Effie had heard before began to come from his open mouth, and his fists clenched and moved toward his chest, almost as if he were trying impotently to beat his breast. His legs straightened, his whole body became rigid, and his back began to bow and rise. It was if an unseen hand had grasped his trouser belt and was lifting him slowly to heaven, until only the crown of his head and his heels were in contact with the floor.

Suddenly, Effie remembered exactly what the symptoms indicated. And she knew that if she was correct, Tapster was likely to die unless the ambulance was equipped with more than the basics, and there was nothing she could do about it.

"Dear sweet Jesus, his face!" cried Patience, and turned away. Billy hugged her. Effie knew what she had seen. As she telephoned for backup, she knelt in front of Tapster's turned-back head so that nobody could see the appalling, inhuman grin that was not the product of any joke but of facial muscles tearing at his lips and cheeks with superhuman strength. It would look even worse if they could see his face the right way up. The spasms had wrenched his eyelids open, too, and the staring pinpoints of his eyes met hers. There was no sexual interest this time. Only the inexpressible pain that scalded every fiber of his body. Aware that Tapster was fully awake, feeling every last ounce of the agony, Effie did not look away.

She saw life drain from his eyes.

The rasping breathing stopped. There was nothing but the silence of the church. The body did not relax, but slumped sideways, still contorted into a rigid crescent.

Effie escaped into professionalism. She tried to take a mental photograph of that moment. The frightened teenagers whimpering together. Billy and Patience Coppersmith holding each other. The other deacons looking down helplessly at the body, apart from Potiphar, who hadn't moved from his seat on the platform. Piltdown looking down from the pulpit. The other worshippers in an outer circle.

Effie looked up at Piltdown and shook her head.

Dying casts a spell. Death breaks it.

Once the soul leaves a body, the watchers remember to react. Piltdown breathed some words into the pulpit microphone about leaving the church, offering the manse and his services. He could not be heard above the rapidly growing noise of the young people wailing, some almost hysterically. Sam Quarterboy sat heavily on a pew and muttered a prayer. A woman communicant fainted and two others ran to help her. Dock walked away, wiping his eyes. Barry Foison made a move toward the Communion table.

"What are you doing?" Effie asked, still kneeling by Tapster's head.

"I'm going use the tablecloth to cover him up."

"No," said Effie sharply. "Stay off the platform."

"We can't leave him like that," said Foison wildly. "It's not right. Can we close his eyes, at least?"

"Perhaps it's better if we all go," said Piltdown, who had descended from the pulpit, skirting the platform. "Let's assemble in the manse. The ambulance will be here shortly."

"No," said Effie again, placing another call on her telephone. "You're all going to have to wait here." She stood up and clapped her hands.

"Listen to me, please," she called. "I'm Detective Sergeant Strongitharm of Scot—of Plumley CID. Many of you know that already. It's very important that nobody leaves my sight until my colleagues arrive. Then we'll take statements. You can go and sit in the pews at the back of the church, if you like, but don't go through the curtains."

She turned to Foison, who was staring at her open-mouthed. What nice teeth, she thought illogically. "Find a towel or something to cover his face, if you like, but don't touch anything on the platform or in the immediate area. Where are you going?"

She addressed the remark to Troy, Michaela's boyfriend, who was heading for the door to the rear of the church. "I need to get to the bog," he said weakly. "I think I'm going to throw up."

"Find a quiet corner of the church and be sick there. I'm sorry." Effie heard a voice on the telephone and asked for Welkin.

"Effie," said Piltdown firmly, above the growing murmurs of protest that had joined the dull sobbing, "this is all happening so quickly, but don't you think there's a chance you're overreacting? If you let me take these people into the manse, I can say some prayers and give them some tea."

"No," she insisted, hearing the distant ambulance siren. "This is a police matter now."

"What makes it a police matter?" he demanded. "Poor Nigel must have had a seizure or something. Now, we've got some very confused and upset young people here. Keeping them in the same place where they witnessed Nigel's death, in view of the body, for God's sake…Well, it's only going to make this worse. I insist that you let me take them out."

"This is a police matter, Paul," she said calmly. "And this church is a crime scene. And I'll tell you what makes it so: the likelihood that your new deacon, Nigel Tapster, has just been murdered."

"You can't be serious!"

"Does it look like I'm joking?" she replied. At that moment, Santa Claus ran into the church. Followed by two more."

Effie's arrival at Edwardes Square at about three o'clock that afternoon was a welcome diversion for Oliver, Geoffrey, and Ben, who had wasted most of the day trying to think of something interesting to do with their Sunday. Oliver had slept in late, and he had been sulking all morning, because his original plans for the day had not included waking up either late or alone. Ben Motley had not woken up alone, but his current girlfriend—a gentleman to the last, he never used any term less respectful than "girlfriend" to refer to his latest companion, even if he had yet to learn her name—had left early. And Geoffrey Angelwine, who always woke up alone, had been unable to go to his office, because it was closed for the weekend for a combined *feng shui* ceremony and asbestos removal. Susie Beamish, who, like Oliver and Geoffrey, rented rooms in Ben's townhouse but who rarely woke up in hers, had already left for work at her latest restaurant, the Generic Café.

Oliver's day had deteriorated further, first when Mallard telephoned again for no particular reason, and then when he discovered that Geoffrey, who had gone out early to buy a stack of Sunday newspapers, had managed to fill in just one clue in each of the seven crossword puzzles that Oliver normally hogged for himself. For the true crossword enthusiast, a puzzle that is only ninety-nine percent your own work is like having a wife who is ninety-nine percent faithful, and Oliver had indignantly accused his friend of breaking the truce on practical jokes. But Geoffrey, fending off blows from a rolled-up *Observer* magazine, had weakly protested that these were all genuine but abortive attempts on his own part to complete just one puzzle.

Ben had proposed going to the cinema after lunch, but their long argument about which film to see was only terminated by an even longer argument about where to have lunch. They had just finished the sliced banana and Brie sandwiches that an exasperated Oliver had eventually concocted by raiding Susie's corner of the fridge, when the doorbell rang. Oliver's utter delight at seeing Effie was rapidly replaced by utter dismay when he saw the misery in her eyes. He whisked her off to the privacy of his room, where she promptly burst into tears and wept for ten minutes on his bed, punctuating her sobs with a brief account of Tapster's disturbing death.

"What made you think it was a murder?" he had asked, toying with the gilded corkscrews of her bushy hair.

"His symptoms," she gulped. "That physical reaction. Poisoning. Or at least, a high enough probability of poisoning for me to suspect a crime. Most likely strychnine. And such an intense reaction that it had to be a fairly big dose. Which means, since that much strychnine would also be fast-acting, it was administered while he was in the church."

"Amazing. Did they teach you that at the Staff College?"

"I think so. But I read it more recently in a mystery novel. Evelyn Greatheart's *Worth a Guinea a Box.*"

"Really? Ah, the debt the world owes to mystery writers. But did you know that in real life, Evelyn Greatheart was my late great-uncle Henry? Bit of a black sheep, actually, in a family shedding the murky wool by the bagful. There was some business about dallying with schoolgirls that was all hushed up."

Effie sat up and grabbed a tissue from Oliver's bedside table. "Ollie, dear, some day you will tell me the story of your extraordinary family from the day the first Swithin fell overboard during the Norman Invasion, but right now, we're talking about *my* day." She blew her nose, while Oliver muttered a few words of apology.

"I can't say I liked Nigel Tapster," he mused, thinking back to his meeting three days earlier, "but that must be an awful way to die."

"It is. Even so, he died fairly quickly, which is a blessing, given the pain he was in. Surprisingly quickly. The spasms can often go on for up to an hour, one after the other, killing the victim through sheer exhaustion. Unless he gets the right treatment. Rigor mortis is instant, so he's stuck in that contorted position until it wears off."

Oliver remembered something. "What if the victim had a weak heart?"

"I imagine the intensity of the muscle spasms could easily put a strain on it, maybe provoke an infarction. I'd have to ask the pathologist."

"Nigel Tapster had rheumatic fever as a child. He told me it had prevented his going abroad as a missionary."

"I'd better make a note of that," she said sadly, reaching for her handbag. She sighed. "Ever the police officer. Thanks for the cuddle, Ollie. I feel a bit better now."

Her eyes were bloodshot and puffy, and her nose was red, and Oliver had never loved her more. He sat beside her and hugged her again.

"That's the first time I've seen you cry," he said gently, hoping the comment wouldn't turn her prickly. "I'm glad I didn't cause it."

"I'm sure you'll get your turn," she replied indistinctly, her face pressed against his chest. "I am allowed to have a feminine side, you know."

"From where I've been sitting for the past four months, every side looks feminine to me. But tell me, what is it about this case that got to you? You deal with murder all the time."

Effie sniffed decisively and stood up, walking over to the window. The day outside was dull and uninviting.

"I've never seen anybody die before," she said quietly, staring out at the untidy garden. "Isn't it silly? All the bodies I've viewed just after their owners departed this life! You get used to it, you insulate yourself from the human emotions. But this is the first time I've been there for the death itself."

Oliver came up behind her and rested his hands gently on her upper arms. She leaned back, and he kissed her head, pressing hard through the dense hair so that she would feel the touch on her scalp.

"But I tell you one thing, Ollie," she said. "I'm glad poor Heather Tapster was spared seeing her husband go that way."

"I suppose Paul Piltdown went round to break the news after the police had finished with him."

Effie turned around. "Oh no," she said. "Tish Belfry took Patience Coppersmith round to do the deed. Paul couldn't do it, because he's under arrest for the murder. Sorry, didn't I tell you? Now, where can I get some lunch at this hour?"

◇◇◇

Susie Beamish worshipped food. The feeling was not mutual, as she should have deduced from her notorious inability to cook, a string of largely imaginary weight problems, and an unbroken record of abject failure as a restaurant owner. Nevertheless, she continued to pursue her chosen career, in spite of all the signs that she'd be better employed in a field as far from the food supply as anyone can get without actually starving.

Susie had decided long ago that the way to the public's heart was through its funny bone. (She might have been more successful if she'd taken the more traditional route through its stomach.) And so she had devised a succession of theme restaurants, each with its own joke, such as an eatery exploring Jewish-Indian cuisine, called Kashmir Tochus, and The C-Food Place, which served only foods beginning with the letter C.

Unfortunately, the fickle eating public regarded each new project exactly like a joke—they groaned the first time and didn't want it repeated. Since the failure in September of Raisin D'Etre, which served only dishes that included raisins, her friends had been dreading the day when they would receive an invitation to the next opening night.

But Susie seemed to have learned her lesson. Since themes didn't work for her, she had deliberately chosen no theme at all. The Generic Café, on Victoria Street, eschewed any suggestion of ethnicity, style, tone, or formality in either its cuisine or its decor. The walls, floor, furniture, lighting, table linen, cutlery, menu, and uniforms were not merely plain, they were aggressively plain, the simplest and most basic she could find. And since Susie's staff were by now quite adept at keeping her away from the kitchen, the plain food was, for once, edible. "Everything about this place is totally average," said the *Independent* restaurant reviewer, and Susie not only took it as a compliment, she even considered having the quote blown up and framed.

The Generic Café was the only place Oliver could think of to take Effie for lunch. Ben had disappeared into his darkroom to work on the pictures he had taken the previous Sunday, but Geoffrey tagged along, partly to hear more about the murder and partly to gaze at Effie, whose preference for Oliver over him he had never fathomed. Effie had repeated her story, picking at a small plate of raw vegetables, the only appetizer she fancied on Susie's spartan menu. She knew from experience that both men could be trusted with the inside information.

"It's an odd experience, seeing it all from the start," Effie reflected. "The Three Wise Men were the first to arrive."

"I thought the shepherds came first," said Geoffrey. "Who are the Three Wise Men?"

"My three male colleagues in Plumley CID. They'd been working undercover on the High Street, because of a rash of pre-Christmas shoplifting. Hearing there was a murder in the manor, they shot over to the church without thinking to change out of their disguises."

"What were they disguised as?"

"I don't want to talk about it," Effie said quickly. "Anyway, they started taking some initial statements. The ambulance crew turned up, but as soon as they verified that Tapster was dead, I had them keep their distance. Then Spiv Welkin and Tish Belfry arrived with some uniformed constables. Spiv took it from there. The science squad showed up next, but they couldn't do much until the duty Scene of Crime Officer arrived. In fact, the pathologist beat him to it, reeking of roast beef and clearly pissed off because the head SOCO was late and his Sunday lunch was congealing. He changed his mind when he saw the body. And at that point, it was all suddenly familiar—taped-off crime scene, forensic picking their way around in sterile overalls,

flashes going off, Tapster carted away in polythene body bag....
That's normally where Tim and I come in." She took a sip of
coffee and then spat it daintily back into the mug.

"I have grown to love Susie Beamish like a sister," she declared,
"but when is she going to learn to make decent coffee?"

"Are you going to be assisting Welkin?" Oliver asked glumly.

"I don't think so. Remember, I'm as much a witness as an
investigator. Just like all the others, I had to give a statement,
although I was out of the church at the most crucial time, chasing the Amazing Disappearing Tina Quarterboy. But Welkin
seemed to be keeping all the fun for the boys. Beginning with
Paul's arrest. Although he's not actually been charged—he's
detained for questioning."

"Let me guess why," Geoffrey offered smugly.

"Go ahead," said Effie, munching on a celery stick.

"If you're right, and Tapster was poisoned, it must have been
given to him shortly before he died. I mean, it wasn't as if he
ingested it with his cornflakes that morning."

"That's right. Strychnine should work within about ten to
twenty minutes."

"Well, the only things he consumed in the ten minutes before
he died were bread and wine, during the Communion service.
So the poison must have been in the bread or in the wine."

"Go on."

"And since Paul Piltdown passed him both, Paul must have
been the killer." Geoffrey folded his arms and smirked until his
small eyes almost disappeared. Oliver considered tipping his
friend's coffee into his lap.

"And so?" Effie asked.

"Er, that's it, actually," Geoffrey concluded nervously.

"What do you mean that's it?" Oliver exploded, attracting odd
glances from the diners at nearby tables. He lowered his voice.

"It doesn't answer anything," he went on rapidly. "Did Tapster
eat or drink anything else during those ten minutes? If he was
poisoned, and the poison is strychnine, can it be administered
some other way, such as through the skin? And if it *was* in the

bread and wine, did Paul know it was there? Could someone else have spiked the sacraments? If the plates had been taken up and down the church first, what was to stop another communicant taking the poisoned pellet or glass? When it got back to the platform, how could Paul know which one to hand Tapster? Was the poison really meant for Tapster or was there a different intended victim? Or any intended victim at all—perhaps it was a random act of appalling mischief, and the lot fell on Tapster? Come on, Geoffrey, Inspector Welkin must have had more to go on than that before he arrested Paul!"

"He didn't," Effie said abruptly, stopping Oliver before he was able to voice his opinion of Geoffrey's higher mental facilities.

"What?"

"It happened exactly as Geoffrey said," she continued airily. "All the witness statements agreed that Paul was the last person to touch the bread and wine before Tapster, so he must have known which was the poisoned glass. Incidentally, we're assuming that the strychnine was dissolved in the wine. It would be easier to isolate a specially prepared glass than a single piece of bread in a big pile, and the alcohol in the wine would go a long way to masking the poison's bitterness."

"Everything all right, darlings?" cried Susie, bustling into view with a coffee jug in each hand. "Anyone for a top-up?"

"'The pellet with the poison's in the vessel with the pestle,'" muttered a distracted Oliver. "'The flagon with the dragon is the brew that is true.'"

"Who are you calling a dragon, you Swithin you?" Susie demanded, although good humor flashed in her chocolate-brown eyes. She elbowed Oliver in the ear and filled their mugs without asking. "This is my special Generic Café brew," she crowed. It has no caffeine, no special flavorings, and no foul aftertaste."

"In fact, no taste whatsoever," muttered Geoffrey, but the others noticed he waited until Susie had flounced out of earshot to terrorize her other customers. He scooped several spoonfuls of sugar into his mug.

"Then how does Welkin think Paul got the poison to Tapster?" Oliver asked.

"He's working on the notion that the poisoned glass was never on the serving trays. That Paul either slipped the strychnine into Tapster's glass just before he took it, or that he somehow had a prepared glass in his pocket or hidden under the table, which he palmed off on Tapster at the last moment. We didn't find anything that would back this up at the crime scene or in Paul's pockets—stuff like empty packets or pieces of cling-wrap or Sellotape. But I have to say, Paul's attitude didn't help his case."

"The vicar a bit bolshy, was he?" asked Geoffrey.

"He was distinctly uncooperative. I had the same sense I had yesterday, when Oliver and I talked to him about Tina's disappearance. I think he's hiding something—even if it's only a suspicion of who's really behind Tapster's death. Paul's just not very good at lying."

"It doesn't make sense," Oliver said thoughtfully. "Even if Paul wanted to murder Tapster—and I know they had an argument the other day—why would he do it there and then?"

"Perhaps it was the only opportunity he would have to pass the poison?" Effie offered.

"No, he only had to inveigle Tapster round to the manse. You've seen how adept Paul is with a kettle and a packet of Jaffa Cakes. Well, not the Jaffa Cakes, maybe. In England, you offer tea to your worst foes."

"And it would be a lot easier under those circumstances to prove that Paul did it," said Effie. "In church, in a Communion service, you've got a full deck of deacons to stand in as the unusual suspects."

"Tapster had no shortage of enemies on that platform," Oliver remarked. "Paul and Nigel were at loggerheads over doctrinal issues, apparently. Old Cedric had just been supplanted on the diaconate. Patience Coppersmith feared for her son. Sam Quarterboy feared for his daughter. Only Dougie Dock seems free of any motive, which is a shame, because I'd like to see him locked up for life."

"And let's not forget all the other communicants," Geoffrey said, warming to Oliver's flight of imagination. "Perhaps all the church members ganged up to protect their children from the Exorcist of Plumley. On Friday night, they make Tapster a deacon, thus assuring him of his place at the Lord's table the next Sunday, when they ritually sacrifice him in full view of the entire Diaconalist congregation."

He broke off. Susie had returned to the table, holding Detective Superintendent Mallard by the arm.

"Look what the cat's dragged in," she sang gleefully, indulging her taste for older men and her affection for Mallard in particular by pressing her body against his and leaving several lip-prints on his neck. As always, Mallard handled it stoically, knowing that Oliver would report the encounter to his aunt anyway. He shook hands with Geoffrey and gave Effie a demure off-duty kiss on the cheek.

"Well, Uncle Tim…" Oliver began, as Mallard pulled a chair up to the table.

"Don't!" Mallard growled, glaring at his nephew.

"I beg your pardon?"

"Don't start with the comments. Why don't I take a seat, have I got to the bottom of this, is there no end to that. I'm sure you've told your friends all about my moment of indignity, and they're dying to join in, but I don't want to hear it."

"What indignity?" asked Geoffrey, seemingly mystified.

"I'm not sure what you're referring to," added Susie. "Did something happen to your…you know…London derriere."

Mallard looked suspiciously around the table. "You didn't mention it?" he asked Oliver, who simply raised his eyebrows quizzically.

"Mention *what*?" Geoffrey demanded.

"It doesn't matter."

"No, come on, Uncle Tim, you have to tell us now," insisted Susie, perching on a chair.

Mallard lowered his gaze. "Oh, well, it was just something that happened the other evening, on the opening night of my play. I had a slight accident with my costume. I'm surprised Ollie hasn't described it. Let's just say…"

"The audience saw your Bottom!" Geoffrey and Susie chanted together, breaking up into howls of laughter. A couple at a neighboring table left without waiting for their change.

"I could have you all arrested!" Mallard thundered, trying to look as fierce as Assistant Commissioner Weed looked when he was mildly peeved. He held the expression for five seconds, then he started to laugh too.

He laughed longer and louder than the others. It was the first time since his enforced vacation and potential retirement that he had permitted himself to find anything funny. Oliver, watching his uncle wiping his eyes with a plain white napkin, knew this, and waited until his chuckles had largely subsided before asking the question that he guessed would be on Effie's mind, too, although he suspected he knew the true answer.

"So what brings you here, Uncle Tim?"

Mallard gave a brisk shrug. "Oh, I was just in the neighborhood," he answered casually. "At the Yard actually, down the road. I called your house, but nobody was in. So I thought I take a chance and see if you'd popped over here for brunch, since I have a bit of time to kill before tonight's performance."

As Oliver thought. Mallard was bored stiff at home. Because of the long hours of murder investigations, Aunt Phoebe had grown used to not having her husband around during the day, and she had adopted a slew of hobbies, activities, and local causes, which couldn't be put aside this side of Christmas. Phoebe had accepted that, apart from an elaborate annual jaunt to an exotic foreign location of her choosing, her quality time with Tim would have to be spent largely in bed at night, and she continued to make sure that they experienced the full range of options offered by that location, as she would often remark on family gatherings to Oliver's general discomfort. However, it did explain why Mallard always made the long trip back to Theydon Bois every night, even during an intense investigation, when his colleagues might have found a cheap hotel or kipped down on one of the Yard's well-used sofas.

"I thought you were on holiday," Effie remarked.

"Oh, I needed to check something with the assistant commissioner's office," Mallard answered airily.

"I'm surprised Weed was at work on a Sunday."

"Er, he wasn't," said Mallard, unavoidably glancing at Geoffrey. "In fact, the cleaners were in." The two men smiled at each other. Oliver dismissed the hint of a conspiracy, on the grounds that Geoffrey Angelwine could not possibly have any secrets worth sharing. He assumed instead that Mallard's visit to the Yard was another abortive attempt to steal his personnel file.

"But enough about me," Mallard said quickly. "How's the case?"

"Do you mean the disappearance or the murder?" Geoffrey asked before Oliver could stop him. He kicked him under the table anyway.

"A murder!" Mallard breathed, his eyes widening behind his glasses. He smoothed his white moustache. "You've had a murder in Plumley! Oh, Effie, tell me all about it."

"Now, now, Tim," she said quickly, "it only happened today, and I was there by accident, still looking for my runaway."

"You mean *you* discovered the body?" he asked, almost drooling in his thirst for information.

"Not exactly. I was there even earlier."

"You witnessed it! By the cringe, Eff, you actually witnessed a murder! So did you make an arrest?"

"An arrest has been made, but it wasn't as simple as that. You see, strychnine was used, and—"

"Strychnine!" Mallard exclaimed, thumping his coffee mug on the table and clutching his head in his hands. A couple of customers who had just sat down tossed aside their menus and headed quickly for the door. Susie ignored them.

"In thirty-five years on the force," Mallard was complaining loudly, "I've never done a strychnine murder. Why, it's positively Agatha Christie. And I take one lousy, unplanned vacation, and you get strychnine poisoning. I'm going to *kill* that Weed!"

Three more tables tried to wave at their waiters, making scribbling gestures. Mallard sat up and pulled his chair closer to the table.

"All right, Effie," he said, "here's what you have to do. Now the first thing to remember is that strychnine is surprisingly easy to find. It's in old medicines and tonics that you can find in junk stores or people's basements, it's been used for pest control, for controlling facial tics—you can even order it over the Internet. Second, people don't die through ingesting strychnine itself, but from the physical reactions it produces in the body. It takes about a hundred milligrams to be sure that somebody is dead…"

"Tim."

"…but under certain circumstances, much lower doses will do the trick. So start by—"

He stopped, partly because it had occurred to him that she had spoken his name, but mainly because she was waving her napkin at him, like a surrendering bandit.

"Tim," Effie said again, "I truly appreciate the advice, and there's nobody on Earth I would rather hear it from, but it's not my case. Detective Inspector Welkin is SIO. I'm only a sergeant, remember?"

"Yes, but I would have thought with your experience on the squad, even those idiots over at Plumley would have made an exception."

"It's not very likely that any murder would be left to a mere sergeant, no matter how respected his or her mentor," Effie said with a gentle smile. Mallard thought for a second.

"But surely young Welkin's made you his number two for this one?"

"No, and I don't blame him," she added quickly, before he could object to his former protégé's apparent loss of reason. "This is a golden opportunity for the new man to train one or two of his regular team, not someone who'll be out of his manor in a week or so. What if the investigation goes on longer?"

Mallard knew she was right, and he sat in silence, distracted by the prospect of the following year. Yes, Effie would be out of Plumley CID and back at Scotland Yard on the second of January, but would he be there to lead her?

"I bet you wish you were in on this one, too, eh?" he said to Oliver in avuncular tones.

"Actually, Uncle, I spent an hour with the victim on Thursday and I visited the scene of the crime yesterday. And I've known the suspected killer since I was five."

"How unlike the home life of our own dear Queen," said Susie merrily, while Mallard gaped at his nephew. She stood up and looked around the deserted restaurant, puzzled. Then she sat down again and poured herself a cup of coffee.

If the bus stop opposite Plumley United Diaconalist Church were a "request" stop, with a red metal flag, a would-be passenger would have to stand on the curbside and raise a hand conspicuously in time for a bus driver to see the signal and come comfortably to a halt. However, it is not a request stop. It is a "compulsory" stop, which means a bus should stop automatically, without being hailed by someone on the pavement. Logically, therefore, there was no reason why the small, elderly man waiting there should have spent the last two hours with his arm more or less permanently raised to shoulder level and stiffly protruding into the path of oncoming traffic. Nor was there any logical reason why at least one of the five buses that had passed during this time should not have picked him up, arm or no arm.

But the little man had long given up on logic, as he had given up on chance, luck, providence, the National Lottery, the British postal system, and—for now—London Transport. For this man was Underwood Tooth, the world's leading expert on being ignored.

Underwood was not at all surprised when the sixth bus shot by without slowing down, its bright headlights cutting through the darkness on this slightly misty evening, dazzling him as the bus missed him by inches. Nor was he bitter, being well used to his role in life after sixty-six years of being constantly overlooked by teachers, waiters, concierges, shop assistants, bank tellers, receptionists, and customer service representatives of all stripes. He merely took the opportunity to rub some life back into the aching muscles of his arm and shoulder and wonder again how long it would take him to walk home. Given the lateness of the hour and the dwindling frequency of the Sunday evening service, he was beginning to think it might be rush hour next morning before a bus would stop to let off a passenger, and he could then make a salmonlike leap for the door before the driver let it slam in his face. A taxi was out of the question; cruising cabs were rare enough in the London suburbs, but since Underwood had never in his life succeeded in hailing one, he had no idea how they operated. He carried some vague impression that all taxi journeys, no matter what the destination, had to pass through Trafalgar Square.

He gazed at the church across the road, its white neoclassical facade looming through the haze. Although Underwood took much comfort in believing that God, at least, was omniscient, he was not a regular churchgoer these days. Whenever he went to a service, he always seemed to find himself without a hymn book. But at least he had never in his life been accosted by a Jehovah's Witness.

However, since this was the last Sunday before Christmas, he had decided to make a rare visit to a place of worship, and a pin stuck in his local Yellow Pages had perforated Plumley United Diaconalist Church, a half-hour bus-ride from his home in Finchley. Long past the habit of phoning ahead for information, he had taken the chance that there would be an evening service at six or six-thirty. But as he had walked toward the building at six forty-five—the bus had taken him three stops further than he wanted—he could see that the front doors were closed and some sort of tape or ribbon was stretched across them. It could have been yellow or white, it was hard to tell the color under the sodium streetlamps. And it had writing on it. No doubt it said "Happy Christmas" or some other seasonal message. He adjusted his glasses. Something about a cross? Surely that was better for Easter. Oh, "Do Not Cross." Good heavens, it was a police notice. But no policeman around to explain it.

Too late to find another church, Underwood crossed the street and began his long wait for the return bus. He was looking forward to a long, hot bath, not simply because of the evening chill, but to soothe his many aches. For him, Christmas was a season of bruises—the crowds in the High Street meant more people bumping into him or unapologetically treading on his feet while he was shopping. But at least there were the pantomimes to look forward to. He could relax there, immune to every other Englishman's terror that some monstrous, superannuated comic in women's clothes or a third-rate novelty-act conjuror would select him to go up on the stage to receive the traditional abject humiliation, a "bit of fun" for the sadistic pleasure of all the other reprieved playgoers. Underwood would never be on the sharp end of the phrase "a gentleman from the audience—perhaps *you*, sir?"

The crime scene tape must also have attracted the attention of the young woman walking past the church. Certainly, she had ducked into the deserted car park and was now approaching the front door. She glanced around, rather guiltily, Underwood thought, as if conscious that she was trespassing. Could you trespass on church property? he wondered. Or did the medieval laws of sanctuary still apply (not that he would ever need them)? And anyway, aren't we supposed to forgive those who trespass against us?

He tittered at this thought, and the woman seemed to look right at him, but had apparently not noticed the small, solitary figure across the street, reminding him again that he'd make a good peeping Tom, if only he lacked the morals. The woman was little more than a moving shadow to him, but he had an impression of long red hair under a beret, and a remarkably short cloak and skirt for the weather. But what was she doing? Was that fake snow she was spraying across the front of the doors, white writing on the black paint? Maybe it was a Christmas decoration, although why she should seem so furtive was beyond him. She shook the can again, and it rattled. Then she added a few more characters and slipped away, almost running down the street past that big Victorian house on the right of the church.

Underwood couldn't help himself. He had to know what she was doing, spraying words onto the church door at ten o'clock in the evening. He glanced both ways, although the roadway was deserted, and scuttled across the street, stopping at the church steps.

Revelation, 11:7

How odd! He would have to look that up when he got home. But clearly not a Christmas text. He knew the Christmas story was split between the gospels of St. Matthew and St. Luke, but thanks to Sunday School Nativity plays and composite versions of the tale for children, he was in his thirties before he found out there was precious little overlap between the two accounts. The vicar of his local church had never given him a straight answer to that observation. Or any other observation, come to think of it.

And it wasn't that plastic snow she had used, but white oil paint. Had he witnessed an act of vandalism? Perhaps he should report this to the minister. His address and telephone number were on the notice-board. Would it be too late to call tonight? Would the church have one of these newfangled push-button response systems that inevitably either disconnected him or left him in an inescapable repeating cycle of the same questions? (At least this was one frustration of modern life that was not limited to him he had discovered, overhearing loud complaining, conversations in elevators between people who thought they were alone.)

He had just produced his pocket diary and was noting the phone number of a Reverend Paul Piltdown, when a bus slowed to a halt on the other side of the street. Underwood ran.

Chapter Six

In This World of Sin

Monday, December 22

Detective Constable Trevor Stoodby without a moustache was a distinct improvement. Stoodby standing in the middle of the CID office and thoughtfully reading a Bible was a greater tribute to Effie's reforming influence than even she could have anticipated.

"If you're looking for a loophole, Trevor, remember that there are ten commandments but only seven deadly sins," she said brightly as she hung up her coat.

He laughed politely, although it was clear that the comment had passed at least fifty feet above his head. "Oh, good morning, Ma'am. I'm checking out last night's graffiti."

"Graffiti?" Effie asked, wondering why all the office chairs had been placed on one side of the large table in the middle of the room, which had been transformed overnight into an incident room for the Tapster murder. Through the glass wall of his small office, she could see Welkin on the telephone, talking urgently and taking notes. She perched on her desk and sipped the tea she had picked up for lunch.

"Yes, last night," Stoodby said swiftly, fighting back an instinctive twinge of appreciation for Effie's legs. "Some time before midnight, somebody spray-painted a biblical reference on the front doors of the church."

"Don't we have anyone keeping an eye on the place?"

"Oh yes, we had a uniformed constable patrolling the perimeter all night, but he didn't see or hear anything. No witnesses have turned up either."

"So what's the reference?"

"I can't make head or tail of it. It's from the Book of Revelation. Listen. 'And when they have finished their testimony, the beast that ascendeth out of the bottomless pit shall make war against them, and shall overcome them, and kill them.' What do you make of that, Sarge? Sounds a bit like a threat."

"Or a prophesy. We need to get a sense of the context."

The door to the room opened, letting in the wispy-haired stick insect (whom she now knew as Detective Constable Graham Paddock) and the bespectacled, chinless chicken (Detective Constable Terry "Tezza" Foot), who had been summoned from their morning assignments by a call from Welkin. This gave Effie a momentary view down the corridor to the public waiting room, where a small man was sitting patiently on a bench. She could have sworn he had been there when she left that morning to visit a succession of outraged and frightened Plumley householders whose homes had been burgled over the weekend. The door swung shut again.

"Anybody looked in on the murderer lately?" asked Foot loudly. Paul Piltdown had spent the night voluntarily in a detention cell and a great deal of the morning in an interview room with Welkin and Stoodby.

"He hasn't confessed and he hasn't been charged," Effie reminded him. Paddock looked at Foot, as if they were confirming a private joke.

"Yeah, I know, Sarge," Foot continued, trying to contain a broad smile, which made it look as if he was leering at her. "But these vicars, they're all the same, ain't they? Bent or randy or both. If their hands aren't in the collection plate, then they're up the verger's wife's skirts. Or some choirboy's cassock."

"That's what you think, is it?" Effie said, with feigned innocence.

Sensing her disapproval, Foot grunted humorlessly and turned back to Paddock, strangely ignoring Stoodby. Tish Belfry hurried into the room, and Effie caught a wisp of Foot's whispered conversation, which included specifying which item of Tish's clothing he would personally like to ascend, preferably on the inside, and the two detectives snickered again. Stoodby shook his head sadly, but if Tish had heard the remark, she ignored it. She stopped dead as she reached her desk.

"Who took my chair?" she demanded.

"Inspector Welkin," Stoodby told her immediately. "And he wants all of us to wait here until he's ready."

Tish looked puzzled. "I hope this isn't going to take too long," she said urgently to Effie. "I need to follow up on something about Tina Quarterboy. I've had an idea."

Effie and Tish had split up for the morning, checking on various weekend incidents that proved there was more to Plumley's criminal underbelly than murdered lay ministers and disappearing teenagers. Effie had hardly spoken to her assistant since the murder. She had justified the previous day's lunch break with Oliver as partial compensation for her late night and for the stress of the morning—and she knew that Welkin would be too busy with the aftermath of the murder to miss her. Afterwards, she had driven back to Plumley, sending Tish off duty and then spending several fruitless hours reviewing every statement taken in the Tina Quarterboy case. But she had yet to follow up on Tina's brief reappearance. A house-to-house of the area around the church seemed the next move, although it had been too late in the day to get that organized. She found she wanted to ask Piltdown more about the missing girl, but even though he was conveniently on the premises, he was off limits to her.

"What's your idea?" Effie asked Tish.

"Oh, it was your idea really. That business of going to the doctor. As you know, I checked, and Tina hadn't been to her family doctor at all. But since Tina was at school on the day she disappeared, I wondered if she might have gone to the school doctor's surgery instead. I called the school secretary this morning—fortunately, she was there even though the school's broken up for the Christmas holidays—and she gave the doctor's number. The doctor was very cagey, and she wouldn't tell me a thing over the phone, not even whether Tina had been there recently. But she did say I could go round and see her this afternoon. She wouldn't suggest that unless she had something to say, would she?"

"Well done, Tish," said Stoodby, who had drifted over and was listening respectfully. Tish ignored him.

"So how did Heather Tapster take Nigel's death?" Effie asked, remembering another assignment that had been entrusted to Tish.

Tish grimaced and put a hand on her sergeant's arm. "Effie, I've never seen anything like it," she confided. "No sooner were the words out of my mouth, than she started howling, bawling uncontrollably, and clawing at the carpet. It was like some animal. I mean, I know my mum loves my dad and would be devastated if anything happened to him, but I thought Heather was going to have a nervous breakdown, right there. Either that or turn into a werewolf."

"How awful," breathed Stoodby.

"Well, she had just lost her husband," Tish conceded.

"I meant for you, having to break the news," he said. Tish looked at him oddly. Inspector Welkin limped out of his office.

Spiv Welkin's morning had begun punctually at nine o'clock, when, at a hastily convened meeting at the area headquarters, his commander had agreed that Welkin could continue to act as senior investigating officer on the Tapster murder. This was an unusual vote of confidence for someone who was a mere detective sergeant less than six weeks earlier. But, as Commander Hoodwink privately admitted, since there had to be a first time for every homicide detective to be SIO, it might as well be on a murder where the prime suspect was already in the hands of the police. And even if the minister had not done it—despite his convictions, Welkin was scrupulous in his account of the investigation—the true murderer was not going to be a random maniac roaming the borough but one of the other four deacons on the platform, none of whom seemed a flight risk. Besides, Hoodwink doubted that any chief inspector in the area would stoop to joining the parade this close to Christmas and at this stage of the investigation, after the elephants had passed. Why not leave the bucket-and-spadework to Welkin and his team?

Welkin had stopped off on his way back to the police station to inspect the graffito on the church and give the young constable who had failed to witness its execution a damn good bollocking. A two-hour interview with Piltdown followed, but though the minister was pleasantly and apologetically stubborn, he had not made any request to leave. Perhaps he thought he was under arrest, Welkin speculated, although he had not yet formally charged Piltdown with anything—not even obstruction. Then he returned to his office, which seemed to have grown narrower and more inadequate overnight, and started making a series of phone calls with increasing self-confidence.

"Good morning all," he caroled, noting that all five detectives on that morning's shift were assembled in the incident room. He pointed at the table he had set up. "Take a pew."

The detectives looked quizzically at each other, and then one by one took a place among the six chairs that Welkin had lined up on one side of the bare table. Effie sat on the far left with Tish beside her.

"Not that one," Welkin cried, as Foot tried to sit next to Tish. He grumpily moved down one place, forcing Paddock and Stoodby to take the remaining seats to his right. Welkin took the empty seat between Tish and Foot.

"I thought you might want to hear the latest on yesterday's murder," Welkin continued. "I need one or two of you to assist me as we go forward, but I'd like all of you to help me with something right now."

He cleared his throat and consulted a batch of notes that he had grabbed from his office.

"First, the initial PM report. Tapster died of a heart attack, brought on by the effects of strychnine poisoning. Traces of the poison were found in his stomach and in his mouth. The other contents of his stomach were the remains of his breakfast, consumed approximately four hours before his death, a minute amount of honey eaten more recently, and some Communion wine. There was also a streak of honey on his left forefinger. The pathologist can't estimate exactly how much strychnine was ingested, but he thinks it was a relatively small dose, perhaps less than seventy milligrams. Enough to bring on convulsions, but not necessarily enough to guarantee death. If Tapster hadn't had a weak heart, and if he'd received the right medical treatment, he may have survived. But he didn't, which is why we're all here."

He flipped a page on his notepad.

"Right, initial forensic reports. Tapster's glass—or at least the glass that was found in front of his seat on the platform—had been emptied, but an analysis of the dregs shows a trace of strychnine. All the other glasses, including the ones that weren't used, were clean. Communion wine only. Ladies and gentlemen, we must conclude that somebody, somehow spiked Tapster's wine glass with poison, and that's how he died."

"Fingerprints?" Tish asked.

"On Tapster's glass, we found his own prints and those of Barry Foison, a church member but not a deacon. And before you urge me to arrest Foison, I should tell you that it was his job to prepare the Communion sacraments, and his prints were therefore on practically every glass in the church."

"Where does he do this preparation?" asked Effie, wondering why Welkin was involving the entire shift.

"I interviewed Foison," Foot stepped in. "He prepares the bread and wine in a sort of side room, right beside the church itself. By 'church,' I don't mean the whole building, I mean the big part of the church, where they have the services."

"Call it the sanctuary," Welkin instructed.

"All right, guv. Anyway, you have to go through this side room to get from the sanctuary to the back corridor, which in turn leads to all the rooms at the back as well as the church's side entrance. You can also get into this corridor directly from a door on the other side of the church."

"And when did the preparation take place?" Effie asked.

"Funny story. Foison says he sets out the glasses and plates and stuff before the service. He buys the bread on the way to church. Yesterday, he left the sanctuary during the third hymn to pour out the wine, but he found only a full bottle in the cupboard, and he didn't have no corkscrew with him. Foison says he could have sworn there was half a bottle left over from the last Communion service, and that would have been enough. Anyway, he cut up the bread and, went back into the sanctuary to listen to the sermon. When it was over, he ran out to his car to get his Swiss Army knife, which has a corkscrew on it."

Of course. Effie remembered watching Foison's slim form rummaging in his car and then slipping around the side of the church, just before she had gone inside the previous morning. She had left that out of her report.

"So basically," Foot continued, "he never took his eyes off the wine between the time he pulled the cork from the fresh bottle until the time he put the glasses on the Communion table in front of everyone. Including Sergeant Strongitharm."

"Did anyone else go into the side room while Foison was pouring the wine?" Tish asked.

"One person," answered Foot. "Guess who."

"Nigel Tapster," said Effie immediately, recalling that she had seen the victim come into the church through the side door just seconds after Heather had left. His wife had barely missed a final chance to see him alive, Effie thought sadly.

"That's right," said Food, slightly deflated. "Foison says Tapster came in during the singing of the last hymn and went on through to the back of the church. Came back a couple of minutes later. Foison assumed he'd gone for a piss."

"There's one thing that puzzles me, Inspector," said Stoodby, as if he were performing the final scene of a whodunit play. "Did

Foison really think half a bottle of wine was going to be enough for an entire Communion service?"

"Let's find out," said Welkin. He limped over to his office and came back carrying a large cardboard box, which he deposited on the floor. He took out two metal platters and placed them on the table. Then he carefully lifted out two more devices, which Effie recognized as the glass holders from the previous day's Communion service, although they now had noticeable smears of fingerprint powder on them. Each holder comprised two horizontal metal disks, roughly a foot in diameter, held about an inch apart, with an arching handle that enabled the holder to be carried. The upper disk was perforated with several circular holes, set in three concentric circles. If a small glass were placed in one of these holes, it would drop through until its bottom rested on the lower disk, and so would be held snugly as the holder was passed around the church, perhaps by deacons who weren't as steady on their feet as they had been in younger years.

From another box, Welkin took out a stack of Communion glasses.

"How many glasses did Foison prepare?" he asked Foot.

"He said he filled the two inner rings, but left the outer one empty."

Welkin counted quickly, then began to put the glasses into the holder.

"That's about twenty glasses in each," he said. "Forty altogether."

"And only half a bottle of wine?" said Paddock. "Stone me, when I take me girlfriend out to a posh dinner, we're lucky if we can get two glasses each out of a whole bot."

"What's the wine list like at Pizza Hut?" asked Foot, laughing so hard at his own joke, he was barely able to articulate. Paddock punched him playfully in the arm.

"All right, let's see," said Welkin quickly, lifting a liter-sized bottle of Communion wine from the box.

"Wassat, guv? Gin?" asked Foot.

"Nah, it's holy water," Paddock cut in, with a guffaw. "Then we're going to say our prayers and hope for a miracle."

"I don't get it," Foot admitted, after a token laugh.

Welkin finished preparing the glasses in silence and held the bottle up to the light. All of the glasses now contained a thimble-ful of water, and the bottle was still half full.

"Big bottle, small glasses," he said, putting the bottle on the floor and taking some index cards from his pocket, which he distributed among the detectives.

"Oh, I see why we're all here," said Stoodby excitedly. "We're going to reenact the crime." He held up his own card, which said "TAPSTER."

"Blimey, Trev, you're gonna be the stiff," cried Foot, brandish-ing his own identification as Potiphar. "That's typecasting. Hey, I wonder how they were planning to get the lid on that coffin. Perhaps it'll have to be banana-shaped, so he'll fit properly."

"The rigor mortis does pass, you know," Effie snapped wearily from the far end of the table. She had received Coppersmith, while Tish beside her was Quarterboy.

"It's a shame his old lady wasn't there to take advantage of the situation for one last time, if you get my drift," Foot continued, nudging Paddock (Dock), who collapsed against him. Welkin stood back, instinctively guessing what was about to happen.

With the self-centeredness of the amateur japester, Foot had started to look around the room, to gauge the effect of what he thought was a barrage of Wildean wit. Trev Stoodby seemed genuinely offended—what had come over that prissy little git in the last couple of days, he used to love a good laugh? Graham Paddock was in hysterics, he's a good lad. Welkin wasn't saying anything; maybe he wasn't such a stuck-up arsehole after all. Tish was looking away, shocked, she probably didn't get it. *Not all she's not getting, I bet, I could show her what she's missing, give her one of Tezza's best boinks. Same goes for Goldilocks Strongitharm, too—thinks she too bloody good for us with her Scotland Yard this, Scotland Yard that, and all that bloody hair. She's the only one looking back at me...*

Effie did not utter a word. Her disapproving, cold blue eyes spoke volumes. Foot felt his brain filling with ideas, images, faster than he could take it in. Somehow, in that moment, he found he knew all about Effie's experiences with murder, about the boundless professionalism of her colleagues, and how in two years of working with one of the best and most admired homicide detectives in the country and with at least two dozen cases under her belt, she had never once heard an investigating officer breathe a word of disrespect for the corpse. There was a dignity to death, no matter how undignified the dying. And he, a petty, pusillanimous man, barely out of uniform, working his first murder case as a detective, was wasting his able mind and everybody's valuable time with the constant quest for the cheap, the mean, the hurtful. He had fouled the code with his first footstep. (It was, after all, his imbecilic idea to keep on those Santa Claus outfits when they entered the church the day before.) A hundred years ago, his brother officers would have left him alone in an anteroom, with a loaded revolver and instructions to do the decent thing.

A millisecond later, he broke from Effie's gaze and stopped laughing. He stood up.

"Sir," he said huskily to Welkin. "Those remarks were really out of line, and I apologize. I especially want to apologize to DS Strongitharm and DC Belfry for the, well, improper implications in my foolish comments. They were indecent and insulting. I'm very, very sorry."

He sat down again, flushing, and stared disconsolately at his tie. Stoodby reached across and gently squeezed his hand. Foot sniffed and fumbled in his pocket for a handkerchief. Sitting between them and turning from one to the other, Paddock looked mystified and slightly nauseous.

"Apology accepted, Terry," said Welkin smoothly, taking his place at the table again and showing them that his index card said "PILTDOWN." He picked up his notes.

"All right, I've conflated all the statements, including Sergeant Strongitharm's account of what happened, although she wasn't in the church when Tapster showed the first signs of poisoning. Surprisingly, there is almost no disagreement among the twenty-odd witnesses, at least in terms of the order in which things happened. We have to assume, then, that it's what's missing from at least one of these statements that will point to the guilty party. Let's begin to find out."

In slow-motion, they reenacted the Communion service, from the point where Stoodby, as Tapster, resumed his seat after singing the strange carol. Welkin/Piltdown passed the bread plates to Tish/Quarterboy and Paddock/Dock, and they dutifully walked around the others and toward the imaginary congregation, returning the same way. Then the wineglass holders were given to Effie/Coppersmith and Stoodby/Tapster, who also walked into the church, removed the right number of glasses for the communicants on each aisle, and returned to the table. They watched carefully, pausing to make notes and comments, as Welkin now took the holder from Stoodby and passed it along the row of deacons. Stoodby drank the water and placed the glass on the table in front of him.

"Strychnine takes a while to work," he commented. "Are we sure the poison couldn't have been in the bread?"

"The forensic report says it was in the dregs of Tapster's wine glass and no other," Welkin answered.

"We're assuming the poison was meant for Tapster, because of all the trouble he was causing in the church," Effie commented eventually. "But what if it wasn't?"

"Let's hear it."

"I can think of two possibilities," she continued. "Number one, it was a totally random act—somebody slipped the poison into the glass not knowing who would take it. And in that case, it could have happened at any time. Barry Foison may have done it. Any of the deacons who were milling around the table before the Communion service began. One of the two deacons who carried the wine to the communicants. Or even one of the communicants, spiking a glass that was still left in the holder. It was pure chance that Tapster took it."

"But if it was one of the deacons," said Tish, "how could he—or she, if we include Patience—have known which was the poisoned glass, so as to avoid it? Assuming it hadn't been taken already."

"I've been wondering about the honey in Tapster's stomach, and on his hand," Effie said. "Do you think there's a possibility that a smear of honey was a way of marking the glass, so the perpetrator would know which one to avoid. From a distance, it would look like a dribble of wine."

"Not a bad idea," admitted Welkin. "I was wondering if the honey had been some way of delivering the strychnine. You know, pour the powder into a blob of honey, wait for it to harden slightly, and then pop your pellet into the wine and hope the mark guzzles it at one go. But I still don't know when it could have been done. What was your other idea, Effie?"

"Oh, this is something I did witness. DC Foot isn't supposed to be here."

I know, Foot agreed privately, I'm unworthy to walk among civilized people, I belong with the reptiles, the vermin, the mollusks of the world. But does she need to rub it in?

"I mean the person he's representing, Cedric Potiphar, wasn't supposed to be on the stage," Effie continued, with a sly grin at Foot's guilty flinch, the only visible sign of his internal soliloquy. "Potiphar had lost his seat on the diaconate at the annual church meeting last Friday. His presence on the platform was a surprise. Perhaps it was a force of habit, perhaps it was a protest, or perhaps he felt the other deacons would all be too polite to tell him to go away, which they were. But that's what caused Tapster to be sitting on the piano stool for his first Communion as a deacon."

"And you think Potiphar was the killer? That the real reason for going up there was to slip the poison into the wine of the man who had supplanted him?"

Effie shook her head. "No, I was wondering if his unexpected presence had somehow thrown off the killer's plans. Was there some method or order to the distribution of the glasses that Potiphar's presence screwed up?"

Welkin looked dubiously at the glass holder in front of him. "That sounds a little far-fetched," he said, absentmindedly prodding the holder. "I know conjurors can make people take a particular card from a pack—it's called forcing it. And I was wondering if Piltdown had somehow forced a glass onto Tapster, by positioning this contraption at a certain angle or distance. But I don't see how you can anticipate the order in which a group of people will pluck their glass from one of these things."

Effie was silent, suddenly aware that this idea only gave them further grounds for suspecting Piltdown.

"Another possibility, sir," said Tish.

"Let's hear it."

"We did a very thorough inspection of the table and platform, and we searched the minister and every deacon, but we didn't find any indication of how the poison was transported to the stage. Every deacon, that is, but one. Tapster."

"If you're suggesting he wanted to commit suicide, Tish, I can think of considerably less painful methods," said Effie wryly, unavoidably remembering the agony in Tapster's eyes.

"Maybe he was trying to kill somebody else on the platform and it all went horribly wrong for him. Perhaps he put his glass down for a second and DC Paddock switched it? I mean Dock."

"You forget that we did search Tapster," Welkin continued, looking though his notes. "Or at least the pathologist went over his clothes at the lab. Let's see, in his pockets he had some loose change, a credit card case, a set of keys, a handkerchief, a guitar pick, a pen, and a comb. Nothing else—certainly nothing like a vial or a small box that could have contained strychnine."

"He could have hidden it in his guitar case," Stoodby suggested.

"We took the case in with the evidence. It contained another plectrum and a spare set of strings. Oh, and a guitar. Which had no secret compartments, incidentally."

"Well, he did go out to the back of the church just before the Communion service," Tish persisted. "Perhaps he picked up the poisoned glass then. Why else would he have left the sanctuary?"

"He was taking a leak!" Welkin exclaimed.

The door opened, and a uniformed policewoman bustled into the room. She stopped dead when she saw the entire CID staff sitting in a row in thoughtful silence, like a truncated *tableau vivant* of Da Vinci's *The Last Supper*. She reversed out of the room again without speaking.

"Let's leave it there for now," said Welkin eventually, climbing stiffly to his feet. "Since we can't fathom the means or the opportunity, I'm going back to the motive. I think it's time to give the Reverend Piltdown another rattle."

"The Reverend *Mr.* Piltdown," Effie muttered pleasantly, following Welkin into his office and closing the door. "You have to use the full title, Sir."

Welkin froze. Effie had called him "sir." She had never called him that in her life. That could only mean she wanted a favor, and now he was petrified in case he couldn't grant it.

"I'll remember that," he said guardedly, wondering if he could anticipate the request. "Thanks for your help, Eff, I appreciated the mental workout. You know you'd be my first choice to assist me on this case, but I feel I should give one of my regular people a test drive."

Effie sat down uninvited and loosened the ribbon that she had used that morning to gather her formidable hair. Oh shit, now he was for it.

"I wanted to ask you a favor, Sir," she said. He shivered. "Do you remember Superintendent Mallard's nephew, Oliver? Oliver Swithin?"

An image of a slightly weedy, slightly toothy, slightly awkward young man with fair hair and cheap glasses flashed into Welkin's mind. Mallard had him in tow last summer, either as a technical advisor or for some perverse form of light relief, he hadn't figured out which. Pleasant bloke, not quite Welkin's cup of tea, but bright enough and prepared to be friendly in a shy sort of way, which is more than can be said for a lot of those stuck-up expert witnesses, flashing their bloody university degrees and strutting around crime scenes like Lord and Lady Muck of Turd Hill. But wait a moment, some half-absorbed memory was leaping to his defense—hadn't Gloomy Gus Moldwarp told him that

Effie and this Swithin geezer have a little romance going on? *Tread carefully, Spiv.*

"Isn't he the one who writes those kids' books about a stoat?" he asked, trying to stay on neutral territory.

"That's the one. You may remember that Tim Mallard thinks very highly of him."

"Well?"

"Well, I happen to know him quite well. In fact, Sir, in the interest of full disclosure, I should tell you that we are very good friends. But my reason for mentioning him is that he is also an old friend of Paul Piltdown, and he knows several of the characters involved in this case, including the late Nigel Tapster."

"Uh-huh." Where was all this leading? Welkin wanted to breathe normally again sometime in this life.

"I was wondering if you'd let Oliver talk to Paul Piltdown while he's in custody. Piltdown may feel more comfortable with someone he knows."

"Technically, Piltdown's not in custody," said Welkin cautiously. "He hasn't been charged with anything yet. If he tries to leave, I probably will arrest him on suspicion, but he hasn't asked to go. Hasn't asked for a brief, either, which suits us down to the ground. He just sits there, refusing to answer our questions."

"All the more reason for putting Oliver in with him," Effie replied, steering Welkin back to the point with ease. "It sounds as if Piltdown's covering up for someone, with some half-baked idea about the sanctity of the confessional, although he told me his denomination doesn't practice confession. On principle, he's not going to break down and reveal all to a copper, but a friend may persuade him otherwise."

"I don't know, Eff. This Swithin's not one of us."

"Oliver's not on our team, but he's on our side. You have the discretion to let him in as a visitor," Effie insisted. She was privately optimistic that Piltdown would reveal more about Tina's disappearance than about Tapster's death, although she wondered how closely the two events were connected.

"All right," Welkin conceded. "Bring him on. What harm can it do? Just as long as you understand that as far as I'm concerned, when somebody won't cooperate with the police, I assume they're hiding their guilt, not their innocence. Piltdown's our prime suspect, and it's not my job to prove him not guilty if he can't be bothered to declare it for himself."

"Thank you, Sir," she said, beaming at him gratefully and playing with a curl. She did not stand up.

"Is that all?" he asked fearfully.

"Well, there's just one other thing…"

Five minutes later, Effie emerged from Welkin's office and strode over to Tish Belfry's desk.

"Let me have the address of that doctor," she commanded. Tish looked surprised.

"I was just leaving," she answered defensively. "If you want to come with me, we can use my car."

"I'm going on my own."

Tish tried to keep the sense of personal offense off her face. Of course, it was probably unreasonable to be possessive over a lead, even though she had discovered it, but she hadn't expected Effie to pull rank quite so abruptly. "Is there some reason why you're excluding me?" she demanded.

"Yes, DC Belfry. You're off the case," Effie told her sternly. Then she laughed. "Tish, you have to work on keeping a straight face. You're off this case because, from now on, DI Welkin wants you to be his principal assistant on the inquiry into Tapster's murder."

Tish rose slowly from her seat. "You're kidding," she said, awestruck.

"Nope."

"I thought he'd stick with one of the lads."

Effie glanced back. Through the glass wall of Welkin's office, she could see him sitting at his desk, staring vexedly into space as if he'd tried to stand up but had winded himself on an unexpectedly open drawer.

"He asked for you," she said simply. "Why don't you go in and report for duty?"

Tish dropped her handbag on her desk, grabbed a notepad and Biro, hugged Effie briefly, and scurried into Welkin's room. Effie picked up the telephone.

Unlike Underwood Tooth, Oliver would not have made a good burglar.

Despite his parents' conviction that the most dangerous creature on the planet is a bored child, there had been a few occasions in their earlier lives when they had been forced to take their offspring with them on prolonged visits to a childless friend or a rarely seen distant relative. Inevitably, a young Oliver would have to use the toilet, and his trip upstairs to the "third door on the right" would take him across the border between the public and private zones of the strange home. Through half-open doors, he could glimpse the old dark furniture and dull wallpaper of uninviting bedrooms, and he would relieve himself while gazing with distaste at baths and basins that were chipped and stained with lime scale, unable to envision his hosts using these chilly rooms with any sense of comfort or fun. He never lingered in this alien world, which smelled of mothballs and washing soda and lavender, and which conveyed an odd sense of guilt and intrusion.

He had the same feeling of trespass now, as he walked through the upstairs rooms in the empty manse, a feeling that was aggravated by seeing how little Piltdown had imposed his own personality on the old-fashioned furnishings that must surely have been in the house before he moved in. Nobody of his generation would have selected that eiderdown, neatly molded to the shape of the bed, or those frilly pillow covers lined up on top! It made him eager to spot something he and Piltdown still had in common, such as the same brand of toothpaste or the same editions of Wodehouse or Golding on the bedroom shelves. Others might have succumbed to the temptation to pry: Did the minister keep a packet of condoms in the bedside table? Was there porn in the bottom of the chest of drawers?

Oliver hurried on, mentally rehearsing a nervous explanation of his presence, in case anyone surprised him, although he was there with his friend's full permission. He had almost called out an apology a few minutes earlier, when he thought he heard movement downstairs. He listened, but there were no further noises.

He found the clean shirt, socks, and underwear he was looking for in Piltdown's untidy drawers, and moved on quickly to the bathroom to pick up his friend's shaving equipment, reflecting that Piltdown's habits—neat on the surface, chaotic underneath—were the exact reverse of his own.

Oliver paused in front of the medicine cabinet. Was his over-scrupulousness preventing him from searching for evidence that would connect Paul to Nigel Tapster's death? Would he find an ancient tin of tincture of nux vomica, left by an earlier minister, or a suspicious packet of seeds that could have supplied the strychnine? Or would he just face the usual disconcerting clues to the secret state of Piltdown's feet, breath, or digestive tract? Already convinced of his friend's innocence, he left the cabinet closed, and went downstairs.

The kitchen was surprisingly tidy, with the plates from Piltdown's last meal washed and stacked on the drainer. That must have been Sunday's breakfast, Oliver speculated, calculating that his friend was certainly due for a change of clothes after more than a day at the police station. Should he go back for pajamas, or would that smack of pessimism? He slipped out of the side door, which Piltdown had admitted was permanently unlocked, and walked round to the front of the house. A policeman was removing the crime scene tape from the church next door.

When the telephone had rung in Edwardes Square earlier that afternoon, Oliver had answered using his celebrated impression of Geoffrey, in case it was his uncle again. Effie's voice was a welcome surprise—he overlooked the fact that she recognized him immediately—and he was overjoyed to have another opportunity to see her, even if it meant trading his planned afternoon of Christmas shopping for yet another tube ride to Plumley. It also gave him an excuse to put off thinking about the direction of his article—now potentially revamped as "Death of a Deacon."

At the police station an hour later, he had been greeted gruffly by Inspector Welkin and informed that Effie was out. He took a seat in the waiting room, glancing at one of the paperbacks that he habitually carried in his battered school satchel and chatting amiably with an elderly man until Tish Belfry led him to an interview room. A bleary-eyed, unshaven Paul Piltdown was waiting for him.

"Let me guess," Piltdown said immediately. "Effie Strong-itharm suggested that I might open up if you were brought in to talk to me."

Oliver took a chair across the table from his friend. Tish had left them alone, and the tape recorder wasn't running, but he could almost feel her eyes on the back of his neck through a suspiciously large mirror set in the wall behind him.

"Let me guess, too," he countered. "You had nothing to do with Tapster's death, but you're convinced you know who did because of something you were told in confidence, and you feel it would be a betrayal of your calling as a minister of God to betray that confidence. Furthermore, you are certain that the poison was meant for Tapster."

"How do you deduce that?"

"Because if Tapster were an accidental or even a random victim, that leaves the possibility that the murderer will strike again. And I don't believe you would stay silent if that were the case."

Piltdown studied the end of his fingernails. "I see we continue to know one another pretty well, after all this time. Now did you bring a cake with a file in it?"

"Paul, why don't you just declare your innocence and ask to leave? The police can't argue with the sanctity of the confessional. Or what do you call it in the United Diaconalist Church, minister-client privileges?"

"No, but they'll arrest me. I imagine my lack of cooperation with their inquiry has given them reasonable grounds."

"Even if they do arrest you, they can only hold you so long before your case goes before a magistrate. You'd make bail before Christmas."

Oliver stopped, a sudden idea dawning on him. "That's it, isn't it?" he exclaimed, his eyes widening behind the wire-framed spectacles. "You don't want any time limits. By staying here voluntarily, even without cooperating, you haven't forced the police to press charges or even formally arrest you. The habeas corpus clock hasn't started."

"And why would I want to stay here indefinitely?" said Piltdown cynically, without looking at Oliver. "Even the cold old manse is more inviting than the cell they graciously let me use last night."

"I can think of two reasons. The first is simple. You're afraid that the real murderer might want to kill *you*, and this is the safest place to hide."

Piltdown showed no reaction.

"The second reason is more complex," Oliver continued. "By concealing the murderer's identity, you're facing the biggest ethical dilemma of your life. So you figure that the most creative solution to this dilemma is to call somebody's bluff. You plan to stay here until the conscience of the killer kicks in, and he or she marches into the cop shop and confesses, just to save your sorry arse."

Piltdown was shaking his head. "If you think this is the biggest ethical dilemma of my life," he said quietly, "then you really don't know me."

Good, thought Oliver, it's reason number two. He really didn't want to believe that Piltdown was driven by mere cowardice. He stood up.

"Of course, there are two flaws in your plan. You've set a moral trap for the murderer and baited it with yourself. Forcing the issue this way hardly preserves your precious ministerial neutrality. So you really have no excuse for not coming clean."

"And the other flaw?" asked Piltdown crossly, slowly stretching his cramped limbs.

"You're assuming the murderer gives a tinker's damn about that sorry arse of yours," Oliver said blandly, checking his watch. "Let's see, you've been here more that twenty-four hours. When I came into the station a few minutes ago, there was only one man sitting in the waiting room. And he wasn't any of your deacons."

The interview room filled with silence. Oliver thrust his hands into his pockets and affected a fascination with the ceiling tiles. Piltdown unbuttoned his clerical collar, removed the stud that anchored it to his gray shirt, and laid it on the table. It was grimy and stained, and he glared at it distastefully. Eventually, he cleared his throat.

"Have you said what you came in for?" he asked coldly.

"Not entirely," Oliver replied swiftly. "I still want to know what happened to Tina Quarterboy."

Piltdown sighed deeply. "As I told Effie on Saturday afternoon, I have no idea where Tina is. If I knew, I would certainly tell you."

"I believe you. But that wasn't the question. Do you know what caused her to run away from home?"

"Yes."

"What was it?"

"I can't tell you or the police without betraying a confidence."

"How did you find out what caused her to run?"

"Same answer as the last question, Ollie. Now, if you've finished playing detective, can you do me a favor?"

Oliver returned with the change of clothes Piltdown had requested just as Effie arrived at the police station. He handed the clothes over to the station sergeant, and then she let him get a snack from the station vending machine before sweeping him into the incident room. Tish Belfry was waiting for Welkin to return from a meeting.

"I'm glad you're both here," Effie said archly. "I have some important news. Ollie, tell me again why you thought Tina suffered from an eating disorder."

"Oh, all right." Good point, why had he thought that? And why ask now, when Effie had just returned from Tina's doctor? He supposed that the doctor must have confirmed his assumption about the girl's health, and Effie wanted him to repeat his reasoning to show Tish why she respected his intelligence. He leaned back in the chair. "Well, Tina said that a lot of food was making her throw up, and that she thought she had been gaining weight, but you only have to look at her to see she's a skinny thing. Plus I don't recall her eating anything at the manse that evening. So given her age, I wondered if these were the symptoms of early anorexia nervosa, or more likely bulimia, given the nausea and the possible vomiting."

"Uh-huh," Effie said. "That's a very perceptive diagnosis, Dr. Swithin. However, according to the school doctor, who examined her last week—"

"She's pregnant?" asked Tish immediately.

"She's pregnant." Effie smiled broadly at Oliver, who dropped his cheese roll. She opened her notebook.

"Tina went to the doctor on Wednesday morning, complaining of nausea and cramps. She examined the girl, suspected a pregnancy, and took some blood to be sure. When the test came back positive, she summoned Tina to the surgery on Thursday afternoon and delivered the good or bad news, according to your role in the affair."

"Did the doctor tell anyone? Tina's teacher, her parents?" Tish asked. Effie shook her head.

"Tina apparently promised faithfully that she would go home and tell her parents herself, so the doctor didn't feel she needed to act. Since the next day was the last day of the school term, she assumed that Tina would deal with her family doctor for the next few weeks."

"But Tina didn't go home," said Oliver thoughtfully. "Not immediately."

They were interrupted by Welkin, limping swiftly into the room, with the faint aroma of English Pub wafting from his overcoat. He glared briefly at Oliver—having already heard about his fruitless interview with Piltdown—but tolerated the young man's presence while Effie filled him in.

"Do you think Tina did tell the parents?" Welkin asked, easing himself onto an office chair and laying his stick on the floor beside him. "Maybe there was actually some unholy row, and she ran off into the night? Maybe the father lost his temper and did away with her, and they're lying about hearing her voice on the telephone?"

"I've seen Tina, Sir, so we know she's alive," Effie reminded him. "And I really don't think they knew about her condition."

"They did seem very keen to keep her disappearance a secret at first," Tish offered.

"Yes, but I think that was their damaged pride. They were genuinely puzzled by the note she left, in which she said she didn't want to disappoint her father. It's quite clear now what she was talking about."

"So do we tell them they're about to become grandparents?" asked Tish. "Or perhaps they'll insist on an abortion?"

"We have to tell them," said Welkin. "The girl's—what?— thirteen. She's a minor. And let's not forget that whoever put that bun in her oven has committed statutory rape, if not worse."

"With respect, Sir, I'd like to wait until we find Tina before we tell them," said Effie.

"And when's that going to be?" asked Welkin tactlessly. "Let's face it, Eff, now we know what we know, isn't it likely that the girl's run off with the father of her little bastard? *That's* where she went after school on Thursday, to tell him he's going to be a daddy. He's probably some middle-aged schoolteacher with a frigid wife, going through a mid-life crisis. Tina's fallen madly in love with him, and they'll be holed in up a cheap Brighton boarding house posing as father and daughter, until it dawns on him that his girlfriend is too young even to buy him a pack of ciggies."

Oliver coughed in a way that suggested he had no need to clear his throat.

"If I may," he began, "I'm fairly sure I know where Tina went on Thursday evening."

"Go on," Welkin grunted.

"Paul Piltdown admitted to me that he knew why Tina had disappeared. But he wouldn't tell me the reason or how he knew. Well, I think we can safely assume that Tina bolted because she was pregnant and she feared her parents' reaction. Now, Tina left school at four last Thursday and was shut in her bedroom from six o'clock until she ran away in the middle of the night. The only way Paul could have found out about her pregnancy was if she told him, either during the famous missing two hours or after she'd left home. And I honestly think that if she'd gone to the manse after running away, Paul would have been able to persuade her to go home again."

"If that's what he wanted," said Welkin. "But what if it suited him to have her out of the way? What if *he's* the father?"

"Oh, surely not," Effie exclaimed.

"Paul's not the father," Oliver continued calmly. "Tina went to Paul because she likes and trusts him, and because he's the spiritual leader of the church. I'm going to guess she told him that Nigel Tapster was the father of her child."

"Tapster!" cried Welkin. "The dead man? How do you get that?"

Oliver pulled out a chair beside Effie and threw himself into it. "Let's assume Tina did go straight to the manse when she left school at four o'clock," he said smugly. "I'm sure Paul would have listened to her story and then urged her to go home and tell her parents. She leaves. And at a quarter past five, what does he do? He heads straight over to the Tapsters' house and has a blazing argument with Nigel. Paul was just leaving when I got there at a quarter to six. Care to guess what the argument was about?"

"But Tina wasn't part of Tapster's cult," Effie protested.

"How far gone is she?"

"A couple of months."

"A couple of months ago, she did go to some meetings at Tapster's home," Oliver informed them with a mild yawn, "until her parents put their foot down. Feet down. Rather too late."

Welkin struggled to his own feet. "Since you're the expert on what Piltdown's thinking, is it worth confronting him with this information?"

Oliver thought carefully. "I'm sure he'll admit to knowing what you know about Tina's condition," he claimed. "He'll probably admit that she visited the manse that evening. But I doubt that he'll reveal anything else she told him, including the identity of her baby's father. To pass that on to anyone would be a severe violation of his personal ethics and a betrayal of his calling. So if you want to pin Tina's pregnancy on Tapster, you still have to find her."

Welkin surged away to visit Piltdown, with Tish in his wake. Oliver and Effie sat in silence for a while. Then she leaned over, patted him on the head, and began to type up her reports about the morning's burglaries. Oliver wandered aimlessly around the incident room, peering at the crime scene photographs and the notes that had been scribbled on the room's whiteboard.

"What's this about honey?" he asked suddenly.

"Don't call me 'honey' at work," Effie snapped, without looking up. "In fact, don't call me 'honey' at all. I don't like it. It'll be 'hon' next."

"No, no, I mean there's stuff about honey on your board."

"The pathologist found undigested honey in Tapster's stomach and on his fingers. Welkin wondered if it could have been used to carry the strychnine crystals."

"Did you know that Tapster put honey in his tea?" Oliver continued, remembering the exchange of quotations during his meeting with the dead man. He had Lambed Tapster's Exodus, but now it occurred to him that a Brooke would have been a better counter, with extra points for the ecclesiastical theme. "I remember that he got it on his fingers and licked it off."

Effie stopped typing and frowned into the middistance. "Now you mention it, I recall him sucking his finger while he was getting ready to play that awful song. Perhaps some honey had been stuck there since breakfast? If so, it could have been just a coincidence that it was ingested at about the same time as the poison."

"Could the strychnine have been in his breakfast tea?"

"Absolutely not. It must have been given to him no earlier than thirty minutes and probably not later than ten minutes before the first symptoms. So he must have eaten it during or since Paul's sermon. The only things we know he put in his mouth were the Communion sacraments. Besides, forensic found traces of the strychnine in the wineglass."

"You know a lot about poisons, don't you?" Oliver commented idly.

"Oh yes. That reminds me, what would you like me to cook you for dinner tonight? I may be able to get some time off."

Welkin and Tish returned before he could answer.

"That's all settled then," he announced, his Cockney accent more prominent than usual. "Mr. Swithin, you were one hundred percent correct. The Reverend Piltdown knew Tina was pregnant. And she did go to the manse on Thursday evening. He would not tell us who the father of her child is, nor if she had confided this information in him. But he did tell us that he had advised Tina to go home and confess all to her parents. He offered to go with her, but she insisted that she wished to handle this alone, and agreed that she would telephone him if she needed his further help or advice. When Sam Quarterboy called the next day to say he would have to miss the church meeting, Piltdown assumed they were all too upset to come out. The first he knew that the girl had done a bunk was when Quarterboy visited Saturday morning."

"So you're going to let him go?" Oliver asked. Welkin looked at him strangely.

"Let him go?" he repeated. "No, indeed. According to your character assessment, Mr. Swithin, the Reverend Piltdown— sorry, Effie, the Reverend *Mr.* Piltdown—was the only person who could have known for sure that Nigel Tapster was the father of Tina Quarterboy's child."

"What does that mean?"

"It means we have charged him with Tapster's murder. Thanks to you, Oliver."

◇◇◇

When Welkin and Tish left the incident room, Effie immediately turned to Oliver, placed her hand on his head, and lifted it quickly.

"What was that?" he asked, shying in case the hand came down again.

"I'm taking back my pat," she said irritably. "Look what you've done. You got Paul arrested."

"What *I've* done?" Oliver cried. "I didn't suggest for a second that he killed Tapster. I merely speculated that Tapster was Tina's secret lover."

"But you must see that Welkin is just itching to connect the two investigations. He's already decided that Paul had the best opportunity to poison Tapster. Now you've given him the missing motive."

"What missing motive? Slaying Nigel Tapster because he's surging through the parish virgins? Paul Piltdown's a man of the cloth, for God's sake. If anything, he's been more charitable to the Tapsters than any of his church members, despite their challenges to his spiritual authority. It's a big jump from having a few cross words with his nemesis on Thursday night to slipping him a lethal mickey on Sunday morning."

"Exactly. And who's to say those cross words that you witnessed had anything at all to do with Tina's pregnancy? Suppose Paul went to Nigel for some confidential advice on how to handle the girl's confession? Or suppose he just felt annoyed because of what Tina had told him and decided to make the most of his bad mood by confronting Nigel about doctrinal issues? Isn't that what he told you they'd been arguing about?"

"Well, yes…"

The telephone began to ring on Effie's desk. "Your trouble, Ollie," she said, fixing him with her pale blue eyes as she reached for the phone, "is you don't know when to stop."

She picked up the receiver and identified herself. After listening for a few seconds, she covered the mouthpiece and turned to Oliver, who had been soberly absorbing the scolding.

"It's your uncle," she said.

"Is he looking for me here, now?"

"No, he wants me. He says if I can spare him half an hour, he has an idea for me."

"Me too, but I bet I'm thinking of something quite different."

She smiled. "It's a good job I love you, because I would have damaged you by now otherwise. Tim's offering to pay for an early supper. Do you want to come?"

"You know he's only trying to barge into your investigation because he's bored at home. And he'll hate it that I'm involved. When will he be here?"

"He's already here. He's calling from the car park."

Mallard didn't comment when he saw his nephew emerge from the police station with Effie, and Oliver maintained the resentful silence during the short drive to the transport café between Plumley and Edgware, where they could grab an unpretentious bite to eat and still leave Mallard enough time to get to Theydon Bois for the final performance of *A Midsummer Night's Dream*. He parked the Jaguar outside the café, expertly twisting the space-time continuum as he slotted the car into a gap that Oliver was convinced was too small for a tricycle. The three filed inside and found an empty table well away from the other diners. While they were waiting for their food, Effie briefed Mallard on what the investigation had uncovered since they had met at lunch the previous day, then she excused herself. Oliver and Mallard sat together in uneasy silence, trying not to meet each other's eye. The café owner's dog, a harrier called Murray, trotted over and watched them.

"I didn't expect to see you here," Mallard muttered eventually. "Shouldn't you be at home writing about small furry mammals?"

"I'm here because Effie asked me to talk to Paul Piltdown," Oliver told him. "I don't just turn up because I'm having withdrawal symptoms from foul play. Like some people I could mention."

"I happened to be passing," Mallard snapped. "And since I was in the area, I thought I'd see how Effie's murder was going."

"It's not Effie's case."

"It should be. And anyway, she can pass my idea on to Welkin. I do have an idea, you know."

"You astound me, Holmes."

Mallard ignored the sarcasm. He waited for Effie to return and began his explanation. "You remember my performance as Banquo in *Macbeth* earlier this year?" he asked smugly.

Oliver sighed and exchanged a glance with Effie. Social obligations to Mallard had meant that their first official date a few months earlier had been a trip to Theydon Bois to witness Humfry Fingerhood's blood-caked production.

"What about it?"

"Well, Humfry had a rather clever idea for my first appearance as a ghost at the banquet, shortly after I was bumped off. He wanted me to be killed on one side of the stage, collapse in a bloody heap in full view of the audience, and stay there. On the other side of the stage, the table is brought in and set up for the feast. So naturally, the audience is waiting for me to get up and stomp across the stage to take my place at the table in time for Macbeth to see me there. But I don't move from my recumbent posture on the left of the stage. And yet, when the moment comes, a thane moves aside slightly, and there I am, a blood-baltered apparition, already at the table on the right."

"And how was this miracle achieved?"

"By using an old stage magician's trick. Misdirection on a classic scale. That was never me, getting bumped off on the left. Banquo is only onstage briefly before the murderers set upon him. So at that point, my role is performed by someone of my height and build, with his back to the audience. I shout his lines from the side of the stage. He falls there and I go under the stage and pop up through a trapdoor directly beneath the banquet table, getting to my feet behind a thane. Rather clever for Humfry, I thought."

"'Misdirection' sounds like something Humfry Fingerhood would know about," Oliver commented. "So why didn't you do it?"

"We didn't have any available actors who resembled me from the back," Mallard claimed, somewhat proudly, since it must have meant he was noticeably taller and slimmer than the candidates.

"And you're saying that wasn't really Nigel Tapster on the platform yesterday morning?" Effie speculated.

"Don't be absurd, Eff. I was just wondering what's to stop somebody from getting into the church from the side entrance, finding a way under that platform, coming up under the Communion table, which you admit was covered with a large cloth, and creeping out to spike Tapster's glass *after* he'd taken it, while they all had their eyes closed in prayer."

"That suggests the killer isn't one of the deacons. Did you have somebody in mind?"

"Not until a few minutes ago," he admitted, "when I found out about the bun in Tina Quarterboy's oven. If Tapster's death is connected with her pregnancy, who knew about it?"

"Only Paul Piltdown," Effie said, with a caustic glance at Oliver. "That's why Welkin arrested him."

"I can think of someone else," said Mallard. "Someone who was in the church when Tapster was murdered, even though she wasn't on the platform."

"She?" Oliver echoed.

"Yes indeed, and Effie saw her. Has nobody bothered to ask the question what on earth Tina was doing at the church that morning?"

"Oh come on, Uncle Tim," Oliver protested. "Even if you reckon that Tina had the desire to kill her seducer, how would she have got her hands on some strychnine?"

Mallard ignored him. "What do you think, Eff?" he asked.

"Utterly ingenious," Effie breathed, with admiration. Murray's tail thumped against Oliver's leg. "Tina's small enough to squeeze around under the platform. And you're right, Tim, there is a trapdoor under the table."

"So it's possible?" ventured Mallard, with growing excitement.

"Absolutely not," she replied instantly. "The trapdoor covers the baptismal pool—the Diaconalists practice adult baptism, you see. The pool is built of brick and lined with tile, and the only way in or out is through a three-inch wide drain. You'd have to be a little thinner than Tina to fit in. And anyway, at the crucial moment you refer to, Tina was at the opposite end of the church, being pursued by yours truly."

And lost, she added silently. There were now four closed doors on Tina's Advent calendar that should have been opened by now.

Mallard's face fell. "It was just a thought," he mumbled.

"It was a very good thought, Tim," Effie said, patting his hand sympathetically. "And I'm glad you're here, because I need your expert opinion on something."

She began to fumble in her handbag. Murray stood up and wagged his tail, convinced that she was searching for something edible. He looked as disappointed as Mallard when all she produced was a sheet of paper. She showed it to the two men. Oliver read the words aloud.

"'And when they have finished their testimony, the beast that ascendeth out of the bottomless pit shall make war against them, and shall overcome them, and kill them.'"

"Do you know it?" Effie asked, aware that Mallard was a regular churchgoer.

"I've come across it before," Mallard replied.

"What does it mean?"

"Anything you want it to mean, which is the problem with the Book of Revelation. Why don't you ask Paul, since you have captive clergyman on the premises?"

"I'm asking you, Your Holiness."

"Oh. Well, this verse comes from a passage describing two witnesses, sent by God to prophesy for twelve hundred and sixty days—about three and a half years—while the Gentiles are trampling the Holy City. During that time, these witnesses are supposed to be invulnerable, and fire comes out of their mouths to consume their enemies. They can bring drought, turn water into blood, that sort of thing. But then they're killed by a beast from the abyss, which is what your verse describes, and their bodies lie in the street for three and a half days without burial. And then they pop up again, rise to heaven, and an earthquake comes and kills seven thousand people."

"How on earth do you remember that?" Oliver asked him.

Mallard smiled and seem to relax a little. "Actually, it's thanks to your murder victim, Nigel Tapster. The case inspired me to look over some articles on cults this morning, and that passage came up in connection with the Heaven's Gate mass suicide in California. You remember, the poor sods who were convinced that a UFO was lurking behind the Hale-Bopp comet? Well, the founder of the cult and his main squeeze, who died several years before the suicide, believed that they were the two witnesses referred to in that biblical passage."

"What's the significance of the quote to Tapster's death?" Oliver asked.

"Somebody wrote it on the church door last night," Effie told them. "At least they wrote the reference."

"Oh, that's what Mr. Tooth was talking about," said Oliver.

"Who?"

"Mr. Tooth. I met him in your waiting room, Effie. He'd been there since you opened up for business this morning. The station sergeant took his name, but nobody had called him in yet. He was still there when we left. Didn't you see him? Quite a decent chap. Apparently, he saw a woman with long red hair painting something on the church door at about ten o'clock yesterday evening. It set me wondering if this was the same woman whom I saw waiting by the manse gate on Thursday evening."

Effie began to rummage in her handbag again, renewing Murray's interest. "Why the hell didn't someone take a statement from this man?" she demanded of nobody in particular. She located her mobile phone and called the general number of the police station. The dog gave her a filthy look and transferred his affections to Oliver.

"Could this graffito on the church door connect Tapster with the Heaven's Gate cult?" Oliver asked. "I heard they were all dead."

"Marshall Applewhite and Bonnie Nettles, who founded Heaven's Gate, called themselves 'The Two,' in a direct reference to that particular passage," Mallard told them. "They identified themselves as the two witnesses sent by God, although they were actually convinced that they were aliens from a higher level of reality, reincarnated several times and always spending their lives together. They also called themselves Bo and Peep, Him and Her, Winnie and Pooh, Tweedle and Dee, Chip and Dale, Nincom and Poop, and Tiddly and Wink. They finally decided on Do and Ti."

"As in Do, a deer, a female deer, and Ti, a drink with jam and bread?" Oliver asked, scratching the dog's head.

"Exactly. Although Do was the male in this partnership. The pair believed they'd been sent to Earth to rescue civilization."

"Don't we all," muttered Oliver. "So if the Revelation text echoed with them, perhaps it echoed for Nigel and Heather Tapster, who seemed to be on the verge of creating their own cult using all the traditional methods, particularly by rounding up the young and impressionable."

"If you're right about Nigel being the father of Tina's child," Mallard speculated with a slight shudder, "then he would certainly be copying the sexual antics of a lot of cult leaders."

"I think we can safely assume that the graffito is a reference to the murder," Effie responded, putting away her telephone.

"Agreed," Mallard continued. "Then let's look at the possibilities. The verse mentions the death of the Two at the hands of some beast from the abyss. So it may have been a warning from the killer that by killing Tapster, he or she was fulfilling a biblical prophecy, in which case somebody should keep an eye on the grieving widow in case she's next for a toxic tonic. Or it may have been a warning *to* the killer from some nutcase who had identified Nigel and Heather with the Two and was trying to draw attention to the murder's apocalyptic implications."

Mallard needed to repeat the last phrase three times before the consonants came out in the right order.

"Could this mysterious woman with the long red hair be Heather Tapster herself in disguise?" Effie asked.

"No," Oliver answered. "I first saw that girl on Thursday evening, waiting in the street in front of the manse. Paul and I had just left Heather at her house. I don't think she could have changed and rushed over there that quickly."

"Assuming that the graffiti artist is the same girl," Mallard reminded him.

"One thing's for sure," said Oliver, "if this is a threat from the killer, then the killer can't be Paul Piltdown. He was holed up in the police station before the graffito appeared."

"If Welkin had understood the quotation, he might have hesitated about arresting Paul," Effie commented ruefully. "But it won't persuade him to let Paul go. If only somebody had interviewed your Mister Whatsisname earlier."

"Tooth," Oliver reminded her. Their meal was brought over, and Mallard busied himself with adding the right amounts of salt, pepper, and ketchup to his mixed grill. The conversation returned to the mechanics of Tapster's death.

"What about the Communion bread?" asked Mallard, buttering a roll and taking a bite out of it. "Maybe somebody palmed a poisoned pellet off on him?" he continued indistinctly.

"There were traces of strychnine in Tapster's used wineglass," Effie reminded him, sipping her tea. "It always comes back to that. What we can't figure out is how and when it got there."

"How about if that's a red herring?" Oliver suggested. "Suppose Uncle Tim's right, and Tapster was poisoned earlier. The glass Tapster used could have been switched *after* his death with a prepared glass that contained a trace of strychnine. There was plenty of opportunity to do that in the confusion." He cut into his battered plaice.

Effie thought carefully, chewing her pork chop and reviewing what she knew about the case. "Tapster's fingerprints weren't on any other glass, and all the deacons were searched carefully, so they couldn't have been concealing his original glass."

"Perhaps the killer wiped that glass and put it on back on the table?" Mallard suggested.

"That doesn't explain how Tapster put his fingerprints on the substitute glass after he was supposed to be dead. Besides, the pathologist also found both strychnine *and* Tapster's saliva inside his glass. It was definitely the glass he drank from."

"Then could some strychnine powder have been slipped into that glass after he put it down?" Mallard asked.

"There was only a small amount of liquid left, probably not enough to dissolve any strychnine crystals at that point. But this idea still supposes Tapster was poisoned earlier. Let me remind you that nobody saw him consume anything in the minutes leading up to his death, apart from the bread and the wine. And nothing else was found in his stomach, except for a tiny trace of honey, which Ollie thinks got stuck to his hand at breakfast."

"We've agreed that he can't have plopped poisoned honey into his morning cuppa, or he'd have died much sooner," Oliver stated. "But could he have had a cup of tea later than breakfast? How about if he was a little careless with some honey that *he* had poisoned and planned to give to someone else?"

"A drip of honey that's small enough to stay on your hand unnoticed isn't likely to hold a fatal dose of strychnine," Effie said. "And none of this accounts for those traces of dissolved strychnine in Tapster's used wineglass. I'm afraid that the person who was best poised to slip Nigel the lethal liquid is still our prime suspect, the Reverend Paul Piltdown."

Oliver put down his knife and fork noisily. "Paul didn't do it," he declared. The dog loyally panted his agreement.

"Why are you so keen to believe him?" she asked curiously, sitting back and folding her arms. "Because you unwittingly provoked his arrest?"

"I'm not sure that was a bad thing," Oliver muttered. "Paul thinks the real murderer will come forward to save him, and an arrest certainly raises the stakes in that standoff. But I believe he's innocent because he said so. Or as good as."

"Ollie, my poor, sweet, trusting youth, does it occur to you that if your pal Paul did manage to murder one of his deacons, he wouldn't be above telling *you* a porky or two?"

Mallard sniggered into his coffee. Oliver glared at him. So did Murray.

"Paul Piltdown didn't kill Nigel Tapster," he stated firmly.

"Then you'd better find out who did," said Effie, scooping up her last four peas on her fork.

"What?"

Effie paused and looked at him, her head on one side.

"Well, Spiv Welkin's not going to stir himself to find another murderer this side of Christmas. He's perfectly content with the one he's got. I certainly can't go over his head and push on with a parallel investigation, and anyway, I still have to find Tina Quarterboy. Detective Superintendent Mallard is on holiday, and much as I'm sure he's about to volunteer to help you, it would be very impolitic for him to show his face on the streets of Plumley." She made the last point firmly, which caused Mallard to change his mind about speaking up. He slipped the dog an unexpected piece of sausage.

"But you, Ollie, are Paul's self-appointed champion," Effie went on. "You know the players and the details of the death, and you have the perfect excuse to make the rounds of the suspects—your famous article on the United Diaconalists."

"I'd forgotten about that," said Oliver thoughtfully.

"I hate to urge any nonprofessional to play detective," said Mallard, "especially someone who owes his living to a rodent—"

"A ferret isn't a rodent."

"Don't interrupt me when there's a 'but' coming."

"Sorry," Oliver replied, humbly choking back an obvious reference to Mallard's recent Shakespearian performance. Perhaps he was learning some tact at last, he speculated. Murray barked once, seemingly in agreement.

"I was going to say that, in this case, I agree with Effie," said Mallard. "I can't help you, anyway. They want me back at the Yard tomorrow. It seems that Assistant Commissioner Weed's been having a few problems in my absence. So you find out what you can, Ollie, but don't step on anybody's toes."

"Fair enough." Oliver beamed at his companions. "Wow, a detective at last!" he purred. Then the smile faded. "Where do you think I should begin?" he asked the dog.

Chapter Seven

We've Been Awhile A-Wandering

Tuesday, December 23

"Come in, Mr. Swithin. Come in, Mr....er...Angelwine," Elsie Potiphar was saying, nervously welcoming them in from the misty rain.

Swithin and Angelwine. The Adventures of Swithin and Angelwine. The Case-Book of Oliver Swithin, as recorded by his friend and companion, Dr. Angelwine. No, no matter how you put it, they sounded more like a firm of Dickensian undertakers than a pair of tough, renegade cops.

Oliver had selected the Potiphars first in the hope that Cedric's habit of spouting Bible references would make Geoffrey want to go back home. He had made the mistake of telling Geoffrey his plans over breakfast, only to find that his friend had begun his Christmas vacation that day and insisted on accompanying him.

They followed Mrs. Potiphar meekly through the dark entrance hall of the terraced house and into the small parlor, where the solid bulk of her husband was sitting imperiously in an armchair. Cedric rose steadily to his feet and greeted the two men with a solemn handshake, waving them to take a seat. Elsie disappeared, muttering under her breath.

The room had last been wallpapered sometime in the 1970s by a decorator whose taste was still in the 1930s. A pair of end-tables, piled with personal items and set up within reach of Potiphar's well-worn chair, indicated that the septuagenarian spent most of his waking time in this part of the house, although there was no sign of a television or radio in the room.

"My condolences on the loss of your diaconal seat," Oliver began loudly, remembering that the old man had a hearing problem. Cedric acknowledged the sympathy with a slight bow of the head and fixed Oliver with his small, brown eyes.

"'Lo, these many years do I serve thee,'" he began, caressing the text with his Cornish accent, despite his obvious disappointment. "'Neither transgressed I at any time thy commandment.' Luke, chapter fifteen, verse twenty-nine."

Geoffrey was murmuring something as Cedric finished speaking, but Oliver assumed it was another of his friend's inaccurate attempts to finish other people's sentences.

"It's been an eventful few days, I understand," Oliver pressed on. "Nigel Tapster's unfortunate demise, and then the arrest of your minister on murder charges." He presumed the word of Piltdown's detention had spread. "I suppose it puts a bit of damper on your Christmas."

"My helpmeet and I were not planning to celebrate Christmas beyond our religious obligations in welcoming the Christ-Child as Jehovah's unspeakable gift," Cedric intoned. His aging leather-covered Bible was on the table beside his chair, and he patted it piously. "There's nothing in my Bible about Christmas cards or Christmas trees or Christmas stockings."

"Yes, but I'd imagine even tomorrow night's carol service is a bit of no-go, with the minister in jail," Oliver offered.

"If we have to remember the Nativity in our own mansions, so be it, as long as it pleaseth Almighty God. As our Lord said, 'Where two or three are gathered together in my name, there am I in the midst of them.'"

"Matthew, chapter eighteen, verse twenty," said Geoffrey quietly. Oliver was about to whisper a hasty reproach, when he heard Cedric state the same reference. He turned to stare at his friend, but Geoffrey's birdlike face was gazing off into the distance.

"I hate to bring this up," Oliver continued, "but with Nigel Tapster dead, do you automatically reclaim your position as deacon, or does there have to be another church meeting? I need the clarification for my article."

"I do not wish to speak ill of the deceased," Cedric began, and Oliver waited for the citation, but apparently it wasn't a biblical quote. After a second's thought, Cedric clearly reconsidered this posture. "Nigel Tapster should never have won my seat. He was taking advantage of Sam and Joan Quarterboy's absence by insisting that the election went ahead. I'm sure that if we all knew the true reason for their nonappearance, we would have postponed the meeting and supported them in the fellowship of prayer."

"'Wherefore comfort yourselves together, and edify one another, even as also ye do,'" Geoffrey cut in.

Cedric stared at him before allowing a contented smile to cross his broad face. "One Thessalonians, chapter five, verse ten," he declared.

"Verse eleven, actually," Geoffrey answered humbly.

The smile faded. While Cedric tried to find the reference in his Bible, Oliver mouthed a few threats in Geoffrey's direction. The old man located the passage, glared at it, glared at Geoffrey, and shut the book without another word.

"I'm curious about the last Communion service," Oliver said. "You went up onto the platform. Was this a statement that you didn't recognize Tapster's right to be a deacon?"

"The Lord directed my feet, as he has for the last forty years of service in his tabernacle," Cedric stated, clasping his hands and laying them on his belly.

"Yes, well, in this case, it did give you a ringside seat for Tapster's death. Tell me, did you see the Reverend Mr. Piltdown do anything odd with the wineglasses when he served Tapster?"

"My eyes were closed in prayer at that time, Mr. Swithin."

"Well, did you see Tapster eat or drink anything apart from the Communion sacraments?"

Cedric smiled again and fixed his eyes on Geoffrey. "'For he that eateth and drinketh unworthily, eateth and drinketh damnation to himself…'" He raised his eyebrows quizzically.

"One Corinthians, chapter twelve, verse twenty-nine," said Geoffrey immediately. He and Potiphar beamed at each other with mutual satisfaction, while Oliver tried to remember if that verse or some other had been the text for Piltdown's sermon. There was something about eating in it.

"I'll take that as a 'no,' I suppose," Oliver sighed quietly, below the assumed level of Cedric's hearing, feeling suddenly out of his depth. "May I ask you one more question, Mr. Potiphar?" he added with increased volume. "I'd appreciate your thoughts on Revelation chapter eleven, verse seventeen."

The look of affability faded from Cedric's face. He seemed uncomfortable and eyed his closed Bible wistfully. "You catch me a little unawares, Mr. Swithin," he quavered, reaching again for the book. "I may need to refresh my memory…"

"Oh, please, never mind, it's not important," Oliver said quickly, standing up and blocking Potiphar's view of Geoffrey, while he reached behind his back and squeezed his friend's beak-like nose to stop him offering his own commentary.

It was as he had suspected: The Plumley churchgoers took their cues from the Gospels and the Epistles (and could do a lot worse for a guide to life); the magical mystery tour of the Book of Revelation was more the province of heavy metal bands and teenagers who thought painting their bedroom walls black was a statement of profundity. The old man was clearly unfamiliar with the prophecy of the Two.

"We needn't disturb you any longer," Oliver continued, "but I would like a word or two with your good lady before we leave."

In the gloomy passageway that led to the rear of the house, Oliver turned on Geoffrey.

"What was that all about?" he demanded.

"What?"

"The Bible quotations."

"Oh that," said Geoffrey. "My parents were fundamentalist Christians. All through my childhood, we had to learn a new verse of the Bible every day, complete with reference. We were tested over Sunday lunch on the previous week's assignment. We had to get all seven right to earn our Yorkshire pudding."

"How utterly ghastly."

"It was all right. It trained the memory. And an accumulation of well-chosen Bible verses would be marginally more useful on a desert island than knowing the lyrics to every Gilbert and Sullivan opera, which I happen to know is one of your talents."

Oliver paused, aware that he could hear an odd rattling through the closed door of a room that he assumed was the kitchen. He had wondered why Mrs. Potiphar had not returned during their interview with her husband. No doubt she was sitting there, tatting or crocheting tea cozies or whatever else the dutiful elderly spouse of a long-serving deacon was supposed to do to preserve a God-fearing household.

"Now, I should warn you that although Elsie Potiphar seems a sweet old lady," he whispered to Geoffrey, "I fear she suffers from Tourette's syndrome or something like it. Don't be offended if she suddenly calls you, oh, for example, a priggish, irritating, nut-faced little twerp. It's nothing personal."

He tapped on the door and pushed it ajar. Then he stopped, astonished.

Mrs. Potiphar was sitting at a scrubbed pine table in the middle of the large, bright room, staring into the oversized monitor of desktop computer and occasionally clicking the side button of trackball. A skein of cables flowed from the back of the computer and across the tiled floor of the kitchen. From the reflection in her dainty glasses, she seemed to be contemplating a color picture.

She looked up. "I know, I know," she said with a smirk. "There's nothing in the Bible about the Internet. Well, tough titty."

"Do you mind if we ask you some questions?" Oliver asked tentatively.

"Of course not, dear boy. Have a seat, the pair of you."

They took two bentwood chairs on their side of the table, while she shuffled her office chair a few inches to the right and peered affably around the monitor.

"Well, as you know," Oliver began, flipping over a page in his notebook, "I'm writing an article on the United Diaconalist Church and—"

"Oh, I'm not a Diaconalist."

"I beg your pardon?"

"I'm not a Diaconalist," Elsie repeated slowly. "I'm only married to one."

"But you attend the church," Geoffrey observed.

"Oh yes, I do that out of marital obligation. But I don't believe all that Christian guff. Never have."

Oliver and Geoffrey looked at each other.

"Then may I inquire discreetly what you are?" Oliver asked.

She grinned, producing comely wrinkles out of thin air. "I'm a true-blue, dyed-in-the-wool, card-carrying atheist," she declared.

"I don't understand," Oliver admitted helplessly. "You're a church member!"

Elsie pushed herself away from the table and sat primly, her hands in her lap. "Let me explain," she said. "Cedric's been a deacon of Plumley United Diaconalist for the last forty years. It's his whole life, apart from one thing—me. We met during the 1950s on an Aldermarston march, and despite our marked philosophical and religious differences, we fell in love. Neither of us would budge in our beliefs, but we wanted to get married anyway. We made a pact. I would show up at all the church services, prayer meetings, and events and play the quiet, loyal, mousy little wife, so I didn't damage his prospects of earning and keeping his diaconal seat; and Cedric would never, *never* quote the Bible at me in our home. And for fifty years of marriage, we have stuck to that pact." She sniggered. "Of course, I can't help myself if I'm occasionally forced to express my opinion of the morons who cluster around the church. That little turd, Dougie Dock, for instance."

"How on Earth can you stand being there for all those acts of worship if you don't believe it?" Oliver asked.

"Oh, it's not easy being an atheist in this modern world," she answered lightly. "There's so much out there that might shake your faith, what with people claiming to spot angels on every street corner and holy statues weeping blood at the drop of a fiver. I need to go to church regularly to remind myself why I don't believe a word of it."

"I mean no disrespect for your considerable charm, Mrs. Potiphar, but I would have thought someone with your husband's faith would have been severely conflicted about marrying a nonbeliever."

"He was," she declared, with a sidelong glance at the computer screen. "But he found some verse in the Bible that squared it for him. It was the last one I ever let him quote at me."

"'If any brother hath a wife that believeth not, and she be pleased to dwell with him, let him not put her away,'" said Geoffrey idly.

"That's the one, sport," she cried, clapping her hands. "Isn't the Good Book wonderful? You can always find a verse to justify any action. Except maybe coveting your manservant's ass."

"Why did your husband go up to the platform for last Sunday's Communion?" Oliver asked, returning to the list of potential questions he had jotted in his notebook the previous evening. "He says it was God's will."

"God's will maybe, but mine definitely," she answered bluntly. "I may not share Cedric's beliefs, but I love him and I'll fight for him. He was devastated about losing that bogus election on Friday. So I encouraged him in a little civil disobedience. Or perhaps 'uncivil obedience' is a better description of a religious duty."

"A woman was spotted in the area of the church after the murder," he said. "A young woman with long red hair. Does that sound familiar?"

"It doesn't sound like anyone at the church," she answered, fiddling with her own braid of white hair.

"Any idea how Tapster was killed?"

"Not unless words can do it," Elsie replied, her good humor returning. "He passed the wine around the congregation that morning. When he got to me, I told him where he could put it."

She cackled at the recollection but then became distracted by the appearance of her screen-saver. She clicked her trackball button to bring back the image she had been looking at before. Oliver stood up.

"We'd better go and leave you to your work," he said.

"Oh, I'm just downloading pornography," she said, without taking her eyes from the screen. She gestured at the monitor. "Stops my mind from wandering."

"That's very amusing," Oliver replied cordially, strolling around the table to see what hobby she was really tracking through the labyrinth of the World Wide Web. Filling the screen was a picture of a muscular and well-oiled man wearing only a Santa hat and boots, with a sprig of holly decorating his hairless and worryingly abundant genitals. He seemed to be taking his temperature with a candy cane. Oliver backed away quickly.

"The gay newsgroups are the best," Elsie continued, starting to download another photograph. "They take better care of their bodies." She looked up at Geoffrey and let her eyes drift up and down his frame appraisingly. "Why don't you stay, dolly? We could admire the scenery together. There's room on this chair for two, if you stack them correctly."

"No thank you," Geoffrey squeaked, edging for the door.

"Suit yourself," she continued insouciantly, watching the screen. She clicked again, making odd purring noises in her throat, while Oliver and Geoffrey slipped from the room.

"Come in, Mr. Swithin. Come in, Mr...er...Angelwine," Patience Coppersmith was saying. No, no better the second time, thought Oliver, we still sound like the opening lines of a cross-talk act. "Swithin PI" wasn't bad for a solo performance, but despite his near-seduction by a seventy-year-old, Geoffrey had stayed with him for the second appointment, neurotically repeating his desire during the short walk to the Coppersmiths'

flat to do some genuine detective work. They had managed to agree that only Elsie had the capacity and flair to mastermind Tapster's death, although since she would require Cedric as her agent on the platform, the Potiphars were unlikely suspects.

The sitting room was a striking contrast to Cedric's lair, with simple decor and well-chosen furniture. The window-ledge and mantelpiece were lined with dozens of Christmas cards, many of them signed in childish handwriting, and a dense, natural fir tree, peppered with elegant white ribbons, almost scraped the ceiling in a corner of the room. From another part of the flat, they could hear odd sounds, like bagpipes being passed through a rusty mangle, and Oliver assumed that Billy was home and practicing his guitar.

"We really didn't get much chance to talk the other evening," Oliver began. "And so much has happened at the church since then."

"You're telling me," Patience agreed, sitting primly on the arm of a chair and fussing with her neat, gray hair. "And I don't have much time to talk even now, unfortunately. I have to go out in about half an hour."

"Some last-minute Christmas shopping?" asked Geoffrey.

"No, I volunteer at a local hospice. Normally I'm only available for evenings, because I work during the day. But during the school holidays, I like to give a little more of my time, now that Billy's older."

"Very commendable," said Oliver.

She brushed away the compliment. "To God be the glory. But since we're a little pressed, let me tell you immediately that dead deacons and jailbird ministers aren't part of our normal Christmas festivities at Plumley Diaconalist. If you're going to include these events in your story, Mr. Swithin, I want to go on the record as saying I believe Paul Piltdown is completely innocent."

"You can't imagine how he could have engineered the poisoning of Tapster's wineglass?"

"Oh, is that how they think it was done? Good heavens! No, I mean I don't think Paul is capable of killing anyone, not even a vile man like Nigel Tapster. Please don't misunderstand me, I'm very sorry Nigel's dead, and my heart is with poor Heather. But Paul Piltdown was about the only person in the church who seemed to tolerate the Tapsters, despite their challenges to his authority. Since I'm the church treasurer, they trusted me to count the votes at last Friday's deacons election. I couldn't swear to it, but I'm sure I saw Paul's handwriting on one of the ballots for Nigel."

"You do realize that if Paul's not guilty, the killer's still among us."

Patience shivered. "Yes, of course, that had occurred to me, and no doubt I'm a suspect, since I was on the spot *and* I was wielding wineglasses myself. I suppose I shall be quizzed again by those silly young policemen, dressed as a pantomime cow this time. And after I've been trying so hard to shut the details of Sunday morning out of my mind. Excuse me."

She left the room quickly, and Oliver was sure it was not just to see if the kettle was boiling.

"She didn't do it," Geoffrey declared definitively.

"What make you so sure?"

"She was surprised when you told her how the poison was administered."

"Could be a bluff."

"Oh. Well, all right, maybe she did do it. Hey, can I try out some detective's intuition when she gets back?"

"Of course not."

They sat in silence, listening to Billy's attempts to master either "Layla" or "How Much is That Doggy in the Window?" After another minute, Patience returned with a tea tray and with redder eyes than before, followed by a trotting pug with a pained expression. Her stance brought back a memory for Oliver of Tina Quarterboy proudly bearing a tray of cups and saucers into the manse living room, the only time he had ever seen the missing girl. It was hard to think of the skinny, gauche adolescent in any kind of sexual liaison with Nigel Tapster, and he felt ashamed for the explicit image of the entwined, naked couple that sprang unavoidably into his mind. He shifted some magazines on the coffee table to make room for the tray.

"Ms. Coppersmith, is Tina Quarterboy in your class at school?" Geoffrey drawled.

Patience paused, milk jug in hand, and gave Geoffrey a puzzled look. He smirked. "You're probably wondering how I guessed," he continued lazily. The dog stopped investigating the skirting boards and gazed at him adoringly.

"I'm actually wondering who's been giving you the wrong information," she replied, pouring dribbles of milk into the cups.

"Ms. Coppersmith is a head teacher, Geoffrey," said Oliver, glaring balefully at his friend, "and at a junior school, not a senior school."

"That's right," Patience confirmed. She handed Geoffrey a cup of tea, but the pug chose that second to leap into his lap and parade cautiously over his stomach.

"Ah, I see T'Pau has taken a fancy to you, Mr. Angelwine," she said. "I'll leave your tea on the coffee table."

She continued pouring, her actions the same as Tina's at the manse that time. But wait—where did Oliver's memory of Tina pouring tea come from? The girl had certainly brought in a tray and coffeepot, but *Paul* was the one who had poured the beverages, "played mother," as the expression goes. That was it! When he and Effie had visited Paul, the day before the murder, the minister had used that same expression of Tina. But he had described an event that hadn't actually happened. And then he pointedly linked this to her being cast as the mother of God in the Nativity play. Dear Lord, had Paul been sending signals all along—consciously or otherwise, but probably consciously—of what he could not permit himself to utter? Then what else had he talked about that day that may have revealed what he knew of Tina's whereabouts, the father of her child? Confession, Jaffa Cakes, mother hen—there was that maternal metaphor again, anyway.

"Billy must be disappointed about tomorrow night's carol concert," Oliver commented. T'Pau had begun a slow ascent of Geoffrey's rib cage.

"Why?" asked Patience, smiling indulgently at the pug.

"Well, I imagine the whole thing's off, what with the murder and the arrest and so forth."

"On the contrary. Sam Quarterboy went to see Paul in the police station last night and brought back the message that the show was to go on. And Paul fully expects to be up in the pulpit, welcoming the Lord of Christmas."

Another message to the murderer, Oliver assumed, unless Pilt-down assumed he would have made bail by tomorrow evening.

"I've just seen Cedric Potiphar and he didn't mention this."

"Well, poor Cedric's not a deacon at the moment, so perhaps Sam hadn't called him," Patience replied kindly. "And even if he had, there's a chance that Cedric may have forgotten. We're none of us as young as we used to be."

"But what about the music for the service? Surely Heather Tapster's not up to performing?"

"No, she was utterly devastated by the news. I know how I felt when Billy's father was taken from us. I just thank the Good Lord that Heather wasn't there to see Nigel die."

"So with Heather unavailable tomorrow evening, who's going to play the piano for the carols. And for Barry Foison's Nativity play?"

"A friend of Barry's, called Oona. She's actually an organist. So's Barry, incidentally, but he says this Oona is a better musician. They're going to awaken the church organ from its long slumber for the occasion."

"If Barry's an organist, why hasn't he been playing for the church?"

"Because his job sometimes takes him out of town on Sundays. So when Heather Tapster turned up and offered her services as a regular pianist, she seemed a Godsend." She was unable to conceal a slight wince.

"When you went with DC Belfry to break the news to Heather, did she tell you why she left the service before the Communion?"

"The Tapsters had planned to have some of the young people round for lunch. I know Billy was going. I suppose the service was running a little long and Heather went home to start the meal."

"Have you seen her since Sunday?"

Patience shook her head. "I believe the young people in her group have rallied round."

"Billy, too?"

There was a pause. "Not yet," she said. She couldn't avoid the hint of triumph and relief.

"How is Billy?" Oliver asked. "His experience the other day must have been quite terrifying. And I know Nigel Tapster was fond of him. Has he talked to you about his feelings?"

"He's a boy, Mr. Swithin," Patience answered ruefully. "Rapidly becoming a man. These days, he wouldn't dream of talking to his mother about his feelings. I've made it clear that I'm here whenever he needs me, but he's been in his room playing that guitar almost constantly since Sunday. He's strong, though. With no father for many years, he's had to be."

Strong enough to see through the wiles of father figure Nigel Tapster, eventually? Or did ceding his credulity to Tapster relieve him from the pressure of being the premature man of the house? If so, how was he handling the murder?

T'Pau was now planted firmly on Geoffrey's sternum, staring into his face with her dark, fish-like eyes and dribbling onto his tie. He looked around in mild panic, not wishing to touch the panting beast.

"Oh, she really likes you!" exclaimed Patience. "They can sense the animal lovers, don't you think?"

Oliver didn't respond, remembering Geoffrey's acute phobia of horses and wondering if it would migrate to smaller animals. Geoffrey had already had one painful encounter with a frightened ferret, which Oliver had rescued from an animal rights activist, and his subsequent refusal to share a house with the mild and affectionate beast had forced Oliver to give up several days of writing while he found a good home for it with a ferret enthusiast.

"So it's going to be an electric guitar and pipe organ duet for Barry's Nativity play?" Oliver mused. "That's a long cry from Benjamin Britten's *A Ceremony of Carols*, which the choir used to perform at my family's church every Christmas."

Patience shifted in her chair slightly and tugged at the hem of her skirt. "Yes, that's a lovely piece, but we couldn't possibly perform it at a Diaconalist Church."

"Hard to find a Diaconalist harpist? Heaven must be full of them. Or is it the bits sung in Latin? Hitting a little too close to Rome?"

"It's not that," she said uncomfortably. "It's a shame, but, you know, Britten being the way he was…"

What? A pacifist? A conscientious objector? Tonal? The penny dropped. "Gay?" Oliver ventured.

"Well…homosexual, yes."

"Surely that's no reason to disapprove of the man or his music, not in this day and age?"

"The Bible is quite clear on this," muttered Patience primly. "'Thou shalt not lie with mankind as with womankind: it is abomination.'"

Oliver turned to Geoffrey, who was slumped almost horizontally in his armchair and seemed to be frozen in a stare-down contest with the drooling animal on his chest. He shrugged slightly, signaling his unfamiliarity with the reference. T'Pau didn't seem to think the worse of him for this admission of ignorance, even when Geoffrey repeated the shrug several times in a vain attempt to dislodge her.

Oliver decided this was not an appropriate occasion to discuss how fundamentalism became oddly selective as it navigated the less-traveled byways of the Pentateuch. But he was disappointed that of all the church members, it was this pleasant and intelligent woman who had voiced a streak of official intolerance. He hoped Paul was as prudent as he'd implied. Oliver glanced again at the questions scribbled in his notebook.

"A young woman with long red hair was seen in the area of the church after the murder. Any idea who she might be?"

Patience shook her head.

"I wonder if Billy knows," Oliver continued, half rising from his chair. "May I ask him?"

"I don't see why not. But I don't imagine he'll tell you anything you don't already know."

"I'll come too," Geoffrey called weakly. The dog, sensing the competition for his attention, licked his chin wetly.

"No, no, you stay here and keep Ms. Coppersmith company," Oliver replied from the doorway. "We don't want to disturb little T'Pau."

The sound of the guitar led him to a door decorated with pictures of rock groups torn from magazines. Knowing that a knock would not be heard, Oliver pushed the door open gently. Billy was sitting on his small bed, an untidy island rising from the discarded clothes, electric cables, and other debris of youth scattered over the bedroom floor. As he leaned over his guitar, his vest hung loose on his thin body, revealing pimpled shoulders. Watching the teenager's fingers moving rapidly over the fretboard confirmed Oliver's suspicion. Although the cheap amplifier distorted the sound, Billy was simply practicing pentatonic scales, repeating the same patterns mechanistically and leaving too much of his mind available for other thoughts. He saw Oliver and stopped playing.

"I thought you said you weren't a copper," he muttered.

"I'm not."

"Then why are you here asking my mother all those questions?"

Oliver chose not to ask how Billy could know what had been going on in the living room. He noted that the tangle of wires at the boy's feet included a sustain pedal for the guitar, which could probably keep the sound going for half a minute.

"Among other things, I want to know who killed Nigel."

Billy snorted. "She doesn't know."

He played a soft, major-seventh chord, unresolved but inherently rich and haunting. Oliver did not attempt to engage him by pretending to be interested in posters of rock groups he hadn't heard of or the fleet of poorly painted model ships scattered across the chest of drawers.

"What does it matter, anyway?" Billy continued, filling the silence that Oliver had deliberately left. "Can't bring him back."

"Yes, I'm sorry about Nigel. You have my condolences."

The teenager looked up testily. "I didn't think you even liked Nigel."

"I only met him that one time. But I can still be sorry that you lost something special."

"Who says it's lost?" Billy riposted, but only as a sad, petulant gut reaction. Oliver moved into the room and sat on a corner of the bed, mirroring Billy's posture.

"Perhaps you can help me with something. The police are looking for a woman—a girl perhaps—with long red hair. Ring any bells? Someone who came to Nigel's meetings, perhaps, even if she didn't join you at the church on Sundays?"

Billy waved his head slowly from side to side, but didn't answer.

"Did you know Tina was at the church on Sunday?"

"I told you and that policewoman—me and Chrissie hadn't been seeing each other for a while. The last time I saw her... Well, I haven't spoken to her for weeks."

"Chrissie?" Oliver echoed. "I was asking about Tina Quarterboy."

"Yeah, that's Chrissie. That's what she'd decided she wanted to be called. Short for Christina. She thought the name Tina was too old-fashioned, too little-girlish. It was what her mum and dad called her."

No doubt it would be Krissi or the more intellectual Chrissee before she had finished exploring exotic new identities. But this eruption of private individuality seemed out of character for the girl. "She seems to respect her parents," Oliver said guardedly.

"Too much if you ask me. Chrissie really wanted to be part of Nigel's group—she really loved him. But her parents stopped her coming to our meetings."

"Why do you think they did that?"

"She said they were afraid of Nigel's influence on us. But I think they were afraid of Chrissie experiencing something that they were dead to themselves. Nigel said some people were scared of giving themselves up to the power of God's spirit. I think my mum's the same. They all want to get to God with their brains, while he wants to come in through the heart."

That was the quest that had brought Paul Piltdown to the Diaconalist Church, Oliver remembered. Billy played another brief scale on the guitar and let the sound ring out.

"You said you haven't spoken to Tina, to Chrissie," Oliver said eventually. "But when did you last see her? It's very important that we find her."

Billy took off the guitar and leaned it against the amplifier. Even the movement provoked a faint electric reaction from the built-in loudspeaker.

"You telling me the truth about not being a policeman?" he asked, after a pause.

"Yes."

"What about that policewoman you were hanging around with? The one who was there on Sunday when Nigel was killed."

"She's my girlfriend."

Billy looked surprised. "Good for you, Slick. Nice hair. Nice…So if you're not a cop, what do you do?"

"I write books. I was writing an article about your church when all this happened."

"Oh, books. Then you must be pretty clever." Billy swallowed. "Can I ask you something? Something that's been bothering me?"

"Sure."

"Suppose you promise somebody that you'd never mention something. And then that person dies. Do you have to keep your promise?"

Oliver took a deep breath, noticing for the first time the slight, lingering aroma of joss sticks. He hoped they hadn't been lit by the fourteen-year-old to disguise more incriminating smells.

"That's a tough one," he said, trying not to sound patronizing. "I'd say yes, you have to keep a secret. Unless the death changes the circumstances. For example, if you promised Nigel something before he died, you should generally keep it to yourself. But if that information could help track down his killer, then I think you ought to give it to the police."

"It's nothing like that."

But it was a promise to Nigel, clearly. Who else had died? Billy's father, or was that too long ago? And Billy could barely keep the secret from exploding out of his mouth.

"Do you think revealing the secret could help someone?"

"That's just it, I don't know. I don't know if it would hurt someone either."

Oliver took off his glasses and wiped them on his sweater.

"Look, let's try something. Why don't you let me guess your secret? You don't have to say anything unless I'm right. That way, you haven't betrayed anybody's trust. And if I *am* right, I promise I won't pass the information on to anybody unless we both agree it could help."

Billy's intrigue pushed aside the last shreds of reluctance. He turned toward Oliver for the first time, his eyes alive. Oliver shifted to reflect his posture, bookending him across the bed.

"All right," Billy breathed. Oliver replaced his glasses.

"It's about Tina. Sorry, Chrissie." Process of elimination— Billy had already ruled out Tapster's murder, and the girl's disappearance was the only other matter that would have weighed on his conscience. Besides, it was Oliver's question about Tina that had started this thread.

"Yes."

"It's about when you saw her last." Billy had already stumbled over that point earlier in the conversation.

"Yes."

"You saw her since she left school on Thursday evening?" That was easy—an earlier spotting would hardly have been made the subject of a confidence.

"Yes, go on."

Now came the challenge. Did Billy see her before or after her departure from the Quarterboys' home in the early hours of Friday morning? If Tapster was involved, it had to be before Sunday morning, for obvious reasons. The young people had gathered at his home on Saturday night. Had Tina turned up then? Or was the sighting earlier? Oliver knew Billy and Tapster had been together that Thursday evening, during Tina's missing hours. And Billy had reacted more strongly to the last prediction, containing the word "Thursday." Yet logic cried out that girl had been at the manse on Thursday evening, not at the Tapsters'. Oliver took another deep breath and let his gut defy his brain.

"She was at Nigel's house on Thursday evening."

"That's it," Billy exclaimed, grinning broadly. "Wow, Mr. Swithin, you must be a mind-reader!"

"Call me Oliver. No, I'm not a mind-reader." Just playing detective. Effie would have to restore the pat on the head, he reflected.

"I suppose now you know the secret, I might as well tell you everything," Billy went on. The logic was debatable, but Oliver was not going to stop him. "You see, I went to Nigel's house after school on Thursday to rehearse with Heather for the carol service. I got there at about half past four, and just as I was going to ring the doorbell, the front door opened and Chrissie came out, crying. She didn't stop when she saw me, but just ran off down the street."

It all made sense. Tina discovered from the school doctor that she was pregnant. The moment school ended, she ran immediately to the man responsible. Then, for some so-far unexplained reason, she ran away from this man to the minister she trusted. Finally, she went home, while Piltdown rushed straight to Tapster to berate him for impregnating the girl. Oliver could cover the route easily in the two hours, allowing for conversations with Tapster and Piltdown. A thirteen-year-old in an adrenalin-fueled state of near panic would take less time.

"Were both Nigel and Heather at home?"

"No, just Nigel. Heather hadn't got home from work yet. I was early."

"Did Nigel seem upset too?"

"Not really. Actually, he seemed amused."

Amused? Unfeeling bastard! Was that how he reacted to the news of his impending fatherhood? No wonder the girl had headed for the sanctity of the Reverend Paul Piltdown. And no wonder Paul was angry enough to confront Tapster immediately. When Oliver had met with Tapster shortly after that encounter, he had seemed calm and in control. Had Paul witnessed the same demeanor, or was Tapster a damn good actor?

"Nigel didn't tell you why Chrissie had been to see him?"

"He said she was upset about her parents' attitude. She didn't know if she should defy them and come to the meetings. Nigel said he had counseled her to obey them and go home. He said he didn't want Heather to know Chrissie had been to the house, because it might have made her angry at the Quarterboys, and he had no desire to sow any conflict within the church. So he asked me to keep Chrissie's visit to myself, as a personal favor. And I told him a secret in return, to show that he could trust me."

A secret Tapster had literally taken to the grave.

"Now that I've told you, does it help?" Billy asked anxiously.

"I'm not sure. But if you don't mind, I may pass it on to my favorite police officer." Oliver winked at Billy. "She's very discreet."

Although he couldn't imagine what Effie would do with the information. The police could now plot Tina's zigzag path through Plumley that Thursday afternoon—school to Tapster, say fifteen minutes; Tapster to manse, ten minutes at the most, he had walked it with Paul; manse to the Quarterboy's home, no more than fifteen minutes for a child in a hurry—but it hardly changed what they already believed, except to confirm Oliver's assumption that Tapster was the father of her child. If anything, it gave Piltdown an even stronger motivation for doing away with Tapster, casual and callous despoiler of underage virgins.

"Billy, do you have any idea where Chrissie might be now?"

The teenager shrugged. Oliver touched him gently on the arm and stood up. He spotted a Railway Mice book on the floor—featuring Finsbury the Ferret, no doubt, or it would have no place in an adolescent's bedroom—but resisted the temptation to pick it up and sign it.

"You'd better go back to practicing," he said after a pause, realizing soberly that after a morning as a private detective, he was no closer to finding an alternative candidate for Tapster's murderer. "Make your mother proud of you."

"Yeah," Billy grunted. "Hey, thanks for the advice, Oliver."

"No problem. Merry Christmas."

"Merry Christmas, mate."

Only twenty-seven people in Britain can explain why the day after Christmas Day is called Boxing Day, but that doesn't stop millions of workers from celebrating it by not going to work. An intriguing side-effect of thus having two consecutive public holidays for Christmas is that no matter what days of the week they fall on, the British can easily justify taking the whole week off.

Suppose Christmas Day falls on a Tuesday, with Boxing Day on the Wednesday. Well then, what is the point, the contemporary Bob Cratchet cries, of bothering to open up the office or factory on Monday, when we all plan to knock off work by lunchtime because it's Christmas Eve? And it's hardly worth cranking up the heat for a working week that's now been whittled down to just two days. By the time we finish complaining about our ingrate in-laws and the cheesy Christmas television programs and the blatant materialism of our kids, it's time to go home for the weekend. Isn't it simpler for Mr. Scrooge to close the counting house until the New Year? (He can still pay us, of course.)

This creative logic is a little more challenging when Christmas Day is a Thursday, but several Plumley residents had pulled it off, and so Effie found more people at home than she expected for a Tuesday morning, when she finally and single-handedly conducted her house-to-house inquiries near the church. These idle residents' excitement at finding a young, attractive, and increasingly moist detective on the doorstep was quickly dashed when they realized she was not brimming over with juicy details about Sunday's murder, but merely looking for a missing teenager who was last seen in the area.

By lunchtime, she had visited every house on the street where Plumley United Diaconalist Church was located, but she had unearthed no new sightings of Tina, only complaints about milk bottles stolen from doorsteps and other petty thefts, which seemed typical of life in Plumley. Frustrated, tired, and soaking because of the cool drizzle that had descended all morning, Effie knew it was time to take a break when she found that she had rung the doorbell of a large Victorian house three times before she twigged that she was back at the manse, and its usual occupant was in police custody. She picked up her car from the church car park next door and drove back to the police station, annoyed with herself for not having taken a day off for more than a week, which also meant she had not taken off any of Oliver's clothes for the same amount of time. She missed him, more than she could have imagined, and when she found him sitting in the station waiting room, the only thing that stopped her from spiriting him into an interview room for a brief but torrid reminder of her feelings was Geoffrey Angelwine's regrettable presence.

"And it had bad breath," Geoffrey said, concluding his list of twenty reasons why he would never be the proud owner of a pug.

"Serves you right," Oliver retorted. "I asked you not to play amateur detective."

"I got close. Patience said her work ended with the school holidays, and there were a lot of Christmas cards from children on display. So I took a chance. Just because you already knew that she was the head of a junior school, you didn't have to get all smarmy."

"Actually, I had no idea what she did for a living," said Oliver.

"Then how did you guess?"

"From the same clues you had. I just thought about it a little longer. Most of the children who signed those cards printed their names. They had to be below senior-school age. And there were too many for just one class of kids. So I guessed Patience was someone who'd get Christmas greetings from more of the school—the dinner lady, the school nurse, or the headmistress. She's too pleasant to show offense at the way you demoted her, but there was nothing deprecating about her reaction either, so I assumed we had to go up a rank or two."

"Very clever," Geoffrey mumbled. "But if you're going to say it's elementary, I'll throw up."

Oliver told Effie what he had learned from Billy Coppersmith about Tina's odyssey on the preceding Thursday.

"It doesn't look good for Paul," she commented, helping herself to a crisp from Oliver's lunchtime packet. She had already overheard the station sergeant mumbling about picnickers in the waiting area. "I thought you were supposed to be collecting information that exonerated him, not that dropped him further in the manure."

"Maybe if I could talk to him again, confront him with the new information, I could get him to put up more of a defense?"

"No chance, I'm afraid. When I left this morning, Welkin and Company were hauling him off to court. I'm sure bail will be denied, in which case he'll be transferred to a proper prison. He won't be brought back here."

"But he's a clergyman. Won't that count for something with the magistrates?"

"The charge is murder and Paul is still refusing to put up a defense. Nope, he's toast. Unless you and Captain Hastings here come up with something."

She gestured at Geoffrey, but he was no longer paying attention to their conversation. He was staring openmouthed at someone who had just walked into the building. Effie followed his line of vision, surprised to see Sam Quarterboy standing forlornly in the rectangle of dim daylight that filtered through the main door. Tish Belfry had walked in with him and was speaking to him quietly.

"Who's that?" Geoffrey asked breathlessly.

"It's Mr. Quarterboy," Effie told him. "Tina's father."

"Not him," said Geoffrey. "Her. She's beautiful."

"I thought you only had eyes for me," she said scathingly. "That's Detective Constable Tish Belfry. She's assisting DI Welkin on the Tapster murder, so you're practically related."

Quarterboy recognized Effie and marched over, with Tish following. Effie braced herself, but five days without his daughter seemed to have taken the edge off the deacon's thorny self-confidence.

"Mr. Quarterboy," she began. "Can I help you?"

"Hello, Sergeant Strongitharm," he answered gently. "I came over this morning to see if there was anything I could do for our minister. Constable Belfry was kind enough to drive me to the court and bring me back."

"How noble of her," said Geoffrey, gazing at Tish. Effie did not take this as her cue to introduce her friends.

"I don't suppose…?" Quarterboy prompted.

"There's still no sign of Tina, I'm afraid."

"Ah." He bent his head sadly. The waiting room lights reflected off his shiny scalp.

"We know she's in the area and she doesn't seemed to be held against her will," Effie assured him, deciding once again to delay the news of Quarterboy's impending grandfatherhood. "It's only a matter of time."

"Yes, I understand. There have been three or four hang-up calls in the last couple of days. I'm sure she's getting close to returning." He flashed a brief, defiant smile, which failed to relieve the sadness in his eyes. "Joan and I are counting on having our Tina home for Christmas."

It was a statement of hope, but it still couldn't help sounding like an order. So Effie would now have to measure the girl's absence in days to go, rather than days elapsed—a countdown to success or failure. She could use the neglected Advent calendar in Tina's bedroom as a personal scorecard. Relieved that Sam did not want to continue the conversation, she walked over to speak to Tish. Geoffrey hovered a few paces behind.

"Mr. Quarterboy," Oliver said softly, as the man stood in the doorway, staring glumly out at the rain. Quarterboy turned, looking puzzled.

"We've met before, haven't we?" he asked.

"The Sunday before last. My name's Oliver Swithin."

"Of course. Forgive me for not remembering immediately. It seems a long while ago."

"I know about Tina, and I'm very sorry you and your wife are having to go through this. I'm sure the police are doing all they can."

"Short of actually finding her," Quarterboy said and sniffed. He stared out through the open door. "Perhaps that's unfair. I shouldn't hold the police responsible for finding Tina when they didn't lose her in the first place. We did."

"How is your wife?" Oliver had contemplated including the Quarterboys on his itinerary, but decided that his amateur investigation would be too much of an intrusion. Sam's appearance at the police station was an unexpected lagniappe.

"Joan is coping, thank you. We both take comfort in our faith in a loving God. But this is very hard on her. For now, she feels unable to face the community."

"She didn't go to church Sunday morning?"

"Even the comfort of God's word and the fellowship of the Lord's Supper could not entice her from home. I left her watching the morning service on the television. Fortunately, it was broadcast from a Baptist church. And under the circumstances, perhaps it's just as well that Joan didn't witness Sunday's appalling event. The Lord often sends his bounteous blessings in disguise."

He began to search in his coat pocket for his car keys.

"I'm sure Paul Piltdown appreciated your support this morning," Oliver remarked hastily. "Can I assume you don't think he's responsible for Nigel Tapster's death?"

"I have no idea who is responsible. Paul Piltdown is a man of his word and a man of the cloth. If he does not admit to this sin, I must assume he is innocent."

"Do you have any idea how Tapster was killed?"

"None at all. It's a complete mystery to me. Now if you'll excuse me, I really must get back to my wife. There's always the chance that Tina will have called, or even returned home."

Oliver grabbed his umbrella and walked with him as he stepped out into the rain, covering the deacon's bald head. It was worth wet feet to get in one more question. "I hope you hear news of your daughter very soon," he said. "You seem a very happy family."

"Tina was never any trouble. That's what's makes this so hard. We still have no idea why she ran away."

You'll find out soon enough, Oliver thought, feeling suddenly guilty because he had to conceal the answer that Sam and Joan wanted so much. "She gave you no indication that anything was troubling her? I believe you only saw her for a few minutes on Thursday evening."

"Yes, she stayed in her room all evening—told us she wasn't feeling well. I looked in on her, but she was doing her homework, and I didn't want to disturb her for long. We didn't talk about anything personal at all."

They had reached Quarterboy's Escort, parked on the street beside the police station.

"Do you mind if I ask what you did talk about?" Oliver ventured, as Quarterboy stepped out from the umbrella's shelter and scurried around to the driver's door. Quarterboy let a flash of impatience cross his face.

"It was a religious matter, actually," he shouted across the roof. Raindrops bounced off his head. "She wanted me to clarify the church's attitude to abortion. I recall that you and I talked about it the previous Sunday. Perhaps she overheard that and wanted more information." He unlocked the door, but paused, frowning across the car roof at Oliver. "Just a minute, didn't Mr. Piltdown say you were a reporter the other evening?"

"Oh no," said Oliver quickly, hoping the weather made him look vulnerable and pathetic. Nature had given him a head-start. "I'm just writing an article about your denomination, but I'm not a journalist."

Quarterboy didn't seem convinced. "Look, I don't know why you're asking all these personal questions, but my daughter's disappearance is a private matter. I'd better not see anything about it in any newspaper. Good day, Sir."

He climbed into the car and drove away. Oliver hurried back to the shelter of the police station. Effie was still in the waiting room, fielding questions from Geoffrey.

"No, I don't know if she has a boyfriend. Why don't you ask her yourself?" she was saying.

"You'll have to introduce me," Geoffrey insisted. "I couldn't just strike up a conversation. I'd get all tongue-tied."

"Find some reason for her to arrest you," Oliver interrupted. "Indecent exposure is a great icebreaker." He turned his back on Geoffrey and pulled Effie to the side. "I just got another piece of the jigsaw puzzle. When Sam looked in on Tina the evening of her disappearance, she asked him a question about abortion. He probably declaimed the official Diaconalist line on the topic, which is that it's murder, no doubt with a hint of his moral contempt for the kind of woman who needs one—just what a pregnant teenager on the verge of confessing wants to hear from her father. I'm not surprised she changed her mind and ran away instead."

"If she's as ignorant of the facts of life as you've been suggesting," Effie asked, "why should she even think about an abortion?"

"Could the school doctor have suggested it?"

"She told me specifically that she didn't discuss any options. She wanted Tina to talk to her parents first."

Oliver prodded the floor sharply with his umbrella. "Damn it! I bet it was Tapster!"

Effie patted his face softly. "We don't know for sure, Ollie. There were only two witnesses to that conversation. One is dead and one is missing. And finding her is my job. Finding Tapster's murderer is yours. Who's next on your list?"

"Well hell-oo, Mr. Swithin. Hell-oo, Mr...er...Angelwine."

"I'm thinking of having my name changed to Urrangelwine," Geoffrey muttered, as the two men followed Dougie Dock through a door marked "Private." Oliver had arranged to meet Dock at his office that afternoon, but when they arrived at the Plumley Tourist Advisory Centre where he worked, the public area was deserted, which Oliver imagined was not unusual. They had to ring a bell for attention four times before a man who, for the sake of efficiency, had managed to have a scowl etched on his face at birth, lurched from the back of the premises and told them the office had just closed until the New Year. Oliver then required another four attempts to explain his reason for calling, mainly because the man was temporarily tipsy and per-manently possessed both of a speech impediment and a foreign accent, which for some reason affected his comprehension as well as his powers of expression. Eventually recognizing the name "Dock" as one of his co-workers, he disappeared, and a moment later, Dougie Dock appeared in the doorway wearing a yellow paper hat.

"It's a little pre-Christmas celebration for my people in the office," he explained, leading them into a large work area where half a dozen of Dock's colleagues sat sullenly on chairs, nursing plastic cups full of pink liquid. A half-empty punch-bowl stood on a filing cabinet, and plates of potato crisps had been dumped on each desk.

"Now then, now then," he announced loudly, "there's no need to stop having fun just because I've left the room. I'd like to introduce two old and dear friends of mine—Oliver Swithin, who's a very famous writer, and Geoffrey Angelwine. He likes wine but he's no angel."

He laughed heartily at the joke and nudged Geoffrey several times. The office workers all chose to drink simultaneously. The scowling man surreptitiously topped up his cup from a hipflask.

"Oh, I'd never heard that one before," grumbled Geoffrey.

"It always comes down to me to organize these social events," Dock confided in a whisper, handing each man a paper hat. "If it wasn't for my leadership, I think they'd all just pack up and go home early. That's hardly a festive start to the holiday, is it? Now, we're all going to play Consequences."

He spun away and started to hand out pieces of paper.

"Mr. Dock is exaggerating a little when he numbers us among his 'old and dear friends,'" said Oliver quietly to a sour-faced, middle-aged woman.

"Pull the other one," the woman muttered.

"In fact, we've only met briefly," he continued.

"Not surprised, dearie," she said airily and nudged another woman sitting beside her. The second woman grunted and turned her eyes briefly in the direction of the ceiling.

"I'd be surprised if he's even met half the famous people he claims as his bosom buddies," the first woman continued.

"So your boss is a little creative with the truth at times?

The women looked at each other again and exchanged expressions of mock outrage. "If you mean little Dougie, he certainly is," said the first woman. "Especially if he told you he's the boss." They both sniggered.

"Come along now, everyone has to join in," called Dock, trotting across and pressing sheets of paper on the women. "Marge, Cissie—our office beauty queens. And Oliver and Gerald, too."

"Geoffrey," Geoffrey complained to Dock's back.

"If you don't mind, Mr. Dock, I'd prefer to sit this one out," said Oliver.

"Now, Oliver, what did I tell you? I'm 'Dougie' to everyone. If you call me Dock…"

"People might think I am one," crooned his co-workers, in chorus. Unaware of the sarcasm, Dock beamed at Oliver and Geoffrey.

"I think he's one all right," said Cissie, under cover of the general laughter.

"Oh, do you suspect…?" Oliver ventured.

"As a nine-bob note," said Marge.

"As a safety-pin," Cissie confirmed. "Honestly, to hear him go on about the boys they let him take out on hikes and camping trips. I wouldn't let my grandson near him."

Much as he felt Dock deserved some punishment simply for existing, Oliver had never seriously considered him a potential suspect in Tapster's death. All of the other deacons had their reasons for distrusting Tapster, and even Piltdown may have bridled at the challenge to his authority or appointed himself Tina Quarterboy's defender. But was this a potential motive for Dougie Dock, or just spiteful office gossip? A man who was a little too affectionate toward the boys in his care? And what if those boys had grown too old for the Victory Vanguard and passed into the relative safety—given their sex—of Nigel Tapster's circle? Did Tapster's new acolytes confide secrets of their days in the woods with the clownish Dock? Maybe that was Billy Coppersmith's secret, shared with Tapster only a few days before his death. And had Tapster used this knowledge to blackmail Dock into voting for him at the church meeting?

"All right now, pay attention to me, everyone," hooted Dock, jumping onto a chair in the middle of the room. He had collected all the papers. "I'll read our stories."

He unfolded one of the sheets of paper. "This one begins 'Dougie Dock.' Oh, it's about me, how flattering," he declaimed daintily. "'Met Finsbury the Ferret, In a Monastery Garden.' He said..." He paused, trying to make out the handwriting. Then he scowled and screwed the paper into a ball.

"I do wish you'd remember there are ladies present, Clovis," he scolded, glaring at the man who had first met Oliver. "I recognize your writing. And you spelled 'salami' wrong."

He opened the next sheet. "Okay, it's 'Dougie Dock,' again. I *am* popular. And this time..." His voice trailed away once more. "Look, I don't think the day before Christmas Day is a time to be saucy, even though I know it's meant in fun."

"Let me read it," called Marge jovially, getting up from her chair. The others made some encouraging noises. She grabbed the sheets from Dock and passed them out to the other office workers. They began to read them in a giggling huddle.

"Would this be a good time to ask you some questions?" Oliver said, drawing Dock gently away and brandishing his notebook. He tried to mask his newborn distaste for the deacon's potential dark side. "You did say I could drop by."

"What? Oh yes, of course," he answered distractedly. "For your article. Fire away."

"Who killed Nigel Tapster?"

The blunt question gained Dock's full attention. His small eyes became wary behind the thick spectacles.

"You're going to deal with that in your article?" he asked with suspicion.

"Certainly," Oliver answered, with what he hoped was the gruff tones of a seasoned crime reporter. "The murder happened while I was doing the research. I met all the suspects. Why shouldn't I switch gears? This could be the true crime story of the decade!" He leaned toward Dock. "And I'd imagine everyone involved will become quite well known in the district, if you get my drift."

Dock smirked and stroked his blue chin. "Well, I like to think of myself as something of a celebrity already," he purred nasally. "I lecture on local history occasionally. Then there's my work with the Victory Vanguard and the Sunday School. And once a week, I'm a deejay on hospital radio, you know."

"Dougie, you clearly play a central role in this mystery. Why, you were sitting right next to Tapster when he died. You saw everything!"

"Yes, that's true, isn't it?" Dock reflected. "Then I can see why you'd want to interview me."

The group behind them laughed as if on cue, but it was a reaction to something Cissie was reading to them involving Dock and three sailors in a nudist colony. Oliver licked the end of his pencil.

"So let's test that photographic memory of yours, D.D. Take yourself back to Sunday morning. You're in the middle of the Communion service. The wine has been served to the congregation. And now Paul Piltdown serves the deacons. Got it?"

"I think…"

"Good. Now, which tray of wineglasses did Paul use? The one carried by Nigel Taster or by Patience Coppersmith?"

Dock adopted a pose that was so ludicrously like Rodin's *The Thinker* that it had to be intentional. The paper hat was an odd touch.

"It was Nigel's," he said decisively.

"You willing to swear to that in a court of law, Doug?"

"Oh. Well, yes, if it comes to that."

"Why do you think he picked that one, D-man?" Geoffrey butted in. Oliver scribbled an obscenity in his notebook and showed it to his friend.

"I suppose it was because it was the last one to be passed back to him by the server," Dock offered. "Paul just held on to it."

"Now think carefully," said Oliver. "Did Paul deliberately take the tray from Patience first and Nigel second? Or could Nigel have held back, forcing Paul to receive them in that order?"

"It's hard to say...wait, yes, now that you mention it, Nigel may have held back just a little."

"And then in what order did Paul serve the deacons?"

"He started on our side. He went to Nigel Tapster first, then me, then Cedric. Then he walked around the table and worked from the outside in on the other side—Patience, then Sam."

"Interesting," said Geoffrey. "So Nigel Tapster was the last to touch the tray before Paul took it and the first to select a glass. The fatal glass, as it turned out."

"Makes you think, doesn't it?" said Oliver conspiratorially.

"It certainly does," Geoffrey said, matching the tone of Oliver's remark and entirely overdoing the effect. If they had been alone, Oliver would have poked him somewhere sensitive.

"Thank you, Dougie," Oliver said hastily, shoving his notebook into his satchel and scooping up his raincoat before Dock could ask any questions.

"Yes, thank you, Double-Dee," Geoffrey added, before Oliver could stop him. "I'll make sure we spell your name right. Now we have to fly. Deadlines, you know."

"Well, I'm glad to be of service," Dock answered, executing a flamboyant courtly bow while looking around to see if any of his colleagues were watching him, intrigued and envious. They weren't. In fact, they were all putting on coats and gathering bags of gifts that they had surreptitiously exchanged while he was occupied with Oliver and Geoffrey.

"Where are you going?" he asked, with exaggerated amazement.

"Home time," Clovis rasped, wrapping a long scarf several times around his neck.

"But the party's not over," Dock protested. "I have lots of other games for you, conundrums to guess. And we haven't played charades."

"We're sorry, but it's time to go," Marge declared as she buttoned her coat. She and Cissie headed determinedly for the door, arm in arm, while the laggards were forced to sidestep Dock's attempts to waylay them.

"Okay, then what's significant about the information he just gave us?" Geoffrey whispered.

Oliver smiled. "I have absolutely no bloody idea whatsoever," he replied serenely.

◇◇◇

"Come in, Mr. Swithin. Come in, Mr…er…Angelwine," said Barry Foison graciously. "I've just got in from work, so I'd appreciate a chance to slip into some casual clothes. Do you mind waiting?"

He pointed them into the living room of his small apartment, above an off-license not far from the church.

"What is it about me?" Geoffrey griped, throwing himself onto a sofa. "Why is there always that hesitation?"

Oliver gazed at him critically. "Well, right now, I'd say it's because you're wearing a green paper crown. Very festive."

Geoffrey snatched the crown from his scalp and crumpled it into a ball. Oliver yawned and gazed around the room. Foison had managed to cram a large amount of furniture into the small space, including an upright piano and an electronic keyboard, without making the room seem like an obstacle course. Oliver envied that skill.

"Listen, Geoff," he said, with a wary glance toward the kitchen door, "while we have a second, can you remember a biblical verse about taking poison?"

Geoffrey linked his fingers and cracked his knuckles. He thought for a second. "'And these signs shall follow them that believe: In my name shall they cast out devils; they shall speak with new tongues; they shall take up serpents; and if they drink any deadly thing, it shall not hurt them.' Mark, chapter sixteen, verses seventeen and eighteen."

"Well done. That's the one Tapster himself quoted to me."

"Do you think Tapster was giving himself some public test of his faith, to see if he could live up to these predictions? Like the snake-handling sects in America?"

"I don't know. The more I think about the wineglasses, the more it seems that the only man who could have poisoned Tapster's glass with no possibility of error was Tapster himself. But I don't think this was a suicide—not with such a terrible, agonizing method of self-destruction."

"Could he have over-estimated the dosage? Maybe he wanted to produce some of the effects of strychnine poisoning without taking a fatal amount?"

"Effie told me strychnine is all or nothing. In small doses, it doesn't have any effect. And why would Tapster try to poison himself partly? If he wanted to produce some weird religious seizure, I'm sure he could have faked it. No, I think it more likely that if Tapster himself poisoned the glass, he meant it for someone else. But then how did he pick it up again by mistake?"

They broke off the conversation when Foison reappeared, having changed from a double-breasted business suit into a loose sweatshirt and jeans. Oliver explained again that he wanted to change the focus of his article, and he let Foison describe what he had seen of the Communion service from his place in the third row of the congregation. The young man's account matched the briefing Oliver had received from Effie, and confirmed Dock's report of the order in which the deacons had been served by Paul Piltdown. Foison had not noticed any unusual handling of the wineglasses that could adequately explain how the strychnine ended up in Tapster's glass.

"Is there any way the glasses could have been tampered with earlier?" Oliver asked. "Before the Communion service began, I mean, while they were in the side room." He hoped Foison wouldn't interpret the question as an accusation.

"Absolutely not," Foison answered swiftly. "You see, I thought there was an open bottle of Communion wine left over from last time, which would have been enough for all the communicants that morning. But I must have been mistaken or somebody must have taken it, as I discovered when I went out during the third hymn. And I didn't have a corkscrew with me for the new bottle. So when the sermon ended, I nipped outside to get my Swiss Army knife, which I'd left in my car, and then I went back and opened the fresh bottle."

"Perhaps you have a secret lush among the deacons?"

Foison giggled, covering his mouth with his fingertips. "Perhaps, although half a bottle of old Communion wine wouldn't do much for them."

"Too stale?"

"Communion wine is nonalcoholic in the nonconformist church. More like grape juice."

"Interesting," Oliver commented. "And so you were with the wine all the time while it was in the side room."

"Well, I left it for half a minute while I carried out the bread to the Communion table."

"Was anyone in the room at that time?"

Foison placed his index finger over his lips. "Not that I remember," he said eventually. "Oh wait, yes. There was one person. Nigel Tapster himself. But *he* wouldn't have poisoned the wine, unless he was planning on killing himself. And that wasn't our Mr. Tapster's style. He was way too fond of life."

"Nobody else was back there?"

"Dougie Dock was teaching Sunday School in one of the rear rooms, but he always uses the door on the other side of the church. And he was with the children all the time."

"So why do you think Tapster was behind the scenes at that time?"

"As I told the police, I assumed he had just gone to use the toilet."

Effie had forgotten to mention Tapster's appearance in the side room, and for some reason, it struck Oliver as important. He would need to think this through later.

"That reminds me, may I use your bathroom?" Geoffrey asked suddenly. Foison pointed him in the right direction, and Geoffrey left the room, giving Oliver an elaborate wink behind their host's back.

"What did you mean when you said Tapster was too fond of life?" Oliver inquired.

Foison grimaced. "I think Nigel Tapster was an opportunist. And I think he was about to take a few opportunities in Plumley. He should never have won that diaconal seat, and I have no idea how he wangled it."

"So, in a way, his murder came at a fortunate time."

"I would never condone the breaking of a commandment, Mr. Swithin. Well, not that particular one, anyway. But I don't think his demise at this time was a coincidence."

"You think he was killed by someone who feared his growing influence?"

"I do."

Foison tugged at his sweatshirt, pulling it forward in loose bunches, as if he couldn't bear for the fabric to touch his chest.

"When we met the first time," Oliver remarked, "you were about to tell me something in Tapster's past. At a previous church?"

"Oh yes, at Thripstone Central Diaconalist. This all started more than two years ago, before Heather arrived on the scene, you understand. Nigel began to get up to the same tricks there—attracting a group of young people around him, meeting in his home, claiming a new spiritual rebirth, performing exorcisms on confused adolescents. It all got rather cultlike, and the deacons and church members became very nervous. And then Nigel got a little too close to one of his female followers."

"Underage?"

"Borderline. Fortunately, no harm was done, and it sounds as if the little minx flung herself at him in a fit of hero worship—if you can see Tapster as a hero—but he showed less-than-perfect discretion. The church used the incident as an excuse to send him packing."

"And then Heather came back from Brazil, and Nigel switched his affection to someone closer to his own age?"

Foison gave a bray of high-pitched laughter. "Hardly, my dear. They'd already paired up before this dalliance took place."

"Then why did she marry him?"

"I think dear Heather saw her marriage as a business merger rather than two hearts beating as one. She wants to be the mother of a cult as much as he wanted to be the father, for largely the same reason, minus the sex. Oh, I have little doubt that she read him the riot act about keeping his hands off the youthful merchandise in Plumley—at least in the early stages of their master plan—but it was as much for their credibility as it was for marital harmony."

A cynic might speculate that Heather Tapster's convulsive outpouring of grief, witnessed by Patience Coppersmith and Tish Belfry, was not so much for the loss of a beloved husband as for the frustration of her hopes for personal power and glory. Would she have reacted differently, Oliver wondered, if she had known about Nigel's impregnation of Tina? And could the Two Witnesses now operate as One? That reminded Oliver of a question he needed to ask Foison.

"Barry, you live near the church. Have you ever seen a young woman with long red hair either at the church or in this area?"

Foison started a little. "Is this some witness you're looking for?" he asked slowly.

"Possibly. Does it sound like someone you know? Maybe someone who was part of Nigel's cult at Thripstone, if you can remember that far back."

A sudden wave of anger swept across Foison's delicate features. "Oh, I can remember, Oliver," he said emphatically. "Do you want to know why? Two years ago, I was part of Nigel's cult too, singing 'Hallelujah' with the rest of them and listening to the gospel according to Tapster, until Nigel's concupiscence and Heather's manipulative ambitiousness could no longer be ignored. That was quite a fall from grace, I can tell you. If it weren't for Paul Piltdown, I think I would have lost my faith entirely."

He subsided in the chair. Geoffrey reappeared, a broad grin on his birdlike face.

"Barry," he crowed. "I know your secret."

"I beg your pardon?"

"I know your secret. It wasn't hard to guess, when you've had a little experience as a detective."

Oliver groaned and covered his face with his hands. Foison hesitated, flitting back and forth between experimental expressions of bewilderment and umbrage. Then he seemed to deflate slightly.

"What gave it away?" he asked ruefully. "I thought I'd been so damn careful about hiding things, knowing I was going to have visitors this afternoon."

Oliver looked up sharply. Geoffrey walked over to Foison, holding something almost invisible between his finger and thumb. "Here's one of the clues, found on the bathroom floor. The razor in the bathtub was another."

Foison reached out and took the object. "Very clever," he said. "Quite ingenious, in fact. You've certainly done better than the police, Mr. Angelwine, although as soon as they arrested Paul Piltdown, their interest in me diminished."

"Well, you did a good job of covering your tracks, I must say, you sly old dog," Geoffrey said, punching Foison gently in the back.

"Look, I hate to interrupt this lovefest, but will someone kindly tell me what's going on?" Oliver demanded. Foison and Geoffrey looked at each other with polite good humor, and then Foison passed the object to Oliver.

It was a long red hair.

"What your perceptive friend has discovered, Oliver," Foison began, while Geoffrey sat down behind him and beamed sickeningly at Oliver, "is that I am a preoperative transsexual."

For some reason, the smirk vanished from Geoffrey's face and was replaced with an expression of pure mystification. Not noticing, Foison continued his story.

"Strangely enough, it all follows from what I was just telling you. My unhappy experiences at Thripstone caused me to take a good, long look at myself, and with help from a psychiatric counselor and spiritual guidance from Paul Piltdown, I determined what I had unconsciously known all my life, that I am really a woman trapped in a man's body. This acceptance of my sexual identity has been the truly transformative experience of my life."

Geoffrey, who had been shaking his head and mouthing the word "no," now looked as if he were about to interrupt the tale.

"Er, where are you now in the...sex change?" Oliver asked quickly.

"I prefer the term 'gender reassignment,'" Foison said. "It's a little less Myra Breckinridge. I'm taking estrogen and I have started electrolysis on my face, although I still need to shave my legs before putting on a pair of pantyhose. That's why there's a razor in the bath, as Geoffrey so cleverly spotted. And for the moment, my glorious hair is merely a wig."

"So you're already living as a woman for part of the time."

"Life experience is essential to the process, before I go under the knife."

Oliver and Geoffrey crossed their legs.

"And I already have boobs," Foison continued, "thanks to the hormones. I have to be careful what I wear when I'm still dressed as a man. Loose clothes only. Yes, I'm rather proud of my pert little knockers. Do you want to see them?"

He sat up and gathered his sweatshirt at the waist.

"That won't be necessary!" Oliver said hurriedly. Geoffrey looked disappointed.

"Fair enough," said Foison, leaning back in his chair. "Just don't change your mind when Oona has them. She would slap your face."

"Oona is your alter ego, I take it."

"Oona is my future," he purred. "She's a gorgeous, lithe young redhead who takes no shit from anyone. Quite a contrast to squeaky, effeminate Barry. I have to become Oona several times a week. I often visit Paul Piltdown as Oona, after dark. I was on my way there last Thursday when I saw you and Paul coming along the street and decided it would be better for his reputation if I made myself scarce."

"I trust my old friend Paul has always behaved toward Oona like a perfect gentleman?"

Foison laughed again behind his hand. "My dear, I can assure you Paul has no interest in Oona whatsoever. And vice versa. Although why bring vice into this?"

"And Oona is going to play the organ at tomorrow night's service?"

"Yes indeed. She's a much better musician than I am. The fluency of touch that Oona liberated at the keyboard, despite her false fingernails, confirmed that I was better off in every way as a woman. I couldn't be the regular Plumley organist as Barry, you see, because the preparation for the transformation kept me away from church too much."

"You hope the Diaconalists of Plumley will be overcome with the Christmas spirit and welcome Oona with open arms?"

"I hope my fellow congregants won't realize it's me. Not this time. I really want them to judge my organ playing on its merits. There'll be time to see how they react to the transgendering later. With Christian love and tolerance, I trust."

Oliver nodded and idly wrapped the stray hair from Oona's wig around his forefinger. "Barry, I really appreciate your assistance and your candor. Please be assured that Geoffrey and I will respect your confidence. Before we leave you, however, I have one last question." He closed his notebook sharply and leaned forward. "Why did Oona paint a biblical quotation on the church door last Sunday?"

On reflection, Oliver had to admit to himself that the question didn't quite have the impact of "Where were you on the night of the twenty-fourth?" or "When did you last see your father?" In fact, it sounded like the sort of ludicrous phrase dished out for one of Dougie Dock's party games, in which one team had to conclude a story with that sentence, while the other was striving to get to "And with a gurgle, Colonel Milkthistle unplugged his toaster and jumped into the millpond." But the effect on Foison was as electrifying as if Oliver had grabbed the stylish Italian desklamp and shone it into the young man's face. He jumped to his feet.

"How did you know it was her…him…me?" he cried, pacing nervously.

"You were seen," Oliver told him, remembering his conversation with the retiring Mr. Tooth.

"That's impossible, I looked all around!" He wiped a hand across his face. "Oh damn it, I just confessed didn't I?" he added.

"We're not the police," Geoffrey reminded him.

"I know, I know," Foison replied distractedly. "But I shouldn't have done it. Doesn't it come under the heading of obstruction of justice?"

"That depends on why you painted it," Oliver observed, remembering the analysis of the prophecy. "Was it meant as a threat against Heather?"

"Good heavens, no! Is that what the police thought?"

"Either that or the opposite—a defiant prediction of Nigel's resurrection."

Foison stopped, aghast.

"I never thought of that either," he stammered.

"Then what was it supposed to mean?"

"It wasn't supposed to mean anything," Foison said with exasperation. "It didn't really matter what it said. What mattered was that it was there. I thought the police would assume the murderer had painted it, as a crazy reference to the notions that Nigel and Heather had about themselves."

"Why?"

"Why?" Foison frowned, as if the explanation should have been unnecessary. "Because if you thought the murderer was still loose, you'd know that Paul wasn't guilty. I did it to help him. I know Paul. He didn't kill Tapster."

But did you? thought Oliver. Although at the end of his day of detection, he was still too polite to ask. And too confused to know the answer.

They arrived back at the police station at six o'clock and took their former seats in the waiting area. Effie came out to meet them, and Oliver went over the additional information he had gleaned that afternoon, although he confessed that none of it had brought him closer to identifying the murderer.

"Look, Ollie," Effie was saying, "if Paul is innocent, then one of the people you interviewed is lying to you. Which one?"

"I have no idea," Oliver admitted. "If pressed, I'd say they were all telling the truth. Even if we had to prod a bit to get it. Congratulations on that, Geoff, by the way."

Geoffrey acknowledged Oliver's compliment with a distracted grunt. His attention was riveted on the door that led to the CID section in the hope that Tish Belfry would make an entrance.

"What happened?" asked Effie.

"Oh, after my warning Geoff to stay away from the amateur detective stuff, he defies me completely and discovers the elusive Oona lurking in Barry Foison's bathroom. It was utterly brilliant."

"Well done, young Angelwine," Effie said generously.

Geoffrey grunted again, but seemed unwilling to pursue the conversation.

"Any progress on the Tina Quarterboy front?" Oliver asked.

Effie's face fell. "Nothing came out of this morning's house-to-house around the church. I've circulated Tina's description to the doctors and hospitals in the area, in case her pregnancy drives her to seek medical treatment. But I'm beginning to think we won't see that young lady until she decides to come home of her own accord. I just hope, wherever she it, that she's getting the right nutrition for herself and for her baby."

"Are you working tonight?" Oliver asked quietly. "I could ditch the Angelwine and we could have a nice romantic supper."

Effie leaned closer to him. "I can't get away just yet," she answered, "but I'm off tomorrow afternoon until the day after Boxing Day. I know you're going down to your parents for Christmas. Will I see you before then?"

"I thought I'd go to tomorrow evening's carol service at the church. Will you join me?"

"It's a date," she said, kissing him swiftly on the nose. Oliver watched her walk away, appreciating the rare opportunity to view her from this angle.

"Ollie," said Geoffrey softly.

"Yes."

"Can I confess something?"

"You mean that you had no idea Barry Foison was a transsexual?"

"That would be it, yes." He smiled weakly. Oliver patted him on the arm.

"Well, what did you think when you came bounding out of the bathroom, brandishing a hair and shouting 'Eureka!'?" he asked.

Geoffrey sighed. "I thought his big secret was that he was secretly living with a woman out of wedlock. I imagined the hair was hers. And what would a man want with a razor in the bathtub?"

"Lots of men shave in the bath or the shower. The water softens their bristles. Someday, when you start shaving, you'll appreciate that. No, if you want to check on the number of people in a household, count the toothbrushes."

He checked his watch. Too late now to go shopping for Effie's Christmas present. He would have to purchase it tomorrow and give it to her at the carol service. There would be time now that his day as a detective was officially over—unless he hit upon the solution to the baffling crime in the meantime. "Shall we go home?" he asked wearily.

Geoffrey sighed again—a deeper, love struck sigh this time, which seemed to have magical powers, since Tish Belfry suddenly walked in through the front door, arguing with a tall, balding man. Given a forced-choice test, Oliver would have categorized him as a detective rather than a stick insect, but it was a close-run thing.

"He's under arrest and bail was denied," Tish declared as they passed. "Let the courts deal with him."

"All I'm saying, Tish," Detective Constable Paddock replied condescendingly, "is that DI Welkin could have got a confession out of him if he'd tried."

Tish stopped, eager to end the discussion before they reached the incident room. "Welkin did try, Graham. I was there," she stated, glaring up at Paddock. "He gave the vicar every opportunity to admit to the murder."

"Oh yeah? Well, all I can say is that he didn't try hard enough. *Hard* enough, get it?" Paddock slammed a gloved fist into his other hand. Then he feigned a look of profound puzzlement. "Or perhaps you don't?" he added with an unpleasant smirk.

Tish flinched with sudden humiliation. She became aware of Oliver and Geoffrey watching them, and lowered her voice as she continued the conversation.

"Quick, introduce me!" Geoffrey hissed.

"What?"

"That nasty scarecrow just insulted Tish Belfry. I must defend her honor. Introduce me to her, and then I can tell him to stop talking to my beloved like that."

"I'm not going to interrupt Tish while she's talking to a colleague. Wait until she's finished."

"That'll be too late," Geoffrey muttered, standing up and approaching the two detectives.

"...don't appreciate that kind of humor," Tish was saying, staring intently at her colleague. "I never have."

"Oh, lighten up," Paddock countered contemptuously. "Bloody policewomen, can never take a joke."

"Police *officer*, Graham, just like you."

Paddock stood back and looked pointedly at her chest. "Now, now, Tishy, I can think of couple of ways you're not a bit like me."

He was about to look up at her face again, a twisted leer on his own, when Geoffrey slid in between them.

"Detective Constable Belfry," he began, "my name's…"

Geoffrey stopped, intercepting the full force of Tish's carefully prepared expression. Behind him, Paddock gasped as he too made eye contact with Tish, and an initial flash of abject shame gave way to a host of memories parading through his mind—mainly incidents of disreputable behavior toward the opposite sex, which he now deeply regretted. Geoffrey's mind went blank. Having experienced very few non-imaginary incidents involving the opposite sex, disreputable or otherwise, he simply reeled as if he'd been slapped in the face with a large haddock, and staggered back to the seat beside Oliver.

"Double-barreled," murmured Oliver approvingly, with a nod toward Tish.

"You know, Ollie, you're probably right," Geoffrey panted, trying to recover his breath. "It *is* impolite to speak to a lady before you've been properly introduced."

◇◇◇

The hallway telephone was ringing when Oliver and Geoffrey arrived home that evening. Geoffrey ignored it and headed straight to the kitchen cabinet, where he kept a small bottle of cooking sherry. Oliver picked up the phone.

"Battersea Dog's Home," he announced.

"Ah, good, it is you, Ollie." Mallard's voice, jovial for once. "I'm calling from the Yard."

"What are you doing in the backyard?" Oliver asked. "And shouldn't you be backstage in Theydon Bois, preparing your rebuttal?"

Mallard was clearly so happy to be back in his spiritual home that he was prepared to overlook the jokes. "I gave my final, farewell performance as Bottom last night," he declared. "I thought I'd see how your day went, before I set off for home."

"Why are you at work? Oh yes, you said something about helping your archnemesis, Assistant Commissioner Weed. I thought he was the one who was trying to keep you away from the place. What's that all about?"

Mallard paused, and Oliver could hear his breathing down the line. "Look, Ollie, this is strictly confidential, of course. It seems that Weed is developing a little…personal problem. It all began Saturday night, when he started to notice an odd smell in his office. He got the cleaners to go in on Sunday, but the smell was still there yesterday morning. So during the day, Weed had the maintenance people go through the duct-work and the heating system to see if they could find a dead mouse or bird, because that's what it smelled like, frankly. They didn't find a thing. But the pong is still there and, oddly, it's only noticeable in his office. Well, naturally, some of Weed's less-than-charitable colleagues are beginning to hint that it's not the office but the incumbent who might be the source of the aroma. So yesterday, just before I met you and Effie, I called to offer Weed some confidential diagnostics, based on that special project I did on the relationship between bodily odors and nutritional imbalance."

"You never did any project like that!"

"Maybe, but Weed doesn't know that. I popped in this afternoon to do my assessment."

"And the pong?"

"Strong. And getting stronger, according to DS Moldwarp, who's been monitoring the situation with great glee, although you'd never think it to look at him. So I left out a few petri dishes filled with chemicals overnight, and tomorrow I shall give the assistant commissioner my analysis. He is most grateful for my discretion, as you can imagine."

"How grateful, exactly?"

"Not as grateful as I intend him to be. So how was the day of detection?"

Oliver told his uncle what he had learned from the suspects, repeating his conviction that they had all been telling him the truth, perhaps not the whole truth, but certainly nothing but the truth.

"Ah, what is truth?" Mallard intoned. "But did you come across anything that might exonerate young Paul?"

"I feel there's a two and a two somewhere in my notes that are screaming to be made into a four, but I can't put my finger on it. I need to give it some thought."

"Good idea," said his uncle. "Sleep on it."

Chapter Eight

Unto Us a Child Is Given

Wednesday, December 24 (Christmas Eve)

Although Oliver occasionally deplored Susie's morals, he admired their consistency. It was a matter of honor that, no matter where she spent the rest of the night after she closed up her restaurant, she always came home for breakfast. "I may be a slut," she would declare happily, "but I'm not a trollop," a distinction that was crystal-clear to the three men who shared the house.

When Oliver stumbled into the kitchen, Susie was standing at one of the counters, staring at a packet of cornflakes and apparently looking for instructions.

"You're up early!" he said huskily.

"I haven't been to bed," she trilled. "Or rather, I haven't been to sleep. I just got home. Want some of my special coffee?"

"No thank you," Oliver answered very quickly. "I'll make myself some tea."

"I'll put the kettle on for you," she offered. Oliver watched her dubiously. It was just possible that Susie could burn water.

"You're early, too," she said, abandoning the cereal box and filling the kettle.

"I woke up cross. I was dreaming, I think."

"Ooh, goody. Something juicy to start your Auntie Susie's day with a bang, although you're already too late for that? It's not that dream where you and Geoffrey Angelwine are climbing Cleopatra's Needle, is it?"

Oliver overlooked the comment and sat down at the kitchen table. "'I have had a dream…past the wit of man to say what dream it was.'"

"What?"

"Shakespeare. *A Midsummer Night's Dream*. It's Bottom's speech, when he wakes up after losing his ass's head. Uncle Tim did it rather well last week."

Susie glared around the room, in search of the coffeemaker. It may have been a trick of the light, but it seemed to Oliver that the machine was trying to shrink back out of sight between the biscuit tin and Susie's broken food processor.

"Well, midsummer's day is traditionally June 24," she said. "Today is Christmas Eve, exactly six months later, so perhaps this was your Midwinter Night's Dream. Was is bleak?"

Oliver rubbed sleep from his eyes. "It's already fading. I think it had a lot to do with this murder and all the people I was talking to yesterday."

Susie spun around and pointed at him with a spatula. "Quick, what's the one thing that was on your mind when you woke up?"

"Breakfast."

She sighed. "All right, I'll make you breakfast," she said dejectedly. "But I meant what one thing did you remember from the dream?"

"That's was it—breakfast," Oliver maintained, now fearful that Susie's misunderstanding might sabotage his digestive health for the entire Christmas holiday. "Breakfast was somehow in my dream. And I woke up asking how did the strychnine get into the glass."

"Yes, but you probably went to sleep asking that one. It's been on your mind since Sunday. But you know what they say: When you have eliminated six impossible things before breakfast, whatever remains, however improbable, must be the truth.

Now you just sit there, and I'll whip you up a cooked breakfast. Do you want some orange juice? I'll leave out the strychnine."

Oliver sat, nursing his glass of juice, and repeating the question to himself, while Susie foraged in the refrigerator.

How did the strychnine get into the glass?

He had asked them all the day before—all the people on the platform who had the opportunity to lace the wineglass with the deadly poison. They had all denied it, and all denied seeing Piltdown tamper with the glasses, and it had sounded like the truth. But what is truth? said jesting Pilate; and would not stay for an answer. At least Pilate washed his hands. And who wrote that crack about jesting Pilate?

"Bacon," he murmured, remembering.

"We don't have any," Susie answered. "I'm frying some tofu sausages instead."

How did the strychnine get into the glass? Tapster's reaction was more or less instantaneous, yet strychnine took time to work—ten minutes at least, usually longer. Yes, you could cut the time to the bare minimum by delivering it dissolved in something, especially something that would disguise its bitterness, such as alcohol. But wait—the Communion wine didn't contain any alcohol, that wouldn't work. The more Oliver thought about it, the more it seemed an impossible crime. And yet, when you have eliminated the impossible…

How did the strychnine get into the glass?

Did the strychnine get into the glass?

Well, yes. The police scientists had found it there, with Tapster's dying spit. But was it the only source? What if Tapster had ingested the poison earlier, within the fatal ten to twenty minutes needed for it to take effect, which meant it had to be after he had walked into the church that morning? What else could he have eaten? Maybe he chewed a breath mint or munched on a stale Jaffa Cake while he was taking a piss—no, when the pathologist sliced open the dead man's stomach, he found only his breakfast. Then maybe that trace of breakfast honey he licked from his fingers was big enough to hold the fatal dose of strychnine, or maybe…

"Breakfast!" he exclaimed.

"It's coming, sweetie, don't get your undies in an uproar," called Susie, attempting to beat a large cast-iron frying pan into submission.

"Thank you, Susie, but I have to pass. I need to go somewhere."

"Really?" she said in a disappointed voice, as he jumped up from the table and headed for the hallway telephone before the smoke caused his eyes to water. "Then did I solve the mystery again?"

"Naturally."

"Oh, good," she chuckled, reaching for the kitchen fire extinguisher as a precaution.

◇◇◇

An hour later, Oliver was sitting in another kitchen, waiting for Effie. He was hungry, but he had already guessed that the pantry had been emptied of anything readily edible, and an inspection proved him right.

He had last been in the manse only two days earlier, but a tour of the upstairs today revealed a marked deterioration in tidiness, even though the house's only regular occupant was still in prison. The disorder had to be the result of a thorough search by Detective Inspector Welkin's minions, no doubt sanctioned by a warrant issued after Piltdown was formally arrested, on suspicion of being the murderer of Nigel Tapster.

Whoever had searched downstairs had been less disruptive, perhaps conscious that the reception rooms and kitchen were often in the service of the church. Or perhaps somebody else had come in and tidied up afterwards. Oliver knew the church could not afford to provide its minister with a housekeeper, but it was possible that a benevolent churchgoer knew about the unlocked side door, which he had used himself a few minutes earlier.

The doorbell rang. He walked through the house and pulled Effie inside as quickly as possible, out of the morning's freezing rain. She kissed him once—deep and crisp and even was the description that sprang to his mind—then pushed him away.

"We're alone, but I'm on duty," she explained as he led her back to the kitchen. "So that was my compromise." She glanced at the room. "I see the lads have been through here."

"How can you tell?"

Effie ran a hand along the front edge of the sink. "It's been dusted," she said, holding up a powdery finger.

Oliver sat down on a kitchen chair and gestured for her to take another seat at the table. She draped her coat over the chair, but began to wander around the room.

"I took Uncle Tim's advice," he began. "I slept on it. And I woke up this morning with an idea or two that I'd like to bounce off you. If I'm right, this may get us closer to wrapping up more than one case."

Wrapping up. Blast, would he still have time to think of, purchase, and wrap a gift for Effie before the end of the day? She had paused behind him.

"Dearest Oliver," she said thoughtfully. "One of those cases must be Tapster's murder. Would I be right in thinking that Tina Quarterboy's disappearance is the other one?"

"Yes."

"Aha. Take off your glasses," she said, strolling enticingly around him.

"What?"

"Take off your glasses," she repeated seductively. He removed his cheap spectacles, a precaution he often followed before he and Effie indulged in some serious mutual lip manipulation. Perhaps, out of advance gratitude for his help with Tina, she had reconsidered her earlier compromise?

Puzzled, he watched Effie's dim outline dart across the room and grab something from the kitchen sink. He only just had time to fling his arms over his head before she began to flog him across his shoulders with a tea towel.

"Oliver…Chrysostom…Swithin!" she fumed, punctuating each name with a highly accurate thrash of the cloth. "If you know where Tina Quarterboy is and you've been holding out on me, I swear I'll stuff the turkey with you! Or vice versa!"

She switched her target area and swatted his unprotected kneecaps several times. Then she paused, out of breath, glaring at him.

"Can I answer now?" he whimpered, lowering his arms cautiously. Effie thought for a second, then nodded.

"I didn't figure it out until I woke up, I promise. And the very first thing I did was call you and get you to meet me here."

"Why here?" she demanded.

"Because Tina has been here."

"I know she's been here—Tish Belfry told me her fingerprints were all over the sitting room piano. Piltdown was the local vicar. He had a lot of his parishioners in for tea."

"No, no, I mean Tina's been here since she ran away," Oliver answered swiftly, choosing not to correct Effie's religious terminology. "In this house. In this kitchen. That's what I wanted to tell you, in private, so you wouldn't have to let Welkin know that I've been helping."

A well-aimed flick of the tea towel cracked uncomfortably close to his left ear. "Oliver," she said in a cold, low voice, "I don't give an aerial knee-trembler *who* gets the fornicating credit for this, just as long as we deliver this frightened, pregnant teenager to a doctor sooner than is humanly possible, and I get to go home and spend some quality Yuletide with whatever's left of my boyfriend. Now talk."

"Fair enough. You see, I woke up thinking about breakfast."

"What?" she asked, with a flawless balance of menace and astonishment.

"Breakfast," he repeated. "Even though I still haven't had any, incidentally. And it was appropriate to both cases, but I'll start with Tina—Nigel Tapster's already dead, he won't mind waiting."

"Will you please get to the point!" Effie was wrapping the tea towel around her hand, testing her grip.

"Well, when I came here last Thursday, after visiting Tapster, I spent a merry half-hour with Paul doing the washing up at that very sink, possibly employing that very tea towel. He hadn't touched the dishes since the previous Sunday. But on Monday afternoon, when I was getting Paul a change of clothes, I noticed that his breakfast things from the previous day were already washed up."

"Perhaps you shamed him into turning over a new leaf?"

Oliver snorted scornfully. "Not Paul. He only had a short time between finishing his breakfast and starting the morning service in the church. I can guarantee that he wouldn't have used that time to do the washing up. And nobody was supposed to have been in the house since Sunday morning, including Paul, who's been under arrest. Also, his bed was made—trust me, no single man living alone would stop on a Sunday morning to make his bed. Certainly not one whose drawers are as untidy as Paul's. I'm referring to his chest of drawers, of course."

Even at a less tense moment, Effie would have ignored the joke. "So you think Tina Quarterboy is Paul's phantom housekeeper?" she asked.

"Yes. The one time I saw her, she couldn't do enough to help him in the kitchen."

"And she's been hiding out here in the manse all the time?"

Oliver shook his head. "I don't think she's been spending her nights here, and she's certainly not here now—I checked all through the house before you arrived. But I do think she's been raiding the larder when she got hungry. She must have known about the unlocked side door. Remember Paul's apologies on Saturday for being unexpectedly out of Jaffa Cakes and other foodstuffs that he thought he had? And I'm sure I heard someone moving about downstairs when I was here on Monday. That must mean Tina's somewhere in this area, and if she's stealing food she's probably not staying in somebody's home."

"That would tie in with the complaints I was getting yesterday about milk and other groceries disappearing from doorsteps in the neighborhood," Effie speculated. "If you're right, I bet Tina herself is responsible for the thefts."

She dropped the tea towel on the table. "You can put your glasses on," she said, resuming her catlike prowling of the kitchen. "I've decided to like you again."

"So did I help?" Oliver asked her eagerly.

"Well, I'd say a more intensive search of this neighborhood is warranted," she conceded. "I'll have to see who Welkin can spare this morning. We'll need to check sheds and garages, empty houses, old warehouses, that sort of thing."

"How about the church next door? The side door to the building and the side door to the manse are practically in line. Tina could easily get from one to the other by climbing over the fence, and she wouldn't have to show her face on the street."

"Yes, but the church is kept locked, isn't it? And I don't know where she could hide in there. She disappeared Friday morning. The building was in use Saturday—we were there, remember?—and it's been a crime scene since Sunday afternoon. Even the Plumley plod would have noticed signs of an illegal occupant."

Oliver stood up and produced a key, which he dangled in front of her face. "Want to check?" he asked.

The cavernous church was cold and damp. Since Oliver and Effie did not know where the light switches were located, they sat in the gloom, in the same rear pew where Effie had witnessed the Communion service three days earlier. A tour of the rooms behind the sanctuary had failed to produce Tina.

"Where did you get the key?" she asked softly, maintaining the obligatory reverent hush. "Paul said he'd lost his set."

"I called on Barry Foison before I went to the manse. Oona answered the door. She's not the worst thing a man could lay eyes on first thing in the morning," he added mischievously.

"You *were* a busy little bee before I arrived," Effie muttered. "So how about breakfast?"

"Oh splendid, if you have time," Oliver said gratefully, reaching for his coat. "I'm starving."

"I meant you were going to tell me how breakfast affects the Tapster case," she said. He dropped his coat.

"It's about the traces of honey on Tapster's fingers," he began. "I first thought he had besmirched himself when he was sweetening his breakfast tea, just as he did that evening when I went to see him. But then yesterday, Barry Foison told me that Tapster went to the toilet just before the Communion service on Sunday morning."

"We think that's why he went out of the church, but nobody's one hundred percent sure. Why?"

"Tapster was a cleanliness freak. If he *had* gone to take a pee, he would certainly have scrubbed his hands clean afterwards."

"Then where did the honey come from?"

Oliver stared ahead at the dim outlines of table and chairs on the deserted platform, trying to conjure the ghostly figures of the suspects and their victim performing the solemn Communion rite, like a clutch of Banquos taking their places at a feast. "If I want to kill someone with strychnine," he continued, "I need to disguise its bitter taste. There are classic cases of murderers using brandy or other alcoholic drinks to slip it to their victims. Then Communion wine, perhaps? The problem is that Diaconalist Communion wine contains no alcohol. And while strychnine is a fairly fast-acting poison, we're all agreed that Nigel's symptoms appeared too soon after he had drained his glass."

He turned to Effie. "But what better medium for strychnine than a taste of honey? Tasting much sweeter than wine. If the poison is already dissolved in something when it's administered, the body will absorb it more quickly. It should work in about ten minutes."

"But, Ollie," she said impatiently, "we always come back to the same objection. The pathologist found strychnine in Nigel's glass. And we know he drank from it, because it also contained traces of his saliva."

"Yes, I've been thinking about that. How did that saliva get into the glass? The communicants get a thimbleful of wine in a tiny shot-glass. They don't sip it daintily—they drain it at one go, like Cossacks drinking a vodka toast, although they balk at tossing the glasses into the fireplace. They certainly don't gargle with the blood of Christ and then dribble half of it back into the glass. Unless, of course, something makes them. Such as the first onset of the effects of strychnine, administered ten minutes earlier. An involuntary cry of pain or a loss of sensation in the jaw."

"But if the strychnine was administered earlier, how did it get in the glass?"

"Spat out with the wine and the saliva. Some of the strychnine-laced honey could easily have stuck to the inside of Tapster's mouth, washed out when he drank the sacrament."

Effie considered this for a few seconds. "It's like the stage-trick that Tim told us about," she declared. "A classic case of misdirection. Everybody thinks the poison was put in the wine, but it's already hard at work in the victim's digestive tract." She playfully ruffled Oliver's untidy fair hair. "Okay, Ollie, is this the point where I sit back baffled while you amaze me by naming the killer?"

"Hardly," he lamented, "since I still have no idea how the honey was slipped to Tapster or who did the slipping."

Effie threw an arm around his shoulder and hugged him awkwardly. "Hey, your mission was to exonerate Paul Piltdown, and if you're right—and please note I'm saying 'if'—Paul is clearly innocent."

"How do you know?"

"I was here, remember? I was off chasing Tina when Tapster first exhibited signs of poisoning. But if the strychnine was administered ten minutes earlier, then I was a witness. And I could swear that Paul didn't have any contact with Tapster during the critical period."

"What can you remember?"

Effie let go of him and sat forward in the pew, gripping the back of the row in front, as if riding a roller coaster. "I didn't get here until the final hymn," she reported. "It was 'O Little Town of Bethlehem,' one of my favorites. After it ended, Paul said a benediction, then we all sat and prayed. He walked through the church to the narthex, behind us, and some other people got ready to leave, including Heather Tapster. Oh, Dougie Dock and some Sunday School kids came in through the door on the right, the pulpit side."

"When did you first spot Tapster?"

"I don't remember seeing him until he emerged from the back room, through the door on the left—this was after Heather had departed. She'd been in the church the whole time, anyway, playing the piano. The deacons milled around at the front of the church until Paul returned from the narthex."

"Would Paul have had time to slip down that alleyway to the side entrance, meet Tapster, and then run back again?"

Effie's curls shook dismissively.

"The deacons all took their places on the platform," she continued. "Oh, Nigel Tapster had to get the piano stool, because Cedric Potiphar was an unexpected visitor to the stage, and they had run out of the ceremonial chairs."

"Ah, ze old poisoned piano stool ploy," Oliver said with a grin and an unimpressive French accent.

"Hardly, I didn't see Nigel chewing it. Well, the Communion service started, Nigel sang his song and…Wait!"

Her voice echoed off the bare walls.

"You've remembered something?" he asked.

She cocked her head on one side. "Nigel's guitar was out of tune," she stated.

"So it was the previous week. The guy had Van Gogh's ear for music. Did he make a big song and dance about tuning the instrument, complete with silly jokes?"

"Yes. Only I remember that he was looking really pained, just before he started singing."

"You're quite sure it wasn't just after?" Oliver asked sardonically.

"No, he was grimacing, wincing as he strummed the guitar. But it was in tune by then, so that can't have been a reaction to what he was hearing."

"Although it might have been a response to a sudden nasty taste in his mouth?"

"Yes!" she cried. "And that was also the point when I saw him suck on his finger—or maybe he was trying to brush away a strand of sticky honey he'd found on his lips."

"How much time passed before the first visible sign of poisoning?"

"Oh, at least ten minutes. There were a lot of prayers in between. Your friend Paul can really let rip when he wants to, and there were long readings as part of the order of service. Yes, Nigel must have eaten the poison at the very beginning of the service, just before his song. Possibly slightly earlier. The killer must have been counting on the fact that Nigel was giving a public performance—he couldn't stop and spit out whatever was tasting so foul, he'd just have to swallow it and get on with the show!"

"But you didn't see him put anything in his mouth?"

She thought hard. "No," she concluded sadly.

They sat in silence, oppressed by the drabness of their surroundings. There had been no Christmas tree erected in the church, and there were no signs yet of any preparation for the evening's service. A shifting in the low rain clouds caused the space to brighten, but only momentarily. Effie stretched self-indulgently, craning her neck back over the pew and staring at the balcony above her.

She froze. Then, illogically, she began to sing, in a soft, pure, childlike voice, the last lines of the carol she had heard on the morning of the murder.

"We hear the Christmas angels,
"The great glad tidings tell..."

Oliver had never heard her sing before, apart from half-hearted attempts to join in with rock music on her car radio, and to his disappointment, she broke off before she finished the verse.

"Ollie," she whispered excitedly, leaning in closely to his ear. "It's Christmas Eve. Do you believe in angels?"

Was this the moment that Effie had chosen to reveal some aspect of her personal theology? "I believe people think they see angels," he said diplomatically.

Effie got to her feet and began to edge her way out of the pew, watching him with an amused expression on her face.

"Danni saw an angel the other day," she said. "Remember? Right here, in a sunbeam."

She beckoned him silently. Intrigued, he followed her through the heavy curtain at the back of the sanctuary, across the narthex, and into the shallow vestibule, tracing the path that she had followed while pursuing Tina on the one occasion when she had seen the girl in the flesh. But this time, she didn't run out through the main church doors, which were closed. Instead, Effie turned to right and approached a locked door that nestled against the side wall of the vestibule. She peered at the lock.

"I left my bag in the pew," she hissed. "Give me a credit card."

Oliver fished out his wallet and mutely passed over his American Express card. She prodded it into the space between the doorjamb and the lock. The door sprang open. Oliver found himself tensing as Effie eased the door toward her.

Behind it was a closet containing an electricity meter and a dead mouse.

Without a word, she marched to an identical door on the other side of the vestibule and repeated the operation. The door opened on the fourth attempt. She handed back his card and carefully pulled the door open.

A narrow flight of wooden steps began behind the door and turned sharply left, ascending into darkness.

They began to climb, single file in the confined space, holding tightly to the crude handrails, Effie's low-heeled work shoes making more noise than Oliver's Nikes. The stairs turned back on themselves. Above them, a dim rectangle grew larger until it surrounded them, and they emerged at the back of the dusty, disused balcony, high above the church floor and level with the tops of the largest organ pipes, far away on the opposite wall. The space was well lit, with more daylight coming through the clear circular window behind their heads. Four rows of high-backed pews dropped steeply away between them and the balcony's parapet. There was an odd smell, mostly unpleasant.

Oliver made a move to walk down the single aisle between the pews, but Effie placed a hand on his arm.

"Tina," she called gently. "You can come out now."

Nothing happened at first. Then there was a faint rustle, and a small pale face appeared above the back of one of the pews, blinking in the light. The girl's dark hair was matted, and she was damp with perspiration.

"I'd prefer to be called Chrissie," she said. Then she vomited prodigiously.

◇◇◇

By the time Oliver returned from Plumley High Street with several Egg McMuffins and two pints of milk, Tina had taken a long, thorough bath and was sitting in the Manse kitchen wrapped in Paul Piltdown's terry bathrobe, with wet hair hanging in tendrils down her back. Effie had found an electric heater in Paul's bedroom and had brought it downstairs, and the girl was waving her slender bare feet in front of the glowing coils and talking. The breakfast, which she attacked gratefully and gracelessly, despite her earlier nausea, did little to slow her down.

"I spent a lot of Friday just wandering about during the day—I had already hidden my suitcase behind the church, early that morning, because I know nobody goes there, at least not until after dark, when it's best not to ask about the sort of things that take place, if you ask me. I'd taken some food from my mum, but it was all gone by the end of the day and I didn't have any more money to buy stuff, but when I came back to get my case later that afternoon—I was up the High Street during the day—I remembered that the manse door over there was always open. Paul must have been upstairs, so I snuck in and took some stuff from the pantry and then I decided I'd hide in the church for the night."

"Specifically, Chrissie, it was finding Paul's keys that gave you that idea, wasn't it?" Effie said, her eyes sparkling.

Tina looked shamefaced. "Will I get into trouble for all the stuff I've taken?" she asked humbly.

"No. I'll make sure everything's all right. Go on with your story."

Tina took a long gulp of milk. "Okay, well, the church was all right as a hideout. It was empty a lot of the time, and I could use the toilet. It got pretty cold at night, but I found some old blankets in a cupboard."

"And a half-finished bottle of Communion wine?" Oliver ventured.

"Yeah. Boy, that stuff was gross, really made me want to puke. Anyway, I knew when people were going to come in, 'cause my dad's the church secretary and he keeps track of meetings and stuff. There was a big church meeting on Friday night, which they held in one of the Sunday School rooms, and then there was that rehearsal on Saturday—I should have been there, I half thought about coming out, I'm a much better Virgin Mary than pigging Kylie Fenwick. All I had to do at those times was go up to the balcony. Nobody's been up there for years, you should have seen the dust and cobwebs I had to clear away."

"So it was you that Danni saw during the rehearsal on Saturday?" Oliver remarked, understanding Effie's earlier question about angels.

"I stood up to get a better view. I ducked down again before anyone else spotted me. You two were there then, weren't you?"

"Yes."

"Yes, I remember Sergeant Effie's hair. That's why I came down on Sunday, the next day, while you were sitting in the church. I could only see the top of your head from the balcony, and I wanted to see if it really was you. I got a bit distracted by seeing Nigel on the stage and you nearly caught me. I hid pretty quickly though, didn't I?"

"You certainly had me fooled," said Effie. The girl's timeline had reached Tapster's murder, but she wanted to curtail it for now. "It must have been really lonely in the church, all by yourself."

"I had my journal," she said stoically, through a mouth stuffed with french fries. "I've been writing. And for the last couple of days, I haven't felt very well, so I slept a lot, although I do feel a lot better now I've eaten a nutritious meal. When you're a writer, you lose all track of time, you know! There aren't enough hours in the day." She spoke authoritatively, which made Oliver feel strangely guilty.

"Oliver's a writer, you know," said Effie.

"Oh yes, he told me when I met him the other week. I explained then how much I like to write and how much I want to be a writer. And I told him the sort of things I like to write about."

"I was thinking that, maybe, you could ask him about his books?" Effie added tentatively. Tina paused, gazing at Oliver and considering the question as if it had never occurred to her.

"Are you two married?" she asked.

"Let's go back to Thursday evening, when you went to Nigel Tapster's house," said Effie hastily. "Did you go to see Nigel because he was your baby's father?"

Tina looked startled. "Oh, you know about that?"

"Afraid so."

"Babies are a gift from God," Tina declared. "When the doctor told me I was pregnant, I knew it was a special gift for Nigel and me. That's why I ran over to his home as soon as I found out. I wanted to tell him our good news, that this meant we could be together, no matter what my mum and dad said."

"But what did you think he would do about Heather, his wife?" Oliver asked gently. Tina glared at him as if he had spat in her ear.

"She didn't care about Nigel," she snapped. "She wasn't a good wife. I loved Nigel, I'd have made a wonderful wife, and a great mother for his baby. Heather wasn't giving him no babies—I'd heard her say as much. And she would laugh at him. She laughed when he sang to us, but I liked his voice. She used to say he couldn't keep in tune and he didn't know, because he didn't have perfect pitch like she did."

Oliver frowned.

"She thought she was a much better musician," Tina continued, "just because she could play the piano. But Nigel was a good guitarist too, much better than Billy. Heather was jealous, she used to make jokes, pull tricks, she'd even make his guitar go out of tune on purpose, I saw her. And she'd bash that tambourine too loud, so you couldn't hear him. I could tell Nigel didn't really like her. He would have taken me with open arms, if it weren't for her."

"Is that what he told you when saw him on Thursday?"

The girl did not answer, sullenly staring at her thin legs. Her eyes filled with tears.

"What did Nigel say?" Effie insisted.

"He thought it was a joke!" she burst out. "He said I had to be mistaken, but if I was going to have a baby, it had nothing to do with him. He even talked about me having an abortion. I heard my dad talk about abortions, and it's a sort of murder, isn't it? I thought Nigel wanted to kill me. He was the father of my baby and I thought he'd be pleased, but instead he wanted to kill me. So I ran away from him."

She began to weep noisily. Effie tore off a paper towel and passed it to her.

"And this is the same story you told the Reverend Mr. Piltdown when you went to see him?"

"Yes," Tina sniffed, wiping her eyes.

"You didn't go to Heather and tell her you were going to have Nigel's baby?" Oliver asked.

"I never saw Heather. I don't talk to Heather."

"You promised Mr. Piltdown that you were going to tell your parents about the baby when you got home."

"Uh-huh."

"Did you mean it?" Effie pressed before the girl lost her ability to speak, although Oliver was sure it would be a very temporary loss.

Tina nodded, talking in gulps. "Yes, but I really wasn't feeling well, and I wanted to understand what Nigel had told me, and when my dad looked in, I asked him about abortion and he told me it meant murder and he said what he thought about girls who got pregnant. It was as if he knew about me before

I told! That's when I decided to run away. They all hated me, apart from Mr. Piltdown!"

She gave herself up to sobbing, hunched over, her damp hair sticking to her shoulders.

"No wonder Paul was pissed off at Tapster," Oliver whispered to Effie, as they moved aside to give the girl time to recover. "Shouldn't you be taking her home? I have a feeling this interview is not quite kosher."

"I'll call the Quarterboys now," Effie conceded. "You're right, we certainly can't ask her anything about the murder, in case we need her answer as evidence in court later. She couldn't have seen anything I couldn't have seen, anyway."

"I'm not so sure about that. But I need to check on something. I'll call you in about an hour."

"You're leaving?"

He smiled. "You've solved your case. Mine's still open."

They talked further in low voices until Tina blew her nose noisily and Niagarally and attacked another McMuffin.

"Chrissie, let me ask you one more question before I go," said Oliver, pulling on his coat. "This is going to seem very odd and very personal, and I wouldn't ask it if it didn't really matter…"

◇◇◇

A rapid review of the last seven days told Oliver this was the eighth time he had made the trip to or from Plumley Central by tube. Normally he would have passed the half hour or so on the Underground train engrossed in one of the two novels that he always carried in his old leather satchel. Today, he was too excited to focus on anything more intellectually challenging than counting Underground trips and reviling Tina Quarterboy for eating his McMuffin. He hurtled through Tottenham Court Road station when he had to change from the Northern Line to the Central, and leaped off the second train when the doors opened at Holland Park, narrowly missing the three middle-aged ladies with beehive hairstyles who were jostling to get on. With no taxis visible on

Holland Park Avenue, he opted to join the well-swaddled joggers in the park and made it to Edwardes Square within five minutes, breathless and sweating, despite the frigid rain.

Susie Beamish had vacated the kitchen, leaving havoc in her wake, but Geoffrey Angelwine was sitting at the table, staring moodily into a coffee cup.

"Ah, Oliver," he said. "I need some advice. Do you think Tish Belfry would be impressed if—"

"You tattooed her name over your heart? Probably. Is Ben busy?" He didn't wait for the answer but stole Geoffrey's bacon and egg sandwich and clattered up the stairs to Ben's studio.

"That wasn't what I was going to say," Geoffrey mumbled to himself. "It's not a bad idea, though."

The studio door was closed. Oliver waited for a moment on the landing, emptying his mouth and trying to recover his breath, then he tapped on the door. There was no answer, but he became aware of the creaking of bedsprings, accompanied by high-pitched yelping.

"Ben," he hissed.

The rhythmic moans went on, going up a notch in volume on every third occurrence, with an occasional cadence that suggested their perpetrator was getting a series of progressively more pleasant surprises.

"Ben, it's me—Oliver. I need to talk to you."

Still louder, still higher in frequency, in both meanings of the phrase. Oliver could hear a deeper, percussive accompaniment, too, as if a headboard were beating time on an internal wall.

"Come on, Ben, knock it off," Oliver called out. "It's Christmas Eve, I know you don't have any clients."

The noises continued. Oliver sighed.

"Look, Susie told me about those times you pretended to be at work, just so I wouldn't bother you," he shouted. "Well, pack it up, I need your help."

The screaming was much more pronounced now, almost frenzied, joined by the snap of wet flesh slapping against more wet flesh.

"Very funny, Ben. It doesn't even sound like a real woman. Look, this is urgent! Okay, I don't want to embarrass you, but I'm coming in."

He thrust open the door, which wasn't locked, and strode into the studio, with a loud yell of "Caught you!"

There was one very long scream.

Three seconds later, Oliver was back on the landing, blushing. Ben shot out behind him, wrapping a hastily grabbed bed-sheet around his nearly naked body.

"I ought to rend you limb from limb!" he was growling.

"I'm sorry, I'm sorry, I didn't think you'd have a real client in there," Oliver stammered. "Although I don't know how you can operate the camera in that particular position. Was it strapped to your foot?"

"That's not a client, you dolt, it's my girlfriend. I was getting an early Christmas present."

"Giving one, too, by the look of it. At least it was wrapped."

"That's just it, I didn't invite you to look," Ben fumed, gathering the sheet around his middle. "What are you, some kind of pervert?"

"Hey, you're the one who keeps his socks on!"

"It's cold in there, and…Never mind why I keep my frigging socks on!"

"Well, you only have yourself to blame. Remember what happened to the boy who cried wolf?"

"He was eaten," Ben muttered wistfully.

"Exactly. You shouldn't have pretended to be on the job all those other times. It's your own fault!"

"What the hell do you want anyway?" Ben demanded.

"I need to see the contact sheets from the photographs you took at Plumley United Diaconalist Church."

"And if I give you these, will you leave me alone? Or do you plan another bout of Swithin Interruptus on this Christmas Eve morning?"

"I shall not trouble you further, Benjamin," said Oliver starchily. "But give me a magnifier, too. For a better view of Tapster's performance, not yours."

Ben slid through the doorway. Oliver heard a brief, whispered conversation inside and then his friend reappeared, with a stack of oversize contact sheets and a loupe.

"Oh, and Helga has a request," Ben said sheepishly, passing over the photographs. "Can you wait, say, twenty minutes and then burst in again like that? She found it oddly arousing."

Oliver called the number of Effie's mobile phone.

"Scully, it's me," he declared, when he heard her voice. "Where are you?"

"With the Quarterboys, Mulder. Patience Coppersmith and Elsie Potiphar are here, too, rallying round."

"How did they know Tina was back?"

"They were already here, helping Sam and Joan keep vigil."

"Can you talk?"

"Yes, I went into a different room to answer the call."

"How did it go?"

"It'll be all right. A few tears, some mild scolding, but a hell of a lot of love and joy. You'd have been proud of them."

"Do they know they're going to be grandparents?"

"Yes, Tina told them. Chrissie, I should say. They took it pretty well, considering. I think they wisely chose to postpone their reaction until Patience and Elsie have left. Sam and Joan are taking Chrissie to see her doctor shortly, but she seems in pretty good health."

"I don't suppose Chrissie-Tina had any insights into Tapster's death?"

"It came up. She killed him."

"What?"

"That's the way she put it, although she denies being the instrument. The poor lamb is convinced that God killed Nigel Tapster on her behalf as retribution because—in her mind—he wanted to kill her. This comes down to her misunderstanding of abortion. So I've volunteered to give her a quick, belated lesson in the birds and the bees—the mechanics, not the morality. Mum and Dad have accepted my offer."

"I'm sure you could teach them a thing or two, as well."

"I can still teach *you* a thing or two, bub, and don't you forget it! I can also wise Tina up to the fact that Tapster was murdered by somebody less than divine."

"Did she witness his death?"

"No, thank goodness! She was hiding behind that door in the vestibule for a good fifteen minutes after I chased her, in case I could hear her footsteps climbing the stairs. So she was spared a lot of that unpleasantness."

"Good. And it's what she saw before she came down from the balcony that really matters. I got the pictures from Ben, and I can confirm what we suspected. Make your arrest, Sergeant Effie."

"Not me. It's not my case. I'll call Tish Belfry with the information and let her take it from there. You get back here as soon as you can with the evidence. I'll meet you at the police station."

Oliver checked his watch. "I'll leave in ten minutes," he told her. "I've got to do a little favor for Ben Motley first."

◇◇◇

At one o'clock that Christmas Eve afternoon, Detective Inspector Lenny Welkin of Plumley CID, assisted by Detective Constable Tish Belfry, arrested Heather Tapster at her home for the murder of her husband, Nigel. She confessed immediately and specifically asked that the Reverend Paul Piltdown, who had been remanded in custody for the same crime, be released in time to lead the annual Christmas carol service at Plumley United Diaconalist Church, later that day.

◇◇◇

"Go on, Tish, tell us what gave her away," said DC Stoodby eagerly.

Tish Belfry looked abashed. "It was Inspector Welkin's collar," she explained.

"Yeah, but we know he had it pinned on the vicar," DC Foot cut in, "till you showed him the error of his ways."

"That's not fair," Tish protested. "The inspector was always open to the possibility that Piltdown was taking the fall for one of his parishioners. I just passed on some information that helped pinpoint which one."

"You do yourself a disservice, Tish," said DC Paddock. "You must have had some inkling it was the missus who done it."

Tish glanced at Oliver, who was sitting contentedly beside Effie's desk in the CID room, eating a banana, while Effie filled a shopping bag with the personal items she'd collected in her week at Plumley. He smiled at Tish and made a courteous gesture for her to continue.

"Well, a lot of this is guesswork," she said nervously. "Heather Tapster has confessed to killing her husband, but she hasn't uttered a dicky-bird since she got herself briefed up."

"But we know she wanted to kill her husband because she thought he'd been f—" Foot looked suddenly terrified and checked himself. "He'd been fooling around with little Tina?"

Tish sat down, facing the three policemen, who were sitting side by side at the table, which still stood in the middle of the room. "No, Heather didn't want to kill Nigel. Of course, she was furious when she discovered that Tina was pregnant—she apparently overheard Paul Piltdown's angry shouting match with her husband. But she was still convinced that Tapster was genuinely doing God's work. So rather than just confront her husband, she devised a little test. She fed him some strychnine immediately before his first official appearance as a deacon. She didn't know that a dosage big enough to bring on the convulsive symptoms—which was what she wanted—would be enough to kill him, especially since he had a weak heart."

"How was that a test?" asked Paddock, hanging on her every word.

"It had something to do with a biblical text," she replied. "About true believers being able to drink poison without harm. Heather believed all this stuff, and she was convinced that if Nigel was the genuine article, he wouldn't be affected by the strychnine. But if he did react, then he was clearly a fraud, and he'd be justifiably humiliated in front of his followers and in front of the whole church. At the crucial moment, though, she decided she couldn't watch it herself, so she went home and waited, either for Nigel to come home in triumph or for someone else to bring news that he'd been carted off to the hospital. She didn't expect a third alternative—me, telling her she's a widow."

"I said you were very brave to do that," Stoodby murmured. The others nudged him to be quiet.

"Why didn't Heather come clean at that point, when she knew Piltdown had been arrested for Tapster's murder in her place?" asked Paddock.

Tish shrugged. "She's not saying. I think it's because she's still totally convinced that she's doing God's will, and she was waiting for some kind of sign as to how to act."

"So how did you figure out how Heather slipped Nigel the strychnine?" Stoodby was so excited, the seat of his trousers had lost contact with the seat of the chair. Tish looked uncomfortable.

"As far as that goes," she began hesitantly, "I owe a lot to Sergeant Strongitharm's interview with Mr. Swithin."

The three men turned simultaneously and glared at Oliver with profound hostility. There was clearly a limit to the courtesy that could be invoked by the Strongitharm-Belfry Look, Oliver reflected complacently, and it didn't extend to interfering civilians in the incident room.

"Wait, there was something else I wanted to ask," said Stoodby, turning back to Tish. "Oh, what was it?" He covered his eyes, racking his short-term memory. On his right, Paddock unconsciously smoothed some remaining strands of hair down over his ears. Foot, sitting on the other side stifled a yawn with his hand.

Welkin limped into the room at that point. He paused, staring at the trio with amusement.

"Thanks for the reminder," he said. "Monkey house—the zoo—animals—reindeer—Santa Claus—Christmas. Everywhere in town is getting dark, so get your lazy arses out onto the High Street and catch some last-minute shoplifters! All except

DC Belfry, who is an example to you all. She can take the rest of the week off, starting now."

The three male detectives scurried away. Welkin headed for his office.

"I feel really guilty taking all the credit for this case when it was all down to you and Oliver," said Tish, wandering over to join them.

"Don't," Effie replied. "If Inspector Welkin knew what Oliver had been up to unofficially, and that I sanctioned it, he'd never trust me again. So while there's some credit going spare, you might as well take it."

Tish smiled, and kissed Oliver swiftly and chastely on the cheek. It was a good job Geoffrey wasn't there, he reflected. As Tish cleared away her desk, Welkin emerged from his office without his walking stick and hobbled over.

"Let me see the pictures again," he asked. Oliver handed over the contact sheets and the loupe, and tentatively directed him to one or two specific images.

"Ben Motley was very close to Tapster when he took these, the week before the murder. It was the moment when Tapster found his guitar was out of tune. You can clearly see that he goes off the platform, gets a pitch-pipe from his guitar case, and blows a tuning note."

Welkin studied the images.

"Nigel went through the same palaver about tuning his guitar on the Sunday he was murdered," said Effie. "I saw him leave the stage and go to his guitar case, but I couldn't see or hear what he was doing from where I was sitting—the piano was in the way. But Tina was still up in the balcony last Sunday morning, just before the Communion service. From that high position, she could see over the piano. And a few minutes earlier, she saw Heather deliberately fiddle with the tuning heads of Nigel's guitar, so he would have to retune it before singing. That was also the time that Heather—while pretending to be looking for some sheet music—must have dipped the mouthpieces of the pitch-pipe into a little tub of honey, laced with strychnine, and laid it back in the guitar case. And nobody saw her do it. She even managed to get Nigel out of the way by suggesting he should use the bathroom before Communion."

"Ten minutes or so later, the poison goes to work," Oliver commented. "Coincidentally, just as Nigel is drinking the Communion wine."

"Coincidence?" echoed Welkin. "Could Heather have planned it that way to throw us off the scent?"

"Unlikely. I think it was pure blind luck."

"Well, it clearly wasn't an act of God," Welkin muttered. "Where do you think she got the strychnine?"

"Oh, I'd guess it was left over from her time as a missionary in Brazil. She used to practice homeopathic medicine, and there's a popular but misguided belief that small doses of strychnine can help prevent intestinal worms."

With a final wave, Tish Belfry left the room.

"Listen, Effie," said Welkin, as the door closed, "I want to congratulate you and Oliver on a job well done. Tim Mallard said I could trust you two to get to the bottom of the Tapster murder."

"Tim?" Effie echoed.

"Yes. I'd never come across a suspect who behaved quite like Piltdown, so I called my old boss, Superintendent Mallard, for advice on whether to arrest him or not."

"But you were so insistent that Piltdown was guilty," she exclaimed. "That was why we…"

Did Spiv Welkin wink at her or was it a trick of the light?

"Merry Christmas, Eff," he said and limped away before she could reply.

The carol service was due to start at half past six, but every pew in Plumley United Diaconalist Church was full at least half an hour earlier. Despite the competing temptations of one more beer with the less inhibited office secretaries or one final attempt to determine which two bulbs in the string of Christmas tree lights had burned out, the people of Plumley seemed unable to resist a religious service at a recent crime scene, conducted by a man just released from prison following a murder charge. Oliver and Effie were standing inside the rear curtain, nervously weighing the competing indignities of sitting separately or asking strangers to squash up and make room for them, when Oliver heard his name called from a side pew. Tim Mallard waved and indicated that he was guarding some space, with the deft use of an overcoat, some papers, and a disdainful expression for any hopeful worshipper who dared to approach him.

"What are you doing here on a Christmas Eve?" Oliver asked him as they slipped into the pew.

"Ah, dear Nephew, I have much to be grateful for," he answered happily, hugging Effie with an off-duty warmth as she squeezed past him. He bundled his coat under the seat and lifted the papers onto his lap, forcing Oliver to sit on his other side.

"I mean, I thought you'd be at your local parish church," Oliver said.

"I will be. Midnight mass starts at eleven o'clock, and I shall be back in Theydon Bois and in your aunt's delightful company by that hour, I trust. But I'd heard so much about this place that I had to come and see it. Not at all what I expected from your description."

He was gazing in admiration around the church, and with good cause, because it was a building transformed. There were still no seasonal decorations, no Christmas tree, and no bunches of red-berried holly, Sellotaped to architectural features.

But there were the candles.

Hundreds of them, burning slowly and steadily and filling the space with a warm, golden light, which filtered away all the Victorian hulk's drabness and decay that was so conspicuous in cold winter daylight. Multi-branched candlesticks the height of a man had been placed at intervals along each of the two aisles, and cramped colonnades of candles paraded across the window-sills and the top of the upright piano, now closed and pushed against the side wall. At the front of the church, the balustrade over which Tapster had tipped so spectacularly was lined with tall tapers, more candlesticks surrounded the acting area on the platform, and several yellow-flamed sconces had been placed on the ledge of the high, bulging pulpit to the right. There was even a stray menorah, just in front of the organ.

A thin blanket of smoky haze was floating under the high ceiling, softening and masking its distance from the worshippers. The church was warm and inviting on such an icy, damp evening.

"Magical," Mallard sighed. Oliver noticed he was toying with the papers in his pal.

"Is that…?"

"A little Christmas gift from Assistant Commissioner Weed," Mallard whispered. "My long-lost personnel folder."

"Sounds like Weed had much to be grateful for, too. I take it you diagnosed his personal problem?"

"Ah indeed. And the Mallard remedy. Guaranteed to work overnight. Unfortunately, not strictly legal, despite the best efforts of many well-known celebrities, which is why the assistant commissioner made no bones about giving me the paperwork."

It took Oliver a moment to process the confession. "You gave Weed weed?" he asked with astonishment.

"Let's just say God may not be the only one on high this Christmas."

Oliver spluttered with laughter. The man in front of him, who had last set foot in a church in 1962 and who had been searching for a hassock for five minutes, turned and glared at him piously.

"But can you guarantee that the odor will be gone?" Oliver asked quietly.

"Of course. As soon as Weed left for the day, I slipped into his office and removed the small piece of liver sausage that I asked Detective Sergeant Moldwarp to tape to the underside of Weed's chair last Saturday. Understandably, it had ripened somewhat in the meantime."

"Diabolical," said Oliver with admiration.

"And all thanks to young Geoffrey Angelwine," Mallard informed him. "One of the better pranks he'd dreamed up for that new book of yours. Nobody thinks to look under the chair.

Geoff was most helpful when I consulted him on the issue—in the strictest confidence, of course. I didn't even have to divulge the family secret."

"What family secret?" asked Effie, looking up from her hymn book with interest.

"Hell-oo!" cried a voice from the aisle. "If it isn't my dear old friend Ollie and the charming Sergeant Strongitharm."

Dougie Dock leaned in with hand extended. He was wearing a bow tie with a pattern of Christmas crackers and a sprig of mistletoe in his buttonhole. Oliver reluctantly greeted the deacon, and introduced his uncle, leaving off his police title.

"Oh, duck!" said Dock with a look of mock terror, and dipped suddenly, covering his balding head with his hands.

"What?" asked Mallard. Dock stood up again, grinning.

"Duck!" he cried, repeating the action.

Mallard looked at him blankly. Then he allowed an expression of enlightenment to cross his face.

"Oh I see, you want to say 'duck' because my name's Mallard. Mallard being a breed of duck. Oddly enough, I do believe I knew that."

"What, people are always making wise-quacks, are they? Here, you're Duck, I'm Dock. Now where's Dick? Ah-hah hah hah hah."

The staccato laughter continued while Mallard resettled his glasses on his nose and peered at Dock carefully.

"'Dock,' you said your name was?" he said. "Have you lived in this area all your life?"

"Well, not yet," Dock replied, nudging Oliver and beginning another round of self-congratulatory chortles, although his eyes showed wariness.

"There was a Dock, I remember," Mallard mused, half-turning to Effie. "Of course, that was a while ago, and I was only a detective sergeant. Let's see, what was the charge?"

"Oh, you're a policeman, too?" said Dock nervously, without his usual interest.

Mallard didn't answer, but continued talking to Effie. "Public nuisance, was it? That covers a multitude of sins. No, something more specific. I think sex came into it...."

The man in the pew in front, who was about to turn round and complain that the conversation was disrupting his meditations, paused and listened. But Dock was already halfway to the front of the church.

"Did you really arrest him?" asked Oliver.

"Never seen him before in my life," Mallard confided.

"What family secret?" asked Effie.

The murmur of voices in the church dropped away noticeably as a striking woman in a forest-green business suit strode proudly down the opposite aisle, a long ponytail of red hair floating behind her. She climbed to the highest tier of the platform until she reached a small chamber built into the side of the massive church organ, which held the instrument's two manuals and pedal board. A curtain blocked her from view, but a few seconds later, a slow melody—a free variation on the Coventry Carol—wafted down from the gray pipes.

"There's another reason why I'm here," said Mallard. "I wanted to congratulate you both on a job well done. And Welkin got the Tapster woman to confess, which means a much neater and tidier trial."

"It's a good job she did, because we're rather short of evidence," said Effie. "We still can't find that poisoned pitch pipe. It wasn't found on Tapster's body, it wasn't dropped anywhere on the platform or round the piano, and it wasn't in his guitar case."

"Could Heather have taken it with her?" Mallard asked.

"She left the building before her husband even used it," Effie told him. "I expect she thought she'd get a chance to recover it later."

"Then could an accomplice have removed the pitch pipe?"

"That's what it looks like, although before Heather clammed up, she was adamant she acted alone. But we searched all the people in the church before we let them leave the building. A pitch pipe is about the size of a pack of cigarettes. It's not that easy to hide, even from a pat down. Ollie and I have an idea, however."

Oliver glanced at his watch. "Time to go," he said.

"Go where?" asked Mallard, but Oliver rose from his pew, pushed his way through the crowded narthex and walked out into the cold night. The rain had stopped and the sky had partly cleared, but the sallow street lamps still had halos of lemon-colored mist. The temperature was close to freezing.

Oliver turned down the quiet alleyway beside the church, ignoring the wet nettles that brushed against his trousers. He reached the side entrance to the church and opened the door into the long corridor that ran behind the sanctuary. At the far end of the corridor, several of the children in the Nativity play were chasing each other excitedly. He knocked briefly on a door marked MINISTER'S VESTRY and pushed it open without waiting for an answer.

Paul Piltdown was sitting at a long table covered with a coarse cloth, which almost filled the dark room. The walls were covered with framed photographs, and Oliver could see a large marble fireplace at the far end of the room. The air was cold.

"Welcome home," Oliver said, closing the door behind him and leaning against it. His breath was misty.

Piltdown tried to suppress a look of mild irritation. He smiled briefly and dragged a hand through his unkempt hair. "I only just made it in time. The police dropped me off at the manse a few minutes ago. I changed clothes and here I am. Now, Ollie, much as I love you, I must prepare for the carol service."

He looked up at a sizeable clock over the mantelpiece, which showed that seven minutes remained before the service was due to begin.

"You knew it was Heather, didn't you?" Oliver said softly.

"Can't this wait?"

"No, it damn well can't!" Oliver snapped.

Piltdown raised his eyebrows and shifted his burly frame in the chair.

"All that time in the police station," Oliver went on, "you weren't waiting patiently for the guilty deacon to run in and confess. You knew all along that they were innocent and that Heather Tapster killed her husband."

"How could I possibly know that?" Piltdown asked, wearily stretching out the sentence.

"Because you saw her. You saw her dip the pitch pipe into the poisoned honey. Then she detuned Nigel's guitar, so he'd have to use the pipe. She thought the piano shielded her from everybody's view. It certainly shielded her from the congregation. But not from Tina, hiding up in the balcony. Nor from the pulpit, where you were sitting, supposedly in prayer. You saw her very clearly, through one of those little decorative spyholes you were boasting about last week. I don't think you knew what she was doing at the time, but when the strychnine started to work, you put it all together. And your every move from that point on was to protect her. Why, Paul?"

Piltdown picked up a stray rubber band that had been left on the table and stretched it over his fingers.

"Being Tina Quarterboy's confessor put me into a privileged position, Oliver," he said, not meeting his friend's steady gaze. He wrapped the band below the first knuckles of his index and middle fingers. "I knew the kind of monster Nigel Tapster had become. When I confronted him last Thursday evening, after I had sent Tina home to face her parents, he actually tried to convince me that she was lying about being pregnant. I know Tina. She wouldn't know how to make up something like that. But there was Nigel, mocking her as a false witness or a slut or worse, dismissing my accusations, betraying and deceiving his wife. I have no idea how Heather found out about Tina, but the moment I realized she had poisoned her husband, I knew why she'd done it. That's why I waited for her to come forward after my arrest. I could hardly show your girlfriend's rather dim colleagues the error of their ways without betraying Tina's confidence. Does that answer your question?"

Piltdown opened and closed his fist swiftly. The rubber band seemed to jump to the ring and little finger. At another time Oliver would have asked him how he did it. He looked at the clock. Two minutes had passed. Five minutes to go.

"You only had to tell the police what you saw," Oliver remarked. "You weren't obliged to suggest a motive for Heather's actions. And anyway, you continued to keep quiet *after* we found out about Tina's pregnancy. Why did you risk your own neck to protect Heather, a woman who'd broken one of the more serious commandments? For that matter, why did you nurture both of them? If Nigel Tapster was such a monster, as you say, why—only one day after you found out that he had impregnated the thirteen-year-old daughter of a trusted deacon—did you cast the deciding vote that made Tapster a deacon himself?"

Piltdown glanced up sharply, fury on his face—but he did not deny the charge. "What do you think, Oliver?" he asked. "Give me your answer."

Oliver leaned back in his chair cautiously. This would not be the time to topple backwards.

"I think the Tapsters found out you were gay, and they were blackmailing you, threatening to tell the deacons. You'd be thrown out of the church here, probably out of the ministry. Though God knows why, since your church members seem to turn a blind eye to Dougie Dock and Barry Foison, two men who are clearly homosexual."

Piltdown began to laugh humorlessly, staring at Oliver.

"Dougie and Barry?" he repeated, with exaggerated astonishment. "Dougie's not gay. His problem has always been a fondness for the female sex. He calls it gallantry, but these days it would be called unwelcome touching."

"His coworkers think he's too keen on the boys in the Victory Vanguard."

"Then they're small-minded bigots. Like any good Christian, Dougie loves children. He maintains a vision of childish innocence that's positively Victorian. And completely chaste. Trust me, Oliver, I would not let him lead the Sunday School or the

Victory Vanguard if I thought otherwise. Any suspicion of an untoward interest in the boys is a reflection of your own dirty-mindedness. I'm surprised at you."

Oliver absorbed the rebuke.

"But what about Barry?" he riposted. "He's a transsexual, for God's sake!"

Piltdown laughed again. "Yes, I'm not sure how the members are going to react when they discover Oona's true identity," he said pensively. "Barry may be effeminate, but he's heterosexual as a male and so Oona will be homosexual as a female. He was confused about his sexual identity, not his sexual orientation. They're not the same thing—I thought you'd have known that, being a sophisticated man of letters. No, Ollie, I'm the only queer here. And that's still our little secret. Nigel and Heather had no idea."

"Then for God's sake, why *did* you tolerate them?"

Piltdown hooked the rubber band around his thumb and let go, shooting it away into the darker corner of the room.

"I suppose Christian love won't do as an explanation," he answered ruefully and sighed. "When I first encountered Nigel Tapster, he seemed to epitomize everything I wanted in my spiritual life. When Nigel closed his eyes in fervent prayer, when he fell senseless in the presence of the Holy Spirit, he made you believe he was experiencing something truly transcendent. But it didn't take me long to realize Nigel was a fraud, a humbug, a flimflam merchant, with his own ambitions for worldly power and worse. I heard about the trouble he'd caused at his last church and I gambled that he'd do less damage in Plumley as an insider than as an outcast. If I could bring him into the fold, then as a minister, I still had a pathway to the children who came under his spell. And if that meant sacrificing old Cedric's unbroken record on the diaconate, so be it. The alternative was to watch the Tapsters rip the church apart on their way out and use the shreds to knit their cult."

"That doesn't explain why you went on protecting Heather *after* Nigel's death," Oliver said, silently noting his friend's first admission that the Tapsters were indeed building a cult.

Piltdown leaned across the table, scratching at the harsh cover.

"I tried to be a good shepherd to my flock," he stated, his eyes blazing. "But then Heather had a better idea. Kill the wolf. So don't I owe her something in return? Not for my sake, but for the sake of my people? My good people!"

He paused, holding Oliver's gaze. Two minutes to go.

Oliver stood up abruptly. "You arrogant son-of-a-bitch," he said and walked to the door.

"Here endeth the lesson," muttered Piltdown, watching him with surprise.

Oliver spun around. "Here's the lesson, Paul," he said bitterly. "Nigel died because Heather thought he was up to his old tricks. She claimed she found out about Tina's pregnancy when she overheard you confronting her husband in their home. But I went to the house that evening, only a few minutes after you left. There was no way that Heather could have heard your conversation, because of the racket she and Billy Coppersmith were making. You said yourself it was going on all the time you were there. Heather didn't even hear you leave. And when she greeted me that evening—after I'd had to hammer on the door—she didn't behave like a woman who'd just overheard that her husband had betrayed their marriage and screwed up their ambitions."

One minute.

"So who told Heather about Tina? Only three people at the church knew of Tina's condition. Tina herself, and she denies speaking to Heather. Nigel, who was so terrified of his wife's reaction that he swore Billy to secrecy about the girl's visit. And you, supposedly bound by your ministerial code to keep her pregnancy a secret. But you didn't, did you?"

Thirty seconds.

"When Tapster laughed in your face that Thursday evening, you were furious—I saw you afterwards. That's why you returned to the house. Not to guide me to the manse, but to tell Heather that her husband had been hooking up with a thirteen-year-old disciple. Tina confided in you, Paul, because she trusted you more than anyone. But you used her as a pawn in your match with the Tapsters. It was an irresistible opportunity to divide and conquer your enemies, and you took it. And it led directly to murder."

"I thought Tina was going home to tell her parents about the baby," Piltdown whispered. "I thought the whole church would hear about it soon enough! How could I have known she'd run away, keeping her secret? And how could I have known Heather would kill Nigel?"

The minute hand reached the half-hour mark with a louder click.

"You'd better get ready for your public," Oliver murmured sadly and left the room.

◇◇◇

Piltdown was in the pulpit before Oliver had time to return to his seat. He felt the minister's eyes on him as he moved into the pew and stood beside Mallard.

Piltdown abruptly announced the first carol, and Oona played the opening chords of "O Come All Ye Faithful" at twice the normal speed. A quick march, not a dirge. Oliver liked it. As they began to sing, trying to keep up with the unfamiliar tempo, Oliver noticed that Effie wasn't using the words printed in the hymn book.

> *"How did it go back there?*
> *How did it go back there?*
> *How did it go back there?*
> *Does he know what we know?"*

Oliver started to sing back, but gave up instantly. The three trooped out to the narthex, which still held some latecomers. Sam Quarterboy and Patience Coppersmith were on duty to distribute hymn books.

"Effie filled me in while you were gone," Mallard informed Oliver, once they had formed a huddle out of the deacons' earshot. "So Paul admitted he clammed up to stymie the police investigation? Because he felt guilty?"

"He didn't just clam up, Uncle," Oliver said ruefully. "We're pretty sure it was Paul who made off with the murder weapon, the perfidious poisoned pitch pipe. He was the only person who saw Heather tampering with it earlier."

"He had plenty of time to creep across and grab it from the guitar case in all the confusion over Tapster's death," Effie recalled. "Paul was most insistent that we all go over to the manse, immediately after Nigel died. He wouldn't shut up about it. I believe he planned to smuggle the pipe out of the church, before the police arrived. But he must have stashed it somewhere in the meantime, or it would have turned up when the police searched him. But God knows where—Welkin's crew were all over the crime scene."

"Tonight is the first time Paul has been back to the church since the murder," Oliver added. "That's why we chose to confront him, but without saying that we know he hid the pitch pipe. We hope it'll force him to dispose of it now, while he thinks the coast is still clear. Let's hope he doesn't try to lick it clean of fingerprints!"

"Effie, are you sure you didn't see Paul leave the area around the body?" Mallard asked, stroking his white moustache. "Even for a moment or two?"

Effie looked away, replaying the tape of Tapster's disturbing death in her mind. On the other side of the curtain, the carol reached the final verse. "Word of the Father, now in flesh appearing." She smiled. "There was one moment when I looked up and Paul was in the pulpit. It was odd, because he'd conducted the whole Communion service from the table. I assumed he was using the pulpit microphone to address the people in the church."

"Wouldn't the police have searched the pulpit?"

"The victim hadn't been near it, so I doubt that they'd have given it more than a cursory sweep," Effie replied. "If Paul tucked the pitch pipe well out of the way, they could have missed it. Thank you, Tim."

The carol ended. Mallard peeked through the curtains that separated the narthex from the main sanctuary. "He's still up there," he reported. "So I suppose our job now is to grab him and arrest him as soon as he comes down, before he gets a chance to destroy the evidence."

"Well, we'd certainly like to find the murder weapon," said Oliver, "but do we really care about punishing Paul?"

Mallard bristled. "Covering up a crime, concealing evidence, interfering with a police investigation—these are serious offenses," he declared starchily. "It's not just a puzzle, you know, with no consequences." He turned to Effie. "Weren't you planning to arrest him, Detective Sergeant Strongitharm?"

She shrugged. "Spirit of Christmas, Tim. I would imagine Paul's already plagued with guilt over his inadvertent role in Tapster's murder, no matter how much he personally gains from it. And that's nothing to the guilt he's going to experience when he finds out the whole truth."

"You mean there's more to come?" Mallard exclaimed. Sam and Patience both turned and glared at him.

"Perhaps we'd better talk about it later," Effie whispered. She and Oliver slipped back into the sanctuary, with Mallard reluctantly following, knowing he would have to wait until the service was over to get an explanation. The Nativity play had already started, and as they scuttled back to their pew the arrival of the angel Gabriel was being heralded by a sudden explosion of sound from guitar and organ, which the congregation could feel as well as hear.

Billy Coppersmith had set up his amplifier at the back of the platform, and Oona had pulled the organ console's curtain aside so they could share cues, giving the audience a side view of her long shapely legs on the pedal-board. Billy seemed preoccupied, as if it was dawning on him that Oona seemed somehow familiar. The leather-clad Kurt bolted through the door on the left of the sanctuary and swaggered onto the stage, to delighted snickers from the audience.

"Yo, Mary!" he shouted, as Tina Quarterboy appeared on the stage.

"Ah, this must be the Schubert setting of the 'Yo Mary,'" Mallard murmured, opening a note that Effie had passed him. He groaned and handed it to Oliver. It said, "What family secret?"

The play progressed mercifully quickly until it reached the scene with the shepherds, which Oliver and Effie had already witnessed in rehearsal. Barry/Oona could do no more than glare down from the organ bench when she noticed Kylie was carrying a soft-toy lamb, and Garth—who had heard about the detectives at the church the previous Sunday—had not only kept his cotton beard, but had traded his entire policeman's uniform for a Santa Claus outfit. Then the heavenly host—in their Victory Vanguard caps—marched swiftly across the front of the platform, bugles in hand, looking about as angelic as a police lineup.

The angels' instrumental hymn of praise started loud and got louder, causing the shepherds to welcome the news of the Christ Child with their hands over their ears. Many of the congregants in the front rows, showed signs of restlessness, if not actual pain.

At last, the music ended on a thunderous final chord, with Oona stretching her legs far to the left to scoop the deepest bass notes from the sixteen-foot organ pipes. High up on the fretboard, Billy sustained a trill that only dogs could hear. The wall of vibrating air swept through the church, causing the floor and pews to tremble and candleholders to judder and slide on the windowsills. A tall metal candlestick on the platform began to sway.

Time stood still for Oliver.

The hollow, multitiered platform was acting like a sounding board, throbbing in sympathy with the growling organ pipes. The candlestick tipped past its center of gravity and fell, landing on the edge of Tina's dress. She yelped and dropped the spirit lamp she was clutching. It shattered, showering methylated spirit over the floor. A bluish flame shot up from the platform's cheap carpeting.

A man in the stunned congregation stood up and shouted "Fire!" Oliver reacted, sliding toward the aisle, but counting on somebody much closer to the platform to get to the children first. The organ chord continued.

Below the platform, a dribble of flaming spirit had trickled into a pile of paint-splattered rags stained with turpentine. Flames gathered themselves, feeding lazily on half-empty cans of paint and jars of cleaning materials. Then they crept toward several stacks of dry, out-of-date hymn books. They could afford this moment of patience—they had waited a long time for this one.

There were more shouts of "Fire!" and screams, as the congregation realized that fireworks were not part of the play. People stood and moved into the aisles, which quickly became clogged with panicked worshippers hurrying to get out of the building. Oliver was halfway to the front of the church when he was pushed aside by the stampede.

On the stage, Garth pulled Kylie and Danni off the platform. They followed the Victory Vanguard boys, who had fled to safety through the open side door. Joseph ran after them, clutching the baby Jesus doll in a misguided act of heroism. Behind the sanctuary, Dougie Dock directed them out of the church and into the night air.

The platform began to smoke in several places.

Paul Piltdown, deep in agonized prayer in the pulpit, had been slow to react to the commotion. He stood up, blinking, and wasted several seconds trying to appeal for a calm exodus, but he was too late and too quiet. He hurried out of the pulpit, leaving behind the plastic pitch pipe that he had gingerly picked up and wedged under the lectern last Sunday.

At the same time, Billy Coppersmith opened his eyes and instantly stopped playing his deafening trill. He tried to get to Tina, who was standing still, staring in horror at the small pool of flames near her feet. But he forgot that he was tethered by the guitar. The cable tautened, dragging him off balance, and he fell. The cheap amplifier crashed onto the platform, sparked, and died.

The organ stopped.

Like Billy, Oona Foison had been oblivious to the shouts and screams of the fleeing mob while she was still playing. Then she smelled smoke. She struggled to slide off the organ bench, her panty hose ripping on the wood. The smoldering amplifier lay across the console steps, and she edged around it. Her wig snagged on the curtain rail.

Billy quickly untangled himself and threw his beloved Stratocaster aside. The fire was almost burned out, although the smoke streaming from the carpet's crumbling backing was finding its insidious way into his lungs. He walked over and put an arm around Tina.

"It's okay, Chrissie," he said gently.

"All right, Billy?" asked Piltdown, standing at the edge of the platform with a few nervous congregants who felt the likelihood of being roasted was considerably lower than the likelihood of being trampled to death. Hovering behind the minister, they seemed relieved that the fire was out as quickly as it started. Behind them, the melee in the aisles continued, as slower pensioners and handicapped people were pushed aside by more able-bodied Plumleyites, still fearing an inferno at their backs. Joan Quarterboy stood silently in a pew near the front, her eyes fixed on Tina.

Oliver managed to get through and joined Piltdown. Trapped in her seat, Effie was calling the emergency services on her mobile telephone. Mallard had let himself be carried to the vestibule, trying to remember the rules of crowd control.

"Everything's under control, Reverend," said Billy, leading a trembling Tina forward. He was wrong.

When the cries of "Fire!" broke out, Sam Quarterboy had almost been thrust out of the narthex by the fleeing sea of people. Fearing for Tina's safety, he had run around to the building's side door, arriving just as Dock was ushering the children out of the building. He pushed past them and opened the door to the sanctuary.

The scorching air below the platform now sensed the escape route. It rushed instantly for the cold night, swirling and egging the nursling flames on. A jagged streak of newborn fire blazed spitefully through the platform. It split, part of its middle tier dropping away in an eruption of sparks. Bright tongues of flame roared up angrily through the hole, spitting heat and screaming abuse at the watchers.

A wigless Foison managed to reach the side door, just ahead of the fire that was catching at his high heels. New bubbles of flame burst through the carpet with every second.

Billy, partly blinded by smoke, knew he only had a short time before the entire platform collapsed. He grasped Tina's hand and stepped across an unburned pathway of fuming carpet. But as he jumped onto the lowest tier, the floor gave way beneath his feet. He disappeared. The fire gave a great screech of victory and blew furiously toward Oliver and Paul, who had stepped forward to intercept the teenagers. They were forced back, coughing.

Tina squealed and leaped away from the edge of the hole. Bushes of fire bloomed on two sides, and thick smoke surrounded her.

"Oh dear God, no!" moaned Quarterboy. He ran toward his daughter, but the flames slapped him back disdainfully. Joan screamed.

"Get Billy!" shouted Piltdown to anyone.

He tore down the "Jesus is Lord" banner from the front of the pulpit, took a large breath, and sprinted straight into a new rampart of flame that had blazed up in front of him. Staggering across the remains of the platform, he managed to reach Tina. He flung the banner over her head and hurtled back the same way, carrying the girl like a swaddled baby.

At the same time, Oliver ducked under the railing and jumped down into the smoke-filled baptismal pool, where Billy had fallen, momentarily protected from the fire outside by its tiled walls. The long, unexpected drop had shattered Billy's thigh, but Oliver got him upright, and the braver worshippers lifted them both out before flames crept around the front of the pool.

They carried the boy to the back of the deserted church. Sam Quarterboy followed, now carrying Tina, leading his trembling wife. Piltdown came behind, wondering when his body's own natural painkillers would go to work on his burned hands.

It was three minutes since the fire had first broken out. The last section of the old wooden platform staggered and fell, and the triumphant flames took their thirst to the pulpit.

Chapter Nine

Good Tidings We Bring

Thursday, December 25 (Christmas Day)

"An act of God," said Oliver skeptically. Nobody else was in the bathroom, or he wouldn't have dared utter the phrase. He tried to add more hot water to his bath, but his toes weren't dexterous enough to work the taps. The action provoked another coughing fit.

A simple accident. That was a preferable explanation. Although to an insurance company, acts of God and accidents often boiled down to the same thing. (Was a church more or less likely to be insured against an act of God? he wondered.) One thing was certain: The fire was no *deus ex machina*, with the timely arrival of a deity or two to solve everybody's problems. The Plumley United Diaconalists had greeted Christmas morning with half their historic church burned to a cinder and the other half about to fall down. And if Piltdown's heroism had helped his sagging reputation, he'd paid for it in minor burns. No, there were still plenty of problems in Plumley.

Of course, there was that odd blackened lump of molten plastic lying amid the charred remains of the pulpit. Or so Oliver imagined…

Really, not a bad bathroom, he thought, looking around. There was a lot to be said for the thoughtful touches only Effie could have provided, such as the thick towels and the supply of soothing bubble bath. It was the first time he had woken on Effie's territory. He had visited her tiny apartment in Richmond, but up to now, she had always treated it as a distant extension to her office, a place to go to sleep alone or pick up a change of clothes when her work pushed him to the side. Last night, after the ambulances and fire engines had departed, she had led him to her car, brought him home and put him to bed, still coughing. It was past three o'clock before his lungs let him fall asleep.

He had crawled from the bed at nine and telephoned his parents to say he would not be joining them for Christmas lunch.

"Why not?" asked Effie sleepily. He covered the mouthpiece to muffle their conversation.

"There's only one train on Christmas morning, and I've already missed it," he whispered.

"I can drive you there."

"It's eighty miles from London. Besides, you have your own plans for the day."

"No I don't."

"Oh." Oliver had informed Effie weeks ago that his presence at the senior Swithins' country house was an established Christmas tradition. He had assumed that Effie would spend the day with her own parents.

"In that case, come to dinner with the Swithin clan," he said warmly. "Always room for one more."

What he could see of her face reddened. "Oh no, no, I'm sorry," she stammered. "When I offered you the lift, I wasn't trying to invite myself. I didn't think. Look, forget about it."

He took his hand away. "Mother—" he began.

"Tell Effie we're dying to meet her," his mother cut in excitedly. "Your Aunt Phoebe and Uncle Tim have told us so much about her. They'll be here, too. Apparently, Tim's been home from work for a week, and he's getting on Phoebe's nerves, so

I invited them to give them somebody else to talk to. Join the party, the pair of you. We can all play Murder in the Dark. So much more fun with professionals. Stay the night. You can have your old room."

"Where will Effie sleep?"

There was silence.

"Mother?"

"Sorry, Oliver, just checking in the hall mirror to see if I was green. Good God, boy, I was at Woodstock, you know! Now, I have to go, your father's perilously close to complete consciousness."

Oliver found himself staring at a humming telephone.

"Welcome to the family," he announced. Effie covered her head with a pillow to hide her embarrassment.

It took half an hour for Oliver to convince Effie that he was convinced she had not manipulated him into introducing her to his parents, and for her to convince him that she was convinced he had not bulldozed her into the same prospect. Then they each attempted to convince the other that meeting parents was not a big deal for their relationship, while making it equally clear that they secretly knew it was and they had no problem with it. After that, Oliver was faced with the choice of exploring why Effie was not planning to visit her parents—although he knew that her father had never forgiven his only child for not being male—or taking the bath she suggested. Exhausted from diplomacy, he opted for the bath.

The warm water soothed the muscles he had strained lifting Billy Coppersmith from the baptismal pool. Billy, too, had demonstrated that he had the right stuff during the fire. Just as well, Oliver had remarked casually to Mallard, as they watched the ambulance ease its way through the crowds that had come out on Christmas night to watch a burning church, since the fourteen-year-old was about to become a father.

◇◇◇

"I trust that this is the one thing you and Effie haven't told me," Mallard had replied.

Oliver nodded. "Billy is responsible for Tina's pregnancy, not Tapster. The result of an evening of experimentation behind the church a couple of months ago."

Mallard stared at him.

"So why on earth did she say Tapster was the father of her child?" he asked, when his nephew had finished one of his frequent bouts of coughing.

"She thought he was," Oliver gasped.

"Because he, too, had seduced her?"

"No. Nigel never touched her."

"Then what was the silly girl talking about?"

Oliver paused while his lungs pulled in more air. Mallard's warrant card had left them inside the invisible boundary that the Plumley police were trying to maintain, keeping the spectators away from the blazing building. Several television crews had now arrived to capture the conflagration—it would make a pleasant change from the standard interviews with last-minute shoppers and live coverage of midnight in Bethlehem. Fire hoses snaked across the cleared street, and three fire engines were blasting cascades of water over the roofline. Sparks and burning papers, ascending in the heat, flew up into the night sky like tiny angels.

Piltdown had been taken to the casualty ward, and Patience had accompanied Billy in the ambulance, but the remaining deacons had gathered in a forlorn flock, watching their church crumble. Sam and Joan Quarterboy held an unharmed Tina between them. Oliver pointed to the family group.

"The Quarterboys had the best intentions in the world," he said sadly.

"Well, you know what they say about the pathway to Hell," Mallard responded, glancing ironically at the dying flames.

"Sam and Joan wanted to preserve Tina's innocence in a world that, unfortunately, preys on innocence. When she asked them where babies come from, she was told they were a gift from God to the parents. And as the actress playing the Virgin Mary, this seemed to make perfect sense of the Christmas Story. She hadn't learned the facts of life from her school friends, who regarded her old-fashioned piety as a bit of a joke. So when the school doctor told her she was going to have a baby, she never connected it with one time she let Billy Coppersmith do that odd thing in the dark that he was so keen to try. Tina didn't know what sex was for. And she didn't know sex was wrong. She's just what her parents wanted—the last innocent thirteen-year-old in England."

"Why did she name Tapster as the spiritual father?"

"She had a God-Almighty crush on him. Nigel made a big impact on the young people who were swept into his circle, and Tina was no exception. But her parents forbade her to go to the meetings, which made her puppyish longing for him even worse. By now she had broken up with Billy, because the sex had been messy and painful. She prayed that God would give her a way back to Tapster. And lo and behold, God plants a baby in her belly, a condition that she's been told is an answer to prayer. In her mythology, Tapster had to be its father, appointed by God."

"So when Tina went to see Tapster that evening, his astonishment and denial were totally genuine?"

"Exactly. And when she ran to Paul, she truthfully answered the only question he posed: Who is the father of your baby? Effie put it the same way. I'm afraid I was the vulgarian who asked her a different, blunter question: Who did you have sex with? And after I'd explained what that meant, the lot fell on Billy Coppersmith. I should have guessed. Billy said he 'broke up' with Tina—Chrissie, as he calls her—and later he talked about not 'seeing her.' Those words don't apply to a mere friendship."

"Do you think Tapster really told Tina to get an abortion?"

"I think he may have mentioned it. No matter how sincerely you believe abortion is wrong, it must be heartbreaking to stare a frightened, skinny, pregnant thirteen-year-old in the face and tell her that she has no godly option but to carry the child to term."

"Then Tapster was also telling the truth when Paul Piltdown confronted him shortly afterwards?"

"Absolutely. Although I believe something had happened in the meantime. Even though Tapster knew he was guiltless, he also knew that his wife might not give him the benefit of the doubt, because of his dubious past. He thought it would be politic to keep Tina's visit from Heather, until he found out more, such as whether the girl's pregnancy was real or imagined, or even if she had been put up to the accusation by people who wanted to undermine his bid to become a deacon. Billy Coppersmith was the only witness, and he was sworn to secrecy. In return, Billy proffered a secret of his own, and I have little doubt that it was the loss of his virginity with Tina. Billy, of course, had no idea that Tina was pregnant, and Tapster didn't tell him. But now Tapster guessed who was the real father of Tina's baby."

"But he didn't tell Paul?"

"No. Naturally, he denied his own responsibility for the pregnancy, but he kept Billy's secret. Even from Heather. And she, in turn, chose not to confront him after her conversation with Paul. She opted to test his holiness instead."

"Why didn't Tapster say something after Tina ran away?" asked Mallard, waiting while Oliver coughed again.

"Because he didn't hear about Tina's disappearance until Saturday evening, when Heather got home from the rehearsal. Perhaps Tapster was planning to talk to Sam or Billy or Patience after church on Sunday morning. He didn't get the chance."

Mallard scratched his moustache sadly. "So all in all, Nigel Tapster comes out of this quite a decent fellow. And he'd still be alive if Paul Piltdown had kept his mouth shut."

"Paul has yet to find out that he accused Tapster wrongfully. When he does, I don't imagine he'll want to stay on as minister of this particular church. Not that there is a church anymore."

"No church?" said a voice.

Oliver had not noticed that Sam Quarterboy had joined them. The deacon reached for Oliver's sooty hand and shook it firmly. "I've just heard that you played a part in finding our Tina and bringing her home, Mr. Swithin. There are no words to tell you how grateful my wife and I are."

Oliver looked across to the group Sam had left. Patience Coppersmith had returned from the hospital and was holding hands with Joan Quarterboy, watching the light die within the building's core. Tina hovered in front of them. Behind them, a crowd of people stood and stared.

"But don't think there's no church," Sam continued. "The church is not the building. It's the people. We'll rise again."

"Hot enough for you?"

Effie's voice startled him. Was that really how it ended the previous evening, or had the warm water lulled him into a half-dreaming state? He did remember the little group of church members staring at the smoking remains, neither crying nor smiling, and singing a carol together before fading away into the night. Good people.

Effie walked up to the edge of the bath and studied him critically while she tied back her unruly hair with a ribbon. She was wearing a dressing gown, but being submerged, he was wearing nothing, and he felt oddly self-conscious. He fluttered his hands under the water, hoping to encourage more bubbles.

"What's all this about a family secret?" she demanded.

"I couldn't possibly tell you."

"Why not?"

"Because it's a secret?" he suggested lamely.

She thought about this answer, head on one side. Then she untied the dressing gown and let it fall from her shoulders.

"Would this persuade you to talk?" she asked. The dressing gown was all she had been wearing.

"Tim lies about his age!" Oliver blurted instantly, gazing up at her.

"Go on," she said, stepping cautiously into the bath. Oliver sat up and moved his legs back to make room for her, but she turned and tied something to the showerhead.

"About twenty years ago," he told her, "the Met put all its personnel records onto a computer. Somebody keyed in the wrong birthdate for Tim, making him five years younger than he really was. He's never reported the error."

"You'd better not be fibbing," she said menacingly, hands on her hips. The water washed her shins.

Oliver swallowed. "Not at a time like this," he gasped. Effie lowered her slim haunches gently into the suds. He noticed that a sprig of mistletoe now hung from the showerhead.

"Eff, you took the end with the taps," he said. "It must be love."

"Never mind that. Why didn't Tim report the mistake?"

"By then, Uncle Tim was already a detective inspector and completely dedicated to police work. He thought the retirement age for detectives was ludicrously early, and he shrewdly speculated that the error might one day give him five more years doing what he loved. And he was right, as it turned out. Is that your foot?"

"Were you expecting somebody else's?"

"Ah. Well, the problem was that all of Tim's paperwork from the Yard's precomputerized days still had his original birthdate. So he…er…arranged for an ambitious clerical assistant to lose it accidentally on a trip to the Criminal Records Office, as it was then. Until last week, that was the only unethical thing he'd ever done in his career. AC Weed found the long-lost file the other day, but I have a feeling Tim's going to lose it again. So Superintendent Mallard's back on the job for a few more years."

"That tickles."

"Sorry."

"Did I tell you to stop doing it?" Effie lay back contentedly in the water and handed Oliver a flannel and a bar of soap. "All right, because you were honest, you may wash whatever parts of me you can reach."

He leaned forward and set about the task with gleeful concentration, his tongue protruding slightly from the edge of his mouth.

"I hate to bring up Geoffrey Angelwine's name at a time like this," she said, "but he called just after you got into the bath."

"What does he want, Tish Belfry's telephone number?"

"As a matter of fact, yes. But he also had a message about your article for that website about Sundays in London."

"*Celestial City*? Oh, well, I know it's late, but I've certainly got a story now—intrigue, blackmail, murder, sex-changes, heroism, fires…"

"It's off," she said abruptly.

"Huh?"

"*Celestial City* folded after its first edition. According to Geoff, nobody on the editorial staff could think of anything to do on a London Sunday."

"Oh. Well, I didn't really want to write the article, so that news makes a rather nice Christmas present." A sudden thought troubled him. He dropped the soap and sat back.

"Er, Effie. What would you say if I'd just remembered that I didn't get you anything for Christmas?"

She sat up and considered the statement, resting her elbows on his shoulders.

"I'd say you were a sweet, sensitive, thoughtful boyfriend who knew that I had no time to get you a gift because of my workload at Plumley, and who wanted to spare me the shame of receiving without giving. And I'd say that, as far as I'm concerned, I can't think of a better present than the present—having you all to myself on Christmas morning. Now, I'm fed up with the taps sticking in my back."

"Okay, we'll swap," Oliver said, relieved enough to put up with any discomfort for this extraordinary woman.

"No, stay there. I'll join you at your end." She pushed him back into the water and slithered up his soapy body until their faces were inches apart.

"Merry Christmas, Oliver," she said softly.

"Merry Christmas, Effie."

◇◇◇

"Of course," she said, a little later. "It's understood that, on the day after Boxing Day, you and your credit card will be first in the queue at the nearest jeweler's."

"Of course."

Author's Note

Religion is a touchy subject. It's quite possible that a believer could read this book and see it as a vindication of his or her faith, while another could declare its mere existence a case of blasphemy in the first degree. Similarly antithetical views could be held by a brace of atheists. That's why I can't emphasize enough that this is not a religious book but a murder mystery that—like many, many others—has a religious setting. As characters, Oliver Swithin and his friends have their own opinions about the varying and occasionally conflicting beliefs held by other characters in this story. As a narrator, I have tried, and probably failed, to remain terminally neutral.

Behavior is different from belief, however. Because of the setting—chosen because it was a very familiar aspect of my childhood and youth—all of the murder suspects have to be devoted churchgoers. If the intense scrutiny of their private lives reveals behavior, physical or mental, that seems at odds with the Christian faith as you understand it, dear reader (and, short of actual murder, most of the incidents and opinions I recount are based on my own observation, although naturally, the characters themselves are entirely fictitious and they know it), please judge them not as representatives of any faith, but as the fallible human beings we all are. Or don't judge them at all. Lest…you know.

I'd like to thank the resourceful Luci Zahray, who gave me generous assistance with the technicalities of certain poisons (and whose story of what happened when her dog ate yeast and chocolate chips is too astounding to make its way into a work of fiction); if I still have the details wrong, it's entirely my fault. And I'd like to thank my friend the Reverend Peter Carey, who donated the best joke in the book, and who is hereby absolved from accountability for any other part of it, religious or otherwise.

To receive a free catalog of Poisoned Pen Press titles, please contact us in one of the following ways:

Phone: 1-800-421-3976
Facsimile: 1-480-949-1707
Email: info@poisonedpenpress.com
Website: www.poisonedpenpress.com

Poisoned Pen Press
6962 E. First Ave. Ste 103
Scottsdale, AZ 85251